THEIRS BE
THE GUILT

THEIRS BE THE GUILT

A Novel of the War Between the States

by UPTON SINCLAIR

War to the hilt!
Theirs be the guilt,
Who fetter the freeman
To ransom the slave!
—CONFEDERATE WAR SONG

Twayne Publishers · New York

Preface

An earlier version of this novel was written in 1903 and published a year later as *Manassas*. Its author was twenty-four, living in two tents in the hills north of Princeton, New Jersey. It was to have been the first volume of a trilogy, the other two to be called *Gettysburg* and *Appomatox*. These were never written. As the publisher of *Manassas* explained sadly, the public was tired of historical novels.

But I felt that I had written more than that, and various critics supported my opinion. Charlotte Perkins Gilman, author of many feminist books, told me of having loaned the novel to a Civil War veteran who had expressed skepticism, saying that no mere youngster could tell *him* anything about the subject. He had come back to her with shining eyes, exclaiming: "It's the war! It's the war! And he wasn't even *born!*"

I had moved to that hillside woodland in order to have the use of the fine Civil War collection at Princeton University Library. They allowed me to take home a dozen volumes at a time, and I would rent a farmer's horse and buggy for $1.00 a trip and drive down from the hills to load up a week's groceries and an armful of reference books. I must have studied over 200 volumes during the writing of this novel.

Also, I had another source from which to draw. Having been born in Baltimore, of a Virginia family, I had spent my early life amongst a proud people who still smarted from defeat. On my father's side my grandfather and seven of my uncles and cousins had been Confederate naval officers; my great-grandfather, Captain Arthur Sinclair, U.S.N., served as a model for the "Grandfather Montague" of this novel. The riots on the streets of Baltimore were described to me as a boy by my maternal grandfather who was an official of the railroads concerned in the affair.

Very oddly, the lady who became my second wife was born and brought up in the midst of just such family plantations as the one here described. While I was writing the first parts of the book in New York, she was attending a "finishing school" on Fifth Avenue, New York, partly under the chaperonage of Mrs. Jefferson Davis, who lived in that city. At that same time I was receiving information from Mrs. Davis as to conditions in Mississippi prior to the Civil War.

When my parents first moved to New York we lived for several years in a family hotel patronized by refugees from the war's devastations; and here I listened to the reminiscences of army majors and colonels. Later I visited Boston, where the reminiscences had a distinctly northern bias. Oldtimers such as Julia Ward Howe, author of *The Battle Hymn of the Republic,* and Thomas Wentworth Higginson, colonel of a Negro regiment throughout the war, added to the background from which the novel grew.

Now the centennial of these events is at hand, and Americans are once again reading historical novels about the period. I have taken this opportunity to give *Manassas* a thorough revision, moderating some of the exuberance of the earlier version. The title has also been changed, as I feel that the years have dimmed the significance of the name "Manassas." A generation removed from the actual era of the conflict is more concerned with the overall picture of the war and its causes than with individual battles and incidents.

BOOK I

The Morning

❧

CHAPTER I

The house stood upon a gentle slope, from which you might look down a broad, sun-flecked avenue into the forests which lined the creek. Two-storied, with double porticos upon three sides and great white pillars about which a man's arms would scarcely go, it was hidden in a grove of pecans and magnolias which had the depth and stillness of cathedral archways. The ground beneath was soft and glossy, and one wondered if the deep, rich green had ever been trod by a foot.

It was March, and Southern springtime. The magnolia trees, some of them a hundred feet high, were in the full tide of their splendor, of crisp, green foliage studded with cream-white flowers. Here and there on the lawn were rose trees of more than a man's height, flashing like beacons with their weight of cloth-of-gold roses a span across, crimson and orange, with petals soft and heavy as velvet. About the lawn were scattered banana trees, pomegranates, and huge scarlet lobelias. Tall hedges of jasmine and sweetbrier ran around the house and along the sides of the lawn, while beyond them on one side stretched a grove of orange trees in full blossom, a sea of flowers which loaded the breeze with sweetness. On the other side was the flower garden, whose riot of color and perfume had gathered the bees and humming-birds from miles around, filling the air with a sound as of distant machinery.

It was high noon, and the air was heavy with sunlight. In front of the mansion everything was stillness, save for a slowly moving old Negro who was tending the trees. Through the open doorway there came into view a group of figures, an aged, white-haired gentleman, an almost equally aged Negro, and four white children; they descended the steps slowly and came across the lawn. The first-named towered above the group, a striking figure; he moved with trembling step, yet holding his spare frame stiffly erect. His hair was snow-white and his face withered with age, but still full of power—with high forehead, prominent nose, and alert expression. He carried his head high, and sniffed the air as he went, learning thus of the springtide about him—for he was blind.

The old Negro tottered alongside, carrying his shawl and cane. The two oldest boys supported him with their shoulders, taking step for step.

"Grandfather," said the child in advance, a little girl, "let us go to the orange tree."

"I will try," he responded.

A few rods farther on was a great gnarled orange tree, with rustic seats about it. "I'll spread your shawl, grandfather," said the little girl, running ahead.

They reached the seats, and he sank down with a sigh; the old Negro sat near him, and the children gathered about his knee.

"Now!" the girl exclaimed, "and what are you going to tell us?"

"Breath, dear!" smiled the other. "Play awhile first. How are the oranges, Plato?"

"Mos' ready, Marse 'Dolph," said Plato, gazing up at the golden fruit left from the year before to ripen, and shining like jewels amid the blossoms. "Few mo' days in de sun, Marse 'Dolph."

"Grandfather, the new governess is coming to-morrow," put in the handsome blond boy called Allan. "Did they tell you? She wrote from New Orleans."

"Tell us about King's Mountain!" broke in the girl.

"No, no, about Sir Leslie!" said Allan.

"I say General Coffee!" cried another of the boys, the black-eyed and arrogant one named Randolph for his grandfather.

There was a debate, above which the little girl kept crying insistently, "King's Mountain!"

"But, Ethel dear," said the old man, "I told you all that only three days ago."

"It was a week ago, grandfather, and I've forgotten all of it."

The grandfather hesitated. "Did you ever meet Sevier before?" asked Allan, suddenly.

"Not until the day before the battle, my boy."

"Did he know you?"

"No, indeed, Allan. How should he have heard of me? I was only a boy of eighteen. But I was on guard when he and his men rode up to the camp."

"How did they look, grandfather?"

"I thought they were Indians," answered the old man; "they wore belts of beads, and fringed hunting-shirts and leggings, and tomahawks. Ah me, but they were fighters—wild, gaunt men, with grim faces that promised a battle!"

"And Sevier?" asked Allan.

"Sevier?" said the grandfather. "He was the handsomest man I ever saw—you had only to hear him laugh once and you would follow him forever. Think of a man who fought thirty-five battles and never lost one, and never got a wound!"

Marse 'Dolph paused a moment; the children seemed to know that he was safely started. "I think," he began again, "that was the blackest hour of our Revolutionary War. It was blackest of all in the South—the British had conquered Georgia and captured Charleston. When I left home, Cornwallis had swept through all North Carolina with his Tories and his blood-thirsty Indians; he had overwhelmed General Gates at Camden, and Tarleton had wiped out Sumter. But over in the mountains in Tennessee were the Holston settlements, where the backwoods fighters lived, and the British threatened that if they took part in the war their homes would be burned. And ah, you should hear men tell of the fury that message roused! It was the brutal Ferguson who sent it—a man who had been burning and hanging through three colonies. Sevier and Shelby passed the word; the Holston men flew to arms; and two thousand of them, facing the cold on the snow-covered mountains, without tents or baggage, marched for a week over into North Carolina. There it was that our party met them and told them where Ferguson had camped. They were almost exhausted, but they picked nine hundred of their best, and we marched all night. The next day we came upon the regulars and Tories—a thousand of them—at King's Mountain."

Here, before the great event, the story-teller always paused, and raising one knee upon the other, he would say with slow preciseness: "Here is the mountain, and here is the North Carolina border, and here is the way we approached. Here, by Allan, is where Sevier was, and here were Shelby's Kentuckians. Colonel Cleavland's men were to get round the mountain, but somehow the British discovered us too soon, so we had to ride like fox-hunters, headlong through the forests and the thickets, over rocks and ravines. But we got there, I tell you!"

All these things the children knew quite by heart; but they never failed to listen spellbound. Gradually the old man's memory would kindle, as scene by scene the panorama unrolled itself before memory's eye. The passion of the battle would seize hold of him; he would hear the music and the storm, "the thunder of the captains and the shouting." Once more he was shoulder to shoulder with these heroic men, striding to their heroic deed; weakness and old age fled away and a new world leaped into being, a world to which he belonged, and in which he was not blind. So as with swift words he poured out his eager tale to the little group around him, it was like the waving of an enchanter's wand. They sat lost to all things about them, tense and trembling, clutching each other's arms when he made a gesture.

For now the British have discovered the approach; their pickets are firing and dashing up the hill; and Sevier, lifting himself in his stirrups, is shouting the word, and the mountaineers are bounding up the slope, making the forest echo with their war-whoops. Far ahead one can see the redcoats forming their line, dragging out wagons to make defences—and hear above all the din the shrill silver whistle which tells that the hated Ferguson is there. Now and then one of the backwoodsmen stops, and, crouching low, takes aim; until, as the firing grows faster and the fight hotter, the crashing volleys thunder from the British lines, and the combat is swallowed in rolling clouds of smoke.

But still the men press on, firing as they can, hurling their tomahawks before falling back to reload. When the red-coated lines sweep forward, as again and again they do, the frontiersmen turn and flee, for, being without bayonets, they cannot meet a charge. Every time the British halt they are after them again, however, hanging to their very heels. "No troops in the world ever fought like that before," says Grandfather Montague; "but these are Americans, and every man of them is there to win or die.

"There were terrible things happened in that battle," the grandfather would continue; "you would go groping up the hill through the smoke, and suddenly it would break away and bayonets leap out of it at you. But it was not an hour before their fire began to slacken, and our men seemed to find it out all at once; they yelled and went over the summit, teeth and claws, and just tore 'em up! They raised a white flag, but it was a long time before we saw it, in all that smoke and din. When we did see it and knew it was victory—oh, my children, what a yell went up!"

There were many other stories of battle which Grandfather Montague could tell; to go all the way back to England, there was the first Sir Leslie Montague, who had defended his king so bravely at Marston Moor, and had nonetheless been captured by a plain Commonwealth soldier, who called himself Captain Otis, but was nothing but a Shropshire miller for all that. Quite wonderful it was to hear how Sir Leslie had broken loose in the night-time, and, freeing two of his companions, had seized the captain, flung him on a horse, and dashed out of camp with him; also how the gay cavalier had let him go again, out of pure devilment, or because, as he declared, he had so sturdily refused to go back to his mill and call himself a captain no more.

There was also a second Sir Leslie Montague who had come to Virginia and had been a famous Indian fighter. He was the father of the old man now talking. He had earned wealth and reputation as a lawyer, and later had moved to the far South, into lower Mississippi, and bought ten thousand acres of the swampy bottomlands of Wilkinson County. Here he had brought his Negro slaves and cleared his plantation—Valley Hall; from here he had raised his company when war broke out with England again in 1812—and when the men of Wilkinson County had to be drafted to stay at home.

Sometimes, after long dwelling on the past, the deeps of the old man's soul would break open, and the children would sit trembling. For his journey was almost done; he gazed into the face of death, and about him there hung a touch of awe. When he told of these heroes he had known: "Some of them trod this very spot," he would say, "and laughed and sang here, in their pride. And their lives were precious to them, they loved the world; they had wives and children, and hopes unuttered; and yet they marched out into battle and died for their country—to make her, and to keep her, free. Sometimes at night I seem to see them, and to hear their voices crying out to me that it must not all be for nothing! When I am gone, too, the lives that they lived, and the dreams that they dreamed, will be gone forever. Yet it was all for you, that you might reap where they had sowed and be happy where they lay dying. So I wonder sometimes if I have told you enough, if I have done all I can to make you love your country, to make you realize how precious it is. My children, you may live ever so nobly, you may die ever so bravely, but you will do nothing too good for your country! All the hope and all the meaning of the ages is in it, and if it fails there will never be any success. Tens upon tens of thousands have laid down their lives to win its freedom; and freedom is first of all things, and best. So it is that you may dream your noblest dream and hope your noblest hope—but your country will be greater than that! You may dare any peril, you may suffer any pain, but you will not do too much for your country. There is nothing that can ever take the place of it—not friendship, nor love, nor anything else in life can be so precious."

CHAPTER II

~~~~~~

Two sons had been born to Grandfather Montague, and both lived still at the old place: the elder, Henry Montague, state senator from Wilkinson County, with his one child, the boy Allan; and Hamilton, the younger brother, with his wife and their three children.

The senator was a lawyer, and had gone North to study. Grandfather never wearied of telling of the wonderful coincidence, how when he had taken the boy to Harvard to start him on his new career, the first professor whom they met was named Otis; and how when he invited them to his home in Boston, the first picture they saw in his parlor was of an ancestor of the family, that same Shropshire miller whom the earlier Sir Leslie had fought in England.

Seven years, altogether, Henry Montague had spent North; ten years later he had returned again, and when he came home that time he brought with him as his bride the youngest daughter of the Otis family, the lovely blonde Lucy, as yet still in her teens. That had been a decade ago, but the darkies of Valley Hall still discussed the festivities which took place on that home-coming.

For just a year the beautiful Lucy had been the life of Valley Hall; and then one night she died in childbirth, and there was left only a painting—and the boy Allan. Allan's uncle, Hamilton Montague, had brought his wife to Valley Hall to become the mother of the orphan and the mistress of the household. Of their two children, Randolph, tall and imperious, was three years older than Allan; Ralph, the younger, was just his age. Little Ethel had been born after they came.

Besides these there was generally a numerous company of guests, and relatives. Also, of much importance to the boys, there was "Uncle Ben" Handy, a brother-in-law of Hamilton Montague —a gentleman without income or occupation, but nonetheless a welcome member of the family. It was one of the characteristics of the old Southern feudalism that all members of a family must be provided for.

Allan's father was a lawyer, riding the circuit, and burdened with the cares of state besides; Hamilton Montague was charged with the management of the plantation, with two overseers and about six hundred Negroes. He was a grave and unbending man, and so it was that Uncle Ben Handy was the chief grown-up companion of the boys. It was Uncle Ben who told them stories and played jokes with them on others. It was Uncle Ben to whom they turned whenever they sought amusement—who could carve beautiful walking-sticks, and make traps with which to catch birds and willow whistles to make noises.

A wonderful place was Valley Hall for children, a universe in itself. There were squirrels and birds without end in the trees, and the yards were full of chickens, ducks, and turkeys, pigs, cows, sheep, horses and dogs. There were two great stables, one for the work horses and mules, and one for the family stud; every person in the family owned a horse, to say nothing of the children's ponies and the four black mares which were hitched to the family coach. The plantation was divided into two farms, each worked separately, and one had to walk half a mile to the villages of the field-hands; but the quarters of the house servants, a row of whitewashed cabins, stood in the rear of the "Big House" and here was an innumerable collection of playthings: all ages and sizes, from toddlers up to overgrown wild boys and girls in their teens, young darkies for the children to muster into regiments and drill and quarrel with, as to which should be the Americans and which the ever-defeated British. There was very little distinction of master and slave between the white children and the black ones, as these latter belonged to Aunt Jinny the cook, Taylor Tibbs the coachman, Pericles the butler, or Thomas Jefferson the head gardener.

Within the limits of the plantation the children might ride their ponies to their hearts' content. It was rich bottom-land with deep, black soil. Its slope ran down to Buffalo Bayou, where were tangled cane-brakes and dense forests, swamps of cypress draped with gray moss and hiding parasitic flowers of gorgeous hues. Into these no child might venture, for here were alligators and moccasins, wolves and bears, and sometimes at night a yelling panther. But there was Ned the hunter, a great giant of a man, the only Negro on the place who was allowed to carry a gun, whose duty it was to creep through the forests and bring back at night upon his shoulder a load of wild ducks or turkeys, or a runaway pig.

Upon the cultivated part of the plantation were the fields of cotton, which brought Valley Hall its wealth, stretching as far as the eye could reach. Here, at whatever hour of the day one came, one found the gangs of field-hands at work, men and women, in the early spring breaking up the black soil with their heavy hoes, the drivers, whip in hand, watching them to see that none shirked. They were picturesque from the distance, but not when one rode close, for they were brutelike and unthinkably filthy.

The countryside was occupied by wealthy cotton planters—there was no other population from Homochitto Creek until you reached Woodville, the pretty little court town ten or fifteen miles from the Hall. Most of these neighbors were of aristocratic blood and so were welcome at the Hall; but not all, for there were some nouveaux riches, ex-overseers, Negro-traders, or what-not—vulgar persons who had made fortunes out of cotton; one spoke to them on the road, but one did not know their wives.

Such as were welcome came whenever they could, and stayed as long as they could be persuaded. There was rarely a time when there were not half a dozen guests at dinner, which made Aunt Jinny's life a perpetual adventure. Huge dinners they were, and Hamilton Montague sat at the head of the table and carved the great turkey or the saddle of venison or mutton, while Mrs. Montague presided at the foot over the silver coffee-urn.

Once or twice a year Mrs. Montague and the children went in the family coach upon a miraculous excursion; by riding all afternoon along roads lined with goldenrod and spending the night at a friend's or a kinsman's home, and then riding all next day, one came at last to Natchez, to the marvelous little city, with its streets blocked with cotton bales and its wharves where the river steamers came to be loaded with these cotton bales. The steamers in those days were floating palaces; you saw one go by in the night-time, a mass of gleaming lights, the throb of its machinery beating back in echoes from the tree-lined banks, and your soul went after it, into faery lands not forlorn. Or to watch them loading by flaring torchlight—the broad-backed, half-naked Negroes and the long chutes down which the bales of cotton leaped madly to the deck! "Niggers above and paddies below," was the rule at that game. "Niggers too precious to risk," men said; "you don't have to pay for the paddies." And last, but not least, the great Mississippi river—the children would have stayed all day to watch it, with its tangled driftwood, the long rows of cotton-wood trees on its banks, the mud-flats with pelicans and herons stalking along.

And then there was the annual trip to Pass Christian. Once a year, when the hot season approached, there began to be a stir in Valley Hall—a giving of orders and a packing of trunks, and one morning the great coach appeared, followed by all the other vehicles available, and servants and family, trunks, boxes and bundles, rolled away in a long procession, the men-folks riding ahead like Arab sheiks leading their families and herds in search of pastures new. Pass Christian was a gulf-coast resort, where the aristocracy of the lower South had their summer villas; the Montagues spent a week in reaching it, always camping out of doors at night when the weather was fair.

Then also there was Christmas: looked forward to for months by old and young. There were parties and balls, winter and summer, at the Hall, but none of them was anything like the Christmas party. Then the guests journeyed from far states, and there was fattening of geese and turkeys for weeks beforehand. On Christmas Eve there were bonfires as big as the smoke-house, and whole beeves roasting before them; and inside every room was crowded, and there was dancing and feasting and egg-nogg to make one's head reel. The next morning there were stockings over the fireplace, and after breakfast a raid upon the brick "storehouse," from whose depths Mrs. Montague and her children brought presents for the servants. In the afternoon there was a great hunt for the gentlemen, and much blowing of horns and barking of dogs; in the evening more dancing and singing and brewing of punch. These festivities lasted for ten days, and during that time no guests went away and no work was done on the plantation except by the cooks and other house servants.

Such was the children's world, and they knew little about any other. To be sure, they had an English governess and they read Sir Walter Scott and dreamed of chivalry. Also they knew of the North from Allan's father; an unpleasant sort of place, where it snowed half the time and no cotton grew, and the people thought only of money, and the servants were Irish instead of black people! Worst of all it was the North that was the habitat of the monster called *Abolitionist*. And whenever the grown-ups were not discussing plantation affairs, and the price of Negroes and cotton, and the horse races at New Orleans, they talked politics—and Abolitionists!

The Abolitionists believed that Negroes were as good as white men, and that they ought to be free. They were always holding meetings and "resolving" and publishing articles to say that slaveholders were brutal men who beat the Negroes cruelly and wantonly; some Abolitionists came down from the North to stir the slaves to revolt, and to steal them and carry them off to Canada. At first people had tried mobbing these intruders, and the Southern legislatures had put prices on the heads of the worst of them, but neither of these methods seemed to do any good. They had gone on just the same for fifteen years now, and had even become so bold as to send petitions to Congress, which had, of course, refused to receive them—only a terrible old man, ex-President John Quincy Adams, who had been in Congress since nobody could remember when, kept making a disturbance about it. So things went from bad to worse, and naturally the people of the South got more and more angry.

There was a question which was much discussed at Valley Hall—never in the presence of Grandfather Montague, who would not stand it, but often when the neighboring planters stopped by at the office. One of the neighbors of the Montagues was a Mr.

Davis, who lived a mile or two outside of Woodville; he had once been a lieutenant in the United States Army, but had retired many years ago and turned farmer and student of politics; two years ago he had come out of his retirement and been elected to Congress, at the same time that Allan's father had been sent to the state senate.

Jefferson Davis was a very dignified gentleman, with a spare figure and face, precise and stately in his manners, but irritable, and when excited both eloquent and imperious. He had thought a great deal about this question of Abolitionists, and took an alarming view of it. In his opinion the North was preparing to make war upon Southern institutions; and day by day, with endless iteration, he pointed out the ever growing signs of this. It was of no use, he asserted, to believe that Congress could not interfere with Slavery. The struggle would come over the territories; the North meant to exclude slave owners from their rights in the new lands they had fought to win, and if the North once got political control, could it not amend or override the Constitution as it chose? Mr. Davis was beginning to question whether Congress had any right at all to exclude slaves from a territory—or, if this view seemed too radical, whether the exercise of the right was not a danger from which the South ought to protect itself by threatening immediate secession.

There was nothing especially new about these views; Senator Calhoun had been advocating them for years, but men were only now beginning to awaken to their truth. Out of the deepening alarm had grown a crusade which the people of Valley Hall watched with tense interest, and Senator Montague had declared to Mr. Davis that if it failed he should conclude that Mr. Davis was right.

Ten years ago one of the Montagues had given his life for Texas. According to Valley Hall way of thinking, the wretched mongrel inhabitants of Mexico—degenerate illustrations of the consequences of the doctrine of "equality" and of white men's mixing with lower races—a people who had had some forty revolutions in the last twenty years—had been at last swept out of Texas. Ever since, the people of the South had been aiming to bring Texas into the Union. Incredible as it seemed to the South, and in full light of the notorious fact that France and England were intriguing for the state, the North had balked this plan, for the avowed reason that it might bring about a war with Mexico, but really because Texas would become a slave state. And now, when after desperate efforts this state had been saved to the Union, Abolitionist fanaticism was trying to limit its borders, again upon the old pretext that it might bring about a war with Mexico!

The President, James K. Polk, was a good Democrat, elected by Southern votes; but the thing which Valley Hall waited breathlessly to see was whether the pressure from the North, the clamor of the Abolitionist press and pulpit could avail to turn him back. Valley Hall was not afraid of war—was it not the manifest destiny of the Americans to conquer the territory of this "hateful and vicious race of Indian half-breeds and degenerate Spaniards?"

Thus there were days of excitement on the plantation, when all the prophesies of Mr. Davis were scattered to thin air. For first the news had come that General Taylor had been ordered to plant the American flag on the banks of the Rio Grande; and then, one never-to-be-forgotten day in April, Uncle Ben had dashed up the road with foam-covered horse, and shouted that Mexico had fired upon the flag, and that the war was on!

That day Allan's father wrote a letter to his constituents, which was published in the Woodville *Republican,* resigning his seat, and announcing that it was his intention to raise a company. After this there was never an instant's rest at Valley Hall—messages coming and going day and night, and the hum of preparation in the air. Hamilton Montague enlisted, and soon afterward it was announced that Mr. Davis was on his way from Washington to take command of the regiment. It was the famous "First Mississippi," and in it was the flower of the aristocracy of the state; the house was thrown open to Senator—now Captain—Montague's company, and men slept on the sofas and the verandas and put up tents on the lawn.

Never could the children forget the morning the company marched away, and how awful was the silence that fell upon the Hall. There was no one left but Grandfather Montague, the mother, and Uncle Ben. Even the chickens and ducks were gone, and you had to admit that you missed the squealing of the pigs at feeding time. The family lived only for the mail-days after that, and poor Mrs. Montague would whisper to her children that it was the duty of a soldier's family to be brave—and burst into wild weeping while she said it.

The regiment sailed from New Orleans for Point Isabel, the nearest harbor to General Taylor's victorious army. Its war hardships began at once; it was encamped on a bare island, baked by the sun, buried by sand-storms, and frozen by "northers," until forty of the men were invalided or dead. It was August before the army got on the march; General Taylor was a Whig, and the administration could not quite make up its mind to support him.

But alas, the only other commander in sight, General Scott, was also a Whig, so there was no help for it! The start was made at last, and suddenly after months of weary waiting, came news of a victory that set the whole heart of the South pulsating with pride and joy. The Mexicans, ten thousand of them, had fortified themselves in the city of Monterey. They should have held it against ten times that number, for every house was a fortress, low and square, with heavy walls of Spanish masonry, and flat roofs and grated windows; but six thousand Americans had taken it with three days' fighting, capturing nearly twice their own number of men! On the second day General Quitman's Mississippi brigade, the city looming before it in a mist of smoke, had swept forward in one grand charge, and amid a rain of fire had planted its flags on the battlements. The next day the same brigade had marched into the city—to the very centre of it, in spite of a ceaseless opposition from windows and roofs, from ditches, canals, and barricades. Tears of pride ran down Grandfather Montague's cheeks when that news arrived.

Again there was weary waiting; the flabby administration, which by this time had earned the contempt of all men, had somehow come to the conclusion that two Whig heroes might be less troublesome than one, and so the expedition for the march to the City of Mexico was being organized under General Scott. Meanwhile, however, there came from Washington sudden tidings which made men stare at each other in consternation—which sent a pulse of indignation through the South, from Maryland to Texas. Here were Southerners pouring out their life-blood for the benefit of the whole nation, and up in Congress was a Pennsylvania Democrat named Wilmot proposing to pass a law excluding Slavery from all the territory which the war might bring! Fire and fury breathed from the letters which came to Valley Hall when that news reached the army.

General Quitman's brigade was drawn away for the new expedition, but the First Mississippi remained with General Taylor, who, with his forces reduced to four or five thousand, retired to Buena Vista. The people of Valley Hall had come to consider the war over, as far as they were concerned, and Mrs. Montague had grown cheerful again, when one ever memorable night there was a galloping up the road, and excited voices down below, and the children rushed down to hear the tidings of another battle between Taylor's little force and twenty thousand Mexicans under Santa Anna—a battle in which the latter had been routed, and in which Colonel Jefferson Davis's regiment had won for itself everlasting fame. It was the Natchez *Courier* from which the news was read, and it said that Colonel Davis himself had been shot in the foot, and Captain Montague "severely wounded."

It was another week before the family could learn the truth, that the wound was a shattered knee-cap which would cripple Henry Montague for life. But a victory it was! The one paper they had was worn ragged—it had been brought a day ahead, and neighbors on horseback galloped from thirty miles around to see it.

The general and Colonel Davis had been at the rear; when they reached the field the Americans were retreating. Davis had placed himself at the head of his regiment and ordered a charge; down a ravine and up the other side they had gone—double quick —and straight into the very centre of the Mexican line. Scarcely, however, had the enemy been checked, when the regiment was charged by a troop of lancers, many times its own number. The swift action of Colonel Davis at that moment made him a Southern hero. He ordered his famous "V-formation" along the edge of the ravine—a V with the point *away* from the enemy instead of towards him! It was a challenge, and it was accepted; the lancers thundered into the gap, and with one volley the Mississippi riflemen strewed the ground with them and turned their charge into a wild retreat. Yet even that had not been enough; when you read the story it sounded like a mediaeval epic, whose hero gallops here and there about the field and conquers everywhere he goes. Exhausted and depleted as the regiment was, with half its officers wounded, it had turned to another part of the ground, where Bragg's battery was defending itself against an overwhelming force, and taking its foe in the flank, had driven him back and saved the day.

General Scott began his famous march of victory—and meanwhile Mississippi made ready to receive her glorious heroes. Hamilton Montague obtained leave to escort his crippled brother, and by slow stages they brought him home, prostrate and fearfully wan. By the time the invalid was able to be helped about, another Christmas had come, and General Scott was in Mexico City, and Colonel Davis in Washington as Senator from Mississippi, the highest reward that his state could find him. General—soon to be Governor—Quitman, of fiery fame, was also there, doing his best to urge a caitiff administration to hold Mexico forever, now that it had been won. Many Mexicans, even, desired this—it was whispered that General Scott had been offered a million dollars and the presidency if he would only stay and rule them.

But it was a sad Christmas at the plantation—it was as if every one upon it had lost a parent; for Grandfather Montague was dead.

CHAPTER III

Peace had come at last, but no peace for the South. A vast territory had been won for the Union, but the South had to fight for it once more, and in the halls of her own Congress. The Wilmot Proviso hung before her, a perpetual menace; the hordes of Abolitionist fanaticism were aroused, and no one could say what they might not attempt. Men suspected they had been behind the efforts of the Mexican peace commissioner to have Slavery excluded from the new lands by treaty; if so, they had been well rebuked, for Mr. Trist, the American commissioner, was a Virginian, and had declared, in immortal language, that if the offer had been "of the territory increased tenfold in value and covered with pure gold a foot thick," he would not have accepted it upon such a condition.

Senator Davis was now in Washington, vigilant, vehement, and justified by events. Grown wiser by experience, and following the lead of Calhoun, he was now boldly declaring that the Constitution gave Congress no power to exclude slaveholders from their rights in the territories. The first fight was over the bill admitting Oregon; Senator Davis had no expectation that slaves would ever go to Oregon, *but "the principle" was at stake.* His constituents at Valley Hall read his speeches, and wondered how the rest of the world could continue unconvinced as it did.

The year 1848 was the year of the presidential election, and in the Democratic conventions the same battle was fought, by William Lowndes Yancey of Alabama, one of the heroes of the cotton states. Yancey denied the dangerous power of exclusion, not only to Congress, but to the territorial legislatures as well—a distinction with a future before it. Yancey had brought the doctrine safely through in his home state, but he went back discomfited from the convention—the South was not yet awake to its peril. The Democratic party dodged the issue, and Valley Hall gave its votes to its own hero—General Taylor—who was a candidate without a platform, but a Southerner, and the father-in-law of Senator Jefferson Davis besides.

Still another year passed. At home and abroad men discussed these questions, eagerly, passionately, and with growing impatience. For little by little the terrible fact had been becoming plain to the South that the dreaded Wilmot Proviso, which the Virginia legislature had vowed it would "resist at every hazard and to the last extremity,"—that though it had been dropped in Congress it was to be carried out in the territories themselves. Gold had been discovered in California, and instantly there had been a rush of people to that place. One year it had been a wilderness, with a few Mexican villages; the next it was a community with a hundred thousand inhabitants—and all Abolitionists!

Congress had left them without a government, and they had formed one for themselves; now they stood asking for admission as a state, and with a state constitution prohibiting Slavery! Miners from all parts of the world, foreigners and Yankees, most of them, owning no slaves themselves and wanting no slaves to compete with, they purposed to keep the South out of the gold-fields which the South had fought for in the war with Mexico. The issue was plain, and public sentiment was forming quickly. The legislatures of the various states passed resolutions; in Mississippi there was a convention in the fall, and a call was out, engineered from behind by Calhoun, for a convention of the Southern states to meet at Nashville in the spring.

Congress was to meet in December, and thither all thoughts were turned. The hopes of the South in General Taylor were now known to be vain; he was in favor of admitting California, and had come to regard Jefferson Davis, his own son-in-law, as little better than a traitor. When Congress met it took three weeks, amid altercations leading almost to blows, to elect a speaker; and then came endless speechmaking and hurling of defiance. The Wilmot Proviso was up again, and one Giddings of Ohio was resolving that all men were equal; on the other side, Governor Troup, of Georgia, was proposing that his state should march upon Washington and dissolve the government. It was of these breathless events that the boy Allan was reading one morning when his father came into the room, limping upon his cane, and brought the boy to his feet at a bound by the announcement, "My son, we are going to the North."

Allan could only stare and exclaim, "Sir?"

"I say we are going to the North," repeated his father.

"Who, sir?"

"You and I."

"For what, father?" he asked.

"We are going to Boston to live. I have not said anything to you about it; I wished to wait until I was certain. It is my health, in the first place; the doctors tell me that I shall never get perfectly well except with a change of climate. Also you know, my son, you must go to college, some day."

"I don't want to to a Yankee college!" cried Allan.

"You will have to go somewhere," said his father, smiling. "Then, too, remember that you have an uncle and an aunt and some cousins in Boston."

"Abolitionists!" the boy exclaimed.

"I hope not, my son; though I have not heard much from them since your Grandfather Otis died. Also there are matters of business, Allan, which fall in with the plan. Uncle Hamilton and some of our neighbors think we could do a great deal better if we bought our supplies wholesale for ourselves, and they want me to consider the plan of finding a direct market for our cotton. Each one of these things is a motive, of course; so far as you are concerned, it is that you are twelve, and that you ought begin to fit for college."

"When are we going?" asked Allan.

"In a couple of weeks. We shall travel by land, and stop for a while in Washington, so that we can see what is going on there."

Allan looked about him, dazed. Never before in his life had he thought that he might leave Valley Hall.

"Very well, father," he said at last, suppressing a gulp; "I should like to go North, I think."

But a few minutes later, meeting a "woolly-headed," ebony-hued little boy, clad in the cast-off uniform of a drummer-boy of the First Mississippi—Jereboam Anaximenes, his own particular "body servant"—Allan flung his arms about him and burst into tears.

It was the afternoon of the 22d of February, 1850, and Valley Hall was enormously in motion. There were not only all the house servants of the Hall, but all from the Hopper plantation, and from the Masons' and the Hindses' as well; dressed in their finest, and superintended by Pericles, the butler, and Taylor Tibbs in full red, they were hurrying about in a fashion rarely seen at Valley Hall. There was a little platform, and around this four tables, set in concentric semicircles, the outside one a hundred feet around, a length which surely no table in history had ever approached before. Upon them were spread snowy cloths, and to them were borne endless loads of plates and glasses, and knives and forks, vases of flowers, and huge dishes of mysterious cold things, carefully covered, and each with a boy carrying a fan to keep the flies away. At one side, gangs of fieldhands were bringing load after load of firewood and placing them in heaps round about. Yet others were stringing lanterns from the trees, and carrying long benches from some place of storage behind the house.

Amidst all this the children flew here and there, breathless with excitement; yet at times one of them, Allan, would stop and gaze about him, and tears would come to his eyes. Back there by the stables was Taylor Tibbs, Jr., washing off the family coach; for when all this feast was eaten, and all these fires were dead, Allan was to be borne away—away from Valley Hall— for what time and to what future no one could tell him.

There were a few early guests upon the verandas, ladies and gentlemen, chatting and watching the busy scene. Among them was one who had been pointed out to the boys, Mr. Yancey, the famous orator from Alabama; they eyed him furtively, but wonderingly. He was something of a disappointment, a quietly dressed, plain-looking man of short stature, speaking politely when spoken to, but for the most part silent, with tightly pressed lips, and a rather sullen expression of face. He strolled away when unobserved, and Allan saw him pacing up and down beyond the shrubbery, his hands behind him, and his head bowed. Allan wondered just why it had been necessary to send out of Mississippi for some one to make a speech at a barbecue.

Now the sun began to drop and more guests to arrive, some of them having ridden all day; the tables by that time were quite covered with mysteries, and there hung between great poles near the fires a whole ox, a sheep, and quite a string of turkeys. When the twilight had fairly come, the lawns and verandas were alive with throngs of people—a thousand, perhaps. The lanterns were all lighted, and soon the fires began to crackle and then to blaze; before long the scene was as bright as day, and the scent of roasting meat filled the air. Somewhere a Negro quartet was singing, and there came the strains of an old camp-meeting melody, carrying the words:

"My poor body lies a-mouldering in the clay,
But my soul goes marching on!"

It was perhaps an hour before the great repast was ready and the word went round, "To the tables!" From the "Big House" there came a line of Negro waiters, bearing smoking dishes aloft; and soon there was stretched out upon a table the huge body of a barbecued ox. A dozen carvers fell upon him, and in a twinkling, portions of him were on everybody's plate.

So, with laughter, and joking, and calling aloud, and flying about of waiters, the meal went forward. Toward the end you saw, at each table, a huge bowl of punch brewing; and one by one the diners laid down their knives and forks, and the waiters whisked their plates away—and every one settled back and prepared for the real feast of the evening—shouted for it, too, insistently: "Speech! Speech!"

At last the host, Hamilton Montague, rose up—his departing brother, Henry, being the guest of honor. Hamilton bade everyone welcome and with laughter and banter he retorted charmingly to their gay interruptions. Everyone in Mississippi could make a good speech in those days, for there were no theatres, no concerts, and almost no books—only speeches.

But toward the end the orator grew serious. The scene was beautiful, he said, the punch was inimitable, for it was made by his own recipe; but out in the darkness beyond were things of which one dreaded to think—behind every happy face lurked a hidden alarm. One might go on hiding it, if he chose, but wisdom cried out against such a course; in short, there was the peril of the South, and here was a master spirit to point the way. He had taken a long journey; he was awaited with deepest interest; they were at his disposal for as long as he would speak to them: the orator of the evening and the orator of the South—the Honorable William Lowndes Yancey!

And the quiet man whom Allan had been eying with so much curiosity, came upon the platform and waited patiently, bowing in acknowledgment of the applause and taking in his audience.

Then slowly, very quietly and distinctly, he began, and men sat forward electrified—oh, what a voice! Clear and vibrant and mellow, it seized one like the note of a violin, and sent tremblings down to one's very finger tips. This quiet man, standing there without a gesture or a motion, took hold of you, and where he chose to go, you went with him.

It was into the dark and silent future that he chose to take you, and oh, what a future it was! The sight of it filled you with dismay. You hated it, and desperate revolt against it leaped up with you. You flung away comfort and ease—yea, life itself, and rushed forth to battle with this iniquity.

You saw two civilizations: one of them of white men who worked—farmers, mechanics, sailors; the other of gentlemen who did not dirty their hands, but who owned slaves who tilled the soil for them. These two civilizations, having each had a vast room to grow in, had lived side by side for two generations; but now, each of them has filled its own limits. One was "The South," the other "The North." Rebel as you choose, struggle as you may, you cannot help this fact, that between those two civilizations there is irrevocable and deadly war! One is agri-cultural, the other industrial; one desires more land, the other more trade; one grows by conquest, the other by settling on the land; one is conservative, the other endlessly radical. Therefore the instant these two forces meet within the government, they grapple; and there is a struggle—prolonged, perhaps, but sooner or later one of them goes down. When it is down, mark this, down it *stays*. There is no second chance, the victor's heel is upon you. Thereafter the policy of the government is the victor's policy, and one which cuts, sinew by sinew, the power of the loser.

"Men of the South! Men of the South!" The orator was no longer quiet and formal—a fire blazed in his countenance, pas-sion streamed from his aspect, leaped in his ringing words. "Men of the South, hear me!" He raised his clenched hand aloft, and the audience strained forward, breathless, suffering. "That in-stant is come—you face it *now!* That instant is going—you know not when it may be gone!"

He paused, and you heard men gasp, and then they sank back with relief. But again in his quiet, simple manner the orator went on to expound his thesis. Here was the South, with a vast territory, more fertile than any in the world, owning a natural monopoly, cotton, and having the world in its hands. And so they produced enormous wealth; but where was the wealth, where was the wealth of the man who sat here to-night? He had land and slaves to work it, but these were only the tools of wealth; and new land when the old was worn out, and new labor also, these he had. But the profits—where were the profits? Why, once a year he went to New Orleans and spent all he owned for the necessities of life—which came, pray, from where? From the North! He could not get them from where they were cheapest—he must get them from the North! There was a tariff devised for that express purpose—"to encourage domestic indus-tries"—at the North! What had the South to do with industries? The South had no industries, and nobody knew anything about industries, thank God! But it must put its hands into its pockets and pay double prices for everything, to support the industries

[29]

at the North! And the Northern papers marvelled at the prosperity of "the country," and at the number of emigrants which the prosperity brought from Europe—all to engage in industries, supported by the South!

No mere man could ever have imagined such sarcasm as this; the orator was no longer human, he was god, come down from the skies, to tear off the veil from the hypocrisies of men. How deeply must the North despise this people, to mock at them for the same ills it caused them! He, the orator, had resigned from Congress because he would not bear what his colleagues seemed to bear quite easily, namely, to be discussed as a half-barbarous survival of a dark age, to be forever fronted with tables of statistics to prove your inferiority! There were more colleges and books and churches at the North; colleges and books and churches would seem to be among the industries that the South had encouraged! What pride must throb in the bosom of a Southern planter as he realized what a success he had achieved—that the industries he had encouraged were grown actually powerful enough to strike down the hand that fed them!

Look again! For a generation you have encouraged industries, and brought millions of poor white foreigners to serve the North, until the country is crowded beyond even the power of your purse. And what has happened? You, the South, need more territory, and wage a war. It costs ninety million dollars; you, the importing states, pay sixty million of them. You pay, also, private treasure—*and you pay your blood!* The North does not want war, scorns you and jeers at you while you wage it; but now that it is won, here is the land, and the North *does* want the land! You say they shall not have it—pshaw! you are fools, they have it already, before you have got your eyes open. There is this swarming population which you have "encouraged"; it has walked across a continent, it has sailed through two oceans— God help you, there it is! And it votes you out! You, your slaves and your civilization—it votes you out! And it gazes at you with bland innocence, and asks you if all that is not perfectly regular.

Then, too, when you object, the North tells you, "It is only one state, California." Yes, but see, there is a vast territory still at stake, and they propose a law to keep you out of that, too!

They could not pass the law, for it happened that you were still their equal in the Senate. But give them one state more—and they have the Senate!"

At this time the so-called Compromise measures of Senator Clay were before the country; and Yancey shook them into rags. The North cried out at them—but the North would come around, never fear! If the North got California as a "free state," what else mattered? They proposed to give the South a Fugitive-slave bill—a bill they would repeal when they chose, and which meantime they would never enforce. But granting that they would, the South might recover a hundred thousand dollars' worth of slaves thereby; in exchange it would lose a state worth uncounted millions! On the other hand, if Slavery were allowed in California today, Negroes would sell in the New Orleans market for five thousand dollars apiece. The South was to give up that! They were to give up *their supremacy in the nation!* This was the thing never to forget—the South was to give up its supremacy in the nation!

This man played upon his audience as a musician plays on a violin, always controlled, always masterful, with perfectly turned and finished sentences, with few gestures, with the witchery of his marvellous voice, he swept them through the whole gamut of emotions—rage, defiance, tears. He swept them onward toward war! He called upon the spirits of their fathers, the men who had hurled back the British from these shores; and ghostly presences trembled above the auditors, and called upon them for consecration. "To realize instantly the peril!" was his cry. "To gird yourselves for the battle—on the brink of the precipice to make your stand! To reply to Northern aggressions with an instant leap! To make them understand that the first move which tends to destroy your equality in this nation—no matter how they may justify it, is the signal for the ending of the Union by the forcible withdrawal of the South. You say that you can wait and secede at any time—but you cannot! Every day you are in the Union it becomes more difficult, every day the power that is feeding upon your strength will be stronger and more loath to let you go!

"Not then, but now! The future calls, a future of success without an end. Standing alone, and alert to your own interests, what happens at the North need trouble you no more. South of you is endless empire; you have conquered it once, you can conquer it again. There is Cuba, there is Central America, there is another continent beyond—nowhere is there a people able to withstand for one instant the march of your imperial power!"

The orator turned suddenly, and with arms outstretched and voice breaking with emotion, cried out to her who was the queen of these adventurings, the muse of their devotion,—the South, the South! Suddenly, miraculously, she rose before them—born of the starlight and celestial splendors—radiant with the hues of morning, singing in her loveliness, she came, she came! She came with tremblings and quiverings, with choirings and harpings of the universe of things, with fairy footsteps to dance her joy, and breaking showers of light upon her pathway. To her men fled with bosom swelling and arms outstretched—the touch of her robe was madness, her beauty was not to be borne. Queen of their lives was she, mistress of their souls was she, muse and goddess—our fair Southland!

"Oh, take us to thy heart, for thy slaves we are! Bound to thee with chains of fire, by the joys of our childhood, by the ardors of our youth, by the stern, sad vision of our later years, we pledge our faith to thee! The devotion of our mothers is of thy giving, the goodness of our sisters, the sanctity of our loves! The glory of our springtides, the fulness of our summers, the splendors of our mornings, the stillness of our nights, are all of thee! To thee our labors in peace, our courage in battle! For thee we live, for thee we should die with a song! Take us to thy heart, as we come to thee, fair Southland!"

The orator had ceased; but the tempests of emotion he had loosed raged still: men sat with faces uplifted and tears coursing down their cheeks, or buried in their arms and shaken with gusts of weeping. In the hour of that fearful consecration all were brothers—graybeards sobbed on each other's shoulders, and youths rushed away into the darkness with hands clasped to their temples.

But then suddenly one came to, and seeing the orator, with

hands dropped and his head bowed, leaped to his feet and cried out; and at once other men delivered themselves by shouts and exclamations. When the speaker came down from the platform they surged round him, wringing his hands and making incoherent protestations.

But to one—the twelve-year-old boy Allan—such an act was unthinkable; he would as soon have stretched out his hands to the burning bush from which God spoke, as to that most miraculous, most wonderful man. When the storm began to subside, he rushed away; he heard not his own father's beautiful farewell, but lay with arms stretched out upon the ground, pledging with tears of fire his love, his worship, his life, to her, the Southland, who in that wondrous hour had laid her hands upon him. The two other boys had reacted to the oratory with equal fervor, but in their own different ways. 'Dolph, always the bold one, the natural leader, went forward with the grown-ups to congratulate the speaker, the family's guest; and Ralph, as always, followed his lead.

The camp-fires were dying and the moon was up; it was time to start and the coach was at the door, before Allan realized that men were shouting his name. The family was crowded upon the veranda, and the equipage stood ready. He looked about —his last look at Valley Hall! He felt himself embraced by the family and by the sobbing Negroes, and then he was lifted into the coach. It started amid deafening cheers. As the sound receded, he burst into tears upon his father's shoulder.

It was only for a moment for his father whispered suddenly, "Hush!" and from the rear there came faint strains of singing, the old plantation's last farewell:—

> "Away! away!
> Away down South in Dixie!"

When morning dawned they were on a steamer for New Orleans, and while on board Allan chanced to open his little trunk, in the top of which he found a carefully tied package with a note, in a slow, painful hand:—

"Dear Allan,—I give you my hunting nife. I want you to keep it til you come across an abbleitionist. *Then you will know what to do!* Granfather said to die for our country, but I doutt if they would dare to hang a man for kiling an abbleitionist.

DOLPH."

CHAPTER V

In those days the traveller from the Southwest to Washington had choice of two land routes. Captain Montague chose what was called the "Southern route," by way of Mobile and the Alabama River, and thence over the new railroad into Georgia, where stages connected with another road to Charleston. By this route it took five days of steady travel to Washington, without sleeping-cars or berths, and with only five-minute stops for meals.

It was Allan's first experience from home, and to him it was a panorama of wonder: the city of Mobile with its endless rows of buildings and of ships; the blue waters of the Gulf; the magical railroad, piercing deep forests and spanning great stretches of cane-brake and swamp; and the long stage route through the high pine lands of Georgia, where the coach was forever toiling in deep sand, or thumping over corduroy roads, and sticking fast and turning out its passengers to pry it up with fence rails. Here the waste lands were covered with broom-sedge, and one passed endless successions of tumble-down shanties having broken windows patched with paper, and perhaps a lank and yellow man leaning on his gun, and a lank and yellow woman smoking a pipe in the doorway, with half a dozen badly-nourished children peering from behind her skirts. Now and then came a town, with straggling whitewashed houses, and perhaps a court-house, with some Negroes dozing upon its sunny side, or sitting upon the fences, sound asleep. Here the road would be good, and the driver would take out his quid and whoop to the horses and crack his whip and make a show.

It was in the middle of the night that they came to the second railroad; a gang was working upon it by the light of the camp-fires. The passengers had to walk down the track to where the locomotive stood puffing, the trainmen calling "All aboard," though it was nearly an hour before they started after all. In the morning there were the cotton lands and the rice swamps of South Carolina, and then aristocratic Charleston. Next a sea trip and another railroad, and at last the long bridge across the Potomac, and, in the distance, the dome of the half-finished Capitol.

So much had Allan heard of Washington, so many times had he been told of its marvels, that it was scarcely possible that he should not be disappointed. A place where great deeds were done, where even now, today, the fate of the nation was being decided; and here the same loungers at the depot, and the same Negroes in the sun, and the same unspeakable roads and ram-shackle vehicles to traverse them! The carriage which bore Allan and his father was engineered by a tattered darkey who wore a high hat without a top, and had patched out his harness with old rope and rawhide, and had made a bit out of telegraph-wire.

Washington—a combination of a few great marble piles and many shanties! Its streets had no sidewalks, and an unwary pedes-trian might get half way up to his knees in ooze while trying to cross them. Pigs ran about, serving as scavengers, and cows kept down the vegetation; a senator or a diplomatic representative would have to get out of the way of a citizen who sat on his doorstep in his shirt-sleeves doing his milking.

The travellers spent three weeks in Washington, stopping at the boarding-house where the Southern statesmen had their "mess," and where Allan met all the giants of his dreams. Their own Senator Jeff Davis was here, tortured, like Allan's father, with his wounded foot, but stately and grave as ever; his face was become thinner than ever, from suffering, and with his high cheekbones and prominent nose, his look was more imperious and cold. Here, too, was Toombs, the lion-hearted, a wild Georgia man, full-blooded, passionate, and terrible in debate. Toombs was wont to shake his black locks when he was angry, so that his admirers compared him with Danton; but when he sat at the table he was the soul of the party, and his laugh was like a drink of wine. Toombs was one of those old-fashioned American heroes whose joy it was to have their pictures taken with their vests unbuttoned and expansive clean shirt-fronts showing; but later on, Toomb's faithful biographer was to record that his was *not* clean, being stained with tobacco juice, at least on that occasion when he rode over the border into South Carolina to confound an opponent with the torrents of his inspiration. "Genius sat upon his brow," according to the chronicler, "and his eyes were black as death, and bigger than an ox's."

Toombs was a hero among strict constructionists, believing that the Constitution protected slavery, and that the Constitution was sacred. He saw no more reason why the government should carry his mail than why it should carry his cotton; and he denied its power to construct an Atlantic cable, the founding fathers having failed to provide for it. In later years it was Toombs who was to startle the land with his famous "door-sill" speech, crying out to his constituents in Georgia that the foe was on the way, and that they must meet him at that portion of their domiciles.

Here, too, was Alexander Stephens, gentle and lovable, Jonathan to this David; a man of such a tiny figure that he was forever taken for a boy—with huge head, and skin wrinkled and drawn like a mummy. The life of Stephens was one long struggle with death, and yet many held him the leader in the House of the Southern forces in the long battle over slavery. Here, too, was Houston, of deathless fame, whose career had begun when as a youth in the Creek Indian War he had gotten himself transfixed with an arrow, and in that condition had led a charge over the enemy's defences. It was Houston who had whirled the Mexicans out of Texas, and was now representing that state, clad in a catamount-skin waistcoat, ostentatiously displayed, and alternated with another of scarlet silk.

There were truly giants in those days! Their second day in Washington Allan and his father went, silent with awe, to the Senate-chamber, to hear the last dying words of Calhoun, the ancient hero of the South. The aged man crept in, half carried by his friends, pale and ghastly, his long cloak wrapped about him. He could scarcely speak, himself; a friend read his speech while he sat with half-closed eyes. Sometimes, however, at a stirring passage, he would open them, and they would glare like coals. Terrible it was to see him still pleading dumbly, with agony, to a heedless world. He had marvellously foreseen the present; twenty years before, he had foretold the struggle, and the course of history for a generation to come as well. Yet, men laughed at him.

In his speech he showed what Yancey had said at Valley Hall, of Northern encroachment upon the South. He pleaded that these things should cease, proposing as a remedy that there should be two presidents, one from each section. "He is old," said Davis, grimly; "that is as near secession as he dares."

Twenty years before, this man, Calhoun, and another mighty statesman, Daniel Webster, had fought a battle of ideas in the Senate; and for twenty years orators and editors had been doing little more than hammering the arguments of these two into the public mind. Now the hosts they had raised up stood facing each other, and all men awaited breathlessly the issue.

In three days from now, Daniel Webster was to speak, on the seventh of March—Daniel Webster, of Massachusetts, champion of Federal supremacy and of the anti-slavery forces. Captain Montague and his Southern friends awaited eagerly a tirade against slavery—for that, they felt sure, would send the hated "compromises" into the limbo of all shams.

But there were factors which these Southerners had failed to consider, and the orator's speech was far different from what they expected. Perhaps it was really that the great man was stricken with fear at the result of his own earlier course, and was trembling for the safety of his beloved Union; or perhaps it was—as the cynics sneered—that two years ahead was another presidential nomination, and that again he was cringing and plotting for the nomination and the votes. Quite a task will the angels find it on the Judgment Day to pick out the selfish from the unselfish acts of statesmen, and until that day arrives, there must continue to be two opinions among men as to the speech of Daniel Webster on that famous seventh of March, 1850.

Pompous and inflated as he might seem to future generations, his speeches did contain half a dozen passages of magical eloquence, which seized upon the hearts of his countrymen and made the history of a land for years and ages. Terrible he was in his majesty at his public moments, all his weaknesses, his vanities, his vices and ambitions forgotten. For years to come men would tell strange tales of the effects he wrought, with his giant presence and his golden floods of speech.

With astonishment the Southerners heard him deprecating the agitation of the Northerners which he himself had led; with curling lips of scorn they listened while he pleaded, first with the North, that they had got everything of importance, that California was safe, and that New Mexico could never support slaves; and then with the South to accept the compromises. "He thinks to get Southern delegates with a speech like that!" cried Toombs, "but, by God, how he'll find he's mistaken!" And so it proved in the event, and it was said that the disappointment killed him.

Great was the rage of Abolitionism on that seventh of March; but the effect of the speech was only too evident, and the Southerners in Congress recognized that they had but one hope left— the President, who was a Northerner but favored the Southern side. Upon the floor of the Senate was Henry Clay, the great "Harry of the West," indomitable old man, speaking half a dozen times a day, arguing, exhorting, imploring, cajoling, commanding—all for his beloved Union! His fate was to go down in history as preferring to be right than to be President. Often enough he was neither; but now all thoughts of personal ambition were gone; he was feeble and his end was at hand. He had no longer a care but to save the Union—and as Toombs added grimly, "to save it in his own way."

When Allan and his father left Washington the struggle was still far from its end. The last sight which they saw in the Senate was Foote, the colleague of Jefferson Davis, clad in silk stockings and "pumps," backed up against the president's desk with a pistol pointed, and Benton of Missouri, an enormous man with a toga-like cloak, flinging it wildly back and bidding the assassin to fire.

The twelve-year-old Southern boy had seen and heard great history in the making. He had not understood much of what these impassioned law-makers were saying, but he recognized that some of the speakers had stated the case of the South as Yancey had, and so he was for them. Now he was to hear the other side— and for a long time to come; for he was on his way to live in Yankee-land.

Through Baltimore—and out of Dixie! Allan sat with face glued to the window, curious to see what sort of land Abolitiondom was. What he saw aroused in him an increasing sense of indignation against the Yankees. He had just seen endless stretches of his beloved South with its wastelands and its slattern villages and crumbling houses, its forest wildernesses and wasted fields with straggling "snake" fences. This was what they had done to his people with high tariffs; while here, in the land of the Abolitionist oppressors were trim white farm-houses with neat fences and gardens, and level roads and endless ploughed-land and pasture. They had left New York and were speeding through Connecticut and Massachusetts, where you were scarcely out of one town before you were in another. "Father," the boy suddenly burst out, "is *all* the North like this?"

"All New England is," said his father, "and the rest will be soon. There are hundreds of thousands of white emigrants landing in New York every year."

"But, father," exclaimed Allan, "these people aren't foreigners; they don't talk like foreigners."

"They talk through their damned long noses," said Captain Montague.

So to hateful Boston, Allan's home for so many years to come. He had put on several coats, but still he shivered as he drove through the streets. He gazed in awe at the vistas of stores and theatres, and huge public edifices, libraries, museums—who could tell what? Here in Boston all was grim sobriety—a man would be fined if he smoked a cigar on the street, so the father complained. And think of being without personal servants—to have to lay out your own clean clothes! It was only one of a thousand outrages of which a Southerner complained, that he could not take his own servants with him to this part of his own country.

That afternoon they sent their cards to their kinsmen, and meantime Captain Montague set out to find a house. He left Allan to his own devices, and the boy fell straightway into a wonderful and most embarrassing adventure.

He had strolled up the hill from the hotel to the great Capitol building, and at this majestic edifice he stood staring in wonder, when suddenly he heard something strike the pavement at his feet, and, looking down, saw that Dolph's huge bowie-knife, which he had kept in an inner pocket, had slipped out through a hole to the ground. He gave a startled glance around him, and to his horror saw an elderly gentleman standing not ten feet away, staring, first at the knife, and then at him.

Allan flushed scarlet, and, without stopping to pick up the knife, turned and walked away. Scarcely, however, had he taken ten steps before he heard a voice behind him, "Pardon me, my son, but did thee not drop that knife?"

"No," he answered hastily, "I didn't" and hurried on.

But he did not go very far. A burst of rage swept over him. He, a Southerner, a Mississippian—to quail thus at the very outset before the power of the North! To run away—and to lie! He turned sharply on his heel, his lips set, and strode back to where the gentleman stood, holding the ferocious weapon in his hand.

Allan gazed straight into his eyes. "Sir," he said, "I told you a falsehood; that knife *is* mine."

"Oh," exclaimed the other, and held it out to him.

"No," said Allan, "I did not come back because I wanted the knife; I can get another that will do me just as well. I came, sir, because I would not let you think I was afraid of you."

The other's perplexity deepened.

"Dear me!" he said, "What does thee mean, my son? Why should thee be afraid of me?"

He was a very tall gentleman, with a stern but benevolent countenance, and a cut of clothes which made Allan think him a minister. He stood gazing down into the boy's flushed face, while still holding the bowie-knife.

"I have just come from Mississippi," said Allan, with desperate resolution; "my cousin gave me that knife so that if I met an Abolitionist—why—why—"

He hesitated. Wonder, horror, incredulity, and amusement chased one another over the features of his Quaker auditor; in the end he put on a look of much gravity, and laid his hand on Allan's shoulder, and said, "Then, my son, thee may begin with me; for I am an Abolitionist!"

There was a long pause; Allan was speechless.

"Thee has perhaps never seen an Abolitionist before?" asked the stranger, at last.

"No, sir," stammered the boy.

"And perhaps thee did not suppose they looked just like me?"

"No, sir," was his answer again; and the gentleman took his arm and said, smiling, "Let us take a little walk, my son, and talk about it." And so it happened that if any of the people of Valley Hall had chanced to be on hand, they would have seen a faithful son strolling around the Capitol grounds and talking with a "nigger thief"; yes, one who stated serenely that he had helped two thousand runaway Negroes into Canada! Who was, of all persons, the reputed founder of the "Underground Railroad" —the notorious Levi Coffin of Cincinnati!

Allan was dazed, but he listened—for what else could he do? He listened to arguments about the rights of black men, to Abolition talk of black men's sufferings. He listened, because the speaker somehow seemed to be one of the kindest and wisest gentlemen he ever had met in his life. Later on he learned that this man actually gave all his time and wealth to the managing of a store at which people might buy Southern products made by *free* Negroes—so terrible a thing did he consider Slavery! When finally he said good bye, Allan had a feeling that the universe had been turned upside down and shaken vigorously about his ears.

"Let me give thee back thy knife, my son," Mr. Coffin had said. "But do promise me that thee will not kill any Abolitionists!"

"I—I don't think I will," stammered Allan.

CHAPTER VI

Captain Montague rented a house on Beacon Street, and Allan came slowly to realize that Boston was his home.

They visited their relatives, Professor Otis of Harvard College, and his family. The professor was a grave, dignified man, whose conversation opened another new world to Allan, who had very little idea of the thing called scholarship. Otis was a widower, living with his two children and his maiden sister, at whom Allan gazed with wonder—she was so much like the picture of his lovely blonde mother at Valley Hall. She opened her heart to the homesick boy at once; and it was only after he had given himself away irrevocably that he made the desperate discovery that she, too, was an Abolitionist.

Of his two new cousins, Jack, a year younger than himself, a beautiful boy with golden hair and a laugh like a meadow brook, had become his friend on the instant. Little Lucy, three years his junior, had proven more difficult, having sat in a corner all the while, staring with wide eyes—and when Allan made advances to her, having observed, with crushing solemnity, "They tell me that you own slaves!"

His kind Aunt Mary never wounded him, but with Lucy there were daily arguments, not seldom ending in quarrels, concerning biblical sanctions of Slavery and the humanness of all people, regardless of the color of their skins.

When Allan was first worsted by the arguments for Abolitionism, he fled to his father for support; but Captain Montague was bitterly afraid of these new influences on his boy, and Allan learned at once that whatever misgivings he might have upon the subject, in the future they must be hidden in his own heart.

Henry Montague had always been an irritable man, but was doubly so since his lameness. It took all his self-control, he would vow excitedly, to live in this infernal city without losing his temper: a statement which had a strange sound, in view of the fact that he was losing it so often. He could not find a newspaper which was not filled with the clamor of the Boston radicals over the speech that Daniel Webster had made in Washington; and regularly every morning he would fling down the sheet, and, striking his cane on the floor, exclaim: "Let them go on! Let them go on! The South will be out of the Union in another three months, mark my words!"

And so it might have been—had not, at this crisis of the nation's fate, General Taylor died and a "Compromise man" become President.

All through the summer the struggle lasted in Washington; but in the end, measure by measure, the bargain was put through. The country sighed with relief and on Boston Common a salute of one hundred guns was fired. One of the items of the compact, the great concession to the South, was a "Fugitive-slave bill" of relentless strictness, one that bade fair to be enforceable at last. Living in Boston as Captain Montague had been, and perceiving what a bitter pill this was for the North to swallow, he had come, without realizing it, to look upon the bargain as perhaps not quite so one-sided after all. There were said to be twenty thousand runaway Negroes in the free states, and the law might prove of real importance, if enforced.

Allan was now going to school, hoping by two years of hard study to be able to enter the high school with his cousin. He had been told by his uncle Otis that he was a very bright boy and could do whatever he chose if he would try hard. But from the first day it was Allan against a whole environment on the subject of slavery. Perhaps if he had been able to consult with his father, for instance—he might have come through with a compromise. But since that was not possible, he had to fight the battle alone; and somehow, every single day some one struck a blow at the structure of his faith in his beautiful Southland.

At the outset, for instance, he had to change his whole conception of the terrible thing called Abolitionist. Using the word as Allan had always understood it, to refer to anyone who admitted himself opposed in any way to Slavery—literally everyone whom he met was against him; his playmates were Abolitionists, even the servants who waited upon him were Abolitionists. His father had engaged a butler, the first free Negro Allan had ever spoken to, a sedate, gray-headed old man; goaded thereto by the vehement little Lucy, Allan had urged the Negro to tell him his story. He had been a slave in Kentucky, and spent ten years of his life earning his freedom by working at night, and then, being cheated out of it and sold, had finally escaped to Canada and earned it once again.

And what became of one's convictions as to the "place" of a Negro in a city where people assured you there were thousands of them free and wealthy, and among the most respected people in the town? And where they invited you to come to their house some evening and make the acquaintance of one of these!

His perception of the difference between Northern and Southern prosperity had of course not diminished as time went on; but now he met people who assured him that the reason was not the iniquitous tariff at all, but Slavery. Like all dedicated propagandists, they would explain they were quite ready to demonstrate it at length to even a young boy, despite his passionate defence of everything Southern. Allan was told that he was precocious but he began to feel that he was stupid.

The uncomfortable conviction forced itself upon him, that he did not know as much about Slavery as he had thought he did. He knew only the limited side of it he had heard of and seen at home; but now he was told of dreadful things which he could not believe—nor disbelieve.

This statement about the sugar plantations of Louisiana—that it paid better to work the hands to death every seven years and buy new! Was it true or not? This statement that Virginia was nothing but a great breeding-ground from which twenty or thirty thousand Negroes were shipped South every year to make up a deficiency! Stories about Negroes beaten by drunken overseers, about free Negroes kidnapped in the North by ruffians! Allan could only rush away, vowing that he would never let anyone speak to him about Slavery again.

But time passed and history was being made day by day, year

by year all over the country, and it continued to be of passionate interest to the people of Boston and the serious-minded Southern boy living there. Politically, the Slavery question was supposed to be dead; and it might have been so, even in Boston, had it not been for one feature of the Compromise bill, the relentless Fugitive law. The provisions of this act, so the anti-slavery people claimed, set at naught the fundamental principles of our judicial system; they put the burden of proof upon the accused, and denied him a trial by jury. Also, with strange contempt of appearances, they awarded a double fee to the commissioner who decided the case, whenever he should decide against the Negro.

In Boston alone there were thousands of Negroes who had escaped from the South, some of them ten and twenty years ago. Many had married in the North and reared families; and now any day the sword might fall upon them. It was difficult indeed for politicians to persuade anyone to regard such a question as "dead." In the spring of 1851, when Allan had been a year in Abolitiondom, and was no longer homesick, there were wild days of excitement in Boston. First there was a fugitive by the name of Shadrach, who, being lodged in the United States court room over night, was abducted by a band of colored men. When the news reached Washington there were furious debates in Congress. The second case was two months later, when a man named Sims, a runaway from Georgia, was seized. The Abolitionists placarded the town with incendiary manifestoes; but guarded by three hundred police and the militia, Sims was got aboard ship for Savannah.

Yet the finality of the compromise was the platform of both of the political parties in the following year, when they made their presidential nominations. Daniel Webster sought the nomination of the New England Whigs, and most terrible to witness were his efforts for the prize; but he failed overwhelmingly. The Whig party hoped to repeat its previous success with a soldier, and nominated General Scott, "Old Fuss and Feathers," as the army called him. Fat and red as a turkeycock, and fully as bustling and pompous, he travelled about the country making ridiculous speeches, and pouring out his boundless affection for everything and everybody who had a vote. It proved all for naught, however. The country preferred Franklin Pierce, the Democratic candidate, an insignificant personage about whom no one knew anything save that he drank too much.

In this year died the last two of the trio of giants, Clay and Webster, the latter's place in the Senate being taken by a Boston lawyer named Charles Sumner. A trial it was for Allan's father to read the papers on the morning after this man had made his first speech at Washington, a philippic upon the Fugitive-slave law. A lawyer of wide culture and travel, a representative of all that was best in the city of Boston, it was truly a thing of significance when he stood up in the Senate and declared that one might as well try "to check the rushing waters of Niagara" as the antislavery agitation. He, a senator sworn to support the Constitution, hurled his defiance at the Fugitive-slave act. "Beware," he cried, "of the wounds of the wounded souls! Oppress not to the utmost a single heart, for a solitary sigh has power to overset a whole world!"

The words were apposite just at this time. One soul had been so oppressed, the wife of a poor college professor in Ohio. Weighed down by the care of many children, she had yet found time to make one effort to utter to the world her feelings about slavery. Her book, *Uncle Tom's Cabin,* published in the spring of 1852, had proven the greatest event of the literary kind that had ever happened in the country. Three thousand copies of it were sold on the first day of its publication, and three hundred thousand in a year. In England it was published by eighteen separate firms in the same period, and it sold a million or two of copies. It was translated into twenty languages—it was read in the hovel and in the palace, in Armenia and in Finland—the peasantry of Italy were so shaken by "Il Zio Tom" that the Pope had to forbid them to read it. It was turned into a play; it filled two houses in gay Paris, and in this country it left room for scarcely anything else at the theatres. It raised such a tempest, it shook men so, that not even the South could do without it; boys went through the trains and steam-boats in the slave states with armfuls of yellow-covered novels—probably the only piece of Abolition literature that was ever read in the South.

It was very trying to statesmen to have such a work appear—
a work which, said Rufus Choate, "will make two millions of
Abolitionists." It gave a frightful impetus to that "din and roll
and rub-a-dub of Abolition presses and Abolition lecturers," which
was sure to result sooner or later in situations embarrassing to
presidential candidates.

In the midst of this excitement Captain Montague read the
book. Allan heard him vehemently denounce its "degrading Negro sentimentalism." There were many "refutations" of Uncle
Tom composed by the indignant South, and one of these was
judged orthodox reading for Allan. The result was that his
curiosity was so piqued that one day in the Christmas holidays
of the year 1853, seeing an old copy in a bookstore, he bought
it and hid it away in his room.

Allan was now fifteen, and as he read, two emotions seized
him—one of agonized sympathy for human creatures in the grip
of a frightful evil, and the other a dazed realization that this evil
was nothing else than the "peculiar institution" of his beloved
South.

In the past three years Allan had grown quite used to the
abstract statement that slaves had feelings "like us"; but it was
quite another thing to see this in action. He felt as did the senator
in the book who had voted for the rendition of fugitives, but
when one suddenly appeared at his door, shivering and helpless,
he turned Abolitionist and "nigger thief." Allan gave himself up
to the story, and when he read the last scene, the death of Uncle
Tom, he was sobbing convulsively.

He bore the misery about with him for weeks, speaking of it
to no one; at last, however, he could stand it no more, and fled
to his uncle's house. He chanced to meet Professor Otis just
coming out of his door, and caught him by the arm and dragged
him into the parlor.

"Uncle William, you must help me. I have been reading *Uncle
Tom's Cabin!*"

The other uttered a long-drawn "Oh!"

"Yes," Allan told him, "and it's too dreadful!"

The professor put his arm about him gently. "Poor boy," he said, "it must have come hard."

"Uncle William, you must tell me something—the honest truth—you must!"

"I will, Allan; what is it?"

"I want to know if it is true; I want to know if such things can ever happen."

"I fear that they do, Allan," was the answer. "I have known of such cases."

"I can't believe it!" Allan rushed on. "I can't believe it! They couldn't be allowed in the world; people would find out about them!"

"People do find out about them, Allan," said the professor, gravely; "but when they do they are Abolitionists."

"I am going to find out," cried Allan, passionately; "I must know the truth! I must!"

Professor Otis drew the boy toward him, "I tell you what we can do, Allan; I have an engagement to-night, but I will break it and go with you. I remember the date, the fourth of January, and the chance is too good to miss. You stay here to dinner, and this evening we will go to hear something interesting. I won't tell you exactly what, but you shall have a chance to make up your own mind."

CHAPTER VII

~~~~~~

It was a pleasant evening, and so they walked. It seemed to be the professor's wish to keep his nephew from forming any opinions in advance; they came to a lecture hall and entered before he had a chance to glance at the signs outside. The audience seemed to be composed of more refined people than usual, and a sudden thought flashed over the boy; he turned and whispered, "Uncle William, is this an Abolition meeting?"

The professor smiled and answered, "No, not quite," and Allan sat back. He waited patiently, until the audience began vigorously to applaud; then with a jump he sat up and stared. Walking out upon the platform, dressed in evening costume and smiling to the multitude, was "a great, big, woolly-headed Negro."

Professor Otis had his hand firmly on his nephew's arm, as he would upon a restive colt; and Allan sat back in his seat. For perhaps half a minute the Negro stood bowing; then, the audience having at last become still, opened his mouth, and actually began to make a speech!

He was a tall and powerfully built man of about thirty-five, a mulatto; his face was typically African, and yet it was more—it seemed like an idealization, by an artist in heroic mood. Pain and suffering were written upon it, and grim resolution lurked about the mouth; the forehead was broad and bold, and the eyes intense. The man spoke with perfect self-possession, as if he had been used to it all his life; also he possessed a voice of depth and power.

"Ladies and gentlemen," he said, "when they told me that I was wanted to talk once more in Boston, I said to myself that here, at least, would be something new. For wherever I am asked to speak, some one of the managing committee invariably comes to me beforehand and says, 'We wish that you would tell your own story; we are sure that the audience wants to hear that.' And of course, my friends, that is very true, but it is also very hard on me; I assure you that it is a trial to travel up and down the American continent telling the same story night after night for years. And so I said to myself that at least in Boston everybody knows my story, and so I can indulge such originality as God has given me. But, ladies and gentlemen, an hour ago as I sat at dinner I was handed this note which I have in my hand, and which is signed by a very well-known gentleman of your city:

" 'My dear Frederick,—I am coming to-night to hear you and to bring a young Southern friend, who is agitated upon the subject of Slavery. I pray you, do not discuss abstractions to-night— *tell your own story.*' "

The speaker paused, and the audience laughed and applauded.

Allan had turned scarlet, feeling as if every eye in the place was upon him.

"I see my correspondent here in the room," said the orator, as he folded up the letter and put it in his pocket. "So I shall have to comply, I fear; and you, the rest of the audience, will have to make out as you can." The rest of the audience applauded vigorously, making clear that they could stand it.

The lecturer had been a slave upon the plantation of one Colonel Edward Lloyd, in the "Tuckahoe district" of the Eastern Shore of Maryland. The plantation was one of the largest in Maryland, and its owner one of the wealthiest and most aristocratic planters in the State. The speaker had been the property of the steward and had grown up in an isolated spot, with many other children, in a ramshackle cabin under the care of his aged grandmother. He described his life there, quietly and in the simplest language; but not two minutes had passed before he had Allan spellbound. This man had a gift of vision, and his every sentence was charged with an intensity of feeling which took it straight to the listener's heart.

A picture of Slavery—by the slave! And what a picture! You did not know how old you were, or who your father was, or where your brothers and sisters lived! Your mother had to walk twenty-four miles after working all day as a field-hand on the plantation to pay a visit to her boy! You *belonged* to some one, and you did not understand why, or whence, or for what purpose!

The plantation was a little nation of its own, having its own language, its own rules, regulations, and customs. The laws and institutions of the State touched it nowhere; there were no conflicting rights of property, for everything was owned by one man. In its isolation it resembled what the baronial domains were during the Middle Ages in Europe. Grim, cold, and unapproachable by all genial influences from without, full three hundred years behind the age in all that relates to humanity and morals."

The man told the story of his childhood, in its utter loneliness and desolation. He pictured "Aunt Katy," the steward's cook, a terrible virago who fed most of the food allowance to her own children, and left the rest to starve. He told how he had drunk the water the meat was cooked in, and fought for crumbs with the dogs; how at night he slept in the chimney-corner with his legs in the ashes to keep them warm, or crawled in to the meal-sack in the closet, his feet being sometimes so cracked with the cold that one might put a nail into them. Said the speaker: "The close-fisted stinginess that fed the poor slave on coarse corn-meal and tainted meat, that clothed him in crashy tow linen, and hurried him on to toil through the field in all weathers, with wind and rain beating through his tattered garments; that scarcely gave even the young slave mother time to nurse her hungry infant in the fence corner—wholly vanishes on approaching the sacred precincts of the 'big house,' the home of the Lloyds. Here the scriptural phrase finds an exact illustration; the highly favored inmates of the mansion are literally 'arrayed in purple and fine linen,' and fare sumptuously every day. The table groans under luxuries, gathered with painstaking care, at home and abroad. Fields, forests, rivers, and seas are made tributary here. Immense wealth, and its lavish expenditure, fill the great house with all that can please the eye or tempt the taste. Here appetite, not food, is the great *desideratum*. Chickens, ducks, wild and tame, guinea-fowls, turkeys, geese, and peafowls are in their several pens, fat and fattening for the destined gustatory vortex. Swans, partridges, pheasants, and pigeons; beef, veal, mutton, and venison; the teeming riches of the Chesapeake: trout, oysters, crabs, and terrapin; the dairy, too, probably the finest on the Eastern Shore; the fertile garden, many acres in size, with its scientific gardener, imported from Scotland. Baltimore gathers almonds, and juicy grapes from Spain, wines, olives, and brandies from France—all conspiring to swell the tide of high life, pride, and indolence. Behind the tall-backed and elaborately-wrought chairs stand the servants, men and maids, fifteen in number, discriminately selected, not only with a view to their faithfulness, but with special regard for their personal appearance. Some of these are armed with fans, and are fanning reviving breezes toward the overheated brows of the alabaster ladies; others watch with eager eyes, and with fawnlike step anticipate and supply all wants. These servants constitute the black aristocracy upon Colonel

Lloyd's plantation; they resemble the field-hands in nothing except in color; the colored maid rustles in the cast-off silk of her young mistress, while the men servants are equally well attired from the overflowing wardrobe of their young masters; so that in dress, as well as in form and feature, in manner and speech, the distance between these favored few, and ragged and toilweary multitudes of the quarter and the fields, is immense.

"In the stable you will find, kept only for pleasure, full thirty-five horses of the most approved blood for speed and beauty. Over the way from the stable is a house built especially for the hounds—a pack of twenty-five or thirty, whose fare would have made glad the hearts of a dozen slaves. Nor is this all; there is practiced at the Lloyd's a hospitality which must astonish and charm any visiting Northern divine or merchant. Viewed from his own table, and not from his fields, Colonel Lloyd is a model of generous hospitality. His house is literally a free hotel for weeks during the summer months. All that pride, taste, and money can do to dazzle and charm is done. Who can say that the servants of Colonel Lloyd are not well clad and cared for? Who can say that they do not glory in being the slaves of such a master? Who, but a fanatic, can get up any sympathy for persons whose every movement is agile, easy, and graceful, as in the case of the house servants; who evince a consciousness of high superiority? And observe that this is all that visitors ever *do see,* or that the inmates themselves see, for that matter! Colonel Lloyd would not know one of his own field-hands if he passed him; he knows only his steward, who in turn knows the overseer of each of the farms. And who of his guests visits the quarters, where in the night time sleep fathers, mothers, brothers, sisters, all in one room, upon a damp clay floor, wrapped in ragged quilts, crowded together by the dying fire? Who asks about mothers and children, husbands and wives, who are torn apart forever, when Austen Woldfolk, the slave buyer, comes to take away from the plantation its increase? Who tramps to the fields, where vulgar coarseness and brutal cruelty spread themselves and flourish, rank as weeds in the tropics; where a vile beast, the overseer, in the shape of a man, rides, walks, or struts about, dealing blows, and leaving gashes upon broken-spirited men and helpless women just out of childbirth, for thirty dollars a month—a business so horrible, hardening, and disgraceful that rather than engage in it a decent man would blow his own brains out?"

The speaker had grown terrible in his anger; lightning shot from his eyes, and his voice rose like the storm wind—as suddenly he raised his clenched hands to the sky.

"And who are you, what are you, that you dare this infamy? By what right, by what power, do you stand thus upon the backs of toiling human creatures—do you *own* them, as if they were beasts of the field that you might *eat?* By what right do you riot in luxury and spread yourself a splendor, made whole out of the blood and tears and agonies of these thousands of immortal souls? What have you done for *them,* what do you *do* for them, that they should have reared this palace for you—and for your family and your guests, your horses and your dogs? You —young Southerner, slaveholder—what, has it never occurred to you in all your life before—have you ridden out over your teeming acres, watched us toiling in the blistering sun, hour after hour, without rest or hope, seen the lash laid upon our naked and bleeding backs, *and never even dreamed that we had souls?* Look at me—look at me!" (He smote his hands upon his breast.) "Have not *I* a soul? Have not I a will—a vision—a God—like you? Hopes and loves, joys and sorrows—rights—like you? Hath not a slave eyes? If you prick us do we not bleed? If you poison us, do we not die? And yet you dare to sell us with your horses and your dogs!"

The man paused; and the audience burst forth in acclamation, in the midst of which Allan sat shuddering, hardly able to contain his feelings. When the orator again proceeded it was in a low, quiet tone.

"But I must go on to my later years—to the time when I was suddenly, by God's providence, as I have always believed, taken out of this home of all darkness."

The speaker went on to tell of his being sent to Baltimore as the servant of a little white boy; and of his kind mistress, who first taught him to read, and then tried to prevent him, when her husband had shown her its unwisdom. Step by step you saw how the soul of that beautiful and kind lady was turned to harshness and bitterness by this effort to watch and keep down and circumvent another human creature.

Next, the steward died, and the estate was divided, and his lot changed again. This time he found himself in St. Michaels, an oyster-fishing village of Maryland, notable for the drunken and sodden character of its inhabitants. There he became the property of a Captain Auld, who had got religion and taken to singing psalms, but who fed his slave upon half a peck of corn-meal a week. Finding his new slave rebellious, he at last hired him out for a year to one Covey, a savage creature whose reputation as a "Negro breaker" enabled him to hire labor for his farm for almost nothing. The Negro's picture of this character and his ferocious cruelty, made his hearers shiver.

The first day his clothing was torn from his back, and three black-gum ox-goads worn out upon him. "From the dawn of day until darkness was complete at evening I was kept at hard work, in the fields or the woods. At certain seasons of the year we were all kept in the fields until eleven and twelve o'clock at night. If at any time in my life more than another I was made to drink the bitterest dregs of Slavery, that time was during the first six months of my stay with Mr. Covey. Mr. Covey succeeded in breaking me; I was broken in body, soul, and spirit. My natural elasticity was crushed; my intellect languished; my disposition to read departed; the cheerful spark that lingered about my eye died; *the dark night of Slavery closed in upon me, and behold a man transformed into a brute!*"

Allan and his uncle came out of the place and walked down the street in silence. They had left the crowded thoroughfares and were walking through the Common, before the boy at last looked up and asked timidly, "Uncle William, who *is* that man?"

"His name is Frederick Douglass," was the reply.

And suddenly Allan broke out with passionate vehemence, "I hope that you don't suppose that *our* Negroes are ever *starved!*"

"I don't, Allan," said his uncle; "I don't imagine that gentlemen in the South treat their servants any worse than I treat mine. But if every one in the world were a gentleman, my boy, it would solve many problems."

"But I think most slave owners in the South are gentlemen!" declared the boy, in desperation. "And, Uncle William, I tell you, there are some mean Negroes, too. You just ought to see how mean they are to each other! Once when two of them got mad with each other, one of them bit off the other's nose and tore off his ears. They like to fight, and the overseers have a hard time separating them."

"Of course," his uncle answered, "not all slaves are like Douglass—if they were, the evil thing would soon cease, I assure you. Many of them, from what I gather, must be as close to savagery as they were in the jungles of Africa. I think it would be a long time before Slavery ended in this country if only the slaves were to be considered. But we are fighting Slavery, Allan, for the harm it does the white man, as well as for the sake of the Negro."

"You mean because it is wicked to have slaves?"

"Fundamentally, yes; it is a system based upon force, and therefore making impossible the highest types of civilization. Southern society for the past generation, in spite of all its refinement, has been sterile so far as intellectual things are concerned; it has made no contribution to civilization in literature, or science, or art, or philosophy, nor would it in the future, I fear."

Allan, realizing that he had no statements with which to refute his Uncle's, was silent.

"You hear Slavery justified," the other went on, "because the Negroes were so recently savages and are still brutish; but it is not only the Negroes it degrades—look at the poorer classes of the whites. You do not need me to point out the difference between a New England farmer and a Southern 'poor white'; the latter will not work beside Negroes, so he squats on the poor lands, and sinks lower every year, until he becomes almost as degraded as the primitive slave. And the Southern slaveholder tells us that this is none of our business; but unfortunately the slave system is aggressive, and we have come face to face with the fact that either we must put it down or prepare to be put down by it."

That sounded too terrible to the lad. "Uncle William!" he

protested. But then in a low voice he said, "Please go on, Sir. I want to understand."

"You must hear both sides, and judge for yourself. You must know the human side, and also the economic side. A slave is a very wasteful machine; he converts into energy only a small percentage of his fuel. The result is that it pays to cultivate with slave labor only the very finest soil, and when you have raised ten or twenty crops of cotton on a field, then you have to have a new field. Virginia used to be a great exporting state—it used to pay to roll tobacco in casks a hundred miles to market; but now Virginia raises hardly enough for her own population—because it does not pay. So in time it will be with Mississippi and the other states of the far South, and later in Mexico and Central America, if the South is allowed to conquer them. The Mexican War was a slaveholder's aggression, a seizure of new lands. Unprincipled Northern politicians, like Polk and Buchanan, were used as tools. It was the most desperate act that Slavery has yet ventured, and did more to awaken the North to the state of affairs than all the Abolition outcry of fifteen years."

This was hard for Allan to accept. "But Uncle William," he protested again, "it was in that war that the Mississippians fought so gallantly. I remember how proud of them everyone was. It was then that my father was so badly wounded, and Mr. Jeff Davis, too. Do you think they were greedy men?"

Professor Otis answered gently: "Then let us call it needy. They were needy men. Their system of slavery was eating out the heart of its present dominion, and had to have more land or die. The South is poor, Allan, and does not know the reason."

"But Yancey said, the reason was the tariff."

"That is nonsense," Professor Otis replied. "Manufacturers are perfectly established in this country, and there is free competition; except in special cases protection can have little effect under such circumstances. I do not deny that the tariff once hurt the South; it taxes the whole people to support home manufactures. But if the South lost by that, it was simply the fact that you cannot make mechanics out of slaves."

[56]

"*He* said," ventured Allan again, "that the South did not want any manufactures."

"Very well," replied the other, "but then the South must take the consequence, which is simply defeat in the race of life. For whether Mr. Yancey likes it or not, it is a fact which no student would deny, that the manufacturing is a higher stage of civilization than the agricultural; and that a society which cannot take the step upward will be left behind."

They walked in silence for a time, Allan's head in a whirl. "It is terrible to see it so!" he exclaimed. "And you will never get the South to see it!"

"That will not make any difference," said the other, firmly.

"Ah, but it will!" cried the boy. "For they won't stand it, they *won't* be left behind. That's just the thing, just as sure as the Abolitionists keep on, they'll break up the Union—the South will secede!"

"If they do, why, there will be nothing to do but bring them back."

"You mean by force, Uncle William?"

"I surely do," said the other, gravely.

The boy stood still. "You mean to conquer the South?" he gasped.

"I do."

"But—but—" Allan could scarcely find words, "Uncle William you *can't* mean that! Why, the whole world couldn't conquer the South!"

"I know they are a brave people," Professor Otis replied, "but my boy, if the South should try to break up this Union, I do not see what an American who knows the meaning of this country could do except to die trying to stop them. America means freedom and progress; split this country up, and you would have standing armies and European alliances; and just one generation of it would be enough to extinguish every hope and every ideal that our forefathers fought for—including yours, my dear boy.

"I cannot understand," the speaker went on, "how any thinking man can expect this Union to die without a fight. Look, for instance, at the Mississippi. Do you think the Northwest could permit a hostile power to hold its mouth? And the territories— who would get them? And the forts at the South—do you suppose that any administration would dare to give them up. It would be madness!"

"But, Uncle William, the South has a *right* to secede, hasn't it?"

"Constitutionally, you mean?"

"Yes."

"The Constitution says nothing about it, in plain words; but obviously the idea of its makers was to devise something to knit the States together. The process has been going on now for sixty or seventy years, and I assure you some of us think that we are one nation. People who talk disunion have grown up with peace and liberty, and they have forgotten the stern facts of life. For these blessings that we find so fair were won by blood and tears; they were torn out of chaos by grim force, and by grim force they were held above the reach of all the powers of destruction. This thing that you hear called *sovereignty,* believe me, is no mere abstraction; it is the combined self-preservation instinct of countless millions of people—of their ideals, and their traditions. We are quiet-looking men; but take my word for it, Allan, the person who laid a hand on this country's flag to tear it, would stir up a frenzy of execration in this one State—my boy, I think every man in it would march out to die!"

Allan was striding on, his head whirling, his hands clenched tightly in his pockets. "Conquer the South!" he was whispering to himself. "Great heavens! Conquer the South! It couldn't be done, Uncle William!" he half shouted, suddenly. "It couldn't be done!"

"Perhaps not," said the other, quietly. "Goethe says that only man can achieve the impossible. We have our souls, you know, and they might rise to the occasion. That would be the question at issue, Allan—that and that only. Perhaps with our universities and presses and other agencies of light we could summon mankind to the effort and save the nation, and the heritage of liberty and light our fathers left us. Perhaps, on the other hand, we should fail—and have no more part in civilization than the South American states.

"Men who teach this doctrine of secession ought to follow it to its end," went on Professor Otis, after a pause. "If the South may secede, then, may a State secede from the South? I have read all these arguments of Calhoun's, for instance—Calhoun admired the constitution of Poland! Here was a decentralized government—any knight could rise in its assembly and forbid any law, and was not that South Carolina in full operation? But now where is Poland? You see what I mean by the sternness of things; Poland saw it in the end, and all her contumacious knights saw it. We find everything so quiet and peaceful, we forget that there are enemies outside who do not love our ways, who eye us hungrily, and would tear us to pieces if they only dared. Mr. Jeff Davis wants to cut us into convenient sections for the benefit of England and France!"

"Grandfather Montague used to say that," said Allan.

"All the old patriots saw it," said the other. "And all of them hated Slavery, too. Patrick Henry and Washington and Jefferson were every one of them Abolitionists and all of them freed their slaves. But since then the cotton-gin has been invented, and now there is an oligarchy at the South whose power is based on Slavery, and they want to maintain their system. My own course in this matter would be one of passivity; I would give no pretext for aggression, I would only wait. And if the South will only wait, too, then the silent, irresistible forces of civilization will work out freedom in another score of years. We have made sure of almost all of the new territory; thirty-four years ago our fathers saved all beyond Missouri, and now we have California, and will have New Mexico. Every year emigrants are filling up those new lands, and drawing a band of fire around Slavery. If only it can be done quietly and diplomatically, we shall have the ugly fellow caught before he knows it. I pray for that, my boy; it would be so much better than secession and war."

They had come to Professor Otis's house, and stopped. "Do you want me to go on home with you?" he asked.

"No, sir," replied Allan, "I am not afraid, and thank you for teaching me, Uncle William. Good night, sir."

"Good night," said his uncle, and gripped his hand. "These are hard things, I know, but you must learn about them, and the sooner the better."

Allan turned and hurried away. He had heard too much, and his head was in a whirl. He could not sleep, he knew—instead he walked on and on, he did not notice where. The terrible idea of the South being conquered! When he looked about him again he was back in the crowded district of the city, on brightly lighted Washington Street, with its rows of shops. "We shall have the ugly fellow caught before he knows it," he was whispering to himself, "and you and I may sit and watch him suffocate to death!"

Then suddenly he stopped on the edge of a crowd which, murmuring hoarsely with excitement, was crushing forward toward the window of a newspaper office, in front of which was a bulletin-board. The first line on it he could read, and his heart gave a leap. He dug his way forward until he could see it all:

MISSOURI COMPROMISE REPEALED ! !

Report of Senate Committee upon Nebraska throws all territories open to Slavery!

Declares unconstitutional a compact of thirty-four years' standing!

Senator Douglas out for the presidency—bidding for the Southern vote!

And underneath flashed three words more; the crowd did not see them, but they danced a demon dance before Allan's eyes:—

SECESSION AND WAR!

BOOK II

The Crisis

꽃

CHAPTER I

The year 1819 had seen the first dispute about Slavery in the halls of Congress, an event which, as Jefferson wrote from his retreat at Monticello, disturbed him "like a fire bell in the night." In that year the admission of Missouri as a slave State had been contested, and it was finally agreed, as a compromise, that the State should be admitted, but that hereafter her southern boundary —36° 30′—was to be the border-line between Slavery and Freedom. The principle of congressional control of Slavery in the territories had been established already by the "Ordinance of 1787"; but now, while many of the founders were still living, it was given renewed sanction, the cabinet of President Monroe, in which was John C. Calhoun, declaring unanimously the constitutionality of the act.

In February of 1847 that doctrine had first been impugned, by Calhoun himself, who now declared that slaves were "property," to be taken anywhere in the Federal territory. This portentous doctrine was at first not taken seriously by any one. Even Jefferson Davis had not dared in 1850 to stand out for more than a continuation of the Missouri line to the Pacific, and this program his State of Mississippi had found too radical. Now, indeed, it was a portent when, four years later, the wild doctrine of Calhoun was definitely adopted by the Democratic Party which was in power at Washington.

A part of the Compromise of 1850 was the arrangement that Utah and New Mexico were to be allowed to choose between Slavery and Freedom for themselves. On the fourth day of January, 1854, Stephen A. Douglas, chairman of the Senate Committee on Territories, brought in a report declaring that it had been the purpose of the Compromise to establish this new principle—soon to be called "popular sovereignty"—in all the territories. Upon the general quiet and satisfaction which had prevailed in the country ever since 1850, this report broke like a clap of thunder from a cloudless sky. Men stared at each other, asking what it could mean. It was long before the South could persuade itself that it was not some trick; it was convinced only by the clamor which filled all the North, as soon as the meaning of the move was perceived.

In that year there were four men hungrily stalking the presidential nomination: General Cass, of Michigan, who had run against Taylor, and hoped for better luck next time; Marcy, of New York, who was now Secretary of State and was issuing manifestoes to the effete monarchies of Europe; Buchanan, of Pennsylvania, who, at the head of Polk's cabinet, had carried through the Mexican War conspiracy; and, finally, Douglas, of Illinois.

The Democratic party of that time was a combination of the slaveholding aristocracy of the South and the lowest classes of the cities of the North; and Stephen Arnold Douglas was a representative of the latter. He was a public man about whose motives there could be no need to call in the recording angel to decide. Master of all the intricacies of the brutal game of politics, he played it without a scruple and with scarcely a pretence. When he first came to Washington he brought with him the manners of the bar-room; in Congress he "stripped off and cast away his cravat, unbuttoned his waistcoat, and had the air and aspect of a half-naked pugilist." A man of enormous energy, vehement, aggressive, a master of rough-and-tumble oratory, of sophistry as well as of abuse, he now leaped suddenly into the van and seized the banner of Slavery, to rush it to the fore. North and west of Missouri were vast lands, the material for six States; hungry plotters from the West were in Washington, and they had shown him the way. If he did not take the chance, some one else would; and behind the man who took it, the whole South would rally in an instant. The gift of the next nomination was in the hands of the South.

The excitement caused by the Douglas "popular sovereignty" stroke exceeded anything the country had ever known before. The freesoil Democrats in Congress issued a ringing "Appeal" against it, and press and pulpit thundered their protests—in every city of the North there were public meetings, addressed not only by the antislavery leaders, but by all those "conservative" persons who had supported the Compromise. Congress was deluged with petitions. There came one signed by eighty per cent of all the clergymen of New England, protesting against the bill as "a great moral wrong, a measure full of danger to the peace, and even the existence, of our beloved Union."

Douglas, being without moral perception, had had no means of foreseeing these things, and had now no means of understanding them. He saw in them only the plotting of his enemies, and in his first defence of the measure he gave on the Senate floor a shocking exhibition. He must have perceived very soon, however, that he had overshot the mark—he could, so he declared, have travelled from Boston to Chicago by the light of his own burning effigies. But there was no turning back; the representatives of the South in Congress were aroused. With the help of Jefferson Davis, now Secretary of War, the President was prevailed upon to make the bill an administration measure, and to bring to its support the full power of that legalized bribery known as "patronage." Douglas himself fought the fight upon the Senate floor, and in the lobby of the House, for four months and a half.

"The Fugitive law did much to unglue the eyes of men," wrote Emerson, "and now the Nebraska bill leaves us staring." Never before had Boston been so angry, or so unanimous; and on the twenty-fourth of May, two days after the bill had been jammed through the House, came an incident as if devised to put its feelings to the test—a Negro named Anthony Burns was arrested in Boston as a fugitive slave. The news of it was like a handful of gunpowder flung upon a fire; the city was covered with placards calling the people to arms, and in Faneuil Hall there was a furious meeting, in which Theodore Parker and Wendell Phillips delivered wild harangues. In the midst of the excitement the cry was heard that an attack was being made upon the court-house, and the meeting, turned into a mob of two thousand, rushed to assist. They found clergymen and Negroes battering in the door with axes and heavy timbers, and in the struggle which followed, Wentworth Higginson was wounded, and one of the marshal's guards was killed. As a consequence, two companies of artillery were ordered out, and later on marines from the navy-yard, soldiers from Fort Independence, and the militia of Boston; so that when the examination of Burns began, it is narrated that "the court-house had the air of a beleaguered fortress." Crowds were pouring in from all over Massachusetts, and public meetings were being held; in the midst of it, to the consternation of Allan, his father limped grimly out, armed with two pistols, and had himself enrolled in the special guard of the marshal, who watched the prisoner day and night, over a hundred strong. It was strange company in which the heroic Mississippian found himself; Richard Henry Dana, who was the counsel for the Negro, declared that in consequence of its assemblage "the people had not felt it necessary to lock their doors at night, the brothels are tenanted only by women; fighting-dogs and racing-horses have been unemployed, and Ann Street and its alleys and cellars show signs of a coming millennium." For this piece of eloquence the author-lawyer was waylaid and sandbagged by one of the offended posse.

On the second of June the fugitive was adjudged to his owner, and there remained only the task of taking him out of Boston. Along the route of the procession, windows were draped in mourning and flags displayed at half mast, or with the union down; fifty thousand people lined the route, filling the air with hisses and cries of "Shame!"

To keep them in order the route was guarded by the city police, and by twenty-two companies of Massachusetts militia. The way

[64]

for the procession was cleared by a troop of cavalry, and after it came, in order, a United States artillery battalion, companies of marines, the marshal's posse of one hundred and twenty-four ruffians and one Southern gentleman, two more platoons of marines, and then a field-piece and more marines as guard. So escorted, the fugitive reached the wharf, and was put on board a United States revenue cutter, which had been ordered by the President to take him to Virginia.

It had cost the government forty thousand dollars to achieve this feat. One of its consequences was the formation of a "Boston Anti-manhunting League," a secret association of many of the best-known authors, lawyers, and clergymen of the city. Their purpose was to kidnap any slave hunters who might venture to show themselves in Boston; and to this end for nearly two years they met regularly, armed with sling-shots and "billies," and with deadly seriousness drilled themselves in all the tricks of the highwayman and the assassin.

Concerning a previous attempt at Slavery legislation it had been observed that it enacted not a law, but a lawsuit. Of the Nebraska bill it might be said that it had enacted lawlessness. "It puts Freedom and Slavery face to face and bids them grapple," Sumner had said. Apparently it had been the idea of Douglas, so far as he had an idea, that the colonists of the new territories were to dwell together in amity until they had decided the question at the polls; though indeed it was by no means clear whether under the new arrangement they were to have the right to decide it but one way. Keen minds saw this question and asked it—whether the settlers were to be allowed to exclude Slavery if they chose? Douglas preferred to dodge it; but the question was the crux of the whole matter, as time was to show, and the rock upon which his hopes were to split.

It proved, however, to be impossible for anti-slavery and pro-slavery settlers to decide the question at the polls. Southerners and Missourians had not the least idea of taking slaves into the territory, if the slaves might possibly be set free; and Northern farmers had no idea of settling in a district which might be saddled with a slave code. All men understood that the question must be settled at the outset; and in the neighboring counties of Missouri were men who knew which way the settlement was to be. Missouri did not want a free State next to her, and she did want new lands for her sons. Scarcely had the bill been signed than an emigration began—an emigration, as the historian of Kansas was to phrase it, of "amateur emigrants, who proposed to reside in Missouri, but to vote and fight in Kansas." They complied with the law requiring the building of a cabin, by nailing up a few rails, or "posting a scrawl claiming proprietorship and threatening to shoot intermeddlers at sight." It was generally believed even at the North that their measures were destined to succeed.

But to a member of the Massachusetts legislature, Eli Thayer, had occurred the idea of meeting the South on her own ground, by means of organized emigration to the territory. He succeeded in interesting the anti-slavery press and anti-slavery philanthropists in the plan, and a society was formed; in the summer of 1854 five companies, about seven hundred and fifty men, were sent out to Kansas, a proceeding that created intense excitement throughout the South. It was reported that the company had five million dollars capital, and the Democratic convention of Georgia described its stockholders as "the paid adventurers and Jesuitical hordes of Northern Abolitionism."

These whom the matter immediately concerned did not mean, however, to be balked by a few emigrants. On election day "the Missouri expounders of popular sovereignty marched into Kansas to assist—an unkempt, sun-dried, blatant, picturesque mob of five thousand men, with guns upon their shoulders, revolvers sticking from their belts, bowie-knives protruding from their boot-tops, and generous rations of whiskey in their wagons." There were less than three thousand registered voters in the territory; there were six thousand, three hundred and seven votes cast. Before the Congressional Investigating Committee, in the next year, testified one citizen of Platte County, Missouri. "Whenever there was an election in the territory," said he, "they were fussin' roun' an' gettin' up companies to go, an' gettin' horses an' waggins. They come to me to subscribe, but I tole 'em that I was down on this thing of votin' over in the territory, an' that Tom Thorpe didn't subscribe to no such fixin's. They jawed me too about it—they did; but I reckon they found old Tom Thorpe could give as good as he got. They told the boys they wanted to make Kansas a slave State; an' they told 'em the Abolitionists were a-commin' in; an' that the Emigrant Aid Society & Co. was pitchin' in; an' they'd better too. You see, they took the boys over, an' they got plenty liquor, an' plenty to eat, an' they got over free ferry. Lots an' slivers on 'em went. There's Dr. Tibbs, lives over in Platte, he used to go, an' you see they 'lected him. The boys tole me one time when they come back, says they, 'We've 'lected Dr. Tibbs to the legislature.' An' says I, 'Is it the State or the territory?' 'An' says they, 'The territory!' Says I, 'Boys, ain't this a-puttin' it on too thick? It's a darned sight too mean enough to go over there an' vote for them fellers, but to put in a man who don't live there is all-fired outrageous!' "

Four months after the election the "legislature" met, and after first expelling its free-state members, proceeded to pass laws which should perpetuate their victory. To decline to take oath to support the Fugitive-slave law was a penitentiary offence; to question the rights of slaveholding was a felony; to induce a slave to run away was death.

The free-state settlers organized themselves, repudiating the proslavery government—a move at which the latter jeered; but also they sent to the East for consignments of the famous "Sharp's rifles," a move which their foes took more seriously. A sheriff of the proslavery party attempted to make an arrest, and a rescue and a quarrel following, he sent over to Missouri for help. The "border ruffians" turned out in swarms; by the first of December there were fifteen hundred of them in arms, and vowing destruction upon Lawrence, the town of the Emigrant Aid Company. The ensuing campaign, which was known as the "Wakarusa War," got as far as entrenching and night skirmishing, but not to a pitched conflict. It had proven easier to plot dishonesty in the cabinet than to enact it in the field, and the first governor of Kansas had been removed—a procedure which was to be forced twice more upon the desperate state administration. The new governor had an interview with the free-state settlers, and he, too, was won over to their view, that they had a right to be there. The Missourians retired in a rage, and every one knew that the conflict had been postponed only for a time.

The attention of the country was focussed upon this strange drama, where for the first time Freedom and Slavery confronted each other in arms. Facing the new issue a new political organization had arisen, its platform the restriction of Slavery in the territories; and this "Republican" party grew hour by hour, as men came to perceive the desperate situation of the free-state settlers.

Throughout the cold months everything stood still in the territory; all the while, North and South, the storm of civil war was gathering. "Let your young men come forth to Missouri and Kansas! Let them come well armed!" wrote Atchison, senator from the former state and leader of the "border ruffians." The Georgia legislature was proposing to appropriate fifty thousand dollars to be spent for arms. In Alabama, a Colonel Buford had sold his slaves to equip a company, and the women of the South were selling their jewels to send him money. When his party of nearly three hundred started, Bibles were subscribed for them by the devout, and the blessings of the church were solemnly pronounced upon their enterprise. At the North there was even more preparation; with a presidential election only a few months away, the intellectual classes of the North were thrilling with the exaltation of a moral crusade.

This political movement had had its manifestations in the higher realms of literature and thought, of which Allan did not know. At Valley Hall on Sunday mornings the family had been wont to migrate in carriages and on horseback to the little evangelical church eight miles away, where Allan had heard all the mysteries of life explained by revelation, and where he had been taught an ethical code summed up in the quaint old British formula—to do his duty in that state of life into which it had pleased God to call him. But now he was eighteen, and a student in his second year at Harvard College, which at that time was filled full of the critical philosophy and transcendentalism.

He had read Emerson, and come to see that revelations are flowers of the spirit and have their day: a life-discovery which meant freedom and joy to others, but had meant nothing but pain to him. Always beside him, in thought, if not in fact, was his father, watching the books he read and the thoughts he thought. It was an endless tragedy, for he dearly loved his father, who was growing old, and whose health the change of climate had not bettered.

The young man had withdrawn himself from the questions of the hour, and wrapped himself in his studies. He could not attend a political meeting without hurting his father, but he could read Goethe and Shelley.

He had lived thus for three years, aloof from other young people when one morning in April, while the armies were gathering in Kansas, the captain had come rushing into his son's room, his face flushed with rage. He had a newspaper clenched in his hand, and he was vowing that he could stand it no longer, not another hour! Allan had read the paper already and knew what it was—a meeting that had been held the previous day in a church at New Haven, attended by clergymen and by professors of Yale College. After a fiery address by Henry Ward Beecher—which was given in full—fifty Sharp's rifles had been voted for a company of Kansas emigrants.

Allan waited patiently for this storm to pass, as many others had passed; but he found that it was not to be. "It is time we were gone home," cried Captain Montague, smiting his cane upon the floor. "The South needs us; she needs every voice and every arm! A war will be on in another month, and we must be home, sir, home!"

Allan heard him with a startled look. "Home?" he echoed.

"Yes, sir!" the other exclaimed. "I tell you I have stood this thing as long as I can; I have waited and waited, thinking of you and of your studies and what-not. But this is the end—by Heaven, sir, you will have to study at home, and what you can't find there you must do without. I will not stand these infamous Northern papers. I will not stand these people! I want to be among my own people, where I belong, and where I am not insulted every hour of my life. God, sir, I tell you I wish I were home to-day, to talk to the people of Mississippi! What is the matter with them?

What can they mean? What does Hamilton mean, that he and his boys are not up there in Kansas now? Why, these scoundrels will have the South throttled before ever she can stir!"

And so the Captain stormed on, striding up and down the floor in spite of his lame knee, breaking his cane in his rage. To Allan's dismay it became more and more apparent that it was no mere passing fancy, but a resolution which had been forming in his mind for many months. "We are going home, sir!" he shouted, again and again, to every objection that Allan attempted.

It was a bitter hour for the young student, meaning as it did a complete overthrow of his every plan; but he fought the fight swiftly, and silently as ever, burning all his own smoke. He believed that his duty was with his father to the end; and before the other's passion had half calmed down he was saying, "Very well, sir, let it be as you think best."

Scarcely two weeks more had passed before he was driven to the depot one raw and damp April morning, and took his last look at Boston through the windows of a flying train. "They change their skies, who travel over seas," says Horace, "but they do not change their minds."

CHAPTER II

The travellers met with an adventure at the outset; at one of the smaller towns on the road they found the station platform crowded with a cheering throng, and a score or so of stalwart men boarded the train, loaded with knapsacks and blankets, and with canvas-covered rifles in their hands. Captain Montague sat and bit his lip while they sang through the stirring song which the poet Whittier had written for them:—

> "We cross the prairie as of old
> The pilgrims crossed the sea;

To make the West, as they the East,
The homestead of the free!"

The father and son left the train not long after that, Captain
Montague preferring to lose a day rather than witness the ovations
these men received. "Never mind," he vowed to the train as it
sped on, "you may see me again before long!" He was seriously
meditating heading another kind of Kansas company himself,
though this was a project to which Allan did venture to protest.

They went by way of Cleveland and Cincinnati and the Ohio
River, a long and tedious journey then, but full of interest to
Allan, to whom the new West was a place of romance. It was the
season of spring floods, and the river was turbid and yellow; they
had a passage swift, if perilous. These were the palmy days of the
Mississippi steamboat, when the rival lines of the tall, double-
stacked vessels ran races, and city after city turned out to cheer
the victor. A "nigger" always sat on the safety-valve, if tradition
was to be believed; and if you did not blow out your boilerhead
or drive upon a sunken snag, you reached your destination.
Gambling went on in the saloons day and night, and pistol "shooting matches" were an occasional incident.

It seemed strange to be gazing at the shores of Missouri, the
scene of the pending struggle about which Allan had heard so
much. On board men discussed the situation all day, aggressive
pro-slavery opinion being the only kind which showed itself. Of
painful interest to Allan was a sight he witnessed twice after they
entered Southern territory—a coffle of slaves coming on board,
bound for the far South. In the first party there were perhaps
thirty, all men and youths—"prime field-hands,"—fastened on
either side of a long chain which they carried with them. Beside
them walked two white men, one armed with a cowskin whip,
a weapon about three feet long, an inch thick at the butt, and
tapering to a point, stiff and springy; it was red painted, new and
shining, and with it he cut the air playfully as he walked, the
whistle of it being sufficient to make the Negroes "step lively"
up the gang-plank. Painful was the contrast between the alacrity
of their motions and the sullen despair which sat upon their faces.

The other party consisted of several families, the women with bright-colored calico turbans and numerous bundles and babies. They were not chained, but attended by a bustling little man who watched them closely, and who was striving diligently to keep warmly wrapped a little girl who was torn with a racking cough, prodding her listless mother with remarks as to the child's value. This was the kind of care which Allan knew was given to the Negroes at home—it might have been due, as some people said, to the fact that it did not pay to neglect valuable property, or as Allan had believed, to the genuine kindness of their masters. These Negroes were left with the baggage, and camped in the midst of promiscuous heaps of saddles and trunks.

At Columbus, Kentucky, other slaves came on board, but Allan did not notice them. Perhaps an hour after the boat had left the city, he observed his father in conversation with a man whose face seemed familiar; drawing near unobserved, he recognized him as the overseer of a plantation not far from Valley Hall, belonging to a family by the name of Roberts. Allan had no desire to meet the man, whose reputation as an overseer—he was a "Yankee"—was not good. He turned away, after noticing with some surprise that his father was in seemingly intimate conversation with him.

It was a couple of hours before Captain Montague again joined his son, his manner one of suppressed excitement. "Did you see that man I was talking to?" he asked.

"I took it to be Jim Henderson," said Allan.

"Yes," replied the other. "And you should just have heard the story he tells."

"You can't believe a word he says, father," said Allan.

"I believe this," exclaimed Captain Montague, "and a pretty story it makes! Did you notice that yellow boy he brought on board with him? A regular giant—a six-footer, and looks like a statue. Henderson's just brought him down from Cincinnati, and will you believe it, that he had to have him kidnapped?"

"Kidnapped!" echoed Allan.

"Kidnapped, sir. Thumped over the head by two rowdies, and piled into a cart, and taken over the Ohio in a skiff. And I tell you, things have come to a pretty pass when a man has to go over into a free State and take measures like that to get his property."

"I don't understand you, father," said the boy.

"A runaway, sir—a runaway! He left Major Roberts's place nearly a month ago, and Henderson's been tracing him ever since. Said he was bound to get him, if it was only for the satisfaction; a regular devil he is, you can see it in his eyes. He claims to have been a free Negro, over in Maryland. Tried to hit Henderson over the head once with a barrel-stave, and got a bullet in his shoulders that laid him out for three months. Henderson caught him in Cincinnati, just getting ready to skip to Canada."

"But I don't understand yet," Allan said; "why kidnap him?"

"Because it was the only thing he could do, with those infernal Abolitionists in Cincinnati."

"A pretty risky business, kidnapping, I should think," Allan managed to say.

"Risky? Why, suppose one of those fellows had betrayed him; Henderson might have gotten locked up for ten years! And to such lengths the South has to go to secure her constitutional rights!"

Smitten with distress, Allan made his escape at the first opportunity and sought the forepart of the boat where the Negroes were kept. He had no difficulty in recognizing the man from the description that had been given him—"Dutch Joe" he was called, no doubt from the nationality of his father. He was a huge mulatto, an athlete in build, with great bull-neck and heavy sullen face. It was late afternoon of a raw day, and about him the Negroes were crouched shivering; but though his shirt was torn and his chest laid bare, he seemed not to be aware of the cold. His hands were chained in front of him, and a chain with a ball attached bound his leg. Sitting upon a box, and leaning against the side of another, his dull glance fixed upon vacancy, he paid no heed to Allan who gazed at the motionless figure—the heavy shoulders, bowed and crushed, the face smouldering with hatred and defiance; and thinking of his father's quiet sentence—"Claims to have been free over in Maryland"—Allan turned away in grief and pity.

It was two days more before they reached their destination;

during that time Allan went several times to take a look at the slave who claimed to be free. Once or twice he saw him eating. His meal had been set before him on a tin plate and he ate mechanically, not seeming to notice what it was. For the rest of the time he sat motionless, with his dull, fixed stare. Never once did he notice Allan.

Besides Henderson, the overseer, whose drooping black mustache seemed always to have been just moistened with liquor, and who lifted his hat to Allan and sought in vain to enter into conversation, there was another man who seemed interested in "Dutch Joe." Allan saw him looking on two occasions, and on a third he turned away hurriedly as Allan approached, causing the latter to wonder if the man had not been speaking to the Negro. Allan had first noticed this passenger just after they had left Columbus, a young fellow of about twenty-two or three, a Westerner in feature, tall and big-boned, with lanky face and a great jaw which worked incessantly as he chewed and vehemently spat tobacco. For the greater part of the time he strode back and forth upon the deck, holding his head high and shooting swift glances around him, as if he were out on a prairie on the lookout for Indians or game. Something in the man's manner seemed to tell Allan that his was a different point of view from that of the others on the steamer; and once when he saw the man leaning upon the rail and gazing at the shore, Allan approached and tried to open a conversation. To his remark, however, the Westerner replied only with a monosyllable, and then moved away.

The last day had come—they were due at Natchez at noon; and Allan's preoccupation with the unhappy Negro proved at last enough to overcome even his repugnance to the overseer. The Yankee had once been a gentleman, but dissipation had played havoc with his features and given him the manners of inferiority. When he spoke to you, his mouth became set in a deprecatory grin.

"Do you get off at Natchez?" Allan asked him, as he stood chewing on a cigar-stump and eying his prisoner.

"Clarke's Landing, sir," said the other; "got a horse there."

"Going to sell that boy?" continued Allan. (A male slave remained a "boy" until he became old, then he was an "uncle.")

"No, sir—not exactly," laughed the man. "I want him to make an example of."

"What's the matter with him?"

"Just ugly, sir; the very devil in him. You can see that, I reckon, in his face; he's the wildest nigger I ever got my hands on, and I've had quite some experience. But, by gad, I'm going to break him!"

"Father said something about his claiming to be a free Negro."

"Yes, sir," said Henderson; "he says he lived in Pennsylvania, and came into Maryland with a load of wood to sell. They don't allow free niggers to come into Maryland, you know—arrested him, locked him up, and sold him to pay jail fees."

"Oh, I see," said Allan. "Is that the way they do?"

"That's the way they serve 'em, sir; wouldn't do to have free niggers moving round among slaves, you understand."

"You bought him in Maryland?"

"I didn't buy him at all; I wouldn't buy any sulky nigger. But when they come our way, we have to handle 'em, you know, sir. Major Roberts bought this fellow from a dealer in Baton Rouge —paid fifteen hundred for him, too. He's a first-rate carpenter, when you can get him to work."

"Did Major Roberts know he claimed to have been free?"

"Oh, yes," said the other, "but the trader had a good title. He was sorry, though, after the boy had tried to brain me. Wanted to sell him then, but my blood was up. I tell you—a man in my business can't afford to let a nigger down him, sir."

"He looks like a dangerous fellow," ventured Allan.

"I'll fix him," laughed Henderson, grimly.

"What are you going to do? Whip him?"

"No," said the man, "whipping don't do any good with his kind. Why, good God, sir, I've whipped that nigger till his back looked like a skinned ox, but it didn't matter—couldn't even get a groan out of him. You see he broods and fights—they say he left a family up in Pennsylvania, and that's what's the matter with him."

Allan shrank involuntarily. "Oh!"

"Yes," said Henderson, without noticing his change of tone; "but I'm going to keep that chain on him, and put him out in the field and work him a couple of weeks. I'll stand over him myself, and chain him up at night, and feed him kinder slender, and I shouldn't wonder if I broke him pretty soon. 'Tain't in nature, you know, for a nigger to stand anything too long."

"No," said Allan, sharply, "I suppose not."

And then he turned abruptly and strode away, leaving the man staring after him.

CHAPTER III

They landed at Natchez and he forgot his worry for a time. There upon the wharf, amid a crowd of wagons and freight, rapturous with welcome, was Taylor Tibbs, Jr., with the coach. (The elder Tibbs had dropped dead of apoplexy one day in the dining room.) Soon they were off down the familiar road, making the dust fly behind them; winter was gone, and the balm of a Southern spring-time wrapped them, a riot of blossoms strewing the way.

They had ridden about two hours and the landscape was growing homelike when there came from afar the sound of gal-loping hoofbeats, and ahead of them, far down the road, they saw two riders approaching in a cloud of dust. They were racing, bending over their horses' necks, and lashing them like mad. The coach passed down into a hollow, and then as it labored up the opposite slope, the riders burst suddenly over the brow of the hill. They came with the sweep of a tornado and a thunder of hoofs, the horses with nostrils distended and manes flying. In another instant they would have been past, but one of them drew rein with such force as to cause his horse to rear and almost go over backwards. An instant more, the coach having stopped also, the rider was leaning over and stretching out his hand, shouting, "By the great Jehoshaphat, here they are!"

Allan stared. He saw before him a huge young man, more than six feet in height, with coal-black hair and eyes, and a face alight with laughter. He caught his breath in wonder. "It's 'Dolph!"

"Well guessed!" laughed the other. " 'Dolph it is!"

And then at the other side of the coach appeared the other rider, having succeeding in turning his horse. He was nearly as big, and Allan stared again, realizing that this was the quiet and timid little Ralph. "My soul, how you have grown!" he exclaimed.

"Did you think we were pickled, riding like that?" laughed 'Dolph, seizing his cousin's hand, and giving it a squeeze like a grizzly bear. "I wouldn't have known you either, but for Uncle Harry. How are you, Uncle Harry—how's the knee?"

"Bad as ever," said Captain Montague; "bad as ever, 'Dolph. But Heaven help us, what men you have grown up to!"

Randolph continued to laugh while they gazed at him, looking him over from head to foot; irresistibly he drew attention from his quieter brother. He was a splendid-looking man, his black eyes dancing and sparkling, his white teeth gleaming, his whole countenance aglow—and the woods rang with the big, handsome fellow's laughter.

The elder man looked over the three young Montagues proudly. Ralph was almost a reproduction of Randolph, with the same fair skin and brunette hair and eyes, while Allan had the beautiful blue eyes and blonde hair of his dead mother, Lucy Otis.

"Meant to meet you at the boat, Uncle Harry," he said; "swear to God we did; but you know those boats are always late, except when you count on it. But, oh, say, we're glad to see you!"

"Glad to be home, 'Dolph," said the captain. "Glad, indeed. How is the family?"

"Everybody flourishing," said 'Dolph, "and all out on the portico waiting for you. And say, Allan, talk about growing, wait until you see Ethel."

"She's taller than you, I think," put in Ralph; "a regular stunner!"

Allan looked at Ralph; he was the image of his father, grave and silent, even at eighteen. " 'Dolph must be twenty-one, now," said Allan.

"Twenty-one last month," said 'Dolph. "Had a party, and raised Cain, and then came home at midnight and scared every one to death, shouting there was a man in the house."

"And hung your hat over the lamp," said Ralph, grimly. "You better not tell that story!"

The carriage had started up again, and the four rode on in silence for a few moments, gazing at one another, and trying to realize six years of change. "I suppose you've all come back Abolitionists!" said 'Dolph, suddenly.

"Yes, indeed!" laughed Captain Montague, and then went on hastily: "But look here, why aren't you boys in Kansas?"

"Wanted to go," said 'Dolph; "Sam Mason's gone, for one; but the governor wouldn't let us."

"Wouldn't let you!" exclaimed the older soldier.

"Governor's got the sulks," Randolph answered. "Won't have anything to do with it."

"I don't understand you," said Captain Montague. "You mean he doesn't care if the North gets Kansas?"

"Not a bit. He says you might as well try to send slaves to Greenland as to Kansas. Cuba and Mexico are the places for slaves, he says."

"But good Lord, 'Dolph, the North will own the country if we don't stop them. They'll run the Congress so that we will be their slaves, and then I'll wager they'll tell us to keep our slaves and work them for the benefit of the North!"

"Right you are, sir, but father says the thing for the South to do is to get out, and forget the damn Yankees for all time. He wants the South to secede right now."

And so the two young horsemen cantered alongside the coach, laughing and chatting until the carriage swung round a turn, and 'Dolph leaned over to give the horses a cut with his whip that made them leap. Then he went tearing ahead, waving his hat as they thundered across a bridge and swept into view of a long avenue, at the end of which gleamed the great white front of Valley Hall.

CHAPTER IV

Besides the Negroes who poured out of the house and from every building near it, there were four members of the family on the front portico to welcome them. There was Hamilton Montague, his face lighted with affection, coming down the steps with arms stretched out; there was Mrs. Montague, rounder and rosier than ever, crying out in wonder at the sight of Allan grown up, and flinging her arms around him and kissing him; there was Uncle Ben Handy, gay as ever, and not a day older; and last of all, waiting serenely, was Ethel. She was but sixteen, and he had imagined a girl whom he might hug and kiss. Instead he almost feared to take her hand, she was so stately.

Here, on the lawn also, were Negro children grown up into men and women, and recognitions and perplexities without end. These Negroes had been most of Allan's boyhood world; here were the playmates whom he had drilled and commanded, and all the tyrants he had dreaded, the latter now grown suddenly obsequious, and clamoring even for a touch of his hand. Here also were the Negro grown-ups, "Aunt Viney," who had nursed Allan, and Pericles, the butler, who had scolded him out of the pantry, and a great, strapping black man who turned out to be Jereboam Anaximenes, who had wept at his departure, pleading to be taken along, because he "belonged" with Mister Allan.

Allan dreamed that night that he was a child once more, and he wished that he might never waken again to a morrow in which the whole world was not such a place of plenty and delight. It was *his* South, and oh, how he loved it!

In the morning there were a thousand things calling out to him; a new saddle horse to test, old friends and old scenes to revisit; Randolph wanting him to go hunting, and his father wanting him to stay and see the neighbors who would surely be coming in all morning to welcome the prodigals. Allan sought to have a chat with Ethel, but Ethel was interested otherwise; breakfast had scarcely been eaten before there appeared a cavalier, "Billy" Hinds, a neighbor, and one of Allan's old playmates.

"It's a match, I reckon," said Ralph, nodding over his shoulder at them, as he dragged his cousin away to inspect a new colt.

"A match!" exclaimed Allan. "But he's no older than I am."

"I know it," said Ralph; "but he's crazy about Ethel, all the same—over here every day, and never takes his eyes off her. Did you notice how he greeted you?"

"He didn't seem very cordial, I thought."

"He's jealous," said Ralph. "If you'd gone for a walk with her this morning, Billy'd have gone for his duelling pistols."

Everywhere on their way to the stables the servants rushed out to greet Allan once more, made happy if he gave them a glance. The little pickaninnies who were babies when he went North gathered around, staring in awe at the new young master.

That morning he tried out the mare his uncle had given him, riding with 'Dolph and Ralph, and the first sight they came upon was a gang of the field-hands, toiling in the burning sun. This was not a new sight, but now it cut him like a knife; he rode on in silence, scarcely hearing a word of what his two cousins were saying. He was no longer Allan Montague, heir-to-be of half this domain, and who still loved it; he was Frederick Douglass, field-hand—who hated the plantation, its greatness, its luxury, its pride.

As time passed such feelings, which haunted him the first day, seemed to possess him again and again as if they were his own, and not those of the Negro orator he had listened to six years ago in Boston. When he had seen all the place and met all the neighbors, he had done everything there was to do; he grew faint at the thought that he was to stay here forever. The white people were gracious and refined, but what they talked about when they were not talking politics, did not interest him; and their constant obsession with fine food seemed to him almost repulsive. The young men were "fast"—their thoughts were of horses, women, and wine; in the "office," where came the elder men, the talk was of cotton and Kansas. It was painful to be face to face with men, some of whom truly believed that Negroes were "half apes" —to be bought and sold, to be killed, if they became unruly. There was no consciousness of cruelty or wrong in this; these grave gentlemen who were so tender with their own loved ones, discussed this and that overseer, and how many "bales to the hand" he got out of his slaves as if the "hands" were mere machines. Allan thought of the argument of which he had heard so much in Boston—that it was the custom to "work off" the hands on the sugar plantations of Louisiana every seven years; and one day in the office with the gentlemen, he asked the question, in a casual way, and started a long discussion in which some contended that it did or did not pay, adducing cases and citing figures, while the listener heard them in silent wonder that not a soul appeared aware of any other view of the matter. The point they discussed was that there were only three or four months in the year when the cane could be ground; one had either to work his hands day and night during these months—which wore them out—or else support a double set all the year round. It was a question about which opinions differed; but no one denied that according to the statistics the slave population of Louisiana decreased two and a half per cent a year, while that of Virginia where there was no need for death-dealing over-work, increased twenty.

It was when they talked politics, however, that these gentlemen disturbed Allan most. He had never forgotten that eloquent speech Grandfather Montague had made to his grandchildren ten years ago, when, so near his earthly end, he had sat with them on the lawn and told them of fighting the British. Grandfather had meant to impress the children with the ideals of their country, and he had not failed in at least one case, that of Allan. He had said that the Union was for the protection of that freedom for which he had fought in the American Revolution, and again in 1812. Now, here were Allan's Uncle Hamilton, and Allan's father, and their friends making clear that there was no longer any "Union" sentiment at Valley Hall. The South stood apart, and the only question was whether or not the time for her to secede had come. There was only one person there who was not ready, and that was Uncle Ben, who took a good-natured and mildly cynical view of public affairs, disapproving of the violence of the politicians because it interfered with his peace of mind and body.

About the Kansas broil the planters talked for hours, waiting for the news. At that time the marshal of the territory had called for help in executing writs in Lawrence; the Missourians were pouring over the border, and a conflict was a matter of days. Allan realized the depth and intensity of their feelings; once or twice he ventured to set right what he took to be misapprehensions, but the way his words were received showed him quickly their dread and hatred of the North and of everything Northern. Beneath the incidents and accidents of the moment lay the deep distrust of a passionately conservative people for an eager and growing democracy. They hated democracy in all its ways, in all its aspects; they hated its manners, its religion, its literature, its thought. In the furious declamation to which Allan listened, he kept noticing one word—one which was strange to his ear, but which stood for all things horrible at Valley Hall—Jacobinism! In Massachusetts people did not talk about Jacobinism, except as something historical and far off; a man would no more have set out to quarrel with Jacobinism than with Lollardry. It puzzled Allan, until he thought of Burke, and realized that he was living in an English civilization of fifty years earlier—the time of the French Revolution.

The habit of self-repression which Allan had formed in Boston was tested more severely than ever. He could do no good by remonstrating with anybody. The wrong that he saw was deep and terrible to him, but it sat entrenched and unassailable. The memory of the Negro, Douglass, haunted him all the time: he saw it in every dusky face, he heard it in every pleading voice, above all, in the strange, wild singing of the Negroes. He knew that the brutality which Douglass had experienced was not usual, certainly not on the Valley Hall plantation and on those of its neighbors. But if slavery made such cruelty and degradation possible anywhere, then Slavery was a terrible evil. He knew too, that the slave-owning planters had been compelled to discipline the black savages from the jungles of Africa when they first came as slaves. These primitives were at once lazy and dangerous, given to the most brutal forms of fighting. They were completely immoral according to civilized standards, and had no idea of the meaning of the word cleanliness.

There was another slave who haunted Allan's thoughts day and night, and would not let him rest. It was the mulatto he had seen on the boat.

Nearly three weeks had passed since his arrival at Valley Hall, when one morning he accepted an invitation from Ralph to go out for a deer. Armed with rifles they rode three or four miles from home, and tied their horses, and struck into the forest. Venison was plentiful, and there were no game laws; in less than half an hour they had struck a fresh trail, plainly marked in the deep black soil, and set out cautiously to follow it. The forest was swampy, dense with rank vines and gnarled and slimy cypress roots; here and there were all but impassable bogs, and then again higher places covered with live oak and brier thickets. Upon these latter the deer were to be found hiding, and as they always lay watching their back trail, at the first of the high places the two hunters separated, intending cautiously to creep around the knoll, and steal up from the other direction.

Allan had crept perhaps fifty yards, eyes and ears on the alert for a sight of the game, when he came to a slight open space through which he could see to the knoll. He noticed a slight movement in the foliage; and the next instant he started back, his heart giving a leap that hurt. Major Roberts' mulatto slave, "Dutch Joe," had stepped into view on that knoll!

He was at least a hundred yards away, and his back was turned to Allan, but the latter knew him in an instant—that giant frame, that close-cropped bullet head, those great shoulders! A trembling like an ague seized him—the man had run away again, and now what was Allan to do? It must be quickly, the next instant might be too late. The Negro stood turning his head this way and that, as if he had heard something; why did he not keep hidden? If Ralph saw him he would surely hail him, and shoot him down if he ran. With sudden resolution Allan put his fingers to his lips, and blew a loud whistle.

The man dropped as if a bullet had struck him. A few moments later came an answering whistle, and then Allan shouted "Halloo!"

"What's the matter?" came Ralph's voice from over the knoll.

"I started the deer," Allan answered. "He's gone."

"Why didn't you shoot?"

"I was crawling under a log, and couldn't. Stay where you are, and I'll join you."

He set out on a run, and had gone but a short distance when he came upon an unexpected sight—there lay a deer, with a bullet hole in its side, and with a piece cut out of it. "The Negro must be armed," Allan thought swiftly, as he dashed on.

"What in the world did you yell like that for?" his cousin demanded, when they met.

"Why not?" asked the other, innocently. "The deer was gone."

"But there might have been others; you can't tell. You never ought to go around bawling in the woods—we'd have met anyway, and now you've scared out everything for half a mile."

"I'm sorry," said Allan, "I didn't think—I was only mad at losing my shot. Let's strike off, and try again."

As they rode home another surprise met Allan. They rounded a turn and came in sight of a pedestrian—the lanky Westerner he had seen on the steamboat.

He went by them without meeting their eyes; he was still chewing vigorously.

"What do you suppose is the matter with that chap?" remarked Ralph. It was a strange sight to see a white man walking in Mississippi.

"Don't know," said the other; "who is he?"

"I saw him at the hotel in town," said Ralph. "His name is Carter; he's some sort of agent. Queer-looking duck."

Allan assented and rode on. Reaching the Hall and finding the family at dinner, the two hunters cleaned up and reported themselves. "Where's Uncle Ben?" asked Ralph.

"He went to town," answered Mrs. Montague. She stopped and listened. "There he is now."

There came the sound of galloping hoofs, and then Uncle Ben's voice, "Hey, you there, come take my horse!" They heard him come up the veranda steps, and a moment later he entered the room. His face was flushed, and his tone excited.

"Heard the news?" he cried. Then hurried on, "The whole country's up! A man most killed Jim Henderson—that yellow devil he brought back from Cincinnati! He's got away again! Henderson tried to whip him yesterday afternoon, and the fellow turned on him and slashed his face all to pieces. They put the dogs on him and ran him out of the swamp last night, but they lost the trail."

"Henderson told me he was going to keep a chain on him," said Captain Montague.

"That's the worst of it," said Uncle Ben; "the man has a file, and filed the ring through in two places, all but a hair. It was on his ankles, and Henderson didn't see it. The fellow broke it right off before Henderson knew what he was about."

"Jerry!" called Hamilton Montague to one of the servants. "Go tell Taylor Tibbs to saddle the horses. It won't do to have that kind of man loose."

Mr. Handy sat down at the table, but they gave him little chance to eat for their inquiries.

"One of Henderson's boys rode over to town this morning," he told them; "that's how I heard it. They've been hunting along the roads with the dogs to see if they can find where the Negro dismounted, for someone had given him a horse. Major Roberts has a standing offer of three hundred dollars for any of his Negroes who run away, and Henderson has added two hundred more. They say Henderson is crazy; he's out this morning, in spite of his cuts. The devil just missed his eye one time. Henderson had been trying to break him—kept him tied up by the wrists at night, and whipped him for an hour or two; didn't make a bit of difference, either. They've telegraphed to Natchez for more dogs. They're going to beat up the whole country."

Half an hour later the party left Valley Hall—Hamilton, his brother-in-law, the three young men, one of the overseers, and a couple of Negroes with the pack of hounds. The captain was left alone, because of his knee, which would not let him ride.

They found the town of Woodville almost deserted except for the women and children, every one having turned out to aid in the hunt. Since the morning had come a telegraph message from Baton Rouge that a traveller, riding past Woodville, had passed a galloping horseman whom he believed to be the runaway. It had been too dark for him to see his face, but the description of his form tallied. The result of this was to turn the Montagues back to hunt through their own woods.

Allan, after riding with them a short distance, turned off toward the Hall. "If only he can elude them until to-night," was Allan's thought—for he faced the fact that he wanted the Negro to escape. He was certain that the person who had helped the fugitive was the young Westerner who had caught Allan's attention on the boat. Allan had connected the fact of this man's going afoot with the Negro's having had a horse, and Allan dreaded lest Ralph might do the same. The two had come from the same direction, and the stranger had looked dusty and travel-stained. "They intend to meet tonight," Allan thought. "I wish I knew where."

He went to his room to think. But soon he heard a horse galloping, and rushed out at the same moment that his father came limping through another door, followed by Ethel and her mother. Coming toward the house at a furious pace was a stranger, a lad of about fourteen. The horse was covered with foam, and the boy's face showed intense excitement.

"Is this Mr. Montague?" he cried, as he pulled up his mount and raised his cap.

"Yes," replied the captain. "What is it?"

"Father wants to know will you lend us your dogs, sir," said he.

"Dogs!" exclaimed Captain Montague. "They are out already. What's happened?"

"We've got the nigger, sir,—that is, at least, we've got his track, but we can't catch him."

"What do you mean? Can't catch him!"

"We've only got five dogs, sir, and they are all for trailing; they won't seize. And the nigger's got a gun, sir, and he shot one of the dogs. He's down in the swamp where we can't ride, and he gets along as fast as we do."

"Who are you?" asked the captain.

"I'm Jim Henderson's oldest boy, sir. Tom's my name."

"And exactly where is all this, Tom?"

"Down in the bayou, sir; it ain't more'n about three miles from here. We've gone about ten, sir, up and down, since we got the trail."

"And you're sure it's the man?"

"Yes, sir; sure, sir. We've got Tom Murray and his dogs from Natchez, and there's no better in the country. They wouldn't make any mistake. We found a place too, where he'd shot a deer and cut him up."

"Who's with you?" asked the captain.

"Father, and Murray, and a whole crowd from Woodville. They sent me to ask for your dogs; they said you had some good seizers that could follow with the rest and tree the nigger."

"Every one of our dogs is out," the captain told him again. "You'll have to go to Mr. Hinds' place. He's got two boar hounds besides his other dogs, and they'll stop him in no time. Do you know how to get to Mr. Hinds'?"

"No, sir," said the boy.

Captain Montague turned to one of the Negroes. "Tip," he said, "go get a horse saddled, quickly, and ride with this boy to Mr. Hinds'."

The man darted off, and Captain Montague turned to the boy. "How is your father?" he asked.

"Pretty badly hurt," the boy replied; "but he don't mind it, he's so mad. Got his face so tied up he can hardly see, but he's through the swamp ahead of them all."

"How close are they to the Negro?"

"We can hear the dogs," said the boy. "We've got one on a string to guide us, you know."

"How did the man come to get such a start yesterday?"

"He had a pistol hid in his clothes, sir. I was out in the field when it happened—it was just before dark. He wasn't working to suit, and father began to lay his whip over him. The nigger bent down and jerked his chain right off and pulled a knife and went at father. His first cut ran clean across his forehead, and when father tried to pull his revolver, the fellow cut him again.

He'd have killed him, I think, if I hadn't laid on with a club. Then he turned to run, and, of course, just as soon as I saw he had a gun I had to give up and let him go. We got the dogs and put them on, and followed him about five miles. The track stopped at the road, and so we knew he'd got on a horse. Father says it's some of the Abolitionists from up in Ohio helping him, sure as guns."

In a few moments more Tip had returned on horseback; the white boy lifted his cap and they galloped away. Allan turned and went back to his room without a word, leaving his father and the two ladies on the piazza. He paced the floor, frantic, muttering to himself, "Oh, my God, I can't stand this! I won't let them kill the man! I've got to help him!"

Never before had he seen the thing *Slavery* as he saw it now, and it seemed like a demon creature with a grip closing about his heart, with eyes that glared into his and turned him sick with horror. He flung up his hands in the air, all his being a cry: "No, no! You shall not!"

He turned and dashed from the room. He would do something, he would do what he could. He would find the man—if he could do no better he would fight his pursuers himself, the whole crowd of them. He sped out of the house and to the stables. There was no one about, but in the excitement the door had been left unlocked; Allan got out his own horse and put a saddle on him, leaped on his back and away—down the lane, over fences and fields, and toward Buffalo Bayou.

The sun had just gone down; heavy clouds hung low, black and sinister above, red and glaring at the horizon. Beneath, down a long slope, lay the great hollow, sombre and dark; somewhere in its far-stretching wilds toiled an agonized human being, sick and panting, stumbling through swamp and thorny brake, fleeing from savage dogs and relentless men. Allan's soul cried out to God with the horror of this thing—that it should be upon earth. He had heard all the arguments—that the Negroes had been savages in Africa and had to be controlled by force; and what could the slave-owners do if slaves ran away and tried to kill their pursuers? Allan didn't know. At this moment he only knew that he wanted this Negro to escape.

He rode on to the edge of the swamp and there paused, listening. Within the great forest it was still as death. He struck his horse and dashed ahead, along the edge of the cotton-fields. A fence and ditch loomed large in the shadows; he took them at a bound and went on. Then again he drew rein and listened, and now he heard the far-off baying of the hounds, echoing over the wild waste of swampland. Allan was thinking, if only he could get to the man and give him the horse; Allan would stay behind and face the pursuers. But could he get the Negro to trust him and come near?

He turned the horse toward the thicket; but the animal stood still, its forefeet on the edge of the bog. No urging could move it, and Allan saw that the attempt would be madness—he could not ride into the swamp at night. He was helpless, and he turned and rode back to the lights of Valley Hall, which twinkled in the distance through masses of foliage.

He was approaching the place from the rear. There were rows of Negro cabins, scattered outhouses, then the great barn and stables looming, and across the barnyard the rear of the big house with its lights. Allan was just in time to see two figures moving quickly across the yard, one assisting the other. They went to the stable doors, opened one, entered, and slammed the door behind them. At the same moment he realized that the baying of the dogs was growing louder.

CHAPTER V

The hounds arrived, and their outcry awakened the place; horses began neighing, cattle lowing, and Negroes rushing out of their cabins. It seemed but a few seconds before there was a crowd of them staring in fright.

Allan had reined in his horse and sat, trying to think what to do before the men could arrive. His reaction from the intense strain was again despair. The immediate horror had been deferred, but the Negro was still a prisoner, and his fate could be no different in the end. Some of his pursuers might arrive any instant, and they would break in the door, and there was no place the Negro could hide where the dogs would not find him. Under the law the man's life was forfeit; he had resisted his master, and was resisting recapture. Allan recollected a question he had once heard asked, in his childhood, and the answer: "If he's quiet, we call the dogs off; but if he fights, he takes the consequences."

It was dark now, but servants were running from the house with lanterns. If anything was to be done it must be quickly. Allan's thought was to get the man out of the barn; if he could put him on the horse, he might yet get away and join the stranger who had armed him.

Those who were running up were Negroes. He rode toward them, thinking swiftly. Whom should he trust? He could spare only an instant to decide; he saw one of the stable hands, a big, broad-faced, good-natured "black boy," who had been wont to bring his pony in the mornings. "Jerry," he called, "come here!"

The Negro sprang to him and Allan leaped from his horse. "Listen to me, Jerry," he said in a low voice. "Those dogs have got that runaway, 'Dutch Joe,' there in the barn. They've been chasing him about the woods for hours, and he's nearly dead. The men will be here soon, and they intend to kill him. I want you to come with me; I mean to help him."

The Negro's eyes were like saucers. "Help him!" he gasped. "Marse Allan!"

"Yes," said Allan. "What's the matter, are you afraid?"

" 'Fraid, Marse Allan—no, sir!" exclaimed the man, breathless with fear. "But does you mean it, Marse Allan?"

"I mean it," was the reply. "Where is father—is he at the house?"

"No, Marse Allan," said Jerry; "he done got de carriage and rid out to look around, Marse Allan."

"That gives us a few moments. I want you to listen now, Jerry. I will take all the blame; no one will know you had anything to do with it."

"I'll help you, Marse Allan," exclaimed the man. "But what kin we do?"

"We must get him out and put him on my horse—that is the only chance. Some one must go in there and make him understand. I would go, but it would do no good; he won't listen to me. He would listen to a colored man."

"Marse Allan!" gasped the Negro in terror.

"You must do it," Allan told him, firmly. "No one will harm you. I will not let them. I think Taylor Tibbs is in there now."

"I seen him, Marse Allan," said Jerry. "It was Tibbs, but I t'ink he got out, sah. I seen a man climb out de loft window in de back an' run, Marse Allan."

Jerry was still dazed with fright; however, he disappeared in the rear of the stable, and Allan waited, in a fever of anxiety.

At any instant this last hope might be shattered. Was not the whole country riding about this neighborhood searching? And the uproar the dogs were making could be heard on the still night air for miles. Allan rode amongst the hounds shouting at them, but to no purpose; he could drive them back from the door for a moment, but he could not silence them.

Seconds seemed minutes, and minutes ages; then, above the confusion outside and the stamping of the horses within, he made out the man's voice: "Joe! Joe! Whah is you?"

The chorus of the pack drowned out the answer, if answer there was. Allan could only wait. He could hear distant cries and shouts, and had no means of being sure whether they came from the plantation hands or from approaching white men.

"What can be the matter with Jerry?" he blindly asked himself. "What can have happened to him?" He handed his horse to one of the servants, and started around the corner. At the same moment Jerry rushed into sight.

"Kain't find him, Marse Allan," whispered the breathless Negro.

"Can't find him?"

"No, sir; he's hidin'. I called him all roun', but he won't answer—he t'ink it's a trick."

"You were afraid!" stormed Allan, angrily. "You did not hunt!"

"I did my bes', Marse Allan," protested Jerry. " 'Fore God I did, but he doan' know my voice, Marse Allan."

But there the man stopped short, turning in fright. From out of the darkness there had come suddenly a wild yell, followed by a chorus of cries. It was the direction from which the chase was approaching, and a pain like a knife shot through Allan. It was the hunters.

The two stood helpless. There could be no mistake about it; he heard a voice shouting, "Here they are, here they are!" and a figure sprang through an opening left by the Negroes as they recoiled. In the clear light of the lanterns stood Jim Henderson.

Never in his life had Allan seen a sight more horrible than that man. His face and head had once been bound in cloths, and there were still some about his neck and forehead, but those about his face had been torn away, disclosing three frightful newly-sewed gashes. One of them had broken open, and from it the blood had oozed out until the man's face and clothing were dyed with it; it ringed his glaring eyes, it ran from the corners of his mouth, and his hair was clotted with it. He staggered against the side of the stable and leaned there, flinging back his head and gasping hoarsely for breath; he looked to Allan like a fiend out of hell. Three or four others staggered into sight behind him, and he pointed his finger at the door, panting: "We've got him! By God, we've got him!"

The men were so worn out that some of them lay down on the ground hoping for a moment's rest. For a minute there was no move, while Allan was making a desperate resolve.

One by one, more of the pursuers staggered in; there were eight or nine of them, when Henderson started forward, his mutilated face distorted with rage, and yelled: "Come on, boys, come on! Let's have him out!"

He leaped to the door. "Get back!" he shouted to the dogs, kicking them away. Several other men sprang forward, and flung themselves against the door.

"He's locked it!" exclaimed Henderson. "Get an axe there, somebody; hand me that crowbar, you nigger!"

He seized the bar and rushed toward the door again. But Allan stepped in front of him.

"Stop!" commanded a strong young voice. "Stop!" And Henderson stopped, in amazement.

"You can't break in this door," said Allan, firmly.

The other's face convulsed with fury. He whipped a pistol from his belt, and for a moment the two stared into each other's eyes. "I don't think you had best shoot me, Henderson," said Allan, quietly. "And I won't have you breaking into our stable."

"But I want my nigger!" Henderson shouted.

"Your Negro isn't in there," Allan answered.

"Isn't in there!" screamed Henderson. "Of course he's in there!"

"No," was the reply, "he is not. I saw those dogs coming up from the woods; they chased one of our own stablemen in there, and I've been trying to get them away ever since."

"What's that? What's that?" cried a shrill, angry voice. A wizened little Irishman pushed his way in front of Allan. A limb of a tree had cut his forehead in the darkness, and his face, too, was smeared with blood. "My name's Murray, and them's my dogs. You trying to tell me my dogs is got the wrong nigger? I've run them dogs for six year, an' there's no fool can tell me about them dogs."

"I think you don't know whom you are talking to," replied Allan. "And you might just as well understand me. I am in charge of this place while my father and uncle are away, and I tell you that I will not have our stable broken into. There are valuable horses in there, and the first thing you know those dogs will have them stampeded. I know who it is in the barn, and if you will call off the dogs, I will show you."

"I can't call off them boar hounds," cried Murray. "The boar hounds ain't mine."

"If that is the case," said Allan, "there will be nothing for you to do but wait until father or Mr. Hamilton Montague comes home."

"By God, sir," whined Henderson, "that's hardly fair; we've been after that nigger since daybreak and look at my face, Mr. Montague."

"I am sorry," said Allan. "If your Negro is there, he will stay there; he will keep, I fancy."

"When will your father be back?"

"I don't know. He is out helping you now. Some of them ought to be home soon, and if they want to turn those dogs loose in there with the horses, they can say so."

"Spread out, boys," cried Henderson, suddenly. "We'll watch the place and wait."

"Send the dogs round," a man suggested; "make sure the nigger's not got out."

Murray plunged into the frantic pack and dragged out one of the dogs, the one he had had in leash and had just released; he led him slowly round the great building, but the dog gave no sign, and came back and plunged into the pack. "He's still in there," said Murray, adding, with a sneer—"the stableman!"

Allan paid no attention, but stood quietly waiting. None of the men guessed from his demeanor that he was perfectly desperate, and only striving blindly to defer the end. The doom of the Negro was now sealed; Allan knew that his uncle and his father would give the Negro up to his owner. It could be only a question of minutes, also, before one of them appeared. Had not the sounds of the dogs been audible for miles around? He was striving to think what he should do when the crisis came.

"You are sure you recognized the man who ran in there?" asked Henderson, approaching him. Allan could see that his "bluff" had not fallen flat with Henderson—the overseer was plainly alarmed at the thought that while he was waiting here, the fugitive might be making good his escape.

"I am certain," Allan answered. "I was riding up myself, and I saw the dogs coming."

"Why doesn't the fellow call out then, Mr. Montague?"

"I don't know," was Allan's reply. "I've been shouting to him, but he hears the dogs, and I think he is still frightened by them."

"I don't know what to make of it," exclaimed Henderson. "By thunder, it'll be pretty tough if we're to lose that man after all. There's a stranger somewhere around, ready to help him."

Allan made no reply. Then a wild idea came to him. "I tell you what I will do, if you want me to," he said, "I will see if I can get in there and find him."

"I wish you would," the other replied.

Allan turned. In the crowd of Negroes who stood about, he saw Pericles, the butler. "Pericles," he called, "come here!"

A stately old Negro approached, and Allan took one of two revolvers from his belt and handed it to him.

"Pericles, I want you to stand here and watch that stable door. Let nobody touch it, mind you now!"

"I see any white trash breakin' into our do'," said Pericles, grimly; and Allan turned and walked toward the rear of the stable.

Once out of the circle of light he broke into a run. He sped straight to the cabin where lived Taylor Tibbs and his wife Tilly, the head laundress, who stood in the doorway, shaking with fright.

"Tilly," said Allan, sternly, "come inside."

She was almost too terrified to obey. Her young master made sure they were alone in the cabin.

"Where is Tibbs?" he then demanded.

"I dunno, Marse Allan—" began the woman, but Allan stopped her.

"Don't lie to me," he said sternly. "Listen. I saw Tibbs go into that stable with the runaway, and I know he came out again. You know it, too. Tibbs is here, somewhere, and I want him—I want him instantly. If he will come out now, I will promise him he will not be punished; but if you don't find him, as sure as he's born, I'll have him sold down the river to-morrow!"

"Marse Allan!" gasped the woman; but before she could say more a board in the centre of the room lifted up, disclosing underneath the yellow face of Tibbs; he was in the "potato hole," the whites of his eyes showing and his teeth chattering with terror.

"Marse Allan—" he began.

"Shut up!" said Allan. "Get up—quick! Listen now, and don't take too long to understand. I want to save that runaway."

"Marse Allan!" gasped Tibbs, again.

"Do you know where he's hidden?"

"Yes, Marse Allan."

"Then come with me, and do what I tell you, quick!"

He turned and dashed away, Tibbs at his heels; when he came within sight of the stables he slowed down, and walked into the midst of the group. "Follow me," he said to Tibbs, and then to Henderson, "Here's our coachman; we'll see what's the matter with that boy in there."

They went around to the rear of the stables, followed by Henderson and several others, and by Murray, sneering. On the ground lay the ladder, which Jerry had used in climbing to the door in the loft.

"Put it up, Tibbs," said Allan, "and go ahead."

The servant led the way, and the two disappeared in the dark hole. "Now!" whispered Allan. "Quick! Where is that man?"

"He clum in de corn bin, Marse Allan," Tibbs responded. "I tole him to dig down an' hide."

"Show the way—quick!" cried Allan.

"He may shoot," panted the other.

"No, it's too dark, but we must chance it. Go on!"

He pushed the reluctant Negro before him, over the deep haymow, and down a ladder, and along a passage behind the stalls, where the horses were stamping and whinnying in excitement. At last Tibbs stopped.

"He was in dah," he whispered, under his breath.

"Call him," said Allan. "Make him understand."

"Joe, Joe!" panted Tibbs. "Joe—whah is you? Here somebody to help you—don't shoot!"

There came no reply.

"Try again! Louder!" whispered Allan.

"Joe!" cried Tibbs. "Hey, Joe! Don't shoot! We want to help you—come out!"

There was a creaking sound, and a muffled voice asked, "Ha?"

"Here's somebody to help you," gasped Tibbs. "Don't shoot, don't shoot!"

"Tell him to take off his shoes," Allan whispered. He had to repeat the message before the puzzled Tibbs could be induced to give it; Allan, in the meantime, was seated on the floor, hastily removing his own.

"Hand them out," Allan commanded, and Tibbs groped his way in the black darkness, and at last brought to Allan a pair of heavy mud-soaked "Negro-shoes." Allan put them on with trembling hands, giving his own to Tibbs, "Tell him to put them on and hide again."

In a moment they were groping their way back. At the loft door Allan halted, and whispered his orders to Tibbs. Tibbs managed to understand at last, "Glory, glory! Marse Allan," he answered.

Allan looked out. The crowd was peering up at him. "Couldn't find him," he said. "I think he must have got out before."

He heard Murray's laugh of derision. "Go on down," he said to Tibbs.

Henderson had seized a lantern; he suspected some ruse— and held it up and made sure that Tibbs was Tibbs. The Negro descended, and when he neared the ground, lost his footing and pushed the ladder so that it fell. "Look out!" he cried, and sprang out of the way; Henderson who held the lantern, dodged, and as he did so Allan swung out and dropped lightly. No one saw the thick shoes he had on.

"I'm sorry," he said to Henderson. "If the fellow's there, he was too scared to come out. You'll just have to wait until father comes back; he'll be here any minute now."

The man turned away with an oath. Others followed him around toward the front door again, and Allan lagged behind. Left in the darkness, he turned and slowly moved away. His heart was leaping madly now; he could scarcely walk in the big, heavy Negro-shoes, but when he had rounded one of the outhouses, he leaped forward and dashed blindly away. It was pitch dark; he sped past the Negro quarters, out through the gardens, over a wall, and then through a field. The heavy shoes hurt his feet, and stuck in the soft soil, but he plunged on.

And meanwhile Taylor Tibbs, repeating his lesson to himself in a frenzy of fear, had strolled to where Murray, the slave catcher, stood with Henderson.

"You fool!" Murray was saying.

"How did I know?" snarled Henderson. "What does the fellow want to lie to *me* for?"

"I don't know," replied Murray; "but I know he lied. I know my dogs too well. How'd he tell, anyway, in the dark?"

"He could tell! He could tell easy!" Taylor Tibbs declared, with a sudden access of courage.

"What do you know about it, you yellow monkey?" demanded Murray.

"Know?" cried Tibbs, gaining in self-importance as he spoke. "I seen him myself! Don't you suppose I knows who belongs in my stable?"

"Where were you?" demanded Henderson.

"Whah was I? I stood right over dah!" declared Tibbs, pointing. "Dat nigger seen dem dogs comin'—an' he no mo'n got in de do', when dey caught up wif him."

"Then where is he?" roared Henderson.

"He clum out dat back window," cried Tibbs.

"What do you mean?" cried Murray.

"I means what I says. I done tole Marse Allan, but he say he seen de dogs go roun' da, an' dey'd smelt him if he'd been dah. But I knows what I seen. I tell you I seen him jump out dat window an' run—an' I tell you dem old dogs jes' ain't no good!"

"You're lying, you're lying!" shouted Murray, shaking his fist in Tibbs' face. But Tibbs would not be silenced—and Henderson seized Murray by the arm.

"Take one of the other dogs," he yelled. "Do what I say! Do what I say!"

And Murray dashed forward and seized one of his yelping dogs by the back of the neck. With the Negroes at his heels he strode around to the rear, underneath the opening, and set it down. The dog gave one sniff at the ground, then raised its head and emitted a howl, and shot away in the darkness. An instant later the whole pack, yelling like a thousand demons, swept round the corner and vanished in pursuit.

CHAPTER VI

For a moment the two men stood staring at each other in consternation.

"What does that mean?" gasped Henderson.

"It means we've been fooled!" shouted Murray. "That nigger got out *since we came!*"

"He did no such thing," said one of the men, "for I've been watching here every minute! There's not a soul come out of that place, except the two you saw yourself—this man Tibbs and young Mr. Montague."

"I believe those dogs have led us wild the whole day," declared Henderson; and without waiting to hear the other's reply, he turned and dashed after the dogs. The rest followed, with a troop of excited Negroes at their heels, shouting and whooping at the sudden new turn of events.

They left the stable yard black and silent, deserted save for one person—Taylor Tibbs. The instant the crowd was out of sight, Tibbs darted to where his master's horse was tied and led him over to the stable door.

"Joe, Joe!" he called. "Come, heah's de horse. Hurry!"

There was a shuffling inside. "Open de do'!" cried Tibbs. "Hurry up—open de do'!"

And a moment later the barrier swung back, and "Dutch Joe" peered out. "Jump!" cried Tibbs, and leaped upon the horse himself. The Negro was behind him almost as soon, and Tibbs smote the animal a blow on the neck that made him leap, and they went across the yard and out into the darkness beyond, like a shot.

In the meantime the men were running after the dogs—out through the garden and the fields. "We'll catch him," Murray was panting. "They're close to him now, don't you hear them?"

But what the pursuers heard was a pistol shot and a dog's yelp of pain.

The dogs were only a few rods ahead, and had halted. "He's up a tree!" Henderson panted. "Look out, he may shoot at us! Keep back with those lights there!"

His warning slowed some of the men, and stopped the Negroes; but four or five of the hunters went on without slackening. Beyond the field was a rough fence, and beyond that the great orchard of the plantation, at the edge of which the dogs were grouped, leaping up and down, barking frantically.

"Hi, yi!" shouted Murray. "Hold him, hold him! Spread round there, boys, so we won't lose him." And then suddenly the man stopped. From out of the darkness had come a loud hail: "Hello, there! What the devil is the matter with you people?"

"Who is that?" Henderson called out.

"It's I, Allan Montague," came the answer. "Those infernal dogs of yours are after *me!*"

The pursuers stood still.

"I say!" yelled the voice again. "I say there, will you call those dogs off, or do you want me to shoot another of them? Speak up quick, for I won't stand much more of this business."

Henderson sprang forward with a cry of fury, seized a stick and plunged into the midst of the pack, laying about him like a mad man. Even the boar hounds were daunted by his onset and gave way, though only for a short distance. They still stood watching warily, and snarling now and then.

"By Heaven, this is too much!" the occupant of the tree was raging. "I tell you those dogs have got to be taken off this plantation pretty quick. Nobody is safe within miles of them."

"How did this happen?" cried the shrill voice of Murray.

"Happen!" echoed Allan. "It happened that I set out to hunt for my Negro they had run into the stable, and the first thing I knew I heard them after *me!*"

"Confound them, anyhow," growled Henderson.

"Now look a-here!" yelled Murray. "There's some trick about this—"

"What do you mean?" demanded Allan, indignantly.

"I mean what I say," shrilled the other. "You've been with that nigger somewhere, and I know it! I know them dogs o' mine. Bring a light, some of you, bring a light!"

Allan dropped swiftly to the ground before his shoes could be seen. "What is it you are trying to say?" he asked, sternly. "You mean that I've been stealing your runaway?"

"Bring the light here," repeated Murray, insistently, and he seized it and clambered up into the tree, peering among the branches. "There's no nigger here," he said, reluctantly. "But I know what I'm talking about, and I tell you there's dirty work been done—"

He stopped suddenly, for out of the darkness had come an angry voice: "Here, here! What's all this about?"

And Allan's heart leaped—it was his Uncle Montague; and back of him came soon a party of horsemen, the expedition which had left the Hall that afternoon.

"What's all this about?" demanded Mr. Montague again.

"This fellow Murray's got his dogs here," Allan told him, "and they've been running our servants all about the place. They chased one of the stable-boys into the stable, and Henderson wanted to shoot me because I wouldn't let him break in the door. Then the first thing I knew the dogs had gotten after me, and I had to climb a tree to get away from them."

"I'm sorry, Mr. Montague," began Henderson, deprecatingly, "but I—"

"I don't want to hear from you," snapped Allan's uncle. "What do you mean, accusing my nephew of stealing your Negro?"

"I didn't say that!" cried Murray. "But I said that I know them dogs of mine, and that there's something wrong. That nigger was in that barn, and I know it, and I tell you—"

Then suddenly young 'Dolph Montague leaped past Allan and strode toward the slave-catcher. "Shut up! *Shut up!*" he cried. "What do you mean, you dog—do you know who it is you're talking to? Don't you let me hear another word from you, or by Heaven, I'll pound you down into the ground so deep you won't get out in a week—you impudent, dried-up, little monkey, you! Hasn't our whole family been out all day chasing your in-

fernal Negro for you, and you stand there and talk at my cousin
—why, by God, if you don't make tracks out of here, I'll shoot
you as full of holes as a pepper-box!"

The hunters dispersed, after agreeing to continue tomorrow.

Allan declined the offer of 'Dolph's horse, saying that he
wanted to be alone to cool off his anger. He thanked 'Dolph
and left with a strange division in his soul; he loved 'Dolph
and was ashamed of having lied to him!

He went to his room by a side door and sank down on the
bed and lay for hours facing the meaning and consequences of
what had happened to him in the last eventful hour. The burden
of the runaway's future now rested on him with an overwhelming
weight, for he knew that he should never give up until the man
was in Canada; and between Canada and Valley Hall was a vast
region full of perils.

Allan had heard of fugitives who, with no guide save the
north star, had travelled on clear nights, hiding by day in the
swamps; of others who had been provided with a compass, and
had put a firefly in its case to light it. He strove to calculate
how long the trip would take, how much food the man would
have to carry in order that he might have to confide in no one.
Allan had also heard of slaves who had bribed steamboat captains to hide them—he thought of this, and figured up his own
resources. He had heard of others who had gone so far as to
have themselves boxed up and shipped by freight—of one fugitive who had been taken by Adams Express Company from
Richmond to Philadelphia in a box two feet eight inches, by two,
by three, and had been stood upon his head for long periods
on the way.

And so on, until after midnight, when he was startled to hear
a low tap on his door.

"Come in," he whispered, and it opened, and the yellow face
of Taylor Tibbs peered in, his eyes wide with fright.

"Marse Allan!" he panted. "Marse Allan! It's de man. He's
terr'ble bad, Marse Allan—I t'ink he die."

"What's the matter with him?"

"I dunno, Marse Allan, but nobody can't manage him."

Allan followed the frightened Negro down the stairs and out of the house. There everything lay silent, in full moonlight. A dog whimpered, but Allan spoke to him and sped on. They ran down a long, tree-lined road, coming at last within sight of the scattered buildings of the quarters, where, through the chinks of one of the cabins, a light could be seen. As they drew nearer they heard low voices within, and Allan cast an anxious glance in the direction of the house of Wilson, the overseer, about a hundred yards away. There, however, everything was still.

Pushing aside the blanket which made up for the deficiencies of a broken door, they entered the cabin, where a terrible sight met their eyes. The place was low and small, with bare floor, and air stifling with the smoke which came from the fagots in the fireplace. They gave the only light in the cabin—the window was covered by a blanket. Against the wall half a dozen black men were crouching, gazing in fear and uncertainty at Allan. The runaway lay on a pile of quilts and rags on the floor in one corner. He was almost naked, what clothing left on him in shreds; his yellow skin had been cut by thorns and the quilts on which he rested were soaked in blood. He lay flat on his back, his mouth half-open, his eyes closed, and about his lips there played a reddish foam.

"How long has he been like this?" Allan asked, softly.

"Ever since he come, massa," answered one of the watchers. "He's been like he crazy—we kain't hardly hold him."

Allan glanced round, noticing that the place was in confusion, the two or three pieces of furniture that were in it, being upset.

"Dutch Joe" bore all the signs of his ordeals. On the portions of his body which were visible, the flesh had been ploughed up with the lash until it looked like the surface of a washboard. His wrists were swelled out as large as his hands; his feet were naked, and about one ankle was the mark of the ring, a terrible sore, and with flies buzzing on it.

For a minute or so there was not a sound save the fugitive's breathing. Allan knelt and put his hand on the forehead of the prostrate giant; it was hot with fever.

He noticed the lips moving and bent low, listening; the Negro's voice was gone, and only the rasping in his throat could be heard. He put his hand on the arm, and the man seized it convulsively, in a grip like a vise. His eyes, now open wide, stared into vacancy.

Then his voice became audible. "Let me go," he cried, "let me go!

"I say I'm a free man," he rushed on. "I tell you I'm as free as you is—I won't let nobody sell me! Don't you hear me—I've got my papers—I'm a free man, I'm a free man! I ain't afraid of your guns—I won't go—dey can't nobody make me! I've lived in Harrisburg fo'teen year—everybody knows me in Harrisburg! I ain't a-goin' to be no slave—let me be! What yo' want me fo'—I ain't hurt nobody, has I? I pays my way; I kin work as good as any man. I was a-goin' back home today, I was —I got a family in Harrisburg—I got six chillun! Who's a-goin' to care fo' my chillun if you sell me? My woman's sick—she can't work fo' dem chillun. Dey's my chillun, an' I tell you I'm a-goin' home! I ain't afeered o' no beatin. You kin cut me all to pieces—it won't do no good. I won't work fo' you—I'll run away de fust chance I git, an' go back to Harrisburg!"

His voice rose louder and louder. "I'll fight, I tell you! You got no right to me!"—and then he stopped and lay panting. Then, after a minute or two, "Git away!" he cried, and struggled to a sitting posture, his eyes wild. "What good yo' t'ink it goin' do yo', to burn me like dat, yo' white devil? Git away, you Henderson! I'll kill you. S'pose yo' kill me—you t'ink dat's all? I wait fo' you!—*I wait fo' you jes' de same,* you Henderson!"

"Dutch Joe" had staggered to his feet, shaking off those who sought to hold him down as if they had been children. His giant frame stood erect a moment—then suddenly he crouched. A wild gleam flashed over his face—the watchers turned in terror, expecting to see the overseer in the doorway. "Ha, you Henderson!" the Negro shrieked. "You never git away from me!" And "Dutch Joe" moved inch by inch upon something which he saw in the doorway. He lunged forward, clutching into space, his voice rising into a scream: "I got you!"

He took two steps before he stumbled and fell to the ground; he rolled over, his eyes starting from his head. His cries were stilled by a gush of blood from his mouth, and he lay motionless.

Allan turned back, where the Negroes still crouched, gazing at him with frightened eyes. "They will never catch him now," he told them; and then, overcome by his own anguish, he hurried from the cabin.

The house of Wilson, the overseer, lay not far to the right. There was a light in one of the windows and he heard some one talking; once he saw a figure pass by the light.

"What's the matter there?" Allan wondered. "What are they doing awake now?"

And then an idea flashed across his mind—Henderson was there.

He tried to put aside the thought; then he started toward the house. Soon he could hear voices in the room—one of them he knew for Henderson's. It was loud and excited—and Allan strode on and pushed open the door and entered.

He stood in the hallway for an instant. He went to the door from which shone the light, and opened it.

He was in Wilson's "office." One side of it was lined with shelves, on which were rows of shoes, rolls of "Negro-cloth," and piles of hats and blankets; on the walls hung antlers and whips. About the room cots had been put up for the night, where Henderson's helpers had been sleeping; now, however, they were sitting up, and by the light of a candle Allan saw that their faces were white. They were listening to Henderson, who was on a bed in a corner of the room. The man's head had been swathed anew in bandages, and he talked swiftly, excitedly. "I tell you, you're fools!" he was insisting. "Don't you suppose I've any sense? I tell you—"

His eyes turned toward the doorway. His body stiffened and he flung up his hands; "Oh, my good God, my good God! What's that? Look at that!" he screamed.

For an instant there was not a sound; then Wilson leaped up. "I say, it's Mr. Allan!"

"Is it? Is it?" Henderson shouted. "Answer me! Answer me!"

"Why—what in the world do you mean?" Allan asked, and Henderson, to his amazement, buried his head in the bedclothes, and burst into sobbing. "Oh, my soul!" Allan heard him moan. "Oh, what a thing to do, what a thing to do!"

"What does he mean?" Allan asked. "What in Heaven's name has happened to you people?"

"You frightened him, Mr. Allan," said Wilson, "he took you for some one else."

Henderson sat up. "How could you do it?" he shouted. "What in hell did you want to come sneaking into this room for?"

"You see, Mr. Allan," put in Wilson again, "Henderson thinks he's just seen a ghost! Thinks he saw that nigger, sir! We're been trying to convince him it was a nightmare."

"You are fools, you are fools!" screamed Henderson. "I say he stood right there! He walked right out of that door!"

"But that door was locked!" cried Wilson.

"The nigger went *through* it, then! It was his ghost—he's dead —that's what's the matter, the nigger's dead! And, oh, my God, I killed him, and he's after me! He stood right there, and pointed his finger at me."

"Look here, Jim Henderson," insisted one of the men—"you're sick, that what's the matter with you!"

"I know I'm sick," moaned Henderson. "I ain't a-goin' to git well, either. I've got my death. That nigger won't ever let me be!"

Allan turned away, and went to the "Big House" numb with emotion.

CHAPTER VII

Six of the Negroes carried the body of "Dutch Joe" out to the swamp at night and buried it; and Allan stood by the grave and told them that when he came into his own all of them should be free. There was nothing more that he could do.

The next day he went for a walk alone down the "big road," and met once more the young Westerner, "Carter," this time riding. Allan stepped out in front of him. "May I talk with you a moment, please?" he asked.

The stranger reined up his horse. "What is it?" he inquired, coldly.

"I believe," Allan began, "that there is a Negro about here whom you were interested in—"

A look of perplexity crossed the other's face. "What Negro?" he asked.

"I mean the runaway," said Allan.

But the stranger only stared at him. "Why in the world should you suppose that I am interested in a runaway?" he demanded.

Allan did not reply for a moment; then he went on resolutely, "It would be too bad if you and I could not understand each other. I know what your danger is, and I want you to know that I do not feel about these things as the people round here do. I want now to tell you that the Negro is dead."

"Dead!" exclaimed the man.

"Yes," said Allan, "he was hiding in our quarters, and he died of exhaustion; they had run him to death."

The Westerner continued to gaze at him innocently. Then he said, quietly, "That is too bad. But why have you not made the fact known to the public?"

"Made it known?" asked Allan.

"Yes," was the reply. "Did you not know that there were rewards of five hundred dollars for the fellow—alive or dead?"

"Rewards?" Allan asked perplexed.

"Yes, of course—you were entitled to them, weren't you? And besides, people are spending their time hunting for him, and the whole country is alarmed about him; and you don't tell them that he is dead! I am sorry to have to say it, sir, but I shall regard it my duty to make known what you have told me. I bid you good morning."

The stranger touched his horse and bounded off, leaving Allan staring after him dumfounded. "What in the world does *that* mean?" he thought to himself. "Have I made a mistake?"

But it was not long before he thought of the other explanation
—that the man suspected a trap. "He saw me with Henderson
on the steamer," Allan remembered. "And my, but wasn't he
sharp about it!"

He weighed the two possibilities, but was left in uncomfortable
uncertainty. He would soon know, of course—he waited through
the day, half prepared for an explosion. None came, however, and
toward sundown he rode into town and learned that "Carter"
had left.

"I was right after all," he said to himself, regretting that he
had not been bolder. "I lost my chance, and I shall never see
him again."

For two days more the neighborhood kept up its search for
"Dutch Joe"—then stopped, and little by little men ceased to
think of him. It was not so with Allan, however; the memory of
the dead ex-slave haunted him, day and night, and poisoned his
life. The plantation was no longer home to him; he had turned
traitor. The Negroes had come to know that he was their friend,
and now they fled to him with all their wrongs, and his every
hour was embittered with new misery. There was no serving two
masters at Valley Hall—you either sided with the owners or the
slaves. Allan was bound hand and foot. What could he accomplish
by interceding? And every day some new fuel was added to the
fire of revolt that was now burning in his soul. Sometimes he
would have to rush away to master himself; and there were hours
when, shrink from it as he would, he foresaw the crisis that was
on the way. He shut his eyes to this future, hoping against hope,
and when the climax came it caught him unaware.

There came a new subject of conversation at the Hall, taking
the place of the runaway: a speech of Charles Sumner's in the
Senate, reported in the Woodville paper the twentieth of May.
This historic oration, "The Crime Against Kansas," seemed to
Allan to come from the heart of a passionate lover of justice.
At the moment of its delivery the news from the territory was
of the closing in of the hosts from Missouri about the free-state
town of Lawrence; and burning with the wrath of the prophets,
the senator from Massachusetts hurled his denunciation of the deed

into the faces of its doers. It was "a Crime without example in the history of the past—the rape of a virgin territory, compelling it to the hateful embrace of Slavery." He denounced the invaders of Kansas: "Hirelings picked from the drunken spew and vomit of an uneasy civilization—leashed together by secret signs and lodges, renewing the incredible atrocities of the assassins and the thugs." He denounced the lawmakers of Kansas—their attempt to "fasten and rivet, by legislative bolt, spike, and screw, the whole usurpation upon the territory." Fronting the authors and the champions of these measures, undaunted by their furious threats, the senator poured out his scorn upon them. Butler and Douglas he pictured as Don Quixote and Sancho Panza.

"The senator from South Carolina has read many books of chivalry; he has chosen a mistress to whom he makes his vows, and who, though ugly to others, is always lovely to him—I mean the harlot, Slavery. Let her be impeached in character, or any proposition be made to shut her out from the extension of her wantonness, and no extravagance of manner and hardihood of assertion is too great for this senator." Douglas he described as "vindicating his labored report"—"piling one mass of elaborate error upon another mass—constraining himself to unfamiliar decencies of speech." His victim followed him with the cry of rage. "Is it his object to provoke some of us to kick him as we would a dog in the street, that he may get sympathy upon the just chastisement?"

The sentiment of Valley Hall about this thing was voiced—vigorously if not coherently—by Mason of Virginia: "I am constrained to hear depravity, exhibiting its loathsome deformities in accusation and vilification against the quarter of the country from which I come. And I must listen to it because it is a necessity of my position, under a common government, to recognize as an equal politically one whom to see elsewhere is to shun and despise." That was the thing which galled them, to be bound up with people who chose such a man to represent them. Might one not just as well have been fastened in the public stocks and set out for them to mock?—"Somebody ought to call the scoundrel out!" 'Dolph cried.

"He wouldn't fight—that's just the trouble," Captain Montague answered. "There would be dozens of challenges if he would accept them."

"But is a man to get the privilege of pouring insults upon our heads merely by professing to despise dueling? By Heaven, Uncle Harry, he ought to be shot down like a mad dog!"

And every one who came to the Hall took the same view of it. To each of them it was like a personal affront—a blow in the face. Allan felt as if he were living above the crater of a volcano—the very air was sulphurous with passion. "We shall wait until the fall," he heard his father saying. "They will elect a Republican President, and that will be the end!"

Such was the program; and meanwhile there was Kansas, the new State which might yet be saved to the South. Men waited hour by hour—one might almost say minute by minute—for the final news from the territory; and a couple of days later, jubilant and breathless, 'Dolph came in with the tidings. Allan had been in the library, and hearing him, came out to the portico and stood listening.

The first blow of civil war had been struck, and the hordes of Abolitiondom were scattered! Seven hundred and fifty heroes from Missouri had made up the party, with the supposed-to-be-murdered Sheriff Jones among them; and the little city of Lawrence, cowed at last, had submitted while he served his warrants. Afterward, pandemonium had broken loose—there were two free-state papers in the town, and the grand-jury of the territory having indicted them as nuisances, the mob wrecked their offices, and dumped their presses into the river. Next came the turn of the great hotel, the stone citadel of the Emigrant Aid Company; a few score of cannon-balls were fired at it, and these failing, kegs of gunpowder were tried, and finally the place was burned to the ground. The house of Robinson, the free-state governor, was fired, and the liquor stores plundered; and so at last the victorious army marched away again, with banners flaunting their defiance upon the breeze—

"Let Yankees tremble, Abolitionists fall;
Our motto is, give Southern rights to all!"

So the black clouds gathered, the thunder muttered, and the air grew dark. It was the South's first taste of victory in a long time; and the young men who came to the Hall were like Iroquois savages doing a war dance. Randolph cursed the luck that had kept him at home while such things were doing. "Do you think it will settle the Kansas issue, Uncle Harry?" he would demand, again and again; he found it difficult to credit the other's assurance that it would take more than that to crush the hopes of Abolition-dom. The sack of Lawrence had taken place at the very time that Sumner was delivering his harangue in the Senate; and 'Dolph laughed gleefully that it was their reply—little guessing how much more was on the way.

The news came that same afternoon. Again it was Randoph who brought it, having gone to town to learn what more he could about Lawrence. He had been gone about two hours, and in the meantime company had come, and quite a party was seated on the veranda, where the tea-table was spread. They were waiting for him and for Captain Montague, who had gone driving with his favorite trotter. Randolph came, wild with excitement, and began to shout almost before they could hear him. "They've killed Sumner!" When he got nearer he qualified it—"Killed him—or almost! Nobody knows yet—but they've given him a beating!" He continued, after he had dismounted and was rushing up the steps: "It was Brooks of South Carolina—a congressman, who did it, got him alone in the Senate-chamber and beat him with a cane—pounded his head almost to a jelly!"

There was stunned silence on the piazza for a moment. Then young Ralph leaped to his feet and shouted: "Served him right! Served him right! Three cheers for Congressman Brooks!"

No one cheered. But no one rebuked the young man either.

"How did you learn this?" asked 'Dolph's father.

"I stood in the telegraph office while the news was read off. It is true—there's no doubt of it. He had a guttapercha stick an inch thick, and he smashed it all to pieces over his head. Sumner tried to get up—he got caught in his desk somehow, and Brooks beat him senseless. They don't know if he's going to die or not!"

"How terrible! Oh, how terrible," an agonized young voice cried out, and Allan stood confronting the assemblage, his face white and his eyes blazing. "To strike a man down when he was helpless, when he was unarmed! And in the Senate of our country, and he a senator! Is there no one here to resent this? Is there no decency left among you? Shame on you, I say—shame!"

And he stopped, choking with indignation; there was a moment of silence—and then from near the steps in tones as furious as his own, came the answer, "Jesus Christ!" Allan turned to see Randolph, his face convulsed with fury, throw his hand up with a knife in it.

There was only one person near enough—Randolph's father. Hamilton Montague flung out his arm in front of his son, and shouted. *"Back!* Stand back, sir, stand where you are! Are you mad?"

Randolph halted and his hand fell to his side. He stood, pale and trembling, glaring at his cousin.

Mr. Montague lowered his arm, and turned to Allan, "You will go to your room, sir," he said, "and wait until your father comes."

But Allan made no move.

"I know what this means, sir," his uncle said. "There is no need to say a word more. We shall wait for your father—he may deal with you as he chooses. You are a traitor to your State, a traitor to your country; and God help you, for it will be the death of him when he hears it—it will break your poor father's heart! Now go!"

Allan turned without a word and went into the house. It had come at last!

CHAPTER VIII

~~~~~~

He went to his room, to await his father. He thought little of himself now. His mind was on the tragedy of the senator, brutally beaten, maybe killed, on the floor of his country's forum. Allan had seen him once at college, a towering figure, six feet and more in height, with the head of an Apollo. Champion of all things free and noble he seemed, and was so considered by those who heard him that day. To them he was the unconquerable defender of every outraged soul; and now beaten into insensibility by a ruthless bully—oh, it was too terrible to be true! And for a difference of political opinion! What was the Congress for? Were the nation's lawmakers to settle the nation's affairs by such means?

Allan saw the truth now as he had never seen it before. No longer was he to be bound by other duties—his love of home, or his love for the South. Indeed, it was the South herself who cried out to him for deliverance, from this haglike spectre of Slavery which rode upon her back, and raised up a son to do such a dastardly deed! Let war and desolation come if it must, let these cities be razed, these fields drenched with blood—even that he would face—so only that this horror be ended, and the spirit of the South set free! He saw her again, as he had seen her in this place when he was a twelve-year-old boy, under the spell of the golden tongued orator, Yancey. She stretched out her arms to him, but now her aspect was wild, her eyes full of weeping; for madness had smitten her sons.

It was late at night before he heard a step in the Hall, and looking up saw Ethel standing in the doorway.

The light streamed about her stately figure, shining on her glossy black hair. She stood motionless, gazing at him; and he rose to his feet, and waited for her to speak. But she remained silent until he said, "I suppose you've come to scold me."

"I have not come to talk to you about that," his cousin answered, trying to control her voice.

"It is something more terrible than that. I don't know how you are to bear it, Allan—we are afraid something has happened to your father."

He started, and she hurried on, "There has been a runaway; the horse has come home with the buggy all smashed to pieces, and he not in it. The men have gone to hunt for him." Ethel stopped and there was a silence.

Then came the sound of men and horses outside; Ethel turned with a low cry and ran from the room and Allan followed. It was faint moonlight, and several horsemen were riding up to the house, dark and ghostly as they came.

They halted, and dismounted, all but one. He bore a heavy burden in his arms, and Allan ran to him and held out his arms. The man gently gave him the dead body of his father.

CHAPTER IX

About ten days had passed since Captain Montague had been buried. His arm had been caught in the wheel of his carriage, and the horse had kicked him. Allan's battle frenzy was gone, and he went about the place desolate, numb with grief. Now and then the fearful truth—that he was alone in the world, that he was never to see his father, never to hear his voice again—would flash upon him with overwhelming force, and he would stand still, sick with despair.

He had lost all the world at once. His family tried for awhile to make it easy for him; but he had committed the unforgivable offence, and they could not hide the truth—that he no longer belonged to Valley Hall, that he had no longer a part in their life. Poor Mrs. Montague was prostrated and under the doctor's care, and he did not see her. His uncles were kind, but the young cousins, including Ethel, avoided him as much as possible. If it had been alone with the family that his outbreak had occurred, and if he had accused only them, it might have been different; but to have had it happen while guests were present, and to include them in his indictment—to have all the neighborhood discussing the fact that a Montague had become Abolitionist—that was unforgivable.

A situation so painful could not continue for long. Allan waited only until time enough had elapsed for his haste not to seem indecent. Then he found Mr. Montague one morning in the office. "I think, Uncle Hamilton," he began, "that I shall return to the North."

"I had presumed that you would," the other responded.

Allen hesitated a moment. "There is something that I have wished to speak to you about first," he said.

"What is it?"

"There are one or two servants here whom I should like, if I could, to arrange to take to the North with me."

Mr. Montague stiffened. "I am very sorry," he answered. "It is impossible."

Allan looked at him in surprise. "Impossible?"

"Absolutely."

"I should hate for there to be any unpleasantness about this, Uncle Hamilton—"

"Have no fear," the other said, quietly; "there will be none."

"But you must excuse me," Allan went on, "if I remind you that half of this plantation does now belong to me."

"It will belong to you," Mr. Montague replied, "when you come of age—or rather it would have under ordinary circumstances. But the circumstances are not ordinary. By the terms of your grandfather's will, his property was divided equally between his two sons. But when your father went to live in Boston, we concluded an agreement by which the plantation was to be operated for our mutual benefit for a period of five years, I managing it here and he conducting its business in Boston. That agreement expired last year, and was renewed for the period of six years. I shall be glad to show you the papers."

"Then, if I understand you," said Allan, "I have nothing to do with it at all?"

"You are entitled to half of its income," said Mr. Montague, "and that you will receive. I am your legal guardian, in the absence of any instructions from your father, and I might, I presume, attempt to control your conduct, and might certainly control your income. I have no desire to do either, however; you may do what you will."

"I thank you," said Allan, in a low voice. There was a short silence; then he resumed, "And what I ask, you could not grant as a favor?"

"I should grant anything that I could," replied his uncle,

"without injuring the plantation—without injuring your interests as well as my own."

"And that would injure them?"

"It assuredly would. Your mere presence here injures them —feeling as you do, and the servants having learned it, as they have. What you propose would injure not only Valley Hall, it would injure the whole community, and the State."

"Explain it to me," Allan said.

"You would want to set the servants free, would you not?"

"Yes," said Allan.

"And what do you suppose would be the effect of this upon those who were *not* set free?"

There was a pause; then suddenly Mr. Montague nodded in the direction of the window, saying, "Look there." The other saw, passing by, the cooper, whom he had so often noticed before.

"There goes a boy," said the other, "whom I have been three years in breaking. He has run away five times, and he has been whipped more than any other Negro on this place. But now at last he has learned that I am his master, and that I rule, and he does his work, and says nothing. What do you suppose would be his thought when he saw some of his companions taken away to be set free? What do you suppose would be *our* thought, knowing that every night he and others were thinking about it—that they were sitting in their cabins discussing it?"

Allan made no answer.

"The legislature of the State of Mississippi," Mr. Montague continued, "has seen fit to prohibit the emancipation of a slave, except with its own special sanction, and for mentioned causes; and what do you suppose is the reason for that? You think it barbarous, I presume; but we have our system and we have to maintain it. We cannot have our servants getting ideas about freedom. And my position as the guardian of this plantation is precisely the same as that of the legislators as guardians of the State. There can be no halfway measures with Slavery—you have to maintain it or it will destroy you. You are going back to Boston, and you can afford to spoil Negroes; but we have to live here among them, and I assure you, sir, this is not easy, as you would find if you had control. If those people you listened to in Massachusetts could be made to come down here and live in Wilkinson County, where there are several Negroes for every white man, they would be turned into proslavery agitators in six months. These primitives need to be civilized—are you aware that they still eat one another in Africa? They are cannibals. You have had none of the burden of trying to civilize a savage people. We live here among them, outnumbered many times. What would happen to our women and children if the black man was not made to understand that the civilized white man is master? So far you have lived here only as a child, while we, your elders, have carried this burden. Now it is too late to undo what the Yankee orators have done to you, and too late to undo what you have done to Valley Hall!"

There was nothing Allan could say. He waited in silence until he could do so without rudeness, and then he rose and left.

It was hard for Uncle Ben to understand that a family was to be broken up by a disagreement about politics. It was Mr. Handy's habit to regard the Slavery question as a "red herring" stirred up by the Yankee politicians. The real issue was that the manufacturing North wanted power in the halls of Congress, and would not let the agricultural South get more power than it already had. "Honestly, Allan," he pleaded, "you ought to be ashamed of yourself not to see through those Yankee tradesmen."

"Do you approve of what we did to Sumner?" Allan asked.

"Sumner?" exclaimed Mr. Handy. "Who is Sumner but a politician, making hay with his constituents? Understand me, my boy," Mr. Handy went on, "I am not defending what one Southern politician did. I'm only telling you not to take politicians seriously. And you should not let yourself be so badly hurt by what is sometimes done to a slave, such as in the case of 'Dutch Joe.' These are barbarous people still, and the overseers are simply policemen keeping order among them on an isolated plantation.

"No, my boy," the lecturer continued, "you've gone and got yourself into a fix, and while you're still too young to know what you are doing! The pity of it! Don't you think you'd better apologize to everyone concerned and start over—here where your friends and family belong?"

"I can't apologize, Uncle Ben; I can't see things as my friends and family do. Maybe I am too young and ignorant as you say, but that's just the point—I must know all the truth about this terrible matter, and only one point of view is tolerated in the South."

So, the next morning for the second time, the carriage bore him away from Valley Hall, on his way to Yankeedom.

Painful was the contrast with his earlier parting, and the memory of it brought bitter tears into his eyes as he drove through the old, beloved countryside. Then the whole county had turned out to see him off with his father; now Randolph had ridden away before breakfast to avoid him, and his uncle, Hamilton Montague, had bade him good-by without even holding out his hand. Only Mr. Handy and Mrs. Montague spoke to him kindly. Ethel had stood by without a word. The world stretched out before him, desolate and lonely—there was no longer any home in it for him, nor any friends to whom he belonged.

CHAPTER X

~~~~~~

In Congress, and all over the country, men were still discussing the Sumner outrage—the North in furious indignation, the South in exulting triumph. The senator was not dead, it transpired—only crippled for life. Mr. Toombs and Mr. Davis had expressed their approval of the assault—and public meetings in the South were presenting Brooks with canes bearing devices such as, "Use knockdown arguments!" and "Hit him again!"

In "bleeding Kansas" the "sacking" of the town of Lawrence had been the signal for the outbreak of local war. One John Brown, an antislavery leader, had made a midnight raid with a band of followers upon a settlement on "Pottawatomie Creek," and taking five proslavery settlers from their beds, had "executed" them, as he termed it, by hacking them to pieces with an old army cutlass. The Missourians were now on the war-path, seeking vengeance for this deed, and guerilla bands were roaming over the territory. When Allan's steamer reached Cairo, the news came that the proslavery men had declared a blockade of the Missouri River, and that persons bound for Kansas who were deemed suspicious were sent floating down again tied to logs.

As the steamer was approaching Cincinnati, he noticed up the river another boat, belonging apparently to the same line, coming from the opposite direction, under the tow of two tugs. "Something out of order," he heard a man near him say, and he stood watching the vessel. As they turned in toward their docks, the other did likewise, and the two landed about the same time. From the passengers who poured off, Allan learned that the boat's machinery had broken down.

While he was engaging a carriage, he noticed coming from the disabled steamer a gentleman and lady accompanied by a young colored woman with a colored baby in her arms. They engaged the carriage next to his, and he saw them again as he entered the hotel. They sat at the same table with him—and Allan noticed that the gentleman was placed where he could keep his eye on the colored woman, who sat in the corridor outside. He watched her closely, and the reason for it was not slow in occurring to Allan—the woman must be his slave. In the States bordering on the Ohio it was generally provided that passengers might carry slaves upon river steamboats which stopped at free-state ports; but if the owner stopped over with a slave, it was at his own risk—at least that was generally the case in late years, since the North had become wrought up on the Slavery question.

They were almost through with breakfast when Allan, who could also see the woman, was startled to notice a man talking to her. The man's back was toward him, and Allan could not tell what he looked like. The master chanced to be speaking to his wife, and for perhaps half a minute he did not notice what was going on; then suddenly he leaped from his seat, and ran into the corridor.

The people in the room stared at him; then, hearing his voice raised, several of them rose and followed him. The lady, flushed with agitation, did the same. Allan, following, was in time to hear the Southerner exclaiming, "Now that's quite enough! I allow no one to talk with this woman!"

The intruder was a tall, elderly gentleman, clad in the sober garb of a Quaker. Allan took one glance at him and realized it was none other than his Abolitionist acquaintance, the "President of the Underground Railroad," Mr. Levi Coffin!

The Quaker held his head high, gazing straight into the other's eyes. "I do not know," he said, quietly, "who gave thee the right to forbid me to speak to whom I please."

"I'll show you about right!" cried the other, passionately. "This woman is my servant, and I will not have her interfered with."

"As to that," said Mr. Coffin, " 'tis for the woman to say—not for thee. If I understand her rightly, thee claims this woman as thy slave; I was telling her that she is free, and that she has a right to leave thee if she wishes. And I assure thee, sir, that if she does wish, no command of thine will be of the least effect."

"By God!" cried the woman's owner, clenching his hands; Allan thought for a second he was going to strike the old gentleman. But people were running toward them from every direction, drawn by the excited colloquy, and this exercised a restraining influence.

The Quaker turned to the Negress. "I tell thee," he said, "that thy master has no longer any right to thee; the law—"

"Maria!" shouted the other, springing between them. "I forbid you to listen to this man! Stand up!"

The colored woman had sat staring from one to the other, helpless with fright, and the child in her arms was starting to cry. "Stand up!" cried her master again, and she rose mechanically.

He grasped her tightly by the arm. "Come!" he said, and they started to the door, pushing roughly through the crowd which now filled the corridors.

Mr. Coffin whispered hastily to one of the waiters, whom he had beckoned to him. Allan saw him slip some money into his hand, and the waiter ran out of the door. Mr. Coffin then hurried forward to the side of the colored woman.

"Listen to what I tell thee!" he said to her. "I will help thee if thee will only let me. Thee said thee wanted to be free. Thee can be free if thee chooses. This man has no right under the law of this state to make thee go a step—"

"Stand back, sir!" shouted the other. "Stand back, I say!"

Mr. Coffin paid no heed.

"It is thy one chance," he told the woman. "If he gets thee on board the steamer, I cannot help thee. Before it is too late, say if thee wants to be free."

The woman was staring into his face, in terror. She began to drag upon her master. "I doan' want to go—" she began, but the other shook her furiously, crying, "Shut up!"

They had come to the door of the hotel. In front Allan saw a carriage standing—the one in which the master had come. He was striding toward it, when around the corner came the waiter, a policeman at his heels.

Mr. Coffin called out to the officer. "This man is trying to kidnap this woman! I demand that thee stop him."

The Southerner halted.

"What's this?" inquired the policeman. "What's the matter here?"

"This woman is my servant," said the Southerner, indignantly. "This fellow has been trying to entice her away from me. She goes with me of her own accord."

And he started for the carriage again; he still gripped the woman by the arm, and she went with him, confused by the excitement, the contradictory commands, and the screaming of the baby in her arms. They were within ten feet of the carriage, when Mr. Coffin sprang in front of them again.

"Officer!" he cried. "I say I demand that thee stop this outrage! Will thee stand by and allow this man to force this woman away?"

"I can't help it, sir," said the officer. "I have nothing to do with it if she chooses to go."

"Chooses?" cried the other. "Don't thee see that the man has frightened her half to death? She doesn't realize what her rights are."

"I can't help it, sir," declared the policeman again, "if she doesn't ask it herself. I have no power to interfere—it rests with her to say."

"Well, ask her, ask her!" cried Mr. Coffin. "Tell her that thee is an officer of the law, and that she does not have to go unless she wishes."

The policeman stood for a moment, uncertain. "See here, sir," he ventured, addressing the Southerner, who had started forward again; but the latter pushed him resolutely. "This woman is my servant and I have a right to take her; it is nobody's business but her own!"

He was in front of the carriage. "Step in," he commanded the Negress, sternly, and Allan thought that he had won. But the carriage began suddenly to back, and the horses to rear and plunge: "Look out there!" he heard the driver shout. "Look out there, you fool!" Turning he saw that another carriage, drawing up at the curb and coming from the opposite direction, was crowding the first one back.

At the same moment the breathless waiter pushed his way through the throng of people, and touched Mr. Coffin on the arm. "Here it is, sir!" he panted. And Mr. Coffin sprang forward and put his hand on the shoulder of the colored woman.

"Maria!" he cried. "Thee told me thee wanted to be free. Now don't let any one frighten thee; thee can choose for thyself. If thee wants to be a free woman, *step into this carriage!*"

The Negress was staring at him, uncertainly. "Step into this carriage!" he cried again; and with a sudden burst of resolution she tore her arm free from her master and sprang away.

"I want to be free!" she panted.

"Officer, thee knows the law; thee has heard this woman speak. Make this man stand back—thee will fail at thy peril! Thee knows who I am, I think!"

The policeman stepped in front of the master. "This won't do, sir," he said—"you can't stop the woman."

"But I *will* stop her! I tell you she's my slave."

"Your slave? Is she a runaway?"

"The woman is not a runaway," declared Mr. Coffin, firmly. "He brought her here of his own will."

"I was on the *River Queen*," countered the master. "The vessel broke down, and I had no choice but to land."

"You'll have to take your hand off her, sir," said the policeman. "I am sorry, but you cannot take her by force."

Mr. Coffin whispered to the Negress, "Step in!"—and the woman tore her arm free and sprang away again. With two bounds she was in the carriage, and the old gentleman leaped in after her. He slammed the door, and the driver lashed his horses, and the carriage went whirling down the street.

The sympathies of the witnesses had all been with the rescuer. There were cries of delight while the baffled slave owner could only threaten the policeman.

"You will find it's the law, sir," was the officer's only reply.

CHAPTER XI

The adventure had put Allan in better spirits. He had thought of Uncle Ben's statement about overseers being policemen to keep order in a primitive community, and wondered if after all, he had not been too ignorant of the slave-owner's side. But here was this Quaker, a gentle and religious man, who declared that slavery was wrong, and that was all there was to it. He went back and changed the order for his luggage and then set out down the street. He had not forgotten Mr. Coffin's invitation to visit him if he was ever in Cincinnati. He would accept it now.

He had no difficulty in finding out where Levi Coffin lived— in a big house on the corner of Franklin Street and Broadway. He was about to ascend the steps when he was surprised to see the old gentleman himself turning the corner—his face still flushed with excitement.

Allan went up to him, smiling, and held out his hand, bidding him good afternoon. Seeing him perplexed, he added, "You don't remember me?"

"I am glad to see thee, friend," said Mr. Coffin; "but I must confess thee is right."

"You once gave me a bowie-knife," said Allan.

The look on the Quaker's face showed bewilderment. "No," he said, "thee has made a mistake in the man."

"Impossible," Allan answered. "Don't you know? It was to kill an Abolitionist with."

And a sudden light flashed over Mr. Coffin's countenance; he stretched out both his hands. "My boy," he cried, "who would have believed it! Where in the world has thee come from?"

"All the way from Mississippi," Allan answered. "And I have turned Abolitionist!"

"No!" cried Mr. Coffin, opening his eyes; then he added eagerly, "Come in and tell me about it."

They turned toward the house. "What became of the woman?" Allan asked.

"Woman? What woman?"

"The one you befriended just now."

"What!" cried the other. "How did thee hear of it?"

"I was within ten feet of you all the time. You were too busy to see me. What have you done with her?" asked Allan. "That is, if it is proper for me to ask."

"I bought her a ticket, and put her on the train. Our own train—the Underground Railroad. Since thee is an Abolitionist, it is safe to tell thee."

"Thank you, sir, for trusting me," said Allan.

"Thee must stay to dinner with us," replied the Quaker. "I will introduce thee to a young man whom I expect to see shortly —an extraordinary person. Since thee is turned Abolitionist, there will be no harm in thee knowing about him."

"Thank you, sir. If it will not inconvenience you. I think I need the company of some Abolitionists just now."

They entered the house, and Mr. Coffin went on telling him about the man he was to meet. "He is the son of the Rev. Elijah Lovejoy, the Abolitionist who was murdered by a mob in Alton nearly twenty years ago. It was that murder which aroused Wendell Phillips. Edward was a child when his father died; but he has pledged his life to the cause of the slave, and he goes down into the South and carries off those who will follow him. It is desperate work, indeed. I do not approve of it myself, but there are those who help him, and all my arguing has not been enough to stop him. He is only a few years older than thee is, but he has been doing this thing ever since the Fugitive-slave law was passed. Besides helping slaves to escape, he gives to the relatives of those who have already escaped. There is scarcely a week that passes that we do not hear of some distressing case— of a mother whose children have been sold—of a husband who has had to flee and leave his wife—of sons and daughters whose parents are dying of old age and neglect. Sometimes we raise the money to buy them—but I have known cases where the owners refuse to sell, merely by way of punishing the runaways. I saw a letter once from a sugar planter in Louisiana, in which he declared that he would flog the husband of an escaped woman to death, unless she came back. When such things happen Lovejoy goes down and helps the slaves to get away. I have not seen him for several months—but I had a note from him yesterday, saying he was coming to see me."

The doorbell rang and Mr. Coffin excused himself to answer it. He came back talking with his guest; and Allan saw that it was "Mr. Carter," his acquaintance of the steamboat, the accomplice of "Dutch Joe."

CHAPTER XII

The Westerner was the first to recover from the surprise. He came forward, stretching out his hand. "So! It was true, after all!"

"Yes, it was true," Allan answered. He added, with a smile, "Mr. Carter!"

"I have many names," said the other. "But now, tell me about 'Dutch Joe.'" Allan told him the sad news, and they discussed the case, fighting their battle over again, and explaining it to their host.

"I was suspicious of you from the first," Allan said, and added, "I almost had the truth out of you there on the road."

"Imagine my situation!" said Lovejoy.

"You were quick about it."

"I have to be, in my business," was the reply. "I have had many people offer me their confidence, but yours was the only case in which I suspected they might be sincere. The reason was a queer one—I had seen you reading books on the steamboat!"

Lovejoy proved to be a person of more education than Allan had supposed. He had been a student at Oberlin, the antislavery and coeducational college of Ohio. He was about twenty-three, but seemed older, spare in face and form, with prominent nose and mouth. He stood erect and eyed one keenly. He had evidently made up his mind as to Allan, and spoke without reserve.

After they were seated, he said to his host, "I came to tell you I have yielded to your entreaties—I am going to give up slave-stealing."

"Ah!" cried the old gentleman, with a warm smile.

"Yes, I have made my last trip South. I am going to start tonight for the West—for Kansas."

Mr. Coffin's smile faded. "Alas!" he exclaimed. "That is worse yet. Thee is going to fight! That is wrong!"

"Going to fight!" echoed Lovejoy, and clenched his hand. "Going to *do* something at last! I was not such a fool as to be unaware of how futile the things were that I was doing—I only did them because I had to do something. But out there in Kansas, trouble is really coming to a head—if we can only blow up the fire hot enough, there will come a war out of that Kansas mess yet!"

"You want a war?" Allan asked, in a shocked voice; and Lovejoy cried, "I want a war.

"Are you one of these who expect to settle this thing by standing up and jabbering about it?" he continued. "Do you think that those people have the slightest idea of giving up, until we have gone in and walked over them—smashed them down so flat that they never dare raise their heads again?" Lovejoy shut his great jaw so tight that the muscles stood out in lumps.

"I understand," said Allan, "but then—I was born a Southerner!"

"Yes," said the other, "I know; and doubtless you love the people—you only hate Slavery, and all that sort of business. But I was born a Northerner, and they murdered my father, and I hate them like the very devil, if Mr. Coffin will excuse me. I hate their pride and their insolence—their blustering and their boasting—haven't I been down there and sat and listened to them talk until I had to go out into the woods and bellow like a bull with rage? Why, good God! there have been times when I have seen myself picking up that whole everlasting slave-driving nation and shaking them until their teeth flew out!—"

The speaker paused a moment, then rushed on, "Take this business of Sumner! Have you heard the opinion of the University of Virginia?"

Allan shook his head. He was shocked, and saw that Mr. Coffin was more so. But Lovejoy appeared not to know or care. He drew a newspaper from his pocket, and after looking through it for a moment, read aloud:

"From the Richmond *Enquirer,* 'Another Cane for Mr. Brooks —We understand that a very large meeting of the students of the University of Virginia was held on Tuesday evening, to take into consideration the recent attack of the Hon. Preston S. Brooks on Charles Sumner, in the United States Senate chamber. Several very eloquent speeches were delivered, all of which fully approved the course of Mr. Brooks, and the resolution was passed to purchase for Mr. Brooks a splendid cane. The cane is to have a heavy gold head, which will be suitably inscribed, and also bear upon it a device of the human head, badly cracked and broken. The chivalry of the South, it seems, has been thoroughly aroused.' "

Lovejoy crushed the paper in his hands angrily and hurled it to the floor. "Now tell me," he cried, "by the Lord God Almighty, is there any sort of an answer for that but bayonets and sabres and an everlasting mash?"

"Yes," said the elderly Quaker. "There is the answer of Jesus."

After dinner the three set out for the depot. The young Westerner now seemed a terrible man to Allan, who still loved the South. But he had to know the facts, and he listened to breathtaking stories of the adventures of an Abolitionist militant. Lovejoy told of an adventure in the mountains of western Virginia; up the Kanawha River he had set free more than a score of slaves, at the solicitation of their relatives in Canada. The relatives had saved money, many hundreds of dollars, and Lovejoy had represented himself as an agent from a firm in Kentucky, intending to engage in the salt trade. He had contracted for the building of two boats, and for the salt to fill them. He had two Negroes who were posing as his slaves, and who sought out those who were to escape. It was early spring, and the river was high and swift; on a Saturday night, after the first boat was finished, a company of the Negroes and one of Lovejoy's "slaves" boarded it, and set out at full speed for the Ohio. On Monday morning Lovejoy discovered his loss, and pretending to be wild with rage, fell to cursing his other servant, accusing him of knowing of the plot. He went in pursuit with horsemen, but only to find the boat tied up on the Ohio shore.

Lovejoy returned, to wait for the completion of the other boat; on the second Saturday night it also disappeared, with his other servant, and another dozen slaves. Again he set out with pursuers, but when they reached the Ohio, became separated from them, and conducted the hidden fugitives by the Underground Railroad to Canada.

When Allan expressed his amazement at that story, Lovejoy promised him a better one yet. "Maybe you won't believe it, but I've got a bill to prove it, somewhere in my pockets—for eighty dollars' worth of wigs. I bought them in Philadelphia—gave out that I was a theatrical agent. I brought out forty-three slaves with them altogether—most of them were friends of people living here in Ohio. They all had to be mulattoes, of course; the first were from Baltimore—I got them together and powdered them up and we took a train for Harrisburg in broad daylight. Then I went to Washington and brought out another company from there, without any one's being the wiser. The third time was at Harper's Ferry—one of these was too dark, and it excited suspicion, and we were almost caught. We took the express for Pittsburgh, but the escape was discovered, and the pursuers engaged a special and overtook us just as we were entering the city. Fortunately we were on the last car, and saw them, and when the train began to slow up we jumped and scattered. There was all sorts of a time after that—nobody was caught, but several of us thought we were going to be. Maybe you read about it at the time—the whole city was crazy with excitement, and the search was kept up a week. But I know Abolitionists in every city, and we were safely hidden. I tell you, though, I still feel shaky when I go into Pittsburgh!"

They had come to the depot and stood by the cars. Then suddenly Lovejoy turned to Allan, gazing at him earnestly.

"Why don't you change your mind?" he asked. "Why don't you come out to Kansas with me?"

Allan shook his head. "I want to be quiet for a while," he said. "I want to think things over. I am still too much of a Southerner."

The other gripped his big hand on Allan's shoulder. "When it's time, I'll come for you! You will fight—wait and see!"

BOOK III

The Climax

❦

CHAPTER I

~~~~~~

While Allan was on his way from Valley Hall to Boston, the political parties were making nominations for the 1856 presidential battle. Stephen Douglas of Illinois had his heart set upon the Democratic nomination, but the fates were unkind to him; he had been favoring concessions to the South, and now the North was reacting with horror over the Lawrence and Sumner episodes. The Democratic politicians, in their alarm went over to Buchanan, who, as minister to England had been out of the country, and so could not be blamed for anything at home.

The Republicans, seeking a hero for their candidate, chose Fremont, the explorer. The campaign which followed surpassed in intensity anything which the country had ever known; meetings were attended by enormous crowds—in some cases by as many as a hundred thousand persons. On the part of the Republicans it was a crusade to save Kansas, and the educated classes of the North, the men of letters, the clergymen, the professors and teachers, were all active in their support. At the South it was freely declared that the success of Fremont would result in the breaking up of the Union, and it was really this which elected his rival.

James Buchanan had been congressman, Secretary of State, and minister to Russia and England, and was now a very old man. He had risen to eminence by life-long plodding, and by a diligent reverence for the commonplace. Stately and formal in his manners, unemotional and reticent in temperament, it was his habit to wait until his party had made clear its precise attitude upon every issue, and then to declare his position, gravely. His party had found him a servant who shrank from no task; and so the chiefs of the slave power had chosen him. They and not he were responsible; for he was merely a muddled old gentleman, proud to be set up for four years to distribute for his party the patronage of the highest office of the land. Under his rule corruption in the government attained gigantic proportions—which he himself admitted in one of his messages, in his own peculiar timid and helpless way.

An event of tremendous moment marked the opening of his administration. In his Inaugural Address he undertook to explain that the dispute about Slavery in the territories belonged "legitimately" to the Supreme Court of the United States—"before whom it is now pending, and [by whom it] will, it is understood, be speedily and finally settled. To their decision, in common with all good citizens, I shall cheerfully submit, whatever this may be." Thus strangely heralded, the "settlement" was handed down two days later—in the form of the famous "Dred Scott Decision."

A Negro man by that name had been taken by his master into territory north of the Missouri Compromise line. He had sued for his freedom, and the case had been before the court nearly a year. Had he, in the first place, a right to sue—was he a citizen of the United States? If so, then was he now free, was the Missouri Compromise constitutional? The court contained at that time five justices from the slave States and four from the free; all of the five and two of the four being Democrats. The opinion handed down was written by the Chief Justice himself, and agreed to by five of his associates. It took a singular course—it first decided that a Negro was not a citizen, and then, disregarding the fact that in that event the court had no jurisdiction and there was nothing more to say, it went on to declare what its decision would otherwise have been: that the territory "was acquired by the general government, as the representative and trustee of the people of the United States, and must therefore be held in that character for their common and equal benefit"; that "the right of property in a slave is distinctly and expressly affirmed in the Constitution"; and that "no word can be found in the Constitution which gives Congress greater power over slave property, or which entitles property of that kind to less protection, than property of any other description." The Missouri Compromise Act was, therefore, "not warranted by the Constitution, and void." Thus was the dogma of Calhoun, forced upon the Democratic party by the recklessness of Douglas, now three years later declared the law of the land by the land's highest tribunal.

The North read the decision with amazement; it soon crystallized the opinion into the sentence that "Negroes have no rights which white men are bound to respect"—a thing which the friends and partisans of Chief Justice Taney took as a shameful wrong. What he had actually said was that our forefathers had believed this—and that as they had embodied the doctrine in the Constitution, it was binding upon their descendants for all time. The distinction was a subtle one, however, and the people could hardly be blamed if they failed to appreciate it.

Roger Brooke Taney was a member of one of the old aristocratic families of Maryland. He had come down from a far-off time, having been an elderly man when he was Attorney-General under Jackson. He was a stern and incorruptible judge, deeply learned in the law, a venerable and majestic figure; but he had seen with deep displeasure the agitation of these newer times, and let himself be persuaded that it was his power and his duty to end it. A slaveholder himself, the thing seemed quite simple to him. "It is not a case of conscience," explains his official biographer, quoting the objections of the agitators—"it is not a case of conscience, but a question of *law*." The words have been used again and again through the ages to provide legal sanction for man's inhumanity to man.

The adverse opinion of Justice Curtis of Massachusetts became the answer of the North in the long agitation that followed. Replying to the assertion that a Negro could not be a citizen of the United States under the Constitution, he showed that prior to the adoption of it, Negroes had possessed the electoral franchise in five of the States. As to the power of Congress to prohibit Slavery in the territories, he cited eight instances in which it had been done: the acts being signed by all the Presidents from Washington down to John Quincy Adams—"all who were in public life when the Constitution was adopted."

The decision at once became the chief issue before the country. By the Democrats it was made a campaign document, and Douglas proclaimed it as a finality. "Whoever resists the final decision of the highest judicial tribunal," he declared, "aims a deadly blow to our whole republican system of government," failing with curious fatuity, or arrogance, to distinguish between resistance to the decision of a court and political opposition to it, two very different things. It was as if the country had been hypnotized—so much talk had men heard of the rights of the South as guaranteed by the Constitution, they seemed to have forgotten entirely the fact that the Constitution provided for its own amendment.

There were far-sighted leaders in the South, however, who were not unaware of this dangerous fact. There was a way of meeting it; if only constitutions could hereafter be made unamendable—at least in one essential particular!

It was proposed to admit "bleeding Kansas" as a State, and an election for delegates to a constitutional convention had been held. The free-state party still holding aloof, the body was all proslavery; and it adopted a state constitution which proclaimed that "the right of property is before and higher than any constitutional sanction, and the right of the owner of a slave to such slave and to its increase is the same and as inviolable as the right of the owner of any property whatever." This being the case, the constitution of Kansas was never to be amended "to affect the right of property in the ownership of slaves."

There was but one obstacle in the way of this consummation. A pledge had been solemnly given that the constitution framed by this convention should be submitted to a vote of the people

—both the governor of the territory and the President of the United States being unequivocally committed to this course. This was a part of the desperate attempts which had been made to patch up Kansas affairs for preelection exhibition purposes. Not all the voters, it was feared, could be expected to take the robust view of those in Washington, who marched in procession beneath a banner which proclaimed, "Kansas and Sumner: let them bleed!"

But the free-state settlers in the territory now outnumbered the proslavery two to one, and this "Lecompton Constitution" would surely be rejected by them if they had a chance. To meet the difficulty the ingenious convention provided for an election at which the voters were to be free to choose between the constitution "with Slavery" and the constitution "with no Slavery"—excepting what Slavery was in the constitution!

Congress assembled, and this plan was laid before it, with the indorsement of the administration. It was going desperately far— too far, as it proved, for many—chief among them being Douglas. The senator was to come up for reelection in the following year, and he dared not have a thing such as this to answer for. He came to Washington, and in an interview with the President declared his opposition to the fraud. The result was a breach in the Democratic party.

Eight years ago Calhoun had pointed out how strand by strand the rope which bound the North and the South together was giving way. He showed how first the Methodist church had split, and then the Baptist, and how the Presbyterian was about to follow. The same thing had since then begun in the political parties; the Whig party had been torn in half, the American party had been torn in half—and now suddenly man stared in amazement at the sight of the Democratic party dividing—and at Douglas, the aggressive proslavery champion of three years before, now suddenly become a hero of the antislavery hosts!

A divinity had shaped his ends, rough-hew them how he would. He was a man of tremendous force—the "Little Giant," his admirers called him; and given a truth at last, he made a stirring fight. The South had turned against him in a frenzy of rage—there was even talk of treating him as Sumner had been treated, and the administration used its patronage openly to defeat him. All through the winter the struggle lasted—men's passions were at fever-heat, and in the House it went as far as a free fight. It was an open secret that bribery was resorted to, that government contracts and government funds were used to influence votes. It was all in vain, however—the Republicans were too powerful, and the plot was defeated. The people of Kansas were given a chance at last to express their will; and when they did so, they rejected the "Lecompton Constitution" by a vote of nearly ten to one.

Douglas was now become the hero of the North. There was talk of forming a new party, which should include his followers and the Republicans. Many even went so far as to advise that no opposition be made to his reelection as senator—influential journals such as the New York *Tribune* were advocating this.

Those whom it immediately concerned, had, however, no idea of adopting such a course. They knew Douglas out in Illinois; and, moreover, they had a candidate of their own. They brought him forward in the spring of 1858, a backwoods lawyer by the name of Abraham Lincoln: long, ungainly, big-boned, an ungraceful speaker, but shrewd and with homely common sense. He had been a life-long rival of Douglas, but only once had he ever been successful—and that success, if gossip might be believed, had proven worse than any failure. They had contested the hand of the same young lady, and the lady was now no longer young, and had developed a terrible temper! Now and then in the man's speeches you might discover a lurking hint of the bitter jealousy which gnawed at him, who had been so hopelessly outstripped by the brilliant senator. Douglas was now in the zenith of his greatness, and when he travelled about the State he went in a private car, and with no end of what his neglected rival sarcastically described as "thunderings of cannon, marching and music, fizzle-gigs and fireworks."

As a debater, the "Little Giant" was a cruel opponent. It was like trying to fight with an invisible assailant—a man could no more hold him than he could a handful of eels. His sophistry was diabolical. He would restate your argument so that you could hardly see yourself where it differed from what you had said—and yet, somehow, different it was! And this monstrosity he would hold up before the people, mock and jeer at it, shake it until its teeth rattled and the sawdust flew out of it; and what had you left but lame explanations and hair-splitting distinctions? Mr. Lincoln had declared it his belief that "this government cannot endure permanently half-slave and half-free." And this, which was a prophecy, Douglas seized upon as a program. "In other words," he cried, "Mr. Lincoln asserts as a fundamental principle of this government, that there must be uniformity in all the local laws and domestic institutions of each and all the States of the Union; and he, therefore, invites all the non-slaveholding States to band together, and make war upon Slavery in all of the slaveholding States. . . . He tells you that the safety of the republic, the welfare of this Union, depends upon that warfare being carried on until one section or the other shall be entirely subdued. . . . My friends, will you ever submit to a warfare waged by the Southern States to establish Slavery in Illinois?"

And when Mr. Lincoln ventured to explain apologetically that he had made a prediction only—"it may have been a foolish one, perhaps"—and to add that he had said a hundred times that he believed there was "no right, and ought to be no inclination, in the people of the free States to enter into the slave States and interfere with the question of Slavery at all"—Mr. Douglas went after that assertion in this style: "Now Mr. Lincoln says he will not enter into Kentucky to abolish Slavery there, but what he will do is to fight Slavery in Kentucky from Illinois! He will not go over there to set fire to the match. I do not think he would. Mr. Lincoln is a very prudent man. But permit me to inquire whether the wrong, the outrage, of interference by one State with the local concerns of another, is worse when you actually invade it than it would be if you carried on the warfare from another State? For the purpose of illustration, suppose the British government should plant a battery on the Niagara River opposite Buffalo and throw their shells over into Buffalo, where they should explode and blow up the houses and destroy the town. We call the British government to an account, and they say, in the language of Mr. Lincoln, we did not enter into the limits of the United States to interfere with you; we planted the battery on our own soil, and had a right to shoot from our own soil, and if our shells and balls fell in Buffalo and killed your inhabitants, why, it is your lookout, not ours!"

Before long Mr. Lincoln, growing desperate, and hoping to pin this slippery adversary better if he got him face to face, ventured to challenge him in a series of joint debates. These occurred throughout the fall; and little by little they began to catch the attention of the whole country, and to force upon it the fact that a new champion had appeared. For this ungainly "rail-splitter" had a way of saying a thing and making it stick so tight that all his opponent's wriggling could never get it loose. What could have been better, for instance, than his definition of "popular sovereignty"—"that if one man wants to enslave another, no third man has a right to object!" Or than his explanation of why Douglas got all the credit for defeating the Lecompton fraud, although he and his friends furnished only one-fifth as many votes as the Republicans—"He says I have a proneness for quoting scripture. If I should do so now, it occurs that he places himself somewhat upon the ground of the parable of the lost sheep which went astray upon the mountains, and it was said that there was more rejoicing over the one sheep that was lost and had been found, than over the ninety and nine in the fold!" Or again than his retort, when Douglas kept repeating over and over a disproven slander about him—"as the fisherman's wife, whose drowned husband was brought home with his body full of eels, said, when she was asked, 'What is to be done with him?'—'Take the eels out and set him again!'"

The South, meantime, was moving fast. In that same year there appeared in the *Southern Literary Messenger* a definition of an Abolitionist—"Any man who does not love Slavery for its own sake as a divine institution; who does not worship it as the cornerstone of civil liberty; who does not adore it as the only possible social condition on which a permanent republican government can be erected; and who does not in his inmost soul desire to see it extended and perpetuated over the whole earth as a means of human reformation second in dignity, importance, and sacredness alone to the Christian religion." And to those who had learned to read the signs, it was plain that only a short time more could elapse before yet a new demand would be formulated, in accordance with this new doctrine. The price of slaves at the South was become enormously high—a "prime field-hand" being worth as much as eighteen hundred dollars. It was clear that if new territory was ever to be opened to Slavery, new slaves must somehow be had.

A few radicals had begun the agitation; it had been continually discussed for nearly two years now, and the public was taking interest. A society was being formed for the purpose of agitating the reform—the "African Labor Supply Association," as it was called—composed of the leading citizens of the South. At a meeting of the "Southern Commercial Convention," a resolution had been offered to the effect that if Slavery was right, "the natural means to its formation could not be wrong"; and demanding, therefore, the reopening of the African slave trade!

Mr. Yancey had spoken at the convention. Mr. Yancey was not prepared to advocate the reopening—it was a question about which his mind was not made up, though he owned that he was leaning toward it. What he did demand, however, and that instantly, was the repeal of the laws which proclaimed the slave-trade to be piracy. To be sure these laws had never been enforced; but that was not the thing—had not the fathers resisted the tax on tea, small as it was, solely for the sake of the principle? Mr. Yancey's objection to these laws was that "they stand on the statute book as a direct condemnation, by our own government, of the institution of Slavery in its moral and social aspects, and indirectly operate to restrict our political power." Furthermore Mr. Yancey insisted that these laws were *unconstitutional*. The constitution provided that the African slave-trade should not be prohibited by Congress before the year 1808. Did that mean that it might be prohibited *after* that? Assuredly not! Were not slaves recognized by the Constitution as property? And as property were they not entitled to the protection of the United States, upon the high seas as well as in the territories? People cried out about the cruelty of it—was not the domestic slave trade precisely the same thing, so far as it was carried on by sea? And did not the passage from Washington to New Orleans often take longer than the one across the Atlantic? Yet tens of thousands of slaves were taken South by this route every year, and no one found any fault with it.

During all these years, of course, the African trade had in reality been going on merrily in spite of the law. Senator Douglas had just been reported as declaring his belief that fifteen thousand native Africans had been brought into the country in the previous twelve months, and it was notorious that wild Guinea Negroes occasionally celebrated their dances in the public squares of New Orleans. In December of the year '58 the country was shaken by the famous incident of the *Wanderer*—a palatial private yacht flying the flag of the New York Yacht Club, which took on board a cargo of seven hundred and fifty slaves at the Congo River and landed them on the Georgia coast. The news leaked out, and there was tremendous excitement, and some arrests—but nothing came of it, of course. The yacht was condemned and sold at public auction, but so deep was the sympathy of the South with the owner that no one would bid against him, and he bought the vessel back for one-quarter of its value.

The Negroes could be bought for fifteen or twenty dollars apiece, on the slave coast, and sold to the South for five or six hundred; there were, therefore, millions of dollars to be made in one successful voyage, and it was no wonder the business flourished. Under the law it was death, and confiscation of the vessel; but even the latter penalty was seldom enforced—as one may gather from the record in the Senate Documents of the Thirty-seventh Congress, in which appears the fact that "the bark *Cora* and cargo" were arrested and bonded in New York on June 23, 1860, and arrested again on the slave coast, December 10 of the very same year! It was declared by the *New York Leader* that "an average of two vessels each week clear out of our harbor, bound for Africa and a human cargo." The London *Times* called New York "the greatest slave-trading mart in the world."

Most horrible were the stories recorded of this traffic; the "slavers" were built as a rule with decks five feet apart, and between these was a shelf, so that two layers of Negroes were laid within this space. Cases had been known, after the trade had been outlawed, in which the wretches were packed in a space only eighteen inches high, and others were seated, each man with another crowded upon his lap. Thus they remained sealed up tight for days, if a storm chanced to arise; it is recorded that the naval vessels cruising on the slave coast could detect a vessel five miles up the wind by the odor. It was necessary, if the "slaver" were to be held, that she should be taken with the Negroes actually on board; and the captain of one, stopped in the night-time, tied six hundred slaves to his ship's cable, and sank them to the bottom of the sea.

This was the new demand which was to be presented to the North. Little by little one might see the signs of it—the *Democratic Review* of New York published an article in which it denounced indignantly the British authorities for allowing their cruisers now and then to stop slavers which were under the sacred protection of the American flag. The article went on to discuss the whole matter—gingerly, but with no uncertain purpose. The writer put the question, "How much better off than slaves are vast numbers of the inhabitants of British territory?" The writer of the article went on to give it as his weighty opinion that "the signs of the times portend and foreshadow the importance of an examination into the warrant of authority from Congress to enact laws prohibiting the slave-trade, a commerce justifiable and lawful under the code of nations."

The article was patently a "feeler." One could almost see the politicians who had put it out, debating it, sentence by sentence—each cunningly constructed, weighed and measured. This must be said plainly—this must be veiled—this must not be mentioned; and now, how will they take it? *What will be the answer of the North?*

CHAPTER II

In the summer of the year 1859 Allan was living at his uncle's home in Boston, and attending Harvard when he received an unexpected visit from Lovejoy. "I have come for you as I promised," was all the Westerner would say.

He was bent on sending Allan on a mysterious errand. "You must go!" he kept saying. "You must ask no questions—just go. The reason is, I want you to go without any preconceptions. I shall only tell you that it is a man I want you to meet."

"Where is he?" Allan inquired.

"It will mean a trip into Pennsylvania," Lovejoy replied. "I cannot go with you, for I am here on business that will keep me I do not know how long. Besides, I want you to have this experience all by yourself."

Allan was silent for a few moments. "You must realize," he said, "that you are asking a great deal of me."

"This man has kept me occupied for almost a year and a half," the other answered, "and it has never been my habit to waste my time. If I ask you to take so much of yours, it must be because I am sure that the event will justify me."

Allan was still seeking all the knowledge he could on Slavery, and Lovejoy was on the inside of events. "I will go," he said. "I put that much trust in you."

"Will you go tomorrow?"

"I will go tomorrow."

Early the following morning—it was a day in August—Allan started for Chambersburg, Pennsylvania. His instructions were to go to the barber shop of Henry Watson, and there ask for "Isaac Smith, the sheep dealer." He bore a line written by Lovejoy.

The journey took him all day, and he spent a night at a hotel, and in the morning set out for his destination. Something unexpected occurred at the outset—as he came from the building a Negro passed by, a tall, commanding figure, walking swiftly; and though it had been six or seven years since Allan had seen him, he knew him at once—it was Frederick Douglass!

Allan sought out the barber shop and found that Henry Watson was a Negro, old and wizened; he inquired for Isaac Smith, the sheep dealer, according to directions. The Negro gazed round his shop nervously, as if fearing lest some one might have heard; then he made haste to close up the place, and left with Allan.

They walked a mile or two, leaving the town behind them, and came to an old stone quarry. The Negro drew close to Allan and murmured, "We'd best be kinder keerful, mass'r. He might shoot."

Suddenly the figure of an elderly white man appeared from behind a pile of boulders, and Watson stood still. The man came slowly toward him, eying them closely. He was clad in rough country costume, very much worn, and yellow with dust; an old hat was pulled down over his eyes, and in one hand he carried a fish pole. "Dat's him," said Watson.

The person strolled toward them, carelessly; when he was near he halted, and inquired, "Well?"

"Are you Isaac Smith?" Allan asked, and took out the paper Lovejoy had given him, and handed it to him. The other took it without a word, and glanced at it. Then he said "Oh!" and held out his hand. "How do you do, sir?" he said.

Allan responded courteously, and the other continued, "I am expecting some one else; let us sit down and wait."

They moved behind the boulders, where they were out of sight of the road. "Isaac Smith, the sheep dealer," laid down his fish pole and seated himself.

He was a man of about sixty years of age, powerfully made, tall and military in his carriage; by his speech he was evidently not quite the boor he was dressed. His head was very long and narrow, and a long beard accentuated his curious features. His hair shot up from his forehead, bristling and straight, and his brows remained knitted as if in intense thought. Beneath them gleamed a pair of pale eyes, keen and restless—the whole face was alert, even wild, in its expression.

He seated himself opposite Allan, and said, "You must excuse me, sir, if I warn you a little in advance of the seriousness of what you are going to listen to here. For twenty years I have been toiling and suffering for the purpose about which I am going to tell you; and never before have I consented that any one should know of it, except one whom I myself knew. In your case I have taken Lovejoy's word for the fact that I may trust you—he seemed to be very anxious for us to meet."

"What is the thing of which you speak, Mr. Smith," Allan asked; but before Smith could reply there was a sound of someone approaching, and he went to meet them. He came back with two Negroes—one of whom was Frederick Douglass!

After they had been introduced Allan said, "I have met you before, Mr. Douglass—a long time ago. I wonder if you remember the occasion when Professor Otis of Boston asked you to tell your own story because he wanted a young Southerner to hear you?"

A light flashed over the big mulatto's face. "I do remember!" he said.

"Perhaps," Allan remarked, "it may please a lecturer to know of a case where his seed fell on good soil."

"Very interesting, very interesting, indeed," put in the "sheep dealer"—in a tone that showed he did not think it interesting at all. "And now, gentlemen, since we're here, and there is no time to lose—to business! Watson, I want you to keep moving round outside, and whistle if any one approaches. Carry that fishpole with you."

"Yes, sah," said the old Negro, moving away.

The four sat down. The Negro who had come with Douglass was named Green, and he sat very quiet, venturing not a word.

"Tell us the plan," said Douglass.

The elderly man burst out impetuously: "I want you to come with me—I want you badly! My bees will begin to swarm—and you are the one to hive them."

So began a strange, and to Allan an appalling story. Said the speaker: "You will never have another chance like this. Think how long I have been planning and toiling—and now at last the hour! I have the means, I have everything; and nothing can turn me, Douglass. We shall prevail, we shall prevail—it has been revealed to me; the hand of God is in it, it is His will! 'And the Lord looked upon him and said, Go in thy might, and thou shalt save Israel from the hands of the Midianites; have not I sent thee?' "

Douglass made no answer; the other watched him eagerly for a moment, then rushed on.

"Do you never weary of all this *talk?* Do you never realize how futile it is? These people will never set your people free—their hand is upon you—they laugh at your efforts! How many years have you been at it—how many will you be at it—before you see it as I see it? I tell you a hundred slaves in Virginia can do more for freedom in one day than a hundred thousand Abolitionists in Massachusetts in their whole lifetime! Why should not your people fight their own battle, as other peoples have done before them? And you—why should you not be their Moses, to lead them out of the house of bondage—you, *you?* What is this temper in you that dreads a blow so much? You shrink from bloodshed—consider the blood of your brothers in Slavery! How many lives could be balanced against the continuance for one more year of this system, which makes every seventh woman of a whole race a harlot? It cannot be the price of a failure that you dread; I know it is not that, Douglass—you are no coward!"

"I wish to see a chance of success. But I see no such chance," Douglass replied, quietly.

"I know! I know!" exclaimed the other, excitedly. "But there will be no chance of success until we make it. We are twenty resolute men with arms in our hands, and we raise our banner—*there* is the chance! Didn't Nat Turner, with fifty men, hold at bay all Virginia for five weeks? That many men today, and I tell you I could shake the system out of the whole State! It is the start that is needed, Douglass, the rallying-point, the call! Do you not think that your people have souls in them, do you not think they will leap to arms when the arms are there? Give a slave a pike and you make him a man; and when he has shown himself a man, the nation will respect him—never before, I tell you. You may lecture, preach, protest—all day, all night, all your lifetime—

and never set free one single man. But once make *war* on the system—once frighten it—*then* see what happens!"

"I think they will overwhelm you before you get started."

"The mountains, the mountains!" cried the other. "Have not the mountains been the home of freedom for all time? I firmly believe that God has put that chain through these States for no purpose but to be used for the emancipation of the slave. And I know these mountains and how long I could keep a body of men there, hiding and fighting—they are full of natural forts, where one man would be a match for a hundred. And do you not think that the slaves would flee to us there? Would they not come trooping in day and night? And do you not see that we have accomplished our purpose when once we have rendered Slavery insecure—when we have destroyed the money value of slaves?"

"What arms have you?" Douglass asked.

"I have two hundred Sharp's rifles—the old Kansas rifles. We have two hundred revolvers, and about a thousand pikes."

"And where are you going to strike?"

"My first move," said Smith, "will be to capture the arsenal at Harper's Ferry."

Douglass stared at him in amazement. The silence spoke for him.

"That is my plan," said the other. "That is where the weapons are."

At last Douglass spoke. "That is not to attack the South, that is to attack the Federal government! It will turn all the nation against you!"

"It will serve as a notice to all the slaves. They will rally to it as to a trumpet-call—and the arms there are enough for all."

"You will be surrounded and cut off in six hours!"

"We will find means to cut our way out. Our first step will be to take the residents of the neighborhood prisoners, and we can hold them as hostages, and dictate terms of egress."

Douglass clenched his fist, and struck it on his knee. "It is madness!" he cried. *"Madness!* They will blow you and your hostages to the skies! Believe me, Captain Brown, believe me— I know them—I have lived among them."

"Listen to me! Listen to me!" exclaimed "Captain Brown," and the excited argument continued. He had thought out his plan in all its details; he had maps and drawings of the neighborhood, and an answer for every argument.

"You will never succeed in it!" reiterated Douglass, again and again. "You are going into a trap, a perfect trap; and once in, there will be no hope for you!"

The other sat with his piercing eyes fixed upon the Negro, waiting while he poured out his protests. Then he proclaimed: " 'Thou comest to me with a sword, and with a spear, and with a shield; but I come to thee in the name of the Lord of Hosts, the God of the armies of Israel, whom thou hast defied!' "

There was a pause; and then Captain Brown went on, "Suppose that you are right—suppose it is the will of the Lord that this plan should fail—do you think that He can find no way of turning it all to His profit? Let them capture me—what then? Might it not very well turn out that I should prove to be worth more for hanging than for any other purpose? Do you think it will be worth nothing that one man has risen up to testify to the crimes of this land, that must be purged away in blood? Do you think that if they were to hang me for it—it would not send a shudder through every slaveholder—it would not show the way to every seeker of freedom, black or white? Verily would it be said once more—'The dead which he slew at his death were more than they which he slew in his life!' "

There was a long silence. "You are prepared for that fate?" asked Douglass at last.

"I am," the other replied; and leaned forward pleadingly. "You won't come with me?"

The other shook his head. "For such a purpose as that," he said, "one will be as good as twenty."

Captain Brown turned to Allan, "And you?" he asked.

Allan could not find a word. He only shook his head. Captain Brown turned away with a sigh—and then suddenly the Negro Green sprang up. "Massa!" he cried. It was the first sound he had made. "I go wid yo'! I been slave all my days—I jes' git free now; but I go wid yo'—even if I die."

It was late in the afternoon, and Allan and Douglass walked back to town alone. "Who is that man?" Allan asked.

"His name is John Brown," the other replied. " 'Old Brown of Kansas,' people call him. He has been in the fighting out there, and it has driven him to desperation. He will be a martyr."

CHAPTER III

Allan went back to Boston like a person in a nightmare. The things he had heard were so monstrous he could scarcely persuade himself they were real, that the madman whose voice still rang in his ears was not a creature of his own sick imaginings. An attack on Harper's Ferry! And an insurrection of the slaves!

He sought out Lovejoy—who gazed at him, smiling innocently. "So," he said, "You found it worth while!"

"Worth while?" exclaimed Allan, incredulously, "Look here, Lovejoy, do you mean to tell me you are going to join in that attempt?"

"I am," answered the other, quietly.

"You must know it is the plan of a maniac," Allan declared.

"Sometimes I have thought so. But if there wasn't some risk, you know, there wouldn't be any fun."

"Fun?" Allan cried, with such vehemence that the other laughed.

"Well," he said, "I don't exactly mean that. But as I've told you before, I want to *act*—I must *do* something, and this man offers a chance." Then after a pause, "You didn't hear him pray, did you?"

"No—but I can imagine it."

"John Brown knows the Bible, chapter and verse, every word by heart; and what's more, he believes in every word of it, the blood and all. He makes us say grace before and after meals; and night and morning, wherever he is, he gets the whole crowd together and prays with 'em. He's a spell-binder if ever there was one! The Negroes just fall down on their faces and roll. I'm not that sort, but the point he makes that gets 'em is that it doesn't matter where we strike—if the Almighty wishes us to win, He will come to our aid and see to it; if He doesn't, it is because it's best for us to perish. What kind of reply can you make to an argument like that?"

"You can keep out of it!" Allan declared, emphatically.

"I'm with him because I see the only chance I ever saw to strike a blow at Slavery. The boldness of it is what will count. Man, it will scare this land like the judgment trump! And when will the slaves ever rise, if they don't rise at such a chance?"

"They won't ever rise! That's the madness of the thing—the wickedness of it—they have no idea of rising!"

"Surely, Montague, you don't mean to deny that a man has a right to strike for his freedom if he can?"

"If it were a slaves' uprising, it would be different. But it's white men going down there and trying to incite them—"

"Going down there and giving them a chance!" broke in Lovejoy. "What chance have they otherwise, with no arms, no communications—bound hand and foot as they are?"

There was another pause; then Lovejoy began to laugh. "It's funny," he said; "I think it's in the blood. You're a Southerner; although you hate Slavery, and call yourself an Abolitionist, you're a Southerner still, and just as bad as the worst of 'em. If it were Poles or Italians who were going to rise up tomorrow, you'd be at the head of them; but it's niggers! So you come away from a meeting with John Brown trembling with horror at what you've heard—and looking as if you'd seen a ghost!"

"Where does the money come from?" Allan asked.

"There's Gerritt Smith, the millionaire philanthropist—he's given thousands of dollars. There's a merchant in Boston by the name of Stearns, and a school teacher in Concord named Sanborn, and Higginson, the preacher, and Theodore Parker."

"Theodore Parker knows of this?"

"Assuredly," said the other—"has from the beginning."

"How long has it been in preparation?"

"About two years—this particular plan. It was to have been

carried out last year, but someone betrayed it. Then we went West again and made a raid, and carried off twelve slaves from Missouri—you doubtless read about that."

"I did," answered Allan.

"The government has a price on his head," said Lovejoy.

"Who are the men with him?"

"Some are his Kansas men; half a dozen are Negroes; there are three of his own sons, and several more that are his sons-in-law, or their brothers. Brown is an Old Testament patriarch—he had twenty children, and every one of them that is left is as full of the cause as he. Some have died for it already."

Time passed, and Allan took to reading bulletin boards and to snatching up the paper in the morning. August passed and September—had they given up again? Then one Sunday morning— the sixteenth of October—came a telegram, unsigned, with the single word, "Come!"

Certainly this was a situation in which it was barely possible he might exert some influence. He knew the temper of both leaders, John Brown, and Lovejoy; but both of them considered him trustworthy. They had taken him into their confidence, and he had not betrayed the trust. Now who could say but that they might listen to him? At least Lovejoy might, and Brown might listen to Lovejoy. It was a desperate idea, but here was a desperate situation, and he was sick of doing nothing. Within half an hour he was on a train.

He reached Baltimore about midnight. There was no train for the West until about six in the morning. He was obliged to wait. He went to a hotel, but could not sleep. Before train time he wandered up to the office of the *American*—there was nothing to indicate unusual excitement. He was on the train and nearly half an hour on his way, before the thunderbolt fell. At one of the stations he heard excited shouts, and saw people running this way and that; he sprang off, as did nearly everyone else, the train men included. There was an insurrection of slaves at Harper's Ferry, and reports of uprisings throughout Virginia and Maryland. The government arsenal had been seized and the arms sent away to the mountains. The bridge was defended with cannon—the wires were down and the tracks were being destroyed. Trains had been fired into, the citizens of the town were being massacred, and an appeal for the militia of Baltimore and Washington was made!

Such were the tidings; the alarm and confusion were indescribable—for some time it seemed uncertain whether or not the train would proceed, and when finally it did, it left a good number of its passengers behind.

Their progress was slow; they stopped for news at every station, finding the depots more and more crowded, the excitement more and more intense. Midway they passed the east-bound train, which had been stopped by the insurrectionists the night before, and only just allowed to proceed. It was after ten o'clock when they neared Harper's Ferry.

The little town lies on a point of land made by the Shenandoah River as it runs into the Potomac. The railroad runs up the Maryland side of the river, crossing to the town by a long bridge. About a quarter of a mile this side of it the train stopped. Armed men could be seen ahead. It was in spite of the protests of the train hands that Allan started toward them. The men ahead shouted to him to surrender as he came within range, and he held up his hands, calling out that he was a friend.

There were three men, one of them a Negro; they were wrapped in blankets—it was cold and rainy—and armed with long "Sharp's rifles." They regarded him with suspicion, which changed only slightly when he said that he was a friend of Lovejoy's.

"Take him to the captain," said one in command—a son of Brown's, though Allan did not then know it.

He marched across the bridge, under the escort of the Negro. At the other side another armed man paced back and forth—a short way up the street was another. There were no other persons to be seen. A few rods on was the iron gate of the armory yard, and as they turned the corner there were more men, among them Brown, rifle in hand.

He recognized Allan, and shook hands with him. "It's all right," he said to the Negro. "Go back to your post."

"Well, sir?" he inquired of Allan. "Have you concluded to help us after all? You see we have been successful."

Allan stared at him. "Successful!" he exclaimed. "How long do you expect to stay here? Don't you know that the whole country is on fire—troops will be pouring in here in a few hours."

"Let them come, let them come!" said the other. "We are ready—we have hostages."

"But how long do you expect to hold the town? When are you going to start for the mountains?"

"Not until nightfall," was the answer.

"Until nightfall!" Allan exclaimed.

"Yes—we must wait for the slaves to come in. I have thought it over," Captain Brown went on. "I cannot change my plan. The Lord's will must be done."

"Where is Lovejoy?" Allan inquired, after a pause.

"He is gone," the other answered.

"Gone! Gone where?"

"He has deserted us, sir. He left about an hour ago—as soon as he found that I was resolved to stay. I was very sorry—but there was no help for it. *I must stay!*"

Allan knew that now he could do nothing. He was dealing with a lunatic or a martyr.

John Brown seemed exalted. His eyes were flashing as he turned here and there, giving swift orders; he was the master of the place, and in a state of almost childish delight in his achievement. He had secured from one of his prisoners a sword which Frederick the Great had presented to General Washington; it enraptured him that he was wielding this in the cause of the slave. He had freed half a dozen Negroes, and armed them; he stopped to walk with them, fondly, paternally—as also with some of the prisoners who were brought in. One pleaded for his wife and children—Captain Brown sent him with one of his men for an escort, to visit them and assure them that no harm was meant. Once he called out: "Do not shoot at that man! Don't you see he is unarmed?" Then he went over to where his "hostages" were cowering, and comforted them, and urged them to keep out of the way of a chance shot.

"What is it that you wish to do, sir?" he said at last, turning to Allan again. "Will you take one of the rifles?"

"I did not come to fight," Allan answered, as quietly as he could.

"Then," said Brown, "perhaps you had best go with the prisoners—you will be safer there. My son Oliver Brown, Mr. Montague. My son Watson, Mr. Montague. Watson, take this gentleman—"

The young fellow came toward Allan, holding out his hand. Suddenly from one of the windows down the street came a blaze of firearms, and John Brown's son pitched forward with a cry. At the same instant another of the men fell dead—with a bullet in his breast.

"Fire! Drive them back there!" shouted Brown, wildly; and sprang toward his son.

The boy was deadly pale. "I'm done for," he gasped. Brown gathered him in his arms and carried him into the building, his lips tightly set, but no other sign of emotion visible.

The firing went on, in a desultory way. Allan, without waiting for more, made his way over to a corner of the grounds, where were gathered all of the prisoners, forty or fifty persons, black and white, old and young, rich and poor. For the most part they were terror stricken, expecting they would be put to death. Among them Allan noticed an elderly gentleman, handsome and aristocratic in appearance, Colonel Lewis Washington, he was told, from whose plantation the precious sword had been taken. The "liberators," as they called themselves, had taken nothing else.

It was not long before there was heard the rapid firing of guns in the distance; it swelled to a volley, and continued as an incessant rattle for several minutes. "They're after them now!" exclaimed a man to Allan. "The soldiers are coming!"

Captain Brown had come out again, grave and impassive, directing his men, who were still keeping back the sharpshooters from the windows. Soon, however, the distant firing seemed to worry him, as well it might; not long after it had died down, a Negro dashed into the place, breathless and gasping.

"They've captured the rifle works!" he panted. "Every one's killed!"

"Killed!" cried Brown. "Who?"

"Kagi—Leary—all of them!" exclaimed the man. "They drove them into the river and shot them there! They're killing Thompson, too!"

Thompson was Brown's son-in-law; the old man put his hand to his forehead. "They have no mercy!" Allan heard him murmur.

The time passed on, the firing continuing here and there. Allan could make out from his position that troops were now surrounding the armory grounds; and the fighting redoubled in fury. Two colored men were killed by shots from near-by windows, and though the little guard still stuck by the gate, they were able to maintain only an intermittent fire. Also there were sounds of a conflict in the rear. Several volleys were heard, and at the same time bodies of troops were seen deploying in front. Brown's other son, Oliver, was struck by a bullet, and staggered into the building to die; so at last it became plain, even to Brown, that the yard could not be held much longer.

Within the enclosure was a compact little stone building, the engine-house. To this the captain retreated, with the remainder of his men, and about a dozen of his "hostages," carefully selected. He nodded to Allan to make his escape with the others, who left the yard at his command. The troops outside were on the watch for them, and welcomed them with huzzas. The last glimpse Allan had of "Old John Brown" was as he stood in the engine-house doorway, holding one of his dying sons in his arms.

Allan had seen only one side of the affair so far; now he saw the frightful panic of the town. Fully a thousand troops, besides numerous armed citizens, now surrounded it. As they realized that the armory yard was won, they rushed up, yelling like madmen. A little way down the street lay a huge mulatto, writhing upon the ground. a great gaping wound in his neck; some men were dancing about him, cursing and jeering. Some were beating him with their canes; Allan saw one man thrust a stick into the wound while the others roared to see the victim kick. A little farther on lay another of John Brown's band—a white man, desperately wounded. He had come out with a flag of truce, and been shot down. He had five bullets in him; but men were shouting for a rope to hang him with.

[154]

The firing grew louder and faster; they were beginning an assault upon the engine-house. Allan did not wait to learn the issue, but hurried away, sick at heart. He came to the hotel—just as a crowd came rushing out. They were young men, their faces white with rage. In their midst was the figure of a prisoner, tightly bound, held by the arms and collar. His captors, silent, rushed him down the street, straight for the railroad bridge. They dragged him into the centre of it and stood him against one of the piers; then there came a crashing volley, and the man toppled and dropped to the base of the pier—fifty feet, at least; but he was still alive, and began to crawl and kick himself along. "Give it to him again!" yelled a voice, and once more the rifle shots rang out. The body splashed into the water, and the current swept it away.

The bridge was held by troops now, and no one allowed to pass. A body of four or five hundred militia arrived from Maryland, and behind them Allan returned to the hotel.

In the night there came the first regular troops, a company of United States marines, under the command of a colonel—a Virginian by the name of Robert E. Lee. Allan was in the hotel-corridor when he entered, booted and gloved, dressed as for a parade, a stately personage, accustomed to command.

"How is this, gentlemen?" he asked, as he came in, addressing the militia officers, who had made the place their headquarters. "Fifteen hundred troops, and these fellows have been too much for you all day?"

"We have not had time, colonel—" began some one.

"Pshaw, pshaw!" exclaimed the other. "Your men have had time to slaughter helpless prisoners in the streets, have they not? How many of the outlaws are there left?"

"We have counted ten killed," replied a voice. "There cannot be more than four or five alive in the engine-house."

"We shall soon settle it in the morning," said the colonel. "The prisoners might be hurt if we attacked tonight. I have ordered my men to replace the guards about the armory—we will not need any help." He paused then, "Lieutenant Stuart!"

Several officers had come in with Colonel Lee. One of them

stepped forward—a big, broad-shouldered lieutenant of cavalry, handsome and dashing, with a fine red-brown beard. He was another Virginian—J. E. B. Stuart by name.

"Lieutenant," said the colonel, "please take a flag and proceed to the engine-house. Demand the surrender of the insurgents—we can give no terms but protection from violence and a trial according to law. Otherwise tell them the place will be stormed the first thing in the morning."

"Very well, sir," said the lieutenant, and added, "By the way, colonel, they say the leader is Ossawatomie Brown, the old scoundrel I once captured out in Kansas."

"You should have held on to him, lieutenant," said the other, quietly. "We will not let him go this time, sir!"

CHAPTER IV

The marines battered in the door of the engine-house and overwhelmed the little band. Captain Brown was kneeling in the centre of the place, feeling the pulse of his wounded son with one hand, and clutching his rifle with the other; a lieutenant of marines leaped down upon him from the engine, twelve feet at a spring, and thrust him a blow with his sword which struck him in the belt and bent the weapon double. Afterward, as he lay helpless, the officer beat him over the face and head with it—so harshly did men think of his deed.

Allan went back to Boston, where he found Lovejoy, the latter having made good his escape, but being not entirely content with himself for his superior wisdom. The city of Boston was in a ferment—the antislavery people were as if they had witnessed a miracle. "There came a sound from heaven as of a rushing mighty wind, and it filled all the house where they were sitting. And there appeared unto them cloven tongues, like as of fire, and it sat upon each one of them!"

There was something out of another world, or at least out of another time, in the faith of John Brown. Crowds had poured into Harper's Ferry on the day of his capture; and they had stood around him, and pestered him with questions as he lay upon the floor, a mass of clotted blood, with a wound in the groin, and one in the breast, and four sabre cuts upon his head. Governor Wise of Virginia came out and was lost in wonder, for he had expected to find a madman or a ruffian. "He is a bundle of the best nerves I ever saw!" he exclaimed. "He is a man of clear head, of courage and fortitude."

Later he lay in a cell, loaded with chains, with two jailers on watch day and night, and two thousand troops to guard him: wounded horribly, believed to be dying, surrounded by the foes he had assailed, and with a nation roaring for his blood in the background. "I do not," he wrote, in a letter, "feel myself in the least degraded by my imprisonment, my chains, or the near prospect of the gallows. Men cannot imprison, or chain, or hang the soul. I would not say this boastingly, but thanks be to God, who giveth the victory through infinite grace."

"This new saint awaiting his martyrdom!" exclaimed Emerson; and went on to predict that he would "make the gallows glorious like the cross." In Concord lived a strange man named Thoreau, who had spent some years in a hut in the woods, and had been put in jail because he would not pay taxes to a slaveholding government; people now crowded to hear him as he pleaded for Brown, and compared him in plain words with Christ.

In the South men seemed beside themselves with terror. The fall in the price of slaves which followed upon the foray amounted, it was said, to ten million dollars. Planters were afraid to sleep on their estates—within one week five barns were burned down near Harper's Ferry, and it was believed to be the beginning of a new insurrection. The guards who were watching Brown had orders to shoot him dead if there was any attempt at rescue; one night the sentinels of the small army which surrounded the town slaughtered a stray cow which approached their lines in the darkness and refused to give the countersign.

The legislators of South Carolina, Missouri, and Kentucky

voted ropes which they prayed might be used in hanging the "old horse-thief," as Senator Douglas had described him. It was rumored that Governor Wise had been so impressed with Brown that he was thinking of pardoning him. "He could never get him out of the town alive," it was said, "not if he came at the head of a regiment!"—"A felon's death!" wrote one Virginian. "Almighty Providence! is man indeed so weak that he can inflict no more?"

There were those who warned the South that man could not inflict even this; a poet was not lacking to call their attention to the fact that "Ossawatomie Brown" might "trouble them more than ever when they'd nailed his coffin down!" But they would not listen. "He came to incite slaves to murder helpless women and children!" cried Senator Davis; and the Richmond *Whig* thundered: "Though it convert the whole Northern people, without exception, into furious, armed, Abolition invaders, yet old Brown will be hung! The miserable old traitor and murderer belongs to the gallows, and the gallows will have its own!"

He was tried and sentenced; and on the second of December, they brought him out to die. Two thousand troops surrounded the scaffold, and cannon guarded the roads. The government had seized the telegraphs, and for days every train that entered the state had been searched and put under guard. It was strange to see all the precautions they took, and how they were baffled— how completely "old Brown" was vindicated in his statement that "men cannot imprison, or chain, or hang the soul!" Even when they were swinging him off, he was beginning to march: during the half hour he hung kicking in the air, all over the North churches were holding services of prayer—bells were being tolled and minute guns fired. In Concord a meeting was being held in the Town Hall, at which Emerson, Thoreau, and Bronson Alcott were speaking; in the excitement of it one of the audience wrote a poem, and sprang up and cried the first stanza of it aloud:—

> "Not any spot six feet by two
> Will hold a man like thee!
> John Brown will tramp the shaking earth
> From Blue Ridge to the sea!"

Wherever there was sympathy with the South, these things were of course read with fury. By way of an offset to them, the President gave on the same day a state banquet to the diplomatic corps at Washington; and when the woman who had been John Brown's wife started home with his body, and wished to stop in Philadelphia to rest over Sunday, the major met her at the depot and ordered her on—the city was in such a tumult.

They took the body on to his lonely home in the Adirondacks, at the foot of old Whiteface mountain, not troubled by tumults. They buried him there, and over his grave they sang the hymn with which all his life he had been wont to lull his babies to sleep— "Blow ye the trumpet, blow!" When it was over, Wendell Phillips, the orator of Abolition, rose up and proclaimed: *"He has abolished Slavery in Virginia!"*

CHAPTER V

The temper of the times was shown upon the assembling of the new Congress, three days after the hanging of Brown. Previously to this it is recorded that those who opposed each other in public life had been wont to meet socially upon friendly terms; but now feeling ran so high that social functions in Washington were difficult to arrange.

In the House the first business was the election of a speaker; the candidate of the Republicans chanced to have endorsed some time before a book published by one Helper, a "poor white" of North Carolina—"The Impending Crisis of the South," an argument against Slavery from the standpoint of the non-slaveholding Southerner. A Kentuckian now moved that it was "insurrectionary," and that no one who had endorsed it was "fit to be speaker of this House."

There was an anecdote of another Kentuckian, who, while narrating the origin of a "personal difficulty," was asked, "Did he call you a liar?" and replied, "Worse than that—he proved it." The trouble with "The Impending Crisis" was the same—what made it so peculiarly obnoxious was the fact that it used, not statements, but statistics. It gave them all, and they were irresistible. It pointed out the fact that though the area of the slave States was greater than that of the free, the farms of the latter were worth two billions, those of the former only one; that the real property of the North was over four billions, that of the South less than three, half thereof being slaves; that the value of the property in eight slave States—which were named—was less than that of the State of New York alone; and that the value of land in New York was $36 an acre, in North Carolina only $3. The taxed property of the nine largest free cities of the North was $754 per capita, that for the nine of the South only $477. The imports of the North were nearly ten times those of the South. Inquiring for whose benefit the South suffered such things as these, he showed that out of a total white population of six millions there were but three hundred and fifty thousand who owned more than five Negroes each.

For these few white owners, the system was maintained and extended, and by them the nation was ruled. Twelve Presidents had been Southern slaveholders, and only six Northern non-slaveholders; moreover, five of the former had served two terms —not one of the latter. They had always had a majority of the Supreme Court, had held the office of Secretary of State forty years out of sixty-seven, the speakership of the House twenty-one times out of thirty-three. Inquiring how they did this—where their power came from—he quoted the vote of "Five Points," a New York slum, at the last election: for Buchanan, five hundred and seventy-four; for Fremont, sixteen. Finally he quoted against Slavery the testimony of Washington, Jefferson, Henry, Madison, Monroe, Randolph, Clay, and Benton.

The politicians of the South never gave clearer evidence of the nature of the fight they were conducting than in the matter of this book. No man could point to a line of it that called for anything but that political action which was held to be the right and duty of every free American; yet a clergyman in North Carolina was sentenced to a year in jail for circulating it, and Helper himself was driven from the State. In the House a representative from Virginia declared that "one who consciously, deliberately, and of purpose lent his name and influence to the propagation of such writings, is not only not fit to be speaker, but is not fit to live."

The result of such a course was set forth in an editorial in the New York *Tribune* early in January. "The orders flow in for the book from all quarters, in all quantities, from one copy to three hundred in a bunch. We do not know how many copies have been ordered, but we have reason to believe the number already exceeds one hundred thousand. The price is now reduced to about eighteen dollars a hundred, in consequence of the extensive sale. The work goes everywhere, through all channels, to North, East, South, and West. Innocent bales, bags, boxes and barrels bound South have each a copy of Helper tucked furtively away in the hidden centre of their contents—if we go about the streets of this most conservative city, ten to one we are delayed at the first crossing by a hand cart or wheelbarrow load of Helper. It is Helper at the stand, Helper on the counter, Helper in the shop and out of the shop, Helper here, Helper there. Helper everywhere!"

Time and again there was almost a physical conflict in the House of Representatives. For eight weeks it was impossible to elect a speaker, and the body was in confusion. Virginia, meanwhile, was arming, knowing not how widespread the John Brown conspiracy might be. "More than fifty thousand stand of arms already distributed," wrote ex-President Tyler, "and the demand for more daily increasing."

"I speak the sentiment of every Democrat on this floor from the State of Georgia," a congressman cried—"we will never submit to the election of a Black Republican President!" One Keitt of South Carolina, who had mounted guard for Brooks while he pounded Sumner, exclaimed, "The South here asks nothing but her rights; but as God is my judge, I would shatter this Republic from turret to foundation stone before I would take one tittle less."

To this Congress had come Owen Lovejoy—"Parson" Lovejoy, of the Princeton District of Illinois—the brother of the "Abolition martyr," and an uncle to Edward. He, too, was soon in trouble. "Slaveholding is worse than robbing, than piracy, than polygamy!" he proclaimed. "The principle of enslaving human beings because they are inferior is the doctrine of Democrats, and the doctrine of devils as well—there is no place in the universe outside of the Five Points of hell and the Democratic party where the practice and prevalence of such doctrines would not be a disgrace!" Pryor of Virginia leaped toward him at this, ordering him back to his own seat. "It is bad enough," he cried, "to be compelled to sit here and hear him utter his treasonable and insulting language; but he *shall not,* sir, come upon this side of the House, shaking his fist in our faces!" Members sprang to their feet, a score or two crowding around the men, shouting, jostling, wild with fury. It seemed as if a fight must come at last—not a man in the body was without a revolver or a bowie-knife.

"Nobody can intimidate me!" shouted Lovejoy. "You shed the blood of my brother on the banks of the Mississippi, twenty years ago, and I am here today, thank God, to vindicate the principles baptized in his blood! I cannot go into a slave State to open my lips in regard to the question of Slavery."

"No," cried a Virginia member, "we would hang you higher than Haman!"

Out of this particular dispute came a challenge to a duel from Virginia's Pryor; a congressman named Potter was the antagonist and he accepted. He had the privilege of naming weapons—and he chose bowie-knives. The fight never came off.

All this was upon the eve of a presidential election—a time when the utmost circumspection is to be expected from politicians —when words and measures are weighed to the smallest grain! Men saw the Southern leaders stalking through the legislative halls, haughty and reckless, flinging caution to the winds. Masters of the art of politics as they were, could it be that they did not realize what they were doing—squandering political power they had been a generation in acquiring, giving up every advantage that their strategy and political skill had won them? Could it be they did not realize the madness of the quarrel with Douglas, who had done more than any living man to keep the Northern

Democracy subject to their bidding? Or was it—a possibility so dreadful that men scarcely dared to face it—that they knew full well what they were doing: they were bent upon wrecking the party.

CHAPTER VI

The time came for the parties to make their nominations. Never before had political excitement in the country been so intense, never had so much depended upon the actions of conventions. In the Democratic convention the great quarrel between Northern and Southern Democrats must come to a head, and discerning men perceived that the issue must shape the history of the country to remotest times.

The convention was to be held in Charleston, stronghold of the slave power; and thither, the last week in April, 1860, came the Democratic politicians from the four quarters of the Union. It was a period of "hard times" in the Northwest—the Douglas men came from a land of famine to one of plenty. The South had never been more prosperous; and here upon the Battery driveway of Charleston city one might see the distilled essence of all its luxury and fashion.

The Douglas men hired a hall, and upstairs were hundreds of cots where they slept, and where each delegation had its private barrel of whiskey. Their consultation rooms were at the "Mills Hotel," and here, in the crowded corridors, filled with clouds of tobacco smoke, they toiled and perspired as politicians do.

At the "Charleston House" were the "fire-eaters," the Southern Democrats. Here might be seen a gentleman with a red cherry face and long, white hair, a New Yorker who had made a princely fortune at the New Orleans bar. He was the power behind the throne. Mr. Buchanan was as wax in his fingers. The name of this gentleman was John Slidell, and his special mission here was to see that Stephen A. Douglas did not get nominated for the presidency. The name of Douglas had come to mean "popular sovereignty," and that meant the emigrants were to be allowed to vote out Slavery from those territories which the South had won by its blood and its treasure. Douglas, to please his Northern voters, was selling out his Southern friends.

No sooner was the convention ready for business than the "irrepressible conflict" broke out. The convention was deluged with resolutions and fiery speeches. The political existence of the Douglas men depended upon their being able to come before the Northern Democrats with a platform which could be construed as a reaffirmation of "popular sovereignty." The Douglas men were in a majority, and so they might easily have had their will; but if they did so, the Southern delegates would leave the convention, the party would break in half, and defeat at the polls would follow.

The Northerners were frantic in their dismay; they found that all the usual convention methods were futile. They had money to spend, and a hundred million dollars a year in Federal patronage to pledge. But it was of no avail. It is said that they promised every office in their gift ten times over—"foreign missions, collectorships, indeed, all the offices within the gift of the President, are the currency here," wrote one. But it was of no avail. The "Committee on Platform" presented two reports. One referred the question to the Supreme Court, which was a way of being ambiguous; the other promised protection to "property," not only in the territories, but "upon the high seas"—which meant recognition of the African slave trade.

There were two days of arguing and expostulating; then the platform of the Northern Democrats was adopted—and one by one the Southern delegations withdrew from the convention. Glenn of Mississippi mounted a chair, his face ashen gray, his eyes glaring in a frenzy of passion. For twenty minutes he spoke, and he brought the Southern delegates to their feet, wild with excitement. "Go your way," he shouted—"we will go ours! The South leaves you—but not like Hagar, driven into the wilderness, friendless and alone! I tell you . . . that in less than sixty days you will find a *united* South standing side by side with us!"

[164]

So they went out, seven States in all.

With this in their ears, the delegates went home—having adjourned their convention to await the action of the Republicans at Chicago, where all men now saw clearly that the next President of the Republic would be named.

For the Republican convention there had been constructed an enormous "wigwam," a wooden building capable of seating ten thousand persons. The new city of Chicago had one hundred thousand inhabitants, and during the convention it had a third as many again. The Republican party was no longer in the hands of enthusiasts—it was grown up, and on the way to power; the office-seekers and wire-pullers were thronging to it in force. The workers for Senator Seward of New York had come by the thousands, decorated with badges and led by a uniformed band; they had barrels of money to spend, it was said, and at their headquarters champagne was as free as water.

The chances were all with the great New York senator. For years he had been the chief man of the party. He was a statesman of intellect; he was popular with the people; and he had not been too fastidious to be popular with the politicians. The trouble was with the doubtful states, which feared him because of his very prominence. He had been the leader of the antislavery agitation; and people were afraid of his "higher law doctrine," as it was called —by which a man was held not bound to return fugitive slaves. Could not some one else be found equally acceptable to the East?

In Chicago the people had one to offer; from all over the State of Illinois they swarmed to yell for him, and to lead them they hired a man whose voice they declared could be heard above any tempest that had ever raged on Lake Michigan. Also they had decorated the city here and there with fence rails which their candidate had split—there were three thousand of them, it was said, down in the Sangamon bottom. "Honest Abe," they called him, and his friends loved him wonderfully.

"Honest Abe" Lincoln had allies in the East, also—a mighty one in Horace Greeley, who was at odds with Seward, and trying to beat him. The great editor was one of the sights of the convention—the crowds flocked round him everywhere he turned; he was sublimely unconscious of it all, having the blessed gift of absent-mindedness. Queer stories were told of this faculty of his —how once in company the hostess, seeing that he could not be stopped in his discoursing, and wearying of offering him refreshments, put the plate of doughnuts into his hands, hoping that he might eat one. He did so, without ceasing his talk—he ate them all, to the consternation of the company.

Twenty thousand people could not get into the "wigwam" when the convention assembled. Upstairs the galleries were reserved for "gentlemen accompanied by ladies"; and frantic was the search for ladies that resulted. Schoolgirls were found in the street, and given a quarter each to see a gentleman in. One of the Seward "irrepressibles"—so they called themselves—subsidized an Irish washerwoman, with a bundle under her arms; and yet another tried to run the gauntlet with an Indian squaw whom he had found selling moccasins on the street. At this, however, it is recorded that the authorities demurred. There was a vehement debate—as to whether or not a squaw was a lady. It was finally decided that she was not, and the applicant went away lamenting the fact that the Republican party was fallen from its high estate.

On the evening of the second day all things pointed to Seward. The balloting began the next morning, and the country was told that his nomination was sure. But through the night, while processions were yelling and bands serenading, the delegations were consulting, and the Lincoln men threatening, cajoling, imploring. The Seward leaders had ceased work, counting the battle won—when Lincoln's managers stole away the delegations of Indiana and Pennsylvania by promises of two cabinet positions for their members. In this they disobeyed the orders of their chief—but later on he thought it best to keep the promise.

A breathless silence prevailed while the roll was called in the morning. At the first ballot Seward had 173½ and Lincoln 102— 233 being necessary to a choice. "Call the roll!" shouted the delegates, and upon the second ballot Vermont came over to Lincoln—and then the Pennsylvania vote was delivered to him, counting 44. The Seward men turned white. The total was Seward 184½, and Lincoln 181. The house was as still as death—every man keeping count for himself; when at the end of the third balloting it was seen that Lincoln was nominated by two votes, a yell burst forth which caused hundreds to stop their ears in pain. A man upon the roof signalled the news to the thousands outside; after that the cannon fired from the roof could not be heard.

To Boston—to Allan Montague, and to all with whom he talked—the tidings of the nomination came as a shock. It was but one demonstration more, it was said, of the weakness of a political system which inevitably passed over the leader, the man of power, for some colorless individual who had not frightened the dull and cowardly by too deep a love of the truth. For a score of years and more the mighty Seward had been fighting this battle of freedom; and now at last, when victory was in sight, to fall back on the argument that your candidate had split rails! Four years had Seward been a governor and ten a senator; and now his party had deposed him and chosen one whom the enemy could call— as did the New York *Herald*—"an uneducated man, a mere vulgar village politician."

Of course none of these things could be said in public; there was nothing for the East to do but to put on a brave face and get to work for "Honest Abe." Seward himself, swallowing his chagrin, toured the country in his rival's support, delivering a series of magnificent speeches. And he was one among thousands. It was the last effort of the long, weary contest to tear the government of the country out of the hands of the slave power. "We judge," wrote Horace Greeley, "that the number of speeches made during the recent campaign has been quite equal to that of all that were made in the previous presidential canvasses from 1789 to 1856, inclusive."

The scent of victory for the Republicans was in the air—the enemy was disorganized and in despair. The Democratic convention had reassembled at Baltimore and nominated Douglas; the seceding delegates thereupon put forth a ticket of their own, with a declaration for congressional protection of Slavery.

The young Republicans organized themselves as "Wide-awakes," and they marched in grand processions of twenty and thirty thousand, wearing caps and capes, carrying torches, singing songs, and shouting for "Lincoln and Hamlin." In Boston there was formed a regiment of "rail-splitters," all six-feet-two in height. At the South men read of *the fanatical diabolical Republican party.* The head of the ticket, having been born in Kentucky, was known as "the Southern renegade"; also they called him the "human baboon" and the "man-ape." The nominee for vice-president, the governor of Maine, chanced to be a man of dark complexion, and on the stump it was freely asserted that he was a mulatto.

"Lincoln will be elected," declared Stephens, in a newspaper interview, "and the result will undoubtedly be an attempt at secession and revolution." The governor of South Carolina had already sent letters to the governors of the other "cotton States" proposing cooperation, and on the day before election he sent a message to his legislature advising secession and threatening war—recommending among other things the preparing of a force of ten thousand volunteers, and the arming of "every white man in the State between the ages of eighteen and forty-five."

Allan discussed the situation one night with his cousin Jack, meeting him on his way home from the armory, and walking back with him. Jack Otis was now in his second year at the Law School, and had just been chosen a lieutenant in the Massachusetts Fifth. He was resplendent in a new uniform and with a silver-mounted sword presented by a college fraternity.

"It's too old a story," he said. "Why, Allan, they have carried elections with it ever since you and I were children! How long do they suppose they can keep it up?"

"But they mean it, Jack!" Allan answered. "They always did mean it, and they mean it this time more than ever."

"I've no doubt they think they do," was the reply. "Wait until we've called the bluff, and see!"

"You think they'll give in?"

"I do," said Jack. "So does every one. So long as it's only talk, the fire-eaters have it all their own way; but don't you suppose that when it comes to *action,* there'll be some men with common sense to be heard?"

"I wish you knew the people as I do," Allan responded.

"You know one family of millionaire aristocrats," was his cousin's retort, "and you call that knowing the South! They may try to, I grant you; but they'll be stopped very quickly. Do you mean to tell me you think that any crowd of slaveholding politicians can wreck this government without any one's lifting a hand?" Jack hesitated a moment, then broke into a laugh. "I promised the governor I'd see this law course through," he said, "but, Lord, how I hate it! And imagine me refusing to go South on a picnic, at the pleasantest time of the year!"

"There may be fighting," suggested Allan, mildly.

"There wouldn't be much, I fear—not enough for me. God knows I'd agree to let them tie me up and whip me, if they'd only hold out till after exams!"

There was no use trying to get Jack Otis to take anything seriously, and Allan made no reply; but he had a picture in his mind of his cousin Randolph, when the debonair Massachusetts lieutenant with his silver-mounted sword came marching into Wilkinson County on a "picnic"!

All things in life had been of the picnic order to Jack—and to most of his regiment, in fact. Theirs was one of the "crack" organizations of the state militia, and most of the officers were young society fellows—college boys, whose ideas of military duty were dress parades and cotillions. Every one of its companies had its own uniform, and a gorgeous one; they owned their armory, elected their officers, and had their own way in general. But their Saturday night drills were things to be seen; and when the files emerged triumphant from some impossible evolution, and the girls waved their flags and cheered, the officers' hearts beat high, and rebellion seemed a hazardous affair for the South.

Gay and full of spirit, open-hearted and affectionate, Allan's golden-haired and handsome cousin was the life of one of these companies. They had made him a lieutenant, and when it came to a dance or to private theatricals, he was a captain by brevet. It was to the detriment of his studies, as his father saw with dismay; but Jack, who was both a little dissipated and still more extravagant, was hopelessly cheerful and clever, and as impervious to rebuke as a duck to rain. When Allan ventured his opinion that the doings of the "Cambridge Tigers"—so the company was called—

was not adequate training for the work, Jack would inquire in what respect Allan's preparations were better.

Then came election day, and Abraham Lincoln received a hundred and eighty out of three hundred and three electoral votes, and carried every free state except New Jersey.

CHAPTER VII

The North had spoken, and the South answered at once. The next morning's papers carried the tidings of furious crowds in the streets of Charleston, with bonfires, cannon firing, processions, serenades, stump speeches. A United States senator had stood in the window of a hotel and harangued a howling mob—bidding them "unfurl the palmetto flag. . . . Fling it to the breeze, and ring the clarion notes of defiance in the ears of an insolent foe!" Business was suspended, and everywhere to be seen were "lone-star flags" and "palmetto cockades"; the judge of the United States District Court and the United States district attorney both formally resigned their offices. And on the following day the legislature of the State called a convention to declare its withdrawal from the Union. Both United States senators from the State resigned, and there were meetings for the ratification of the legislature's action.

Day by day the newspapers of Boston chronicled these events and similar ones all over the South—"The March of the Revolution," as one of them termed it. Alabama and Mississippi called conventions; the legislature of Georgia appropriated a million dollars for the purpose of arming that State. To the latter Senator Toombs had delivered a furious harangue. "I ask you to give me the sword!" he cried. "If you do not give it to me, as God lives, I will take it myself!"

They really meant to secede, then, these wild people! So Allan's golden-haired cousin exclaimed. But what was the matter with them? Was it on account of Lincoln? Why, he was so little of an antislavery man that Wendell Phillips had called him a "slave hound!" And what harm could he do the South anyway?—his party could not even command either branch of Congress! To break up the country upon such a pretext—it was preposterous!

Yet they were in earnest—day by day it was becoming more clear. Some among the Republicans cried "Treason!" and invoked the example of Jackson, who had vowed his "By the Eternal" to hang the South Carolina nullifiers nearly thirty years before. But, alas! poor Mr. Buchanan was no Jackson. For ten or twelve years the old gentleman had made his living by crying "Wolf!" to the Northern States; they had seen fit to laugh at him, and now it was not in human nature that he should be very much enraged at seeing his predictions come true.

In so far as there were any precedents at all in this crisis, the hope of the distracted country lay in a "compromise." There commenced a defection from the Republican ranks, the bankers and merchants leading. The stock market was in confusion, banks were suspending, ruin stared the country in the face.

All eyes were turned upon Congress, which met early in the following month. The first thing was President Buchanan's message—he had taken counsel with Senator Davis upon it, and delivered a long sermon, addressed to the free States, upon the wickedness and folly of their ways. For the troubles which had come upon it, the North had nothing to blame but its own "long-continued and intemperate interference" with the South. So far as the message dealt with the future, its doctrines were summed up by Senator Seward: (1) "That no State has a right to secede unless it wishes to; and (2) that it is the President's duty to enforce the laws unless somebody opposes him." Pitiful, indeed, was the figure of this feeble old man, who after half a century of political time-serving, was now dropped into this seething cauldron of passion. The destinies of a nation lay in his keeping—and he was tossed here and there, helpless. Under the country's political system, he remained President for four months after Lincoln's election.

In the harbor of Charleston were four military works belonging to the United States government. One of them, Fort Sumter, had cost a million dollars, and was now without a garrison, and with hot-headed Southerners arming and drilling day and night in front of it. In command of another, Fort Moultrie, was Major Anderson, with sixty men. He had warned the government of his peril—as General Scott had done before him; but the Secretary of War was a secessionist, and no troops were sent. Troops could do nothing, was the argument—the one hope was in a "compromise."

All the border States were proclaiming this. Foremost among their representatives was Crittenden of Kentucky, the "Nestor of the Senate," the successor of Henry Clay. On December 18th he introduced his measures—calling for six amendments to the Constitution, in the interest of Slavery. It was to be explicitly declared that Congress had no power to interfere with the institution in the slave States; also Slavery was to be recognized south of the Missouri Compromise line of 36° 30' in all the territories "now held or hereafter acquired"—the last phrase referring, of course, to Cuba, Mexico, and Central America, which the Southern leaders meant to subdue. Three days later the South Carolina convention assembled, and passed unanimously its "Ordinance" declaring the dissolution of the Union between that State and the United States of America.

The bells of the churches rang out this news; cannon proclaimed it, and handbills confirming it were scattered about the streets. The people organized themselves into impromptu processions—one band of young men marched to the tomb of Calhoun, where they pledged their solemn vows upon their knees. That evening the delegates met, in the midst of a vast concourse, and the formal signing of the Ordinance took place. Overhead swung a banner portraying the old union as an arch in ruins; and a new one raised about it, of slave States only, with South Carolina as the central stone. The Republicans in Washington stood appalled at the course of events, and in the North men went on praying for "compromise." Abolitionist meetings were once more being broken up by mobs in Boston, a thing the country had not seen for twenty-five years.

Shut up in the harbor of Charleston was Major Anderson with his sixty men. The Major was a Southerner and a "states-rights man," but meant to do his duty as an officer of the United States Army. Before him was a city in which the blare of martial music and the tramping of militia were to be heard day and night; whose newspapers were clamoring for the capture of the forts, and printing the doings of the North under the heading of "Foreign News." He had in Fort Moultrie a line of ramparts to defend, nearly a quarter of a mile in length, and surrounded by sand-hills from which his men might be picked off at leisure; Fort Sumter, on the other hand, was situated upon an island in mid-channel. The Major took a bold resolve, and on the night of the twenty-sixth of December he spiked the guns of Moultrie, cut down the flag-staff, and transferred his command to the other work.

When Charleston opened its eyes the next morning, it rubbed them hard, and then went wild with rage. The governor sent to demand from Anderson his immediate return, which was refused. South Carolina at once seized the other forts, and filled them with troops; also the government custom-house at Charleston, and the arsenal, with all its contents. Commissioners from Charleston were sent to Washington to demand of President Buchanan that Anderson should be sent back to Fort Moultrie and it was said that the President was on the point of yielding. The South Carolinians were vehement with the old gentleman. He pleaded that they did not even give him time to say his prayers.

An expedition was prepared to carry supplies to Fort Sumter, and it seemed then to all men as if a conflict could be only a matter of days. The vessel, an unarmed merchant steamer, appeared off the bar of Charleston harbor on the morning of the ninth of January, and the South Carolinians at once opened fire on her. But Major Anderson found himself unable to signal to the ship because the halyards of his flag were caught; and while he waited, shrinking from the fearful duty of beginning a war, the vessel turned and went out to sea again.

On the same day the papers told that the State of Mississippi had seceded. Florida followed a day later, and Alabama a day later than that. There was a strong sentiment for delay in Alabama, and there had been a bitter fight in the convention; Mr. Yancey had made a furious speech, denouncing the "cooperationists," as the timid were termed, comparing them with Tories, and calling them traitors and rebels, "misguided, deluded, and wicked men."

A week later the withdrawal of Georgia was made known, and that of Louisiana after the same interval. With Louisiana went the government mint at New Orleans, with half a million dollars in coin; and when the State of Texas seceded, which it did on the first of February, a general of the regular army surrendered to it military property worth a million or two more. Well had Mr. Davis calculated when he said, addressing the "compromise men" in the Senate, "With every motion of that clock is passing away your opportunity!"

The swiftness of such events stunned the North. The country was falling to pieces before its eyes, and not a hand raised to prevent it. The administration had sunk into inactivity—there was no more attempt to reenforce Sumter, and none to save the other forts. At the North everything was paralysis and confusion; at the South, aggression and success. Papers in Canada announced that England would recognize a Southern "confederacy," and the Richmond *Enquirer* declared that bands were organizing in Virginia to seize Washington. In Congress a bill was offered to divide the country into four sections; and the mayor of New York now sent a message to the city council, in which he recommended the secession of that city. The metropolis sympathized with the slaveholders, and hated the rest of the State—a population which De Bow's *Review,* the literary organ of the South, had described, in discussing the proposal, as "the vile, sensual, animal, brutal, infidel, superstitious democracy . . . the whole beastly, puritanic, 'sauer-kraut,' free Negro, infidel, superstitious, licentious, democratic population, . . . the immoral, infidel, agrarian, free-love democracy of western New York!"

The Secretary of the Treasury electrified the country by sending a despatch to the commander of a revenue-cutter in Louisiana, "If any man attempts to haul down the American flag, shoot him on the spot!" But the secessionists did not even deliver the message, and the vessel went the way of everything else. In Washington employees of the government and officers of the army were proving disloyal in such numbers that no one knew who could be trusted.

The one idea of President Buchanan had become to bring his administration to its end without war. In this he was at one with the Southern leaders, who needed time to mature their plans; and behind the scenes there was a struggle between them and the radicals of Charleston, to whom the presence of the Stars and Stripes over Sumter was a perpetual menace and insult. Charleston was wild with impatience—secession had somehow not proven a panacea as promised. The value of slaves was now half what it had been before Lincoln's election; business was at a standstill, and the expenses of the military regime were twenty thousand dollars a day. A commissioner had been sent to Washington to demand the surrender of Sumter; and receiving instead one of the interminable disquisitions of the placid President, he fell into a fury, and replied with a letter which must have made that aged gentleman jump. "You next," the commissioner wrote, "attempt to ridicule the proposal as simply an offer on the part of South Carolina to buy Fort Sumter and contents as the property of the United States. . . . It is difficult to consider this as other than an intentional misconstruction. You were told that South Carolina, as a separate, independent sovereignty, would not tolerate the oc-cupation, by foreign troops, of a military post within her limits— and this your Secretary calls a proposal to purchase!"

In Congress men were still laboring for the "compromise." It was now seen that this must mean the loss of the cotton States to the Union; but it might still be possible to keep the border States, and to avert a civil war. Seven slave States had seceded, eight still hung in the balance—Delaware, Maryland, Virginia, North Carolina, Kentucky, Tennessee, Missouri, and Arkansas. In each of them the attempts of the "precipitators" had failed; and now the General Assembly of Virginia, expressing its wish for some settlement, came forward with the suggestion of a "peace confer-ence," to which all of the States were requested to send delegates. These met in Washington, upon the fourth of February, ex-Presi-dent Tyler being the presiding officer; the hopes of the "conserv-atives" were all in this conference, but few of the Republicans regarded it with favor. They perceived that the secessionists were using the convention as a means of blinding the country and gaining time for their preparations.

On the day this peace conference met, another assembled at Montgomery, Alabama, made up of delegates from the cotton States. Their purpose was to form a Southern Confederacy, and they proceeded with resolute swiftness to do it. In five days they had drawn up and adopted their provisional constitution, and had chosen Jefferson Davis their president, and Alexander Stephens their vice-president. The constitution differed little from the one they had left, save that it explicitly recognized Slavery. The African slave trade was prohibited, out of respect for the opinions of mankind: a move which greatly displeased South Carolina, and caused the Charleston *Mercury* to predict a new secession.

In a few days Mr. Davis was inaugurated; he named his cabinet, and then the convention, acting as a Congress, went on to provide for a loan of fifteen millions of dollars, and the raising of a hundred thousand volunteers. It took over "all questions and difficulties" then existing with the old Republic, and it named commissioners to treat concerning them. Also it named others— of whom Mr. Yancey was one—to hasten abroad and secure the recognition of England and the nations of Europe: all of which had a very businesslike and serious aspect. "We will maintain our rights and our government at all hazards," Mr. Davis had said, as he entered Montgomery, now the capital, amid thundering of cannon and deafening cheers. "We ask nothing; we want nothing; and we will have no complications."

CHAPTER VIII

For half a century this thing, Secession, had been like some monster of the deep, rearing its crest from the troubled sea; now, for the first time, its full form was revealed, and men gazed at it, terrified. The country torn in half! The Union severed! Some of its states organized with a new government, a new name, a new flag! There was nothing left of America, there was nothing left in the world that a man could live for! So said many of those around Allan.

For Allan Montague it was doubly hard, for now indeed he had no home. Where did he belong? He still loved the South, her people and especially his own. Yes, the South was "home!" No other place could possibly be. It was no use to try to see it as an abstract question, a matter of the phraseology of the Constitution, the intention of the founders, the rights of the minority, the sovereignty of the states. It was his own personal problem. He must belong somewhere. But why? Again and again he seemed to hear his grandfather's voice, to see his face as he lay dying, but still pleading for the freedoms of the land he had loved and fought in two wars to protect. That land was the "Union." "Cherish it! Guard it!" he had told his grandchildren. "Tens upon tens of thousands have laid down their lives to win its freedom; and freedom is first of all things." What would his grandfather say to him now? What would he say to Valley Hall?

Long ago Allan had flung aside the arguments for "the constitutional right of secession." Even supposing that one were to grant that right to the sovereign States of South Carolina and Georgia—the right to annul the compact by which they had entered the Union; what then of the States of Florida and Louisiana and Mississippi, which now claimed equally the right? Florida, that had been purchased from Spain by the money of the whole nation, and Louisiana and Mississippi that had been purchased from France the same way! It was the military and naval power of the whole nation, such as it then was, that had kept England from gobbling up the last two States, purchase or no purchase.

And where was it to stop, if each State had such a right? How long would it be before new differences would arise—differences between agricultural and manufacturing States, for one thing, leading to the withdrawal of the West? California, bought from Mexico with the whole nation's money, might become a manufacturing state, and secede. The government had just put down a revolt of the Mormons in the territory of Utah—and now all the Mormons had to do was to be admitted as a State, and then secede. And New Mexico, also purchased at a cost of millions of United States money—her population was mainly Mexican, and all they had to do was to be admitted as a State, and secede and then return to Mexico! Why, what would prevent any foreign nation from colonizing the territories of the United States—what would prevent Canadians from filling Oregon—or Russians, or Chinese, if they chose—and then seceding? Or the Germans in Pennsylvania? Or the Irish in New York? One could not trust entirely the disinterestedness of a people which advanced an argument with such consequences as these.

A slave empire such as the South had begun could of course not endure, said many at the North; decay and ruin would be its destiny. "Let them go, then," said some, perceiving this. "Let them go, let them have their way—let them try it! They will come back." Those who held this view watched the stormclouds gather over Sumter with sick hearts. If once it came to fighting, this hope was gone forever; whatever happened then—there would never more be a Union. How absurd was the idea that such passions as actual war excited could ever be quelled between them! The idea that States could be driven back into the Union at the point of the bayonet! Better a thousand times that they should go now— that they should have their will—so only we keep safe and free the institutions the founding fathers left us!

Allan listened to the arguments. What are we going to do about copyrights and patents—about the railroads and telegraphs we own down there—about the two hundred million dollars their merchants owe to ours, and that they are going to sequester? What are we going to do about the tens of thousands of slaves who will come pouring into our borders—with the quarrels and raids that will follow them? Do you not see that if we do not fight, the rebels will never stop until they have walked all over us? These men are *slave drivers!* They know nothing but force, they respect nothing but force, their whole political system is nothing but the incarnation of force! Let them go, and what you will do from the very start, what you are beginning to do right now, is to enter into a race with them in military preparedness; and in ten years you will be as Germany and France are now, and your people will have bent their heads to the yoke of standing armies and conscriptions.

The argument went on: The only hope lies in the fact that our nonrecognition of this rebellion makes it impossible for Europe to recognize it, without committing an act of war. Do you think that the aristocracy of England, and the emperor of France, will not know where their interests lie? You hoped for an era of peace and freedom—do you not see that the one chance for an era of peace and freedom for centuries to come lies in the experiment this Union of States was trying here? How could peace be brought to the world so quickly as by a power such as we were to become— too strong to be attacked, too prosperous to need to attack others? It was our dream to stand to mankind for democratic institutions —to be the hope of the oppressed masses all over the world; and now we are to fall to pieces—and the despotic monarchies of Europe will have centuries added to their lease of life.

So talked the young men of Harvard, with whom Allan discussed the problem. These Bostonians were not given to blustering; it was a sign of the times that now all over the city drill clubs were organizing, that night after night these men were being made into soldiers. They said nothing about it to the young Southerner, until they were asked; then Allan learned that some of them were sleeping on the floor by an open window on winter nights, wrapped only in a blanket. There was one slightly-built young gentleman who had been the poet of Allan's class, and was now married and a father, but walked twenty miles every day, with his pockets filled with lead; he was wealthy, and had been tenderly reared, and he owned that he did not like hardship. But the Union must be preserved.

What Allan asked himself was, *could* it be? Allan knew the South: the first shot that was fired would send the border States out of the Union—there would be fifteen States to conquer, nine or ten millions of white people, as brave, alert and determined as ever lived on earth. And upon their home ground, in the midst of their forest wildernesses, their mountain passes, their eight or nine hundred thousand square miles of territory—to conquer and subdue them would be a task the like of which history had never seen. The wealth of the North would not be equal to it—the lives of its people would not be equal to it. And it was to be done by a people without a principle, without a leader, without a care save for partisan advantage and the state of trade. It was all very well for a few ardent young Republicans to be going to drill clubs; the Republicans had been a minority at the election, and since then nearly all of them had given in to the South, and were offering themselves to the South to be kicked. And the old Conservatives —and the Northern Democrats—were you going to get a war out of them?

"But the new administration!" the young men of Harvard answered, when Allan argued thus. "Will not a bold Administration policy rally the North?" Allan waited to see it. Generally speaking Boston was not prejudiced in favor of six-foot rail-splitters; and his speeches were awaited now with anxiety, and read with dismay. The new President's remarks were full of flippant and tactless sentences. Upon the question of the hour he had nothing better to offer a distracted country than the opinion that there was "nothing going wrong," that there was "nobody hurt," that there was "no crisis but an artificial one." His main theme was the statement that he had not prepared a speech, but had merely come to see the people, and to give the people a chance to see him—and that he had very much the better of the bargain.

Now perhaps it was true, as a diarist noted, that the coming President was "the most ill-favored son of Adam" ever seen; but it was atrocious taste to keep making speeches about it! Also he had developed a fondness for an amazing procedure which he called "putting backs with" people—with the tall men of the communities he passed through—to demonstrate that they were not as tall as he! And finally there was an unspeakable incident of a young girl who had written him that she thought he would be "prettier" if he "let his whiskers grow." Now when she greeted him in the crowd he kissed her, calling her "Grace," and remarking that he had done as she asked. The next morning the New York

Tribune came out with the head-line "Old Abe Kissed By A Pretty Girl." Boston trusted that this was the climax, but shortly afterward it opened its newspaper one morning and read that Mr. Lincon had abandoned his program at Philadelphia, and sneaked ignominiously through Baltimore at night, disguised, so the reports declared, in a "night-cap and a long military cloak!" The truth was that his friends had unearthed a plot, in which the chief of police in Baltimore and numerous Southern leaders were said to be involved, to have his railroad train mobbed by the "plug-uglies" of that city, and himself stabbed to death by a band of assassins. This, however, the country did not know, and the Democratic press jeered derisively, while the Republicans in secret almost wept.

The sporting men of Baltimore had laid wagers, at odds, that he would never get through the city; and in the South it was the general belief that he would never be inaugurated. That the prediction was not realized the country owed to General Scott, who was now the senior officer of the army. The general was a Virginian, but he did his duty as an officer of the United States Army. His troops were not visible, but they were there, and the secessionists who thronged Washington knew also that their guns were loaded with ball. The President read his Inaugural Address undisturbed, and while he read it Senator Douglas stood by and held his hat, meaning this for a sign that he intended to support the administration. Whatever Douglas did, he did boldly, and he had now come out against secession. As he represented a million of voters, the North found this a helpful sign.

The Inaugural speech pleased Boston better. The President took pains to be apologetic to the South; he had no intention of interfering with Slavery in the States, and he intended to execute the Fugitive law. But he denied in clear and unmistakable terms the right of secession. He said that he intended scrupulously to avoid bloodshed and violence, but that the power confided to him would be used "to hold, occupy, and possess the property and places belonging to the government, and to collect the duties and imposts." Addressing the South, he concluded: "In your hands, my dissatisfied fellow-countrymen, and not in mine, is the momen-

[181]

tous issue of civil war. The government will not assail you. You can have no conflict without being yourselves the aggressors."

This was very promising for a start; but to stand still and wait for the South to act proved soon to be impossible. It was discovered that Major Anderson was short of provisions, and that the administration had to choose definitely between supplying the fort and abandoning it. So once more the country was put upon the rack, while the new cabinet wrestled with this problem. It was complicated by the fact that the Virginia convention was in session: the secession sentiment in it ebbing and flowing visibly, day by day, with the rumors of the President's intentions. To attempt to enter Charleston harbor would most certainly mean a fight; and at the first shot the "Old Dominion" would secede.

The President had adopted the singular expedient of making up a cabinet of all his political rivals; Seward was Secretary of State, and Chase, whom Seward hated, was Secretary of the Treasury. Three other disappointed presidential candidates had also been taken in. As a means of uniting the party in a crisis, and of securing the country's best talent to meet it, this was a promising plan; but a man with such a cabinet on his hands bade fair to have a lively time. The confusion became evident at the very first council— the conservatives, with Seward leading, wished to back out of the fort, while the radicals wished to hold it at all hazards. While Seward was exchanging communications with the Confederate "commissioners" who were in Washington, the President was seeking counsel, and striving to make up his mind upon this frightful issue. To make his situation more maddening he was overwhelmed with office-seekers, who had swarmed in from all over the country —twenty of them to every office, it was figured. Seward wrote that they packed the grounds, halls, and stairways of the White House, so that he could hardly get in or out; and the President called himself a man sitting in a building, allotting compartments, "while the structure itself is on fire and likely soon to perish in ashes."

The country looked to the President, and the President looked to the country. "I shall strive to find out what you wish," he had said, "and then I shall do it." So now he waited, and watched, while day by day the issue grew clear. Should he take his stand—

should he hold the fort, and let come what would? Or should he haul down the flag—were they willing to bear the shame of that? For three months now their eyes had been fixed upon it, they had written and prayed and sung about it; and now was it to come down? They would have to face the contempt of the world, they would have to face their own self-contempt; and were they sure that even if they did, it would settle the matter? The government held also Fort Pickens in Florida. Would not the South demand that? And supposing the second demand granted—would *that* be the last?

There was one man at least who ought to have seen it clearly— Seward, who had long ago proclaimed the truth about this struggle: "They who think that it is accidental, unnecessary, the work of interested or fanatical agitators, and therefore ephemeral, mistake the case altogether. It is an irrepressible conflict between opposing and enduring forces!" For half a century they had been debating, quarrelling, threatening; and now they stood face to face, sword point to sword point. Now all of the past was concentrated in one little fort—one tiny spot in an infinity of space where the points of the two swords had come together!

BOOK IV

The Storm

❦

CHAPTER I

~~~~~~

In the last days of March Allan set out once more for Valley Hall.

He had made up his mind that his home was still the South. It had been four years since he had left it "forever," but it had never ceased to be his home; and now, as the ship moved, as the chill mists of Boston vanished, and the breezes began to grow warm, the longing for that home possessed him more and more. The old plantation—he was to see it once again. How plainly it stood out in his memory! And the people—how were they? For four years he had not had a word—some of them might be dead, for all he knew. They had been incensed when he left; but surely time had mellowed their feelings somewhat—it had mellowed his, and he yearned to see them again. He yearned to see the cotton fields, flooded with sunshine. To see the moonlight on the roses and magnolias; to hear the mockingbirds, to watch the fireflies, and drink in the odor of jasmine and sweetbrier at twilight! There was truly a witchery there which no one who had lived there could ever forget. They might disagree with it, they might disapprove of it, yet they loved it.

How gladly would he have escaped from the stern realities of the hour, to enjoy its blessings as he had known them in his childhood! The steamer was bound for New Orleans, and the few passengers were Southerners, and on edge with excitement. The vessel was never far from the coast, and when it was opposite Charleston they listened for the sound of guns. Rounding Florida they passed close to a schooner, and the steamer slowed up while they hailed her. But she had no news, and so by the time they neared the end of the journey, the suspense had become great indeed.

How well Allan remembered that low coast, which he had first seen when he was a twelve-year-old boy going North with his father to the hateful land of "Abolitionism." Those long white reefs, over which flapped the armies of pelicans—it might have been one instead of eleven years ago that he had watched them. But when the steamer neared its destination and the customs boat came out to meet it, here at least was something new —a strange, three-striped flag. How his father would have gazed with happiness upon it!

Allan soon grew used to the flag. It floated from all the public buildings in New Orleans, and from perhaps half the private ones. The lazy old city seemed transformed into a military post; there were tents in all the public places, soldiers parading in the streets—nearly every other man one passed was in uniform. Without end and beyond belief was the variety of the uniforms—there were Turcos, and Zouaves, and Chasseurs—and others without name. Where you would have looked for advertisements and theatre posters, you saw instead placards and announcements of the various volunteer companies; the Lafayette Guards, the Beauregard Rifles, the Pickwick Rifles—for Mr. Charles Dickens was the author of the day; the Moagher Rifles, the German, the Spanish, the Italian volunteers. Many of the "affiches" were in French—the Creole population was even more wild with excitement than the rest. At all of it Allan stared in amazement. He had not dreamed of anything like it. No Southerner had ever dreamed of the South being changed, no matter how long he had been away from it. Now the very look upon the faces of the people was different; they had been happy, easy going, but now the air was full of menace, the bits of conversation one caught upon the streets and in the hotels all had to do with war.

The bulletin boards in front of the newspaper offices were crowded. There were rumors of war, and rumors of peace, but still very little news. The "Illinois baboon" had been in office a month, and had not yet been able to choose a policy; the balance still trembled and swayed.

Allan took the river steamer for Clarke's Landing; he was glad to be out of the turmoil—to see the land as he loved and remembered it, drunk with sunlight, clothed in wonder, endlessly peaceful and still. Here and there were the villas, white, with green-painted blinds, bosomed in trees, orange and lemon trees, myrtles and magnolias, peach trees, and huge moss-draped live-oaks. The land lay asleep, or so he thought—and Allan's soul cried out in grief at the thought that it might ever awaken to the crash of war.

He landed, mounted a livery stable horse, and put it to a gallop. He was going to see Valley Hall once more! To see the boys, to see Ethel and Uncle Ben! And Aunt Jinny, and Pericles, and Taylor Tibbs! And the horses and the dogs, and the quarters and the fields of cotton! The flower-lined road on each side of him fled by—and so for an hour or two, until the landscape began to grow more familiar, and his heart to thump. This was Major Potter's place, and there was the road where you turned in! Allan's thoughts went back a dozen years or more, to the time when his father had made a political speech there. How vivid the memory!—a thunderstorm had burst in the middle of it, and some one had wondered at the bad taste of the powers that managed thunderstorms. Over in that grove was the Hindses' house —and beyond the slope were the woods and the bayou, and at the other side the edge of Valley Hall plantation. Now the little bridge, and the turn—and you saw the house!

He put spurs to his horse, and dashed on. A moment later he started, as out of the deeply shadowed archway of the road came two horsemen, riding rapidly; they were in uniform, blue, with red facings. One was tall, and mounted upon a great coal-black horse; the other was smaller and rode a bay. Allan's pulses began to leap. He was near enough to see their swords shaking as they rode—yes, there was no mistake—it was his cousins!

He gave a yell, and waved his hand, and galloped down upon them. They slowed up, staring at him—didn't they know him? A moment or two more, and he reined up his horse before them and stretched out a hand upon each side to them, crying, "Hello!"

There was a moment's pause—Ralph had half reached out to take his hand; but 'Dolph sat erect, drawn up to his full height. His brows were knit—then suddenly he set his lips together, and gave his horse a cut that made it leap. "Go to hell!" he said, and went by like a flash, and down the road. His brother followed.

They left Allan sitting motionless, dazed. He turned and watched them vanish, his heart beating like a hammer; then he rode on very slowly. He was not angry—he was stunned. Nothing that he had ever seen had seemed quite so much like *war* as that.

By the time that he reached the turn in the road he had become very sober, and felt in truth a little like a fool. He beat back the emotions that rose in him as he saw the house—he rode up to it as he would have ridden up to any other house.

There were two people upon the veranda: one was Ethel, and the other an old colored woman, whom Allan did not know. He saw that the girl was lying back, propped up on pillows. She was very pale, and the Negress was fanning her.

He rode close to the veranda. "How do you do, Ethel?" he said, and raised his hat.

The girl half rose, and then sank back. "How do you do, Allan?" she answered, in a subdued voice. She looked older—but more beautiful than ever, he thought.

There was an awkward pause; then she spoke to the Negress, "Mammy, go and tell some one to come for Mr. Allan's horse."

The woman went away, and Ethel looked at him again, without a word.

"You have been ill?" he asked her.

"Yes," she answered, and that was all.

"And how is every one?"

"They are very well," said she.

Again there was a pause. It was broken by a sound from within the house—the crying of an infant. Ethel started. "Mammy!" she called. "Mammy!"

The colored woman came around the corner of the house, running; she disappeared inside.

"What is that?" Allan asked, in surprise.

"It is the baby," was Ethel's reply.

He dismounted, and gave his horse to the stable-boy, who had come running, and stood staring and grinning. "How are you, Tom?" he said, nodding to him, and went up the steps onto the veranda.

"So you are married," he said, trying not to be aware of her coldness. "Who is he?"

"I married Billy Hinds."

"Ah," said Allan. "Billy" was the young cavalier whose devotion at the age of seventeen Allan had noted when he last visited the Hall. "Where is he?" he inquired. And Ethel answered without looking at him. "He is gone to the defence of his country."

There was silence. Allan knew not what to reply—but suddenly Ethel sat up, and gazing at him angrily, cried out, "Allan, how can you bear it?"

"Bear what?" he asked.

"This frightful situation? How can you bear to see it, and know that you are the cause of it?"

"I, Ethel?" he asked, amazed.

"You! Yes, you! Who is to blame but just such cruel and wicked men as you? Men who hate us—who cannot leave us in peace—who have hounded us out of the Union and now want to hound us back!"

The blood had mounted to her cheeks, and her eyes were big and black, and wild looking. "I wonder that you can come down here!" she rushed on. "Why *have* you come? Is it to gloat over the misery you have caused? Is it any pleasure to you to know that my husband had barely an hour to gaze upon his new-born babe, before he had to go away to prepare for a war? And now he is ill at New Orleans—and I am ill here. And I must see my two brothers start tomorrow! Go among the people around here, people who once loved you—you will scarcely find a family upon whom some such sorrow has not fallen!"

"Ethel!" said a man's stern voice, from inside the house, "you were not to excite yourself."

It was Hamilton Montague standing in the doorway, now. The girl sank back without another word, and closed her eyes.

There was an uncomfortable pause. Then, "How do you do, Uncle Hamilton?" said Allan.

Mr. Montague bowed gravely. "I thank you," he said. "I will see you in the office, Allan, if you like."

Allan bowed, and turned without a word to follow him. The two entered the office and Mr. Montague pointed to a chair. He seated himself by his desk, and fixed his eyes upon his nephew. "I suppose," he began, "that you have come to take possession of your share of this property."

"Yes, Uncle Hamilton."

"Well, sir," his uncle replied, "I have to tell you that you have come to no purpose."

"To no purpose?" Allan asked, doubting his ears.

"You cannot have the property," said Mr. Montague.

"I do not understand you, sir—the property belongs to me," Allan answered.

"It would have belonged to you if you had not chosen to league yourself with the enemies of your country."

"You must explain to me, Uncle Hamilton," Allan said, after a pause; "I really don't know what you mean."

"What I mean is, that after carefully considering it, I have concluded that it would be wrong for me to allow any part of the resources of this State to pass at such a time as this into the hands of its enemies; and, in particular, to allow any of the enemies of our domestic institution an opportunity to interfere in its affairs. Therefore I have decided to remain in possession of Valley Hall for the present."

Allan drew a deep breath. "I see," he said. "And the law?"

"I do not think," said Mr. Montague, "that you would be wise to appeal to the law."

The young man flushed, startled by the tone even more than by the words. "That is a threat?" he asked.

"No," was the response, "it is merely wise counsel."

There was a pause. "You have always been a gentleman, Uncle Hamilton," said Allan, at last.

"I have been too much of a gentleman to defend my actions," was the response. "In this case, however, I am willing to explain that I am not acting for myself, but for my State. The revenues which may accrue in the matter will be at the State's disposal— as also is the property, of course. There is now before the Congress in Montgomery a bill dismissing all law cases in the interest of Northern parties; and it will not be many days after the first stroke of war, I fancy, before all debts due to Northerners, and all property belonging to them, will be sequestered. That will cover the case."

"I see," said Allan, and added, "You take the liberty of anticipating the law."

"In which," was the other's response, "I follow the best of precedents. I am merely holding, in the expectation of a war, a fort which I happen to possess but to which I now have no other right. It is *my* Sumter."

"And if the war should not come?"

"In that case," said the uncle, "I should have neither the right nor the wish to deprive you of your property. Just as soon as the questions at issue are settled to the satisfaction of my country, I shall make you an offer for your share in the estate; and if you do not care to accept that, I shall cause it to be sold, and transmit to you half of the proceeds."

There was a long silence. Allan sat motionless, his heart beating fast. Assuredly, this was bringing the political situation very close "to men's business and bosoms." Then, the respect for his elders which he had been taught took command, and he swallowed his feelings. He rose and stood very straight, gazing at his uncle.

"You hold my portion of this plantation through my father's trust in you," he said, "and I do not believe you are keeping faith with him now. But you have the power, no doubt; and you will not be troubled with any words from me. If you will be so good as to order my horse, I will go."

He bowed and went out. The veranda was deserted; Ethel had taken the opportunity to disappear. He stood waiting until his horse came down the road.

Taylor Tibbs was leading it; and the little yellow man, who had evidently not heard that there was anything wrong, was filled with delight. "Marse Allan!" he cried, and rushed, horse and all, to embrace his young master. But there came a stern voice behind Allan, "Tibbs!"

And Tibbs halted. "Go to the stables, Tibbs," Mr. Montague commanded, and came forward and took the rein himself.

Mr. Montague held the horse in silence, while Allan mounted; then their eyes met, and he bowed in response to Allan's "Good bye." Allan rode away without even a last glance at Valley Hall.

He had not ridden far when he saw another rider approaching. It was his uncle Ben Handy. The old gentleman rode up, crying out his joy, and holding out his hand. "Well, it's Allan!" he exclaimed. "Well, well!"

"How are you, Uncle Ben?" Allan replied, happily.

"You are leaving so soon?" asked his uncle.

"I was not invited to stay," Allan answered, dryly.

"I know, I know," was the reply, and the kind old face of Uncle Ben became sad. "Hamilton told me what he was going to do. And I told him it was a shame!"

"Thank you, Uncle Ben. You can't imagine how much I appreciate that! I suppose I was a fool, but I had not expected such harsh treatment."

"And what are you going to do about it, Allan?" his uncle asked, a little nervously.

"I suppose I'll have to sue—"

The other interrupted quickly. "Then don't talk about it around here!" Mr. Handy reached over and laid his hand on Allan's.

"I don't believe you are even armed," he said.

"Armed!" echoed the other. "Of course not. Why should I be?"

"Listen, sonny," the older man answered. "Take my advice, and don't stay 'round here any great time—and don't do any talking, here or anywhere else, until you're up North again! Holding Abolition views has been made a penal offence now—and not only that, but the people are apt to be violent. I have heard of objectionable people being tarred and feathered, and beaten, and even hung, once or twice. So I beg you, don't try to make any trouble about the business of the property around here."

Allan had never seen his Uncle Ben so serious.

Mr. Handy went on, "I wouldn't even go through Woodville, if I were you, Allan; I met the boys in there, and they told me they'd seen you. 'Dolph's excitable, you know, and he's been drinking today, and he's probably talked some on the streets. You really have no idea of how the crowd about here is worked up!"

Allan had been thinking hard while his uncle was talking. "Uncle Ben," he said, at last, "I consider that I have behaved myself very well, on the whole. And I don't believe that I care to run away now from 'Dolph, or any other man."

There were hoofbeats down the road, and two horsemen came round the turn. "Here they are now," said Mr. Handy, in a low voice.

He moved somewhat in front of Allan who sat motionless gazing at the approaching riders. They had slowed their horses, and were coming on at a walk.

Allan could see that Randolph's face was flushed, and suddenly he lashed his horse, and bounded straight toward Allan. He halted at his side, and demanded, "Did you get what you wanted?"

Allan looked at him, but did not answer. Ralph rode up quickly and placed his horse between the two. "Now, 'Dolph!" he said, gently.

"Let me alone!" cried the other, angrily. "Get out of my way! What does he want down here, anyway? Does he think we're going to let any damned Abolitionist walk off with our Negroes and not say a thing?"

Mr. Handy had driven his horse into the group, and caught 'Dolph by the arm. "Now, see here!" he cried. "Don't be a fool— you are forgetting yourself, 'Dolph!"

"Take your hand off me!" the other shouted, and tore his

arm loose. At the same time he gave his brother's horse a slash with his whip that made it leap out of his way. Then he shook the whip in Allan's face. "What did you come down here for, confound you!" he demanded. "Why don't you stay where you belong? You think we'll have any Yankee spies around us—"

Old Mr. Handy had seized him again, and now his brother flung himself from his horse, and leaped toward him. There was a sharp scuffle, Ralph trying to hold his brother's arm. " 'Dolph!" he cried desperately—"don't you know what father said to you— don't you know what you promised him? You ought to be ashamed of yourself!"

"Ashamed, hell!" yelled 'Dolph. "What does he take us for? What'd he come here for, if he wasn't looking for trouble?"

"Allan," cried Mr. Handy, "*go on!* Why don't you *go on?*"

Allan hesitated, then he started his horse. "Thank you, Ralph and Uncle Ben," he called to them over his shoulder, "and good bye." Behind him he heard Randolph cursing as he tried to get free from the two men who were holding him.

"Go on, you coward!" yelled 'Dolph. "That's like a Yankee— go on! But don't you think you'll get away from us—we'll be up there after you, don't you make any mistake! Ask when you get in to Woodville, and you'll find out the news. Get ready for a fight, coward. You've got to fight, damn you, whether you want to or not!"

And that was the last Allan heard from the man he had so dearly loved. "Ask when you get to Woodville there, and you'll find out the news!" What did 'Dolph mean?

He came to the main street of Woodville. The courthouse bell was ringing, and he saw people hurrying in that direction, and put the spurs to his horse. It was sunset—one would have expected to find the occupants of Woodville's aristocratic villas on their verandas; but the houses seemed empty—the doors standing wide open. He rode on and came in sight of the courthouse square. Here there was a military encampment—the place was white with tents, and a battery of artillery was in front of them, and the "stars and bars" waving above. Directly before the building was an immense crowd—here was where all the town had come. Some one was making a speech—as Allan approached he could catch snatches of the voice between the strokes of the bell and the frantic roaring of the crowd.

A man dashed out from a store, bareheaded; he passed near Allan, who jerked up his horse and called, "What's the matter?"

"It's Sumter!" the man answered. "The Yankees are going to reenforce it! They've got word about it at Charleston!"

CHAPTER II

Allan went back to New Orleans that night, pacing the deck of the steamer and chewing the cud of bitter reflection. What a blow in the face he had got himself!

He knew little of the value of money—having always had more than he needed—and had not yet realized what it would be to have *nothing*. Nor was it his disappointment at the failure of his plans; the freedom of the Negroes of Valley Hall seemed a trivial matter in comparison with the significance of what he had experienced—the light which it threw upon the temper of the people. It had exceeded anything that he could have dreamed. And now the North! What would he find when he got back to Boston?

The news he had heard at Woodville was no mere rumor. The Washington government had sent word to Charleston that it intended to provision the fort—"peaceably," it said, that is, by an unarmed vessel. In New Orleans there was intense excitement, a regiment having just been ordered to assemble and hold itself in readiness. Allan had intended to return North by steamer, but this news changed his plans, and decided him to travel by land, and pass through Charleston.

He left New Orleans the same morning, by the boat for Mobile.

The trip was the same he had taken with his father eleven years before; it required a day and a night—first through Lake Pontchartrain, then along the coast of the Gulf, or rather the narrow passage inside the reefs, beyond which one could see the snow-white surf. On the other side the land was so cut up with bayous that one saw little sail-boats apparently skimming through green meadows.

At dawn they came into Mobile Bay, where, at the entrance, were two recently seized forts, with the blue and white flag of the new Confederacy above them. In Mobile were troops in all the squares, and the din of preparation in the air. Here the news was that a reply had been sent to Washington from Charleston to the effect that the proposed attempt to supply Sumter would be resisted. War vessels which had been fitting out in New York for the supplying were now on the point of sailing.

The steamer which went up the river to Montgomery was called the *Southern Republic,* a significant name; it had borne the name for a long time, a fact more significant still. Allan heard it said that the Irish captain of the *Southern Republic* boasted that he had built it with the proceeds of a lucky stroke in the African trade. It looked like a big three-storied house, and upon its deck was a "steam calliope," which played "Dixie" at every landing. The banks of the chocolate-colored Alabama were so high that nothing of the country could be seen; but there was always a crowd at the tops of the long stairways of the landings to listen to the music and cheer for "Dixie."

The trip took two days—Allan landed in Montgomery early in the morning, the tenth of April. He bought a paper and ran through it eagerly.

Events were marching. United States vessels were reported off the bar at Charleston, and Fort Sumter was exchanging signals with them. Four regiments had been telegraphed for from the Southern states; and President Davis had called upon the State of Alabama for three thousand men.

At midnight Charleston had been roused by the firing of signal guns, calling out the reserves; all night long the streets of the city had echoed with the rolling of drums and the galloping of cavalry —there were said to be seven thousand men and one hundred and forty cannon now surrounding the fort. The Charleston *Mercury* of the previous day was quoted, to the effect that the announcement from "Lincoln's government" was to be taken as a declaration of war. "The gauge is thrown down," ran the article, "and the God of battles must decide the issue between the hostile hirelings of Abolition hate and Northern tyranny and the people of South Carolina defending their freedom and their homes!"

It was furthermore reported that President Davis and his cabinet were now in continuous session, discussing the final and irrevocable step of war. Allan started, realizing that it was here, where he stood, that this was being done; he gazed about him again, the hot and dusty little city becoming suddenly a place of romance. The streets of Montgomery were filled as never in their history before. They were tingling with excitement—one drew it in with the very air. Allan went to the hotel, which he found so crowded that he could scarcely get inside the door. Here were the headquarters of all the politicians and office-seekers of seven States, to say nothing of contractors, speculators, gamblers, sight-seers, military men. Already, before breakfast, they were up and doing; in the dining room the uproar was such that one scarcely heard a company of soldiers that passed outside with their screaming fife and rattling drum.

After breakfast Allan strolled up to the Capitol: a white marble building in the usual Graeco-American style, standing upon an elevation and towering high above all the city. Here also were military encampments and the blare of military music; even that early, people were thronging to the chamber where the Congress met.

Allan entered also and waited for a view of the assembly. Here were the men who had done this deed, and it seemed hard to believe that they could look like other men. He watched them, listening meanwhile to a venerable clergyman who prayed confusion upon their enemies, after the ancient fashion of the British hymn:—

"Confound their politics,
Frustrate their knavish tricks;
On Thee our hopes we fix,
God save us all!"

They were big, broad-shouldered men, these legislators, dressing for the most part in Southern fashion, with wide black hats, black ties and high white collars. Allan noticed that many of them chewed tobacco. Their presiding officer was a Mr. Howell Cobb of Georgia, stout-faced, benevolent-looking, with a full gray beard. Mr. Cobb was one of the big men of the South—he had been Buchanan's Secretary of the Treasury, and owned a million dollars' worth of Negroes.

Presently he observed ahead of him a gentleman whose figure seemed familiar; he walked feebly, but with stiff, military carriage. Allan increased his pace—yes, surely he was not mistaken, it was Mr. Davis—an old-time neighbor at Valley Hall, who had become the hero of the battle of Buena Vista in the Mexican War. It was there that he had been seriously wounded in his leg, just as Allan's father had been.

Allan felt his pulse leaping. All the waiting, the fevered anxiety of a nation—and here walked the man upon whose shoulders the present rested, by whose nod the future was to be decided. As he was waiting, so were thirty million other Americans—hoping and dreading, and all looking to this man. Happiness or misery, life or death for how many of them—all depending upon him! Perhaps even now he was going to decide—perhaps he had decided already! The hand which swung there at his side—perhaps it had already signed the order that was to plunge a continent into war.

They came to the corner, where stood a large brick building with a Confederate flag above it—the "State Department." The president ascended the two or three steps—and as he did so happened to glance down the street.

Allan raised his hat. "How do you do, Mr. Davis," he said.

Mr. Davis returned his bow, studying him closely. "Your face is familiar," he began—

"My name is Montague," Allan said. "I am Captain Montague's son."

"Harry Montague's son!" cried the other cordially, "Why—sure enough!" He came down a step, and held out his hand. "How long has it been since I have seen you?"

"Eleven years," Allan replied; "in Washington."

"Yes," said Mr. Davis, "I remember. And then your father's death. Where are you living, Allan?"

"I live in Boston still," was the reply.

The other looked surprised. "In Boston!" he exclaimed. "You have come home now, I suppose?" he added.

"No," Allan answered. "I still live in Boston."

A shadow crossed Mr. Davis' face. "The South has need of all her sons, Allan," he said gravely.

A sudden impulse seized Allan; his hand had been upon the railing of the steps, and he leaned forward, stretching it out imploringly. "God grant you wisdom, Mr. Davis," he whispered.

The president of the Southern Confederacy looked into the young man's eyes, and his soul seemed to come suddenly into his face. He was very thin from sickness—his features were haggard, and furrowed by care. "My boy," he said, his voice trembling, "if He does not, it is not because I have not asked Him."

Then—Allan scarcely knew how—he was gone, and the door of the building had shut.

The traveler turned away, quivering. How that look had shot through him!

There had been times of late years when he had hated Jefferson Davis—hated him bitterly—for Allan believed that without him this horror could never have been; it was of his making more than any other living person's—his vehemence, his eloquence, his ability, had carried it through. And had it always been his people that he thought of? Had it never been himself—his personal ambition? Allan shuddered as he walked on, thinking that if ever it had been ambition—how the memory of it would some day scorch Jefferson Davis!

He had led the Southern "rebellion" for so long—and now it had gotten beyond his control. It was known that he was dragging back, that he was trying to restrain the radicals of Charleston city. Was that, possibly, why he was so pale and haggard—why the cheek-bones stood out in his face so that it looked almost like a skull? There rang still in Allan's ears a frightful and savage sentence which a member of the Alabama legislature was said to have spoken to Mr. Davis, "They will be back in the old Union in ten days, sir,—the people of this State—*unless you sprinkle blood in their faces!*"

They were driving him into war—yes, that was it! There had been times when Allan, too, had thought he wanted war, but he did not want it now. Could you look into the faces of these people about you and wish to destroy them? They had given him cause for anger, and he had felt it at times; but still they were just pitiful men and women. He thought of Ethel again, and her cry of anguish. How many like her had seen their husbands march away! How many would never see them return!

An idea took possession of him. Why had he not spoken to Mr. Davis—why had he not pleaded with him—poured out his soul to him? Surely he could not have offended him—his heart was too full. To make such an appeal was what he had meant when he had gone to Harper's Ferry to see Lovejoy and Brown— to pour out his soul to them. Had he not a right now to speak to an old family friend? He might possibly have said something to influence him—he might have turned the scale! Mr. Davis was just a man; he was formal and reserved, but he had a heart. Who could say but that in his secret soul he was hungry for some one who would speak such a word?

Allan stopped. His heart was leaping—why might not he do it now? It might not yet be too late! Was it that he was afraid? Could any thought of himself influence him at such a time? Mr. Davis might call him a fool, and send him about his business, but what would that matter? What was *he* at such an hour?

He faced about, and walked swiftly. He was only a square or two from the building; he reached it before his impulse had weakened. He pushed open the door and went in, his hands trembling, his cheeks burning.

He stood in a long, whitewashed hall. There were rows of doors, with the names of officials written on paper and tacked upon them. "Where is Mr. Davis' room?" he asked of a clerk who passed him.

"Upstairs," was the reply, and Allan ascended. Here were more doors, and he went along scanning them. Upon one of them was written: "The President."

He knocked. "Come in," said a voice, and he entered.

There was a large desk by the window, with a chair in front of it; but the chair was empty. In the centre of the room stood a young man, a stranger to him.

"Where is Mr. Davis?" Allan asked.

"He is engaged," was the reply. "The cabinet is in session."

"When will he be disengaged?"

"I do not know. The session will probably last all night. Is there anything I can do for you?"

"No," said Allan, "no—" and turned, and went out. He was too late!

All the rest of the day he waited, lounging about the hotel and the capitol grounds, listening for news, and getting only rumors. It was incredible, what these people seemed to believe—he heard two men discussing Lincoln, and one said that he had once been married to a Negress, and the other that he was drunk all day. The latter statement was frequent in the Southern newspapers, then and later.

That night the traveler left for Charleston. A very small contact with reality had dispelled his dream of swaying the destinies of the nation, and he was inclined to think that maybe he was a fool.

Ordinarily, one took two days for the trip—to Atlanta the first day, and to Charleston the second. But now the pressure was greater, and the trains ran day and night, and straight through. There were several companies of soldiers on the one that Allan took, and they made the trip lively. At every station, even in the small hours of the morning, there were people to cheer, and they turned out on the platforms and roared and shouted in reply. Each one of these volunteer organizations had its own music and generally each struck up independently, so the banging and blaring and confusion were indescribable. In these first companies was all the wild blood of the South—both the officers and the enlisted men were young gentlemen of wealth and fashion out for a lark. It was said that in some companies you could not count the millionaires on all your fingers. There was no Southerner too good to be a private at such a time as this—though of course they were privates in their own way. They had their body-servants and belongings with them; when the companies halted in a city, they often stopped at the hotel; when they went into camp, they brought cases of champagne and boxes of truffles and patés. Now, all night, while the cars thumped along, they played cards, and told stories, and sang songs, and chewed tobacco and smoked it, and drank many bottles of whiskey—"forty-rod," or "sixty-rod," as they called it, according to their estimate of its deadliness.

The next morning, the eleventh of April, they were in Atlanta; and here was more news. Events had been moving the day before —the papers reported that everything in Charleston had been put in preparation for an attack upon the fort. The South Carolina convention had adjourned—and nearly all its members had enlisted as volunteers. The volunteers on the train were disposed to sleep now, and there was less uproar through the afternoon. Allan sat and gazed out the window at the endless succession of half-cultivated fields and half-burned forests, of dreary stations with unpainted wooden shanties and grog-shops in the background, and a ragged, uncouth population assembled—the children barefoot, the men often likewise, but all cheering and excited. These "poor whites" cheering for Slavery!

Towards evening, the train arrived at Augusta. Here there was a veritable *Mardi Gras* celebration—the soldiers turned out of the cars, dancing and singing, parading up and down the platform, with their arms about each other's necks. The news had come that General Beauregard had sent to demand the surrender of Fort Sumter. A bombardment was expected every hour; and all Charleston was gone out to watch it. Allan sat in the car, very still, the uproar sounding far away. Mr. Davis and his cabinet had decided!

The engine whistled, and the passengers piled aboard, and off they went amid a deafening din. There was no sleeping that night —no one could even sit still. Long after midnight everyone kept watch, and at station after station crowded upon the platform, or leaned out of the windows, shouting for the news. There had been some delay—the fight had not come off as expected, and the city had gone to bed again. Could it be that the fort was going to surrender? Or might it not be that the report was untrue after all?

Between stops the warriors sang through their repertoire. These companies were from New Orleans, and their favorite was the *"Marseillaise."* They had versions newly made for the emergency —and new words for all the familiar patriotic airs, for "Dixie" and the "Star Spangled Banner" and other melodies, from "The Minstrel's Lament" to "Sally in our Alley"; and all night they roared them out to the popping of champagne-corks.

Until at last through the open windows of the car a fresh, cool breeze began to blow. It smelt of the ocean, and meant Charleston; a hush fell upon the crowd—they sat listening, their impatience growing every instant. The train had never seemed to creep along so slowly, its stops had never been so exasperating. There came at last a halt of several minutes, and, two or three at a time, the passengers got up and went outside. Allan joined them, glad to have a chance to move about and stretch his limbs.

The train stood upon the low marshy ground just outside of the city; the bay was to the left, and one could hear the dull boom of the surf beyond it. The breeze was, however, the only messenger; it was still too dark to see. But the first pale flush of morning was now spreading in the East, and men strained their eyes, striving to make out the outline of the shore and of the distant fort, which stood in mid-channel. Any minute it might come into view, and then they would know what had happened in the night-time! Men clambered up on the tops of the cars in their eagerness to be the first to learn.

"Oh, say, can you see by the dawn's early light!" All his life Allan had heard the words of that song, and never thought much what they meant; but now their emotion seized him, how poignantly, how vividly! The flag, the flag! He had been like a traveller in the midst of a desert; a sight of it would be to him like a gleam of verdure, a promise of water. So he stood with the words of the song racing through his mind—

Suddenly the crowd whirled about, startled into silence; across

[203]

the harbor there had shone a sudden far-off gleam of fire—instantaneous, like a flash of heat-lightning—close to the horizon. At the same moment a pale spark of light was seen to shoot into the sky. It went up in a curving track, trembling, scintillating; slowly and more slowly it moved—then seemed to stand still—hovering, shaking like a star. And then it fell, faster and faster—and disappeared like a meteor. A few moments later there came across the water a dull and heavy boom—and from the throats of the startled onlookers burst a roar that seemed to lift the roofs off the cars. It was a shot!

CHAPTER III

The edges of the misty bay seemed to leap out in dull red light; but sounds could not be heard, because of the frantic uproar in the train. The passengers yelled, tossed their hats, and fell upon each other's necks and laughed and wept. The train started again; faster and faster it sped into the city; and then some one struck up the "Marseillaise," and a few joined, and then all, and they sang it, verse by verse, in wild exultation, with passion such as surely it had never roused in men since the day when there marched into Paris those "six hundred Marseillaise who knew how to die:"—

> "To arms! to arms! ye brave!
> The avenging sword unsheathe!
> March on! March on!
> All hearts resolved
> On Victory or Death!"

Little by little, as they grew hoarse, and the train slackened its speed in the streets of the city, other sounds began to grow audible, the ringing of bells and the blowing of whistles, and above all, the

[204]

thunder of an incessant cannonade. The men about Allan went wild; then the train began to slow up at the depot, and they poured out, some of them climbing out of windows in their haste. Upon the deserted platform they fell into line; there were a few hasty commands from their officers, and then away they went, double quick, cheering like mad.

It was now light enough to see plainly. The little city was wide awake, lights burning in all the windows, and people thronging into the streets. They were all running one way; by the time that Allan neared the sea-front he was in the midst of a river of humanity, which poured out upon East Bay Battery—men, women, and children climbing over the railings, running over the grass, singing and shouting.

It was a dull misty morning, but one could now make out the solitary fort in the midst of the bay, and the dim shore-line upon each side, whence came the swift bursts of flame and the thick puffs of lurid smoke. Some fifty guns were thundering forth from a circle of batteries; the shells from the mortars bursting in the air about the little fort, crowning it with flame-riven vapor. Above it, the twinkling bombs sped here and there across the sky, cutting tangled curves, and waking the pale dawn to a strange pyrotechnical show. Faster and faster, as the music of the cannon thundered, it beat up the blood of the thronging thousands, and one could see their cheeks aflame with passion. Gleaming now through the rifts in the smoke-clouds, out there amid the crash of shot and shell—was the flag! And for how much insult and outrage it stood to them! How long it had waved there, menacing and defiant! How they had hated it, and writhed at the sight of it—and now it was coming down!

With Allan too, it was the end of a long impatience. The change came so suddenly that he scarcely realized it; it was the tapping of the flask and the coming of the precipitate—it was there, where an instant before had been no sign of it. Secession had brought forth its child—Slavery its grandchild! With Slavery you might parley, with Secession you might hesitate—but with this—ah, God! He stood there with the wild din of the battle in his ears, and all his soul leaped up. No, never—you could not dally with

[205]

this, you could make no terms with this! The Union would have to fight now, and secession would be put down! And, what a relief it was to have brushed aside all the cobwebs, to see the issue plain!

Suddenly Allan realized that to all this cannonade Fort Sumter was not replying. The flag floated on—but the flag was not enough. What was the matter?

"They haven't fired a shot yet," said a man at his side, answering his inquiry.

"Why not, I wonder?"

"I don't know," was the reply; "I guess they're scared and hiding."

It could not be that, Allan knew. But he moved here and there, burning with impatience—what could it mean? Was he to stand there and see the flag fall and the fort torn to pieces—and learn, perhaps, that the wretched politicians at Washington had forbidden Major Anderson to reply?

The truth of the matter was that Major Anderson and his men were then quietly breakfasting upon salt pork and water: having not too much powder, and hence no need of haste. It was broad daylight before finally they fired their first gun. The crowd roared with joy—now there would be a battle!

The bombardment redoubled—the wide spaces of the harbor echoed with it, the buildings of the city shook with it. Before long the whole of the scene was hidden in smoke; it was a raw day, with showers now and then, but through it all the wealth and fashion of Charleston thronged the waterfront. Some one would start a cheer, and it would run like a breaking wave along a beach; now and then a company of soldiers would march down the driveway, or a favorite officer gallop past, and the din would almost drown out the bombardment. Here and there a party would strike up a song. There was a couplet which seemed to give endless delight—some one was chanting it every minute:—

"With mortar, Paixhan, and petard,
We tender Old Abe our Beau-regard!"

Now and then as the breeze would make rifts in the smoke,

Fort Sumter or the batteries would come into view. Allan went back into the city to get a pair of fieldglasses; with these he could see the fort, torn here and there with shot—could see the shells bursting about it, and brick and stone flying now and then as a round shot buried itself in the walls. None of the garrison was in sight—they were firing only the lower tier of guns. Upon the half-dozen surrounding batteries, however, he could see the gunners plainly; they would leap upon the breastworks after each shot, watching to see the effect of it, cheering and waving their caps. The fire of Sumter appeared to do them no particular harm, so far as Allan could see. Upon the island near Fort Moultrie was a village and a summer hotel, the latter crowded with guests, ladies and gentlemen who had gone there to watch this holiday warfare, and to see the gallant sons of South Carolina expel the "hirelings of the North."

All day long the cannonade went on, ceasing only with the darkness. No harm had been done, it transpired—the Southern loss consisted of one old mule! The night fell cold and rainy, which put an end to any street demonstrations; but in the hotels and bar-rooms there was carousing until dawn. All night the guns of Moultrie kept up a slow bombardment, a promise for the morrow, and a warning to the fleet outside, which was prevented by the gale from making even an attempt to reenforce the fort.

Promptly at dawn the next morning the fight began again. The day was fine, and the crowds on the Battery, wharves and house-tops of Charleston, were greater than ever. The besiegers began firing red-hot shot; and in the course of the morning the barracks of the fort took fire. Soon the blaze could be seen, and the sky grew black with the smoke. The guns of Sumter slackened—for a time ceased altogether. The crowds cheered madly, and the surrounding batteries thundered on. Allan, who had spent a sleepless night, stood biting his lip in misery. The fort was going to fall!

Charleston cheered when Fort Sumter opened fire again, admiring the pluck of the garrison. Major Anderson was not personally unpopular in the city; it was known that he was a Kentuckian and a state's rights man, and that his heart was not in the fight—he was only doing his duty. In truth the garrison was

[207]

doing its best—it was outnumbered a hundred to one. In the midst of smoke and flame, and with the magazine in peril, the defenders of the fort were obliged to crawl about on the ground with wet cloths over their faces.

Shortly after noon their flagstaff was carried away, and they nailed their flag to the fragment that was left. Not long afterward, however, their firing ceased altogether; and after some delay the besieging cannon also fell silent. A white flag had been raised upon the fort.

There were complications and delay. It transpired that an officious aide of General Beauregard had rowed over, waving his handkerchief, and offering terms which he had had no authority to offer. Finally, however, it was decided to grant them—the garrison was to salute its flag and march out with the honors of war. The news was placarded about Charleston, and that night the city gave itself up to rejoicing: the streets thronged, and every house blazing with lights, bonfires, torchlight processions, military paradings everywhere, bands of music, and generals and senators making speeches from doorsteps and the balconies of hotels. It was Saturday night; and on the morrow the fort was to be evacuated—there would be services of thanksgiving in all the churches, and in the Roman Catholic church a "te deum" in honor of the glorious victory. In the midst of it all Allan made his way to the depot, and took a train for the North.

He spent that night in Wilmington, North Carolina. The quay where the ferry-boat landed was piled high with cannon-balls, and there was a military camp near by. All through the evening the scenes of Charleston were repeated; and when he got up in the morning he was surprised to find that the uproar was worse than ever. He judged that something new must have happened, and he dressed in haste and ran out to the street. Then a thunderbolt struck in the shape of a newspaper announcement with flaring headlines:—

A PROCLAMATION
By the President of the United States:
"Whereas the laws of the United States have been for

[208]

some time past and are now opposed, and the execution thereof obstructed, in the States of South Carolina, Georgia, Alabama, Florida, Mississippi, Louisiana, and Texas, by combinations too powerful to be suppressed by the ordinary course of judicial proceedings, or by the powers vested in the marshals by law: now, therefore I, Abraham Lincoln, President of the United States, in virtue of the power in me vested by the Constitution and the laws, have thought fit to call forth, and hereby do call forth, the militia of the several States of the Union to the aggregate number of 75,000, in order to suppress said combination and to cause the laws to be duly executed."

It was to be war then—war! The papers were full of it—and here on the streets was a hoarse, surging mob of men, all of them armed—some even with pikes—screaming and yelling. The Abolition hordes were coming! And any one who would climb upon a step and make a speech might have a dense throng around him in an instant—cheering for "Jeff Davis" and the new Confederacy. Allan was the more surprised, because North Carolina had not yet seceded, and was one of the States whose "latent Union sentiment" had been an endless topic at the North.

But at every station it was the same—at every place where the train even crossed a road there was a crowd. At one stop there was a little church with a grove beside it, and a regiment tented beneath the trees; at another a troop of cavalry picketed in the main street of a town, so that one looked down a long lane of horses, prancing in the midst of the wild confusion. At a third place they were raising a "secession pole," draped with bunting— a ceremony which the train honored by waiting until it was over. At still a fourth—a little backwoods station—Allan saw an extraordinary sight. A company of volunteers was gathered there, clad in gray homespun shirts and "butternut" trousers, and armed for the most part with "squirrel guns"; and they were all singing like fury. Standing upon an overturned barrel an old gentleman was leading them—a man with white hair and long white mustaches; he had a sword in one hand for a baton, and he swung it six feet at a beat. His face was dripping with perspiration, and distorted with passion—a more demoniac-looking creature Allan had never dreamed of in his life. The crowd sang one song after him, then he roared for another, and another; as the train rolled out of the depot they were in the midst of a strange composition—

"Want a weapon? Gather a brick—
Club or cudgel, or stone or stick;
Anything with a blade or butt,
Anything that can cleave or cut!
Anything heavy, or hard, or keen;
Any sort of a slaying-machine!"

On Monday evening he came to Weldon, where he learned that his way to Washington through Richmond was blocked by the floods. He would be obliged to wait until morning and go by way of Norfolk. In Weldon was a bulletin-board with a crowd about it. The governor of Kentucky had just telegraphed to the President refusing to comply with his demand for troops; it was said that the governors of Virginia and North Carolina were on the point of doing likewise. In Richmond, the Virginia convention was then in session, and the day had been one of stormy debate; the convention had adjourned until the following day, leaving the question still undecided. It was said, none the less, that troops were already moving upon Washington, which a member of the cabinet in Montgomery had declared would fall by the first of May.

Still more eagerly Allan looked for the news from the North. It was meagre, but what came was startling. Senator Douglas had formally announced his intention to support Lincoln; and in New York, Philadelphia, Trenton, and other Northern cities, immense crowds had paraded, compelling suspected persons to display Union flags, and wrecking the offices of pro-Southern journals. One read it twice before he could believe the news—that the office of the New York *Herald,* "the mob-newspaper," had been mobbed.

The scenes which Allan witnessed in Virginia were like those in North Carolina; he travelled again in a train full of soldiers, and arriving at evening in sleepy little Norfolk, he found it more ablaze with excitement than any place he had seen so far. Companies had been pouring into the city from all over the State; for just across the river was the Gosport navy-yard, one of the largest in the country, and lying there were about a dozen vessels of war, including eight frigates—one of them a huge steam-frigate, the *Merrimac*. Here also were some two thousand cannon, an immense granite dry-dock, and military stores to the value of nine or ten millions of dollars—all without a garrison to protect it! It was known that the government at Washington was alarmed about it, and that work was being rushed upon the *Merrimac* to get her out in safety.

But most of the officers in the yard were Southerners, and hence there had been many delays. On the night of Allan's arrival two vessels were taken out by the secessionists and sunk in the channel to block it.

He found to his dismay that the steamer for Baltimore had been seized, and that his own way was blocked. With the swiftness with which events were moving, the loss of a day or two now might mean that he would never reach the North at all. Already he had heard wild rumors that Washington had been seized; it had long been whispered that one Ben McCullough, the leader of a company of rangers of Mexican War fame, was assembling five thousand troopers in Virginia for that purpose. Merely to inquire about a method of escape was to render one's self an object of suspicion in Norfolk.

There were bulletin-boards and excited crowds about them. He read the dispatch which the governor of Missouri had sent to "Old Abe," expressing himself with praiseworthy frankness— "Your requisition [for troops] in my judgment is illegal, unconstitutional and revolutionary in its object, inhuman and diabolical." On the other hand it was stated that the militia of Massachusetts were that day mustering in Boston, and that one regiment would start for Washington on the morrow. These and other items from the North gave glimpses of a state of affairs in which Allan hardly dared to believe.

In the morning there came a report that President Davis had

issued a proclamation offering to commission privateers; also, on that day, the convention in Richmond ordained the secession of the State—and though the step was supposed to be secret, it leaked out and was whispered in Norfolk. That was a fearful rumor for many, there and elsewhere throughout Virginia. Hers had been the chief part in the making of this Union, and hers the last agonized attempt to save it; now came the word that all hope was gone—and that her soil was to be made the battle-ground of two empires of warring brothers. How many families it rent in half!—there were officers in the military and naval service who had spent their lives in guarding the stars and stripes, and each man now had to choose, either to make war upon the flag, or to follow it and make war upon his home. Not all of them were young, and could say as did one Virginia captain, sent to watch the bridge which led into Washington: "If any rebels come tonight, boys, we'll blow them to hell; but tomorrow be careful, for I shall be a rebel myself!" In Washington was that Colonel Lee whom Allan had seen at Harper's Ferry on the fateful night of John Brown's insurrection; to Robert E. Lee, the most trusted officer of the army, General Scott, also a Virginian, now offered the command of it—and he went away to his home across the river to wrestle with the dreadful problem. That day, also, in a house in Norfolk, there sat two captains of the navy who had given between them a century to the service. They were Virginians both, and they labored with each other, pleading, each of them, with tears in his eyes—through the night, and until the break of day, but all in vain. One of them, Captain Arthur Sinclair, went South to ruin and death; the other went North—his name was David Farragut.

Before that day was gone, Allan's impatience had reached its climax; he found a boatman to ferry him over to Portsmouth, and thence he made his way to the navy-yard. He judged it likely that at a critical time such as this there would be constant communication between the yard and Washington. In the midst of the confusion and din of preparation, he found an officer to listen to his plea. He had letters in his pocket by which he could prove his story; so he obtained permission to travel on a despatch-boat which was to leave that night. It bore a young engineer of the navy, whose errand it was—though Allan knew nothing of it—to carry to Washington the startling tidings that the commandant of the yard had refused to obey the orders sent him, that the *Merrimac* should put to sea. Three days later the vessel, with all the others, and nearly everything else in the place, was in flames.

It was the afternoon of the eighteenth, of that momentous month of April, that Allan found himself at last in Washington. Everything there was feverish with excitement. Union flags fluttered from all the buildings, public and private—how beautfiul these flags had come to be! Allan had not believed the tales he had heard, and hoped that his fears for the capital would vanish when he reached it; but he found now that the city was a whirlpool of rumors, shaken every hour with a new alarm. Virginia was moving on Harper's Ferry, and McCullough's raiders were to strike that night. Ex-Governor Wise was leaving Richmond with troops—uprisings were occurring in Maryland—mobs were sacking Baltimore—bridges were burning, telegraph wires were down. Everywhere he heard a fresh story; and always one terrible chorus, "No troops yet from the North!" It had been three days since the call, and still they did not come! Allan went into Willard's Hotel, which was packed; he could see that nearly all the people there were Southerners, and they talked to each other apart, and in whispers. It was said that General Scott was dreading the outbreak of a conspiracy that night, and had turned the Capitol building into an arsenal for the defence of the President and his cabinet.

Allan bought newspapers, and went down the street, reading them, darting his eyes from column to column, his cheeks flushed and his hands trembling. The country was up! There were public meetings in every city, flags from every house, a universal holiday through sixteen States. Companies were offering from every town, banks lending funds, business houses and public councils subscribing for the support of soldiers. East and West, the fervor was like that in the South. Douglas had come out for the war, so had Buchanan, and even the mayor of New York, who had wanted that city to secede, had issued an address blazing with patriotic ardor for the Union. There were no longer any political parties, no longer any classes; clergymen and college professors were enlisting by the side of day-laborers and clerks, "leaving all things to save the Republic." The very newspapers in which he read these reports were changed—the meanest reporter or correspondent was suddenly become a seer of visions, a man with a duty and a faith, speaking invocations and prophecies. The whole face of America was altered—all the selfishness in it was gone, all the cowardice, the blindness. Even the thugs and black-legs of the Bowery were organizing a regiment, and being presented with Bibles!

The voice of Allan's Grandfather Montague spoke to him again—those lessons which as a child he had only partially understood—how terribly he understood them now: that America was humanity, it was for the brotherhood of man, its hope was the hope of man, and its purpose the purpose of God. The old man had told of the soldiers on both sides of Allan's family who had died for the Union; for it was in union that her strength lay. These things made the North as well as the South Allan's country. He loved both—and now he must fight for both—to keep them one.

From the cities and the farms, from the mountains and the prairies, from the East and the West they were coming at last, to save the heritage of their fathers. And Massachusetts, glorious old Massachusetts, was leading them! They had asked her for two regiments and she was sending five. The banks of Boston had offered the money, and the same night the call had come the troops began to gather. They were pouring into the city from every county in the State and their towns were voting them money, and flags, and clothing, and whatever else they could need. They were quartered in Faneuil Hall—the "Cradle of Liberty"—where Hancock and Allan's ancestor Otis watched over their slumber!

Allan looked for the Fifth Regiment—it was in the Fifth that he had made up his mind to enlist, with his Northern cousin and his friends. He saw no mention of it; but the Sixth had left the afternoon before, and was due in Washington the next morning;

the Eighth had left the same evening, and the rest were close behind. On the morrow the New York "Seventh" would start, the "dandy" regiment of that city.

CHAPTER IV

Allan sent a telegram to Jack, inquiring about the regiment; and when he started up Pennsylvania Avenue he saw a group of officers galloping along, and some artillerymen with a small field-gun. They were going toward the Capitol, and he watched them go by in a cloud of dust, and then set out to follow. But he stopped, because he saw a familiar figure on the other side of the avenue. He darted across, calling, and the man turned—yes, it was Edward Lovejoy!

The Westerner seized his hand. "You got my message?"

"Message. No, I got no message."

"I wired you ten days ago," said Lovejoy, "telling you there'd be war."

"I didn't get it," Allan answered. "But I'm here!"

"You have come in the nick of time. I have been out for the last two hours hunting for men to help save the city tonight!"

Allan stared at him. "What do you mean?"

"We expect an attack," said the other.

"By whom?"

"By every one you see around here! Haven't you seen them whispering in the corners? All day we've been promised troops —and they don't come, they don't come! And right now the Virginians are marching on Harper's Ferry, and all the arms there, and the machine-shops and rifle works, are to be burned!"

Allan was struck with dismay. "Come on," Lovejoy said hurriedly; he started, and Allan joined him. "There's no time to be lost about it. Do you know any one to help us here in Washington?"

"Not that I can think of."

"Well, keep a lookout; you can't tell whom you may meet. We need every true man in the city."

"Who's managing this?" Allan asked.

"Private citizens—Cash Clay for one, and Jim Lane, if you know who he is."

"The Kansas leader?"

"Yes. But talk lower; it mustn't be known."

The name of Lane was familiar to Allan as one of the more violent of the free-state leaders in the old Kansas quarrel—a companion of John Brown. Cassius Clay was a Kentuckian, an Abolitionist who had had various adventures as editor of an anti-slavery paper, fighting duels about it in his native State.

"What are you going to do?" Allan asked.

"We are getting some volunteers to patrol the streets for the night, and to guard the White House. If the capital of the country were to go, and all the archives and the public buildings—don't you see it would ruin us? What more would Europe want for a pretext to recognize the rebels?"

"What's the matter with the President? Why doesn't he do something?"

"What *isn't* the matter with him! The country needs a statesman, a man to command—and we've got a simpleton of a backwoods lawyer! He doesn't know anything about anything; he has no tact, no sense—why, some of the stories that people tell of the things he's said and done fairly make your hair stand on end! It doesn't matter to me if the man hasn't ever been into society, and wears black kid gloves at the opera and horrifies the swells of New York. There are men here who'd stand by him if he went to the opera in his shirt-sleeves. But the man is incompetence spelt in letters a foot high—they say it takes him a week to make up his mind about a country postoffice, and then he changes it overnight."

Lovejoy strode on, his brows knit. "And yet," he continued, "he means well—he's kindhearted, you can see that by just looking at him. I stood in front of him while he read his Inaugural, and I don't think I ever saw anything so pathetic. The poor man was so nervous he could hardly hold the manuscript, and his spectacles seemed to get moist with his agitation. He couldn't see through them, and his hands shook so he couldn't manage to wipe them, and his voice kept breaking—I thought he was going all to pieces."

"All that *is* fearfully discouraging," said Allan.

"No!" the other declared. "No! it needn't be discouraging—not with the temper of the country as it is. It will sweep everything before it, it will find the way—it will find some man to take charge in the end. That is the wonder of Democracy. It simply means that we men who are to do the fighting have got to get in and fight so much the harder. Above all, that we've got to do it quickly or the country'll be bankrupt. Go about in these hotels in Washington and use your eyes—last week they were jammed with office-seekers, but already there's a bigger horde coming down—of contractors! They've come like buzzards—there are droves of them on every train, and they're going to eat the *heart* out of the country."

The speaker strode on angrily. Then, "Do you know anything about Cameron? Well, he's Mr. Lincoln's Secretary of War—a Pennsylvania politician whom Lincoln's managers bribed with a cabinet position to get his delegates at Chicago. He's one of those gentlemen in politics who are honest, and have 'heelers' to do the dirty work. I suppose there's been more rottenness in Pennsylvania politics under his rule than there has been anywhere else in the country outside of New York. And now he's got charge of the pocketbook of the nation, and all the boys are out celebrating. Money will have to be spent hand over fist, you know—the things must be had, and no time to haggle or ask questions. And of course no one will ever know about it—except that you and I who are to do the work will have shoddy blankets, and shoes that fall apart, and guns that won't shoot, and powder that won't burn. For every dollar that buys anything there'll be two stolen besides."

Lovejoy raved on; but soon their attention was attracted by the sound of distant cheering, that seemed to grow louder as they listened. Everything on the street stood still; and then came the faint strains of military music, and Lovejoy gave a yell. "It's the troops! They've come!"

Every moment the music came nearer, an incessant shouting with it. The people on the avenue broke into cheers—the head of a column had swept into sight—and was coming on, in a cloud of dust. There were five companies of Pennsylvania troops. They had come on without waiting for arms—there were arms enough in Washington. They were spread out in open formation to disguise the paucity of their numbers, and they came with music and waving of banners. They enrolled themselves for the night in Lane's "Frontier Guards," which were assembling upon the Capitol grounds. The doors and windows of the Capitol building were boarded up and barricaded, a breastwork of cement barrels piled along the front of the portico, and cannon and sentries guarding every approach. The temporary volunteers were receiving their arms—a motley assemblage, "down-East" Yankees and Kansas frontiersmen, would-be postmasters, farmers, clergymen, travelling salesmen, and sightseers. There was "Jim" Lane himself, talking always as if he were on the stump, brandishing a shiny new sword—a wild personage wearing a calfskin vest and sealskin coat. He had been a lifelong politician, and was soon to be a general of armies; by him the weird command was marched to the White House, and into the "East Room," one of the halls of state of the presidential mansion. Here were gorgeous plush upholstery and hangings, frescoed ceilings, velvet carpets, and glowing chandeliers; and here the volunteers stacked their muskets, unslung their knapsacks and cartridge-boxes, and spread themselves for the night. It was a thing never to be forgotten, this assemblage of men, old and young, rich and poor, big and little, clad in every kind of costume, lined up and in desperate seriousness taking their first lessons in squad drill. Later you might have seen them stretched out in the corners, sound asleep, or with their feet on the sofas, reading newspapers, or squatting in groups on the carpet, playing cards.

No uprising occurred to disturb them or to test their resolution. They had one unexpected experience in the course of the evening, however—a startling one for Allan. He noticed a group gathered in the doorway, and several moving to join it; Lovejoy nudged him and whispered, "Look there!"

In the great doorway there had appeared an enormous figure of a man, reaching nearly to the top of it, his impossible height accentuated by his leanness and by the tall "stove-pipe" hat set upon his head. He was dressed all in black, in a suit that was new but did not fit him, so he looked ill-at-ease, like a farm-hand on his way to a prayer meeting. Out of the sleeves there projected an enormous pair of hands, which he seemed not to know where to put. He wore a loose collar and a carelessly knotted tie, the ends of which stuck out over his coat; and from this collar there rose a scrawny, yellow neck, surmounted by the most peculiar head Allan had ever seen. On top was a shock of dark, rebellious hair—below it a rough stubble of beard. The face seemed to be all nose and mouth between a pair of broad, outstanding ears. Allan could scarcely see the small twinkling eyes. He could see enough, however, to connect the face with familiar pictures; he caught Lovejoy's arm, whispering, "It's the President!"

"It's the President," Lovejoy responded.

Most of the men in the room rose to their feet as Mr. Lincoln, a smile lighting up his odd features, looked about him. "Be careful of my furniture, boys," he said. "It's only mine for a while, you know, and I have to pass it along in good condition."

"We'll take care of it, Mr. President," some one replied.

"Maybe," went on the other, laughing, "the rebels are coming to capture it. I don't care how much you spoil it then."

"They'll never get it!" cried several voices. "Never—don't you worry!" The men were beginning to crowd round the President, whose huge figure towered head and shoulders—plus an enormous cylinder of a hat—above them. Standing in front of him was a little drummer boy, in the uniform of the regular army; Mr. Lincoln put his hand on the shoulder of this small personage, and, with chuckles, demanded: "Any of you people ever heard" (Mr. Lincoln pronounced it "heerd") "the story of the Peterby boys and the mule?"

"No," said several eager voices.

"You fellows have come from so many parts of the world. I didn't know but what there might be somebody from Sangamon County, out my way. If there was, he'd have surely heerd of the Peterby boys and the mule."

"Tell it," some one urged.

"That's what I'm going to do," was the reply; and when the laughter and applause had ceased, the President went on, enjoyment of his own story wrinkling his face.

"There were six of the Peterby boys in the Sangamon Bottom," he began, "and the biggest of them was about twenty, the youngest about eleven, and there never had been any one of them known to do any work. Naturally, they were not good neighbors; and they lived next to an old fellow named Harper—Captain Harper, we used to call him, though I never knew why—who was the crossest old reprobate a man ever laid eyes on, and was always quarreling with the Peterby boys. They used to rob his cornfield, and he'd watch for them moonlight nights with a shotgun—they never let on to him, but many and many a time they've had to pick some of Captain Harper's bird-shot out of each other's backs with their jackknives! Well, it seems that Captain Harper had a mule that was a fearful mule, and would kick a wagon into matchwood whenever he got excited. He hitched it in the town one day while he went into the store to do his trading, and while he was gone the Peterby boys got a bunch of fire-crackers and set it under the mule." (At this point the narrator fell to laughing so hard that he had to stop for a moment.) "They just had them underneath, and everything ready, and Nick Peterby about to touch a match to them—when all of a sudden here comes old Harper strolling out of the store. Of course they got up and lit out for dear life, expecting to be chased; but instead, the old cuss stood in the door without even swearing, so they turned around and stared at him. 'Go ahead, consarn ye!' says he—'blow him to hell, if you like—I don't care what you do to him!' At that naturally they stared all the harder. 'What do you mean?' cries one of them. 'Mean!' yells Harper, 'I mean you can put a barrel of firecrackers under him if you want to. I've jest sold him and the wagon to your dad!' "

And then, while the soldiers roared, the President bent over and doubled up with laughter. When finally he turned and went away, they could hear the sounds of his mirth all the way down the hall, and up the stairway.

CHAPTER V

"You know," said Lovejoy, when the two had gone apart and sat down, "you know there's something great about a man who can come out of the backwoods into the White House and do as that man does. It may be it's nothing but blindness, but it's blindness that's big in its proportion—it's blindness that amounts to genius! Is it really that he is so obtuse that he doesn't know the effect he produces? Or doesn't he care, or is it a pose, or what? I declare I can't fathom him—he's too much for me."

"The crowd seemed to like it," said Allan; "but does he do like that all the time?"

"That!" cried the other. "That isn't a circumstance. I suppose so far as stories go, and smutty stories in particular, the senators and congressmen when they get together socially tell them about as much as any other men. But this man tells them all the time —he doesn't care who it is, a diplomat or a duke or a bishop; and he doesn't care where it is, at some formality, some reception. And he sends them away with their heads reeling—and doesn't seem to have the slightest idea of it at all! They say, though, that sometimes he uses them to get rid of the office seekers—that he positively scares them out of the place!"

After midnight, the poker-playing and story-telling ceased, and the "Frontier Guards" wrapped themselves in slumber on the floor of their palatial quarters. Toward morning Allan received an answer to his dispatch, informing him that the Fifth had not yet been called; this decided him to continue on to Boston, as he had originally intended. He wished to bid farewell to his family

[221]

there before the fighting came on, and the news in the papers was that the Massachusetts Sixth had left Philadelphia the night before and would surely reach Washington that morning—as also probably the Eighth. That meant, Allan judged, that there was no longer need of fear for the capital; and so, soon after dawn, while the company was still fast asleep, he said good-by to Lovejoy and took the train for the North.

The rumors concerning Harper's Ferry had proven true, and one more calamity had fallen upon the startled nation. The cars were crowded with fugitives, mostly women and children, the families of diplomats and correspondents and other residents of Washington, who were taking flight from the scene of the impending conflict. Everywhere one saw frightened faces, and heard whispered rumors of fresh disasters. Allan kept an anxious lookout, for he expected every minute to pass the train bringing South the troops upon which so much depended. It did not appear, however, and he began to feel alarmed once more, and to wish that he had waited another day.

In a couple of hours they were in Baltimore. The trains from Washington came into Camden Station, and thence each car was drawn separately through Pratt Street by horses, to the President Street Station, about a mile and a half away, where they were again made into a train for Philadelphia. There was some delay upon reaching the city, and Allan left the cars and started to walk.

All that he had read had led him to expect that he would find disorder in Baltimore. But he was not prepared for what he found—the depot and the street for a block around were thronged with excited people, and when he got clear of them and went on he found men running up the street and calling to each other, as if something alarming were just then happening. He saw men pointing up Pratt Street, and hearing distant shouting from that direction, started to run himself. Turning the corner he saw a throng in the distance. "It's the soldiers coming!" shouted a man, in answer to his inquiry.

From all the side streets people were hurrying up, and every moment the uproar became greater. They were in a "tough" part of the city, near the water-front where most of the people were rowdy. Allan noticed that many of them carried sticks, and a few of them more dangerous weapons. He ran on, his heart thumping fast.

The dense mass of people up Pratt Street was coming his way; they were shouting, jeering—the noise was like the roaring of a sea, and it grew each moment louder, and more ominous. At first Allan could only see the crowd, but, coming nearer, he made out that in their midst was one of the railroad cars; they were running before it and beside it, shaking their fists at it, throwing stones at it, cursing and yelling. He halted, thunderstruck; surely no one could have been such a fool as to try to send troops through this city shut up in cars! Why in Heaven's name not let them march through? Had there not been warnings enough—secession-meetings and speeches, threats in the newspapers, predictions from the South? The "plug-ugly" of Baltimore, a ferocious rowdy, bred out of Slavery for political purposes, was known by reputation all over the country; and to send the soldiers through the haunts of such a creature, shut up in cars like sheep!

Allan's anxiety was all the greater, for these, he knew, must be the Massachusetts troops. The mob was close enough now for him to see them plainly; they came on at a run—for the horses of the car were trotting—a throng of howling ruffians, old and young, some of them in their shirt-sleeves, some drunk, all with paving-stones or clubs in their hands. The windows of the car were closed, and the curtains drawn, and the inmates gave no sign. The crowd beat upon it, and now and then they would try to stop the horses. The windows of all the houses along the way were open, and from them people yelled imprecations. "Bean-eaters," they called Bostonians, "mamma's darlings, kidgloved soldier boys, counter-jumpers," and innumerable other epithets. Allan stepped into a doorway while the storm swept by, trailing out behind for a block or two. He thought of following, but instead went on, knowing that there would be other cars to come. The result of the criminal folly of those in charge would of course be that the regiment would be split up into two or three dozen sections, instead of marching as a unit.

He was not mistaken; soon he heard the roar of another mob, and saw another car sweep round the corner far down the street. It came on like the earlier one, only this time the crowd seemed more dense and more violent. It went by, and again and again the same thing happened. One could not but conclude that this outbreak was premeditated, for the rowdies were pouring in from every direction, sometimes whole gangs of them flying down the side streets together, and each man of them with a weapon ready to hand. Guns and pistols were becoming frequent, and Allan noticed that several loads of paving-stones had been dumped on Pratt Street, of which the mob was not failing to take advantage. He was in the centre of the whirlpool, and never had he seen such rage upon the faces of men, never had he heard such furious imprecations. Every time a car came by the yelling would swell into a roar, the rush of the crowd become like a charge of cavalry, sweeping everything before it, and there would be no way for him to escape save by running into a side street or an open door-way. Several times he heard shots fired; and once as a car was directly opposite him a man hurled a cobblestone clean through the side of it. At the same time others were trying to drag the driver from his place. Allan followed, feeling sure that the climax was coming now—that the troops would be compelled to come out.

Before long, however, he turned back, for up the street he saw that they were trying to tear up the track. For lack of better tools they had taken an anchor off a schooner which lay in the basin, and whose bowsprit projected out over the sidewalk. When he reached the place, they had dug a hole with a pickaxe and had gotten one prong of the anchor under the track, and were ripping it up. At the same time down a side street came a drunken Irish-man, roaring and singing, driving a mule and a cart full of gravel; this he upset on the track, to the delight of the mob that sur-rounded him. The press was now so great that it was not easy to move on the street—those who had escorted the first cars to the depot had no doubt returned. A little way farther on, Jones's Falls—a creek which ran through Baltimore—crossed the street, and here they were breaking up the planks of the bridge to bar the way. Standing upon an empty barrel was a black-whiskered desperado with a bowie-knife in his hand, making a speech, principally of oaths. "Don't let another one of them get by!" was the burden of his remarks. "Kill the damned nigger-thieves! Send them to hell where they come from!"

The next car came into sight, and the crowds surged on to meet it; every pane of glass in it was shattered already, and one of the horses which hauled it had been shot in the leg and could hardly move; the car had been derailed somehow, and was bumping along on the rough cobblestones. Leaping at the windows of it were men with knives and revolvers, and as it came near Allan there were several shots. A moment or two later there came a blaze of light from the windows of one side, and the mob fell back, screaming with rage. Two men lay rolling on the ground, and a third was dragging himself away from the track in front. A fellow rushed by Allan, cursing, with blood pouring from the sleeve of his coat.

The car thumped on to where the gravel lay upon the track, with two loaded grocery wagons upset beyond it. The doors opened and soldiers rushed out and began to remove the obstructions. They had not proceeded far, before a man ran up to them; he seemed to be expostulating with the officers in command, and Allan heard some one near him say that it was the mayor of the city. In a few moments the excited colloquy ended with the horses being taken to the other end of the car, the soldiers reentering it, and the driver whipping up and returning in the direction from which they had come. At this sign of the victory the crowd surged forward again, roaring with delight.

Allan followed, blazing with anger. They were going to give up, then! They were going to give up and leave the capital of the nation to its fate, because there was no man there with resolution enough to put himself at the head of the regiment and march it through that villainous horde! Would there never be an end to the humiliation, would the nation never find its manhood?

Borne along in the torrent of people he went back with the car to the President Street Station—and there he saw a sight that changed his mood—the rest of the regiment was leaving the train and forming upon the street!

He could not see them, after they had stepped from the car platforms, for the crowd which surged about them. He could see their flags, however—there was the Massachusetts State flag, and there was a regimental flag with their number on it—yes, it was the long expected Sixth! There were four companies left to make the march, some two hundred men in all; much to Allan's relief every man he saw come out had a musket in his hand. Above the uproar he heard the sharp, determined commands of the officers, and a few moments later the crowd surged backwards, and the flags began their advance.

A howl went up from the mob; a man pushed past Allan, a huge brute with the voice of a stentor, and a secession flag nailed upon a pole in his hands. The crowd massed themselves behind him, and rushed upon the troops, jeering, throwing stones, and yelling for "Jeff Davis." Allan lost sight of the man, but he could follow the secession flag; he saw it strike at the flag of the regiment and knock it down; then, running up the steps of a house, he was just in time to see an officer leap out with drawn sword, and slamming the hilt of it into the ruffian's face, knock him backwards. He seized the secession flag, and ripping it from the pole, stuffed it into his pocket.

At the head of the column now marched the gentleman Allan had been told was the mayor of Baltimore; he was exhorting and imploring, and with half a dozen policemen was constantly beating back the throng from in front of the advancing troops. His position was a perilous one, for brickbats and paving-stones were flying, and occasionally there came a shot; Allan saw a man on the roof of one of the houses hurl down a plank upon the column, knocking one of the militiamen senseless. A few moments afterwards he saw another man standing in an upstairs window, with a gun in his hand; he raised it and took aim, and Allan cried out a warning. But one of the soldiers had seen it also, and there was a flash and a report, and the man in the window tottered and pitched headlong to the street.

Fully ten thousand yelling demons were now swarming about the little company, and the din was indescribable. Every now and then shots would be fired, sometimes half a dozen in succession. Allan turned into a side street until the troops had passed, then when the rear of the column was by, he tried to fall in behind it and follow, but it was at least two blocks distant before he could get into Pratt Street. The frenzy of the mob was now demoniac; there were women among them, too, ragged creatures with streaming hair and bloodshot eyes, the women of the slums. Firing was still going on, and from time to time Allan saw wounded men being carried into houses. He saw also three dead militiamen; one with a bullet hole in his face. The mob had stripped him of his weapons, and beaten him with cudgels and paving-stones.

Before long the crowd ahead came to a halt, and from the deafening roar Allan became convinced that the column had been blocked and a massacre begun. There was no way for him to get forward, and so he passed an agonized quarter of an hour before he finally learned what had happened—the mob had succeeded in blocking itself at the bridge instead of the troops; the latter had skipped across upon the rafters, a process which naturally took the thousands who followed a much longer time. By the time Allan got to the bridge the pressure had ceased, and he heard it said that the "nigger-thieves" were on the cars and out of the city. He drew a breath of relief, having no means of knowing the true state of the case—that the tracks had been torn up in front, and that the train was surrounded with a greater crowd than ever.

Allan walked to the station where these troops had come into Baltimore, and where he meant to take the train to Philadelphia. He found there about a thousand Pennsylvania troops, unarmed, with the mob surrounding them; already the latter had driven out the unfortunate musicians of the Sixth Massachusetts, who had been left behind, and who were now flying for their lives through the city. The unarmed men in the cars were in desperate plight, for they could not go forward, and there was no engine to be had to take them back. Quite a crowd of Union sympathizers had gathered about to defend them, however, and Allan, snatching up a stick, plunged into the melee and joined these. They had held the crowd at bay for ten or fifteen minutes, when city police arrived, and these, brandishing their clubs and revolvers, kept up the fight until a locomotive came and the train started off. Allan succeeded in getting into one of the cars—it was not a time to stand upon ceremony. His forehead was cut, and his clothing torn.

When he reached Philadelphia he learned that the telegraph wires were cut; and the bridges outside of Baltimore were said to have been fired. The accounts of the "massacre" in Baltimore told of hundreds of the Sixth having been killed, and Allan had no means of knowing that this was untrue. He boarded the train again, and went with sinking heart, foreseeing that the panic prevailing would cause more delay, and still more peril to Washington. On the way to New York Allan passed a train with some troops on board, and toward the close of the afternoon he arrived in Jersey City. There was a great crowd, crazy for the news. The telegraph wires having been cut, the only way newspaper reporters could get news was from Allan's train, and so they were waiting at Jersey City. From there Allan had wired his cousin to let him know of any sudden orders the Boston regiment might receive. Then he took the ferry-boat to New York City, and was driven to the hotel, where he found a message which Jack had sent him two days earlier. He tore it open, and while the crowd in the corridors stared at his torn and blood-stained clothing, he read the news that Jack's company would arrive from Boston in time to take the train with the New York Seventh.

"What time does the Seventh march?" Allan asked the hotel clerk.

"They may have started now," was the answer. "They were to leave this afternoon."

CHAPTER VI

Allan was sure that the regiment had not passed him anywhere, but still he was anxious, and sprang into a cab and drove in haste to the Armory, on Lafayette Place. He found that he was in time. Friends and relatives of the militiamen were begging to be admitted, and Allan had difficulty in getting by. He learned, however, that the "Cambridge Tigers" had arrived, and when he declared that his errand was to enlist, the doorkeepers let him pass.

The main hall of the Armory was a scene of confusion; there was packing of knapsacks, rolling of blankets, loading of guns; men running in every direction, muskets stacked here and there; piles of baggage, banners, drums, musical instruments, camp-kettles, upon the floor; and above all a babel of voices, shouts and laughter, cries of command. Allan saw the flag of the Massachusetts company in one corner, and made his way toward it. There was Jack, flushed with excitement, talking eagerly; and suddenly catching sight of his cousin he made a dash for him, crying, "Well, old man!"

Then he noticed Allan's condition. "What the devil has happened to you?" he asked.

"I have been through Baltimore," was the reply.

Jack let out a yell. "He's been through Baltimore!" They were surrounded in an instant—the cry went through the place, "A man from Baltimore!" The militiamen shouted a dozen questions at once, which Allan answered as fast and loudly as he could. He could not say how many had been killed and wounded, but he told what he had seen, and men listened with tense faces and burning cheeks. All day they had talked and thought of nothing but Baltimore, and they were ablaze with indignation. If only they had been there—how different it would have been!

The regiment had been on the point of departure for a couple of hours; and now you could hear the orderlies calling the rolls in the company rooms, the last preliminary to a start.

"I'm glad you've come, old fellow!" exclaimed Jack, again and again. "You are going with us, are you not?"

"Is there room for me?"

"Yes, yes, the regulations call for seventy in a company and we have less than sixty."

"All right, then. I am with you."

"We must hurry," Jack said. "You must get a musket here in the Armory. And perhaps you can get a uniform instead of that bloody coat. Come and see Houghton."

Houghton was the captain of the company. "He had a pull, and got us this chance," Jack explained, as they started across the hall. "You've no idea what a time there is in Boston, with all the men and the companies that want to go, and those that want to raise more companies! Our colonel's a slow-poke, and we thought we were left; but then we learned that the Eighth had gone one company short, and Houghton went to beg for the place. There were half a dozen ahead of him, but he was a classmate of the governor's in college, and so he got it. Just think—we only got the notice about four o'clock this morning!"

So Allan's cousin rushed on as they hurried to find their captain. "Five regiments have gone out of Boston in five days—and there are new companies drilling already in every town in the State!"

The formalities of Allan's enlistment were brief. There was no uniform for him, but they were able to give him what would serve for the time—one of those long gray coats which Governor Andrew had gotten himself into hot water for buying three months before. Also they gave him a musket—and how his fingers had itched for a musket in Baltimore that morning!

"How is the family?" Allan inquired, when the two were back in their corner.

"Everyone is well. Father says he's coming down to Washington to see us, if we don't get the rebels cleared out too soon. How happy he'll be to see you and me together."

"I'll be glad to see him, you may be sure," Allan declared.

[230]

The men of the company came crowding around Allan to welcome him. They were an unusual aggregation of soldiers, the "Cambridge Tigers"; there were a few mechanics and clerks among them, but for the most part they represented the wealth and culture of the college town. There were a score or so of the older Harvard men among them, and a few from other colleges.

They soon heard words of command, and the companies began to form and file out. The Massachusetts men were to bring up the rear, and so they waited, watching the others donning their overcoats and slinging their knapsacks, and lowering the two howitzers of the regiment by the rear stairway. As the first of the troops appeared outside, the usual roar from the crowd came rolling in. Allan was used to the cheering now; it never failed to give encouragement to marching men, in the North as it had done in the South.

Allan took one swift glance, and as far as the eye could see there were people waving handkerchiefs and hats and flags, and yelling like mad—the police had tried to hold the crowd back from where the troops were forming on the street; but mothers and sisters and sweethearts had broken through, and every other man had a pair of arms about his neck, and a sobbing face on his shoulder. Most of the volunteers were white about the lips, but they pressed them together tightly, trying hard not to be too much moved. Allan and his company had to struggle all the way to the rear of the march; there were but few friends to see the Bostonians off, but the crowd did its best to play the part—men slapped them on the back as they passed and shouted praise; women waved handkerchiefs, and threw them flowers. As the "Tigers" were in Cambridge, so the Seventh was the *corps d'elite* of New York; its members came from the wealth and fashion of the metropolis, and their friends were here to see them go. Flowers and fruit and sandwiches, bonbons and boxes of candy, cigars and pipes were pressed into their hands—a fellow from the Bowery offered his bulldog, all he had, and there was a soldier who had a purse thrust upon him and afterwards found ten five-dollar gold pieces in it.

Suddenly past the long line there struggled a group of policemen, driving back the throng; and far down the street they heard the strains of the band, and the quick commands of the officers. The men tore themselves free; there were last frantic partings, the crowd scattered here and there, and line by line the regiment swung into column, slowly at first, then faster and faster, then in full swing. They were off!

They swung into Broadway—and what a sight was there! Flags, flags, flags! Flags upon the housetops, flags in the steeples, flags in the windows, flags in people's hands. There were streamers across the street, bunting in the windows—the great thoroughfare was a canyon of flags, and bunting and—people! And countless thousands were singing,

> "Land where my fathers died,
> Land of the pilgrim's pride,
> From every mountain side
> Let Freedom ring!"

There was no man there so dull but felt his heart pounding, shaken with emotions of which he had never dreamed. They were going to war! No holiday parade was this—they were going to war! Within a few hours the regiment would be in the streets of Baltimore, with the furies raging about it, with death stalking its ranks. Allan remembered the stories about soldiers of the Revolutionary War in which Grandfather Montague had fought. "Those soldiers had wives and children, and hopes unuttered," he had said; "yet they marched out into battle, and died for their country—to make her and to keep her free . . . There is nothing that can ever take her place; not friendship, nor love, nor anything else in life can be so precious."

And now the old man's grandsons were marching to protect that freedom—but against each other!

At last they turned off Broadway. Here again were banners, faces, cheers, and far down the street a ferry-boat, sheds, wagons, and—humanity! Whistles were blowing in the harbor, bells were ringing—and the men staggered on, the people surging in, overwhelming them; the regiment was swallowed up, the ranks broken, the march lost. Every man fought his way through as he could, and when at last they were all on board and the crowd forced back and the ferry-boat had swung out into the river, the silence was oppressive.

Allan sat apart, his forehead in his hands, and his face hot. Suddenly he heard a voice beside him, saying, "You have a lot of work to do, comrade, before the end."

He looked up, a little startled. "Who are you?" he asked.

"I am the sergeant of your company," said the man, who spoke with a slight German accent. "When you have had some experience you won't let yourself go like that—one needs all his strength for fighting."

"I suppose so!" Allan answered in a tired voice.

"I have been through a war," said the sergeant. "I know."

BOOK V

The Battle

🌷

CHAPTER I

In Jersey City there were twenty thousand people to greet them; the depot was packed solid, and a platoon of police had to clear the way with clubs. And after they had started, they found a throng all along the railroad tracks, continuing even after they had left the town. There was nowhere a car's length without a person—and this was true all the way to Philadelphia. There were thousands of people at every stop, and enough refreshments offered them for a supper once an hour. The cheering seemed never to cease. At a station they passed at two o'clock in the morning they found a group of old ladies waiting for them with pails of ice-water; and when they came into Philadelphia toward morning, there was a crowd there, and a banquet, disguised as a breakfast, prepared for them at all the hotels.

Here it transpired that their desire to march through Baltimore was not to be gratified. The administration had given way before the frantic demands of the authorities of the city, and had promised that no more troops should come through it! At that hour Baltimore was in the hands of a mob, which had sacked the gun shops and the liquor stores; the streets were barricaded and guarded by artillery and cavalry, and companies of secessionists were hurrying in from the neighborhood. The wildest rumors as to the fate of Washington prevailed.

Here Allan's company joined the Massachusetts regiment to which it was ordered, and came under the command of its officer, one Benjamin Butler, destined to fame. General Butler had been a criminal lawyer, not of the highest reputability, and a pro-slavery Democratic politician whose boast it was that he had voted fifty-seven times for Jefferson Davis in the Charleston convention the year before. But he disapproved of secession, and when the call came for four regiments from Massachusetts, as a general of militia he had been first to apply and get command of them. He was cross-eyed and coarse in appearance, but aggressive and determined, and with a kind of humor of his own. At present he was casting about him for some way of reaching Washington, deciding finally to take the railroad ferry-boat at Havre-de-Grace, and from there steam to Annapolis. Since the colonel of the New York Seventh preferred to sail directly from Philadelphia to Washington, the two regiments now parted, the Eighth Massachusetts leaving the city at eleven in the morning.

Rumor had it that the ferry-boat was in the hands of the secessionists, and so the regiment prepared for a fight; the general came through the train and gave elaborate directions as to their action. The fight did not come off, but the directions were enough to frighten one man so that he leaped from the moving train and dashed into the woods, to the intense amusement of his comrades. Late in the afternoon they boarded the huge ferry-boat *Maryland,* and steamed down the Susquehanna. While they were making the trip, all business in New York was at a standstill, and a half million people were thronged in Union Square, listening to patriotic speeches from men of all parties.

The "Cambridge Tigers" reached Annapolis at midnight, finding the town awake, with lights flashing here and there, and signal rockets in the sky. This checked the ardent general's determination to land, and he cast anchor. Before long an officer of the Naval Academy came on board to say that the governor of Maryland forbade the troops to land. It transpired that the commandant of the place was a Union man, and was in fear of an immediate attack. The frigate *Constitution,* "Old Ironsides," now a school-ship, was moored in front of the town, and the secessionist militia had been drilling in full sight of her daily. Reports had it that the railroad to Washington had been destroyed and the cars removed, and that large parties of the secessionists were gathered in the interior.

Time was precious, but the general hesitated; he fell to parleying with the mayor of Annapolis and the governor of the State, both of whom were on hand, and frantic at the idea of "Northern troops" invading the soil of Maryland. These gentlemen professed to be loyal, in spite of their belief in "states' rights"; the governor was just then keeping the wires hot with his messages to Washington, imploring the Secretary of State to offer a truce, "so that the effusion of blood might be prevented." He went on respectfully to offer his solution of the difficulty—that the British Ambassador, Lord Lyons, "be requested to act as mediator between the contending parties of our country."

The *Constitution* was stuck fast upon a mud-bank, and in the morning the ferry-boat passed the time trying to drag her off. In this it was finally successful, whereupon General Butler issued a stirring manifesto to the regiment. "This is a sufficient triumph of right," he declared, "a sufficient triumph for us," and went on to add that by this the blood of their friends shed by the Baltimore mob was "avenged." The rejoicing over the achievement was, however, somewhat damped by the discovery that the *Maryland* herself had run on a mud-bank, and that the regiment was therefore helpless.

Here it spent the day and night; it had run short of water and provisions—there was only enough for "a biscuit and an inch of salt pork" per man. They were so crowded on board that there was scarcely room to move, and for beds they had nothing more attractive than coal-bags. Exposed as they were to a broiling sun, the young gentlemen of Cambridge, including Allan and Jack, began to see war as a serious matter.

The long wait passed, however, and in the morning there appeared up the bay the steamer bearing the Seventh, which had been out in the ocean and around Cape Charles. More time was now wasted trying to float the *Maryland;* but finally, in the afternoon, the Seventh was landed at the Naval Academy dock, and then the Massachusetts men were transferred to the steamer and landed also. It was said that four regiments of the secessionists were intrenched at Annapolis Junction, and it was believed by nearly all at the outset that not two-thirds of those who marched would reach Washington alive. At this time the North was in a frenzy, owing to news having come that the Seventh had been surrounded by the "plug-uglies" and cut to pieces; this was also published and believed in the South.

While the hours slipped by, and the officers wondered and waited for reenforcements, the capital was in deadly peril. On Tuesday the Massachusetts men, having determined to march by the railroad, seized the depot. In one of the sheds they found an old, rusty engine. "Can any one repair it?" asked the general. "I can," answered a private—"I made it!" In truth there was scarcely a trade which was not represented in that regiment—one of the officers of the Seventh has recorded his opinion that if the orders had been "Poets to the front!" "Painters present arms!" "Sculptors charge bayonets!" a baker's dozen out of every company would have responded.

The rails of the road, which had been dragged here and there and hidden, were hunted out and the track laid; provisions and stores were gotten together, and the Seventh having meanwhile concluded to join, the two regiments made ready, and on the morrow at daybreak set out to march on foot. Four more steamers had arrived in the night, with reenforcements from the North.

It was a beautiful spring day, and the campaign bade fair to be a picnic excursion; of the much-talked-of enemies there was no sign, and the skirmishers who were sent out in front to look for them soon betook themselves to the more profitable task of looking for the hidden rails. Following them came two companies of the New Englanders, repairing the track, and then the little engine, pushing ahead of it two platform cars, with the howitzers of the Seventh, and pulling behind it two more cars, loaded with supplies and baggage.

Before long they came out into the "tobacco country," where the sun beat down upon them, and where they found the march not so pleasant. Repairing the track and building bridges as they went, they could only make one mile an hour, and so there was plenty of time for the weary to rest. The men had been obliged to come without rations, and so there was foraging among the neighboring farmhouses, whose inhabitants had for the most part fled for their lives.

Night came on and found them only halfway to Annapolis Junction. There was a full moon, however, so they kept on, repairing the track as needed; men who were not engaged in this work falling down at each halt and sleeping as they could, many of them three-fourths asleep even while they marched. Those who gave out were taken on the cars, but the rest stuck to it, and at daybreak on the following morning they were in sight of the Junction, which they approached in battle array, only to find it deserted. The road had not even been disturbed, and before long appeared a train from Washington, sent out to meet them. It lacked but a few hours of a week since Allan had left Washington for the North via Baltimore, and in that time no troops but the Sixth Massachusetts had reached the capital. When, therefore, the triumphant Seventh swung into Pennsylvania Avenue that afternoon, with music sounding and banners waving, there was a scene almost as stirring as the Broadway march had been.

The Eighth remained behind to guard the Junction, and to open the way for the army that was coming. That night they slept beneath the stars, and in the early evening when the men were lounging about the camp-fires, singing, Allan made the acquaintance of the German sergeant who had spoken to him on the way from Jersey City. He was sitting apart, puffing at a short pipe, and Allan went over to him. The sergeant looked up and said, "Hello! Sit down, won't you?"

He was a man of about thirty; short, but of powerful build. He had light, wavy hair and clear blue eyes that he fixed on one when he spoke. He was quiet in his ways, and no one in the company seemed to know him very well. His name was Schlemmer,

Jack had said, and he lived in Boston. "I want you to tell me about that war," Allan remarked. "Were you in the German army?"

"Yes," said the other; "but I ran away from it—it is not so that I have fought. I am a Socialist, and I fight only for freedom."

"Where?" Allan asked.

"In many places I have helped," said the other— "wherever there was fighting, in 1848-1849. I was in Poland, and then in Saxony. I was in the street-fighting in Dresden, when we tried to overthrow the monarchy. I was on the barricades—you have heard of all that, perhaps?"

"I have read of it," Allan said.

"I was wounded there," said the sergeant, "and I was nearly caught. I escaped; but many there were caught. There was Bakunin, the Russian, and him they sentenced to be shot. You have heard of Bakunin? And there was Klingel and me, and Wagner—you have, perhaps, heard of Wagner—Richard Wagner?"

"No," said Allan.

"He is a musician," said Sergeant Schlemmer. "You will hear of him some day—Richard Wagner; they laugh at him now, but they will not always. He too is a Socialist, but they have pardoned him since, I believe. He is a man of genius, and they had to pardon him; but me—they would not forgive me. I was in prison a month in Berlin, and then I got away again. I came to England."

"How long have you been in this country?" Allan asked.

"Eight years I have been here," said Sergeant Schlemmer. "When I was married, I came."

"Oh," said Allan; "then you have a family?"

"I have three children."

"But how can you leave them to go to war? What will they do?"

"They have a little," he said—"they will get along. Your people will help them, perhaps, and my comrades have promised."

"And you like this country well enough to fight for it?" Allan inquired.

"When we fight for freedom, it does not matter to us where we fight."

"How long have you lived in Boston?"

"Two years; before that I was in Hartford. I teach music—I play the piano."

"Oh!" said Allan, and added with a smile, "Perhaps you would rather listen to the music now than talk to me."

"I do not teach *such* music," said the sergeant. "Herr Gott!" He puffed on stolidly, whilst the enthusiastic militiamen continued to shout, "We'll meet you on Canaan's happy shore!" Pretty soon the German observed, "You do not smoke?"

"No," Allan answered.

"You must," said the other.

"Must? Why?"

"You are going campaigning. You must have something to do. You don't want to die of boredom."

Allan said nothing, but waited while the other puffed again. He was getting used to his intermittent style of conversation. "I have watched you," the man began again, finally. "You are nervous; you are full of excitements. You must always have something to do. You won't last."

Again Allan said nothing. "A soldier has to learn to wait," the other continued; "he has to wait months, and ask no questions. He mustn't care. That's why they have to drill them so much. They have to be wooden."

Allan laughed uncomfortably; then, his eye roaming through the camp, he replied: "I am afraid a good many of us won't fill your requirements. Perhaps we are too good to be made into soldiers."

"All men are too good to be made into soldiers," said the sergeant, in a low voice. "But it has to be done."

CHAPTER II

The line from Annapolis was soon repaired, and it became a scene of busy activity, thousands of troops arriving every day.

Before long there came the Fifth Massachusetts, and then the "Cambridge Tigers" joined it and went up to Washington. They marched past the White House, and once more Allan had a glimpse of the tall, black-clad figure of the President as he stood in the doorway to watch them pass. Many civilians had now fled the city, going North or South according to their choice. Washington was rapidly becoming a military encampment; the march of troops was heard all day, the galloping of cavalry and the rumbling of cannon. Long trains of army wagons began to arrive, and fortifications to arise on the hills about the city. The Patent Office was turned into a barracks; the rotunda and rooms of the Capitol were filled with troops—they bivouacked in the chambers of the Senate and the House, and the vaults of the terrace in front of the building were turned into storerooms and bakeries, from which before long there came sixteen thousand loaves of bread a day. By the first of May there were ten thousand troops in Washington, and as many more in Annapolis.

The "Frontier Guards" had been disbanded, and Lovejoy came to see Allan and bid him farewell before leaving for Kansas. They were raising a "John Brown regiment" in Kansas, and Lovejoy had been called to take command of one of its companies. Men were hearing a great deal about old "Ossawatomie Brown" in these days; when the country was ablaze with war his deed wore a different aspect from what it had been during peace. A poet had already seen his figure stalking over the ruins of Sumter; and there came a day when one of the new Massachusetts regiments swept into Pennsylvania Avenue, singing a strange, wild marching-song to a tune called the "Hallelujah Chorus," an old camp-meeting melody that Allan had heard many years before. The song spread like wildfire in the camps at Washington, and all over the country the armies shook with it as they poured southward:—

"Old John Brown lies a-mouldering in his grave,
Old John Brown lies slumbering in his grave—
But John Brown's soul is marching with the brave,
His soul is marching on.

"He shall file in front when the lines of battle form,
He shall face to front when the squares of battle form—
Time with the column and charge with the storm,
  Where men are marching on.

"Ah, foul tyrants, do you hear him when he comes?
Ah, black traitors, do you know him as he comes,
In thunder of the cannon, and roll of the drums,
  As we go marching on?"

The Fifth Massachusetts was quartered in the Treasury Building, and Allan got grimly down to the work of being made into a
soldier. Every man there was burning up with enthusiasm, but
few of them were used to hard manual labor, and they found it
a rough business. How they envied the gay young lieutenant, who
had nothing to do but display his uniform and give orders and
make out reports! Allan, for one, had not the first idea of the
duties of a private, and the work kept him upon his feet from
daybreak until night; there was squad drill and company drill,
and regimental drill several times a week, in the wretched mud-
streets of Washington. There was guard mounting, and cleaning of
arms and accoutrements, and cooking of rations; his new uniform
was heavy and hot, his musket weighed—what it weighed he had
no means of finding out, but it seemed a hundred pounds. His
arms ached, his feet and limbs ached, and still they drove him on,
until sometimes his body trembled, and his head swam, and every
nerve screamed its protest.

The rest bore it, however, and he bore it also, setting his teeth
grimly; it was the fault of the worthless life he had lived, he told
himself—how he envied little Jimmy Hotchkiss, the classmate of
long ago, who had been walking twenty miles a day since last
November, and now went about his duties whistling like a bobo-
link! Sergeant Schlemmer was Allan's drillmaster, and, together
with half a dozen other recruits, put him through atrocious
"stretching-out" exercises until his bones cracked. Sergeant Schlemmer was, alas, no longer a quiet and phlegmatic dreamer, but a
Prussian martinet whom there was no pleasing, and whose man-

ners were scarcely to be borne. It was well enough to be strict, but there is a limit to all things, and because a man happened to have been bred a gentleman was no reason for supposing he could not obey orders without being yelled at. It was for the country, of course, and it had to be done. At times he found himself wondering if the country would ever appreciate the miseries these men had borne for her.

In Maryland the legislature was in session, strongly secession in its sympathies, but now held in awe by the manifestations of Union feeling about it; in Baltimore the tide was beginning to turn—the severing of the railroad and the consequent isolation of the city were ruining its business. The line through Annapolis was now in full operation, open to the public as well as to the government; and a few days after this Allan and Jack received a telegram from Professor Otis, saying that he was coming on to attend to his errand.

The following day, when off duty, they went to meet him at the depot, as excited and full of anticipations as two schoolboys. They dined at Willard's, where Allan recollected with wonder that only a week or two ago he had considered the fare atrocious. How short a while had it taken to change his ideas! Willard's was crowded with shoulder-strapped officers, who also found the government table not to their taste.

Afterwards the three took their way to the White House. In the anteroom they found a crowd of people of all sorts; but apparently the introductions of these were from less weighty persons than Senator Sumner, who had armed Professor Otis with a letter. They were soon shown into the gorgeously furnished reception room where Allan had once spent the night.

In the dim light they saw the President standing here. His hands were clasped behind his back, and he gave one the feeling that he was painfully ill at ease; when he bowed it was in a queer, jerky fashion, as if there were but one joint in his body, and when he shook hands his arm went up and down after the manner of an automaton wound up. When the two young men had been introduced, he shook hands with them also, and asked them to be seated. The little gilt chair creaked with the weight of his tall frame as he set them an example.

Professor Otis stated his errand, and in the meantime the two others devoured Mr. Lincoln with their eyes; the chance to meet him was something of which Jack had been dreaming for a week. The President had crossed one of his long legs over the other, and as his foot stuck out one could not help observing that he had on a pair of old, ragged slippers, without any heels—and also that he wore white yarn socks. "Several suggestions such as you make," he was saying, "have come to me already. I have referred them to the War Department. I can see no reason myself why the government should not avail itself of every assistance that may be forthcoming. But I will refer you to Secretary Cameron, and we will see what he says."

Then Mr. Lincoln tapped a bell at his side, and while he was waiting for the response, dropped into general conversation. His manner of constraint seemed to wear off after a little, and the two young men noticed that his smile was kindly. "Two of our deliverers?" he said, looking at their uniforms; and then, suddenly, fixing his glance upon Allan, he added, "Have I not seen you somewhere before?"

"Hardly where you would remember me," Allan answered.

"Ah, but I never forget faces!" said the President. "I have seen you, I know."

"I was here with Lane's volunteers," Allan replied.

"Oh, yes!" said the other. "I recollect." And then, as his secretary entered, he said, quietly, "Please write a note to Secretary Cameron, introducing Professor Otis, and asking him to consider what he has to say."

The secretary went out, after handing the President a despatch. The President excused himself for a moment while he read it, and they saw a frown gathering on his face. "Dear me, dear me!" he exclaimed. "More trouble!"

He looked up again, gazing ahead of him into space for some time, tapping the hand with the paper nervously upon the arm of his chair. "Here I am," he began finally, half as if speaking to himself, "here I am trying to save the government which the people have intrusted to me; and here are men actively engaged in trying to destroy it, making war upon it day and night; and one of my officers succeeds in detecting some of their conspiracies, and arrests them, and every single time it happens some judge or other steps forward with a writ of *habeas corpus* and sets them free! If I object, they tell me that I have no right to suspend the writ of *habeas corpus*—that only Congress can do it—and that if I do it I am violating the Constitution and the liberties of the people! Now what in the world am I to do in a case like that?"

The President seemed to be asking their advice, and there was a moment's awkward pause. Jack, who had completed nearly two years in the law school, now found himself for the first time in his life regretting that he had not done more studying—so that his mind need not have been a blank in this crisis. Professor Otis, whose department was mathematics, was on the point of attempting to smooth over the difficulty, when suddenly the President began to laugh gleefully. "I heard such a funny story today," he said. "Wilson sent it to me—do you know Henry Wilson, Professor Otis?"

He was referring to the colleague of Senator Sumner—the "Natick Cobbler," as he was known to the country.

"I have met him," said the professor.

"Well, he sent me this story by a friend," went on the President. "It seems they've been arguing this constitutional question up there in your State, and the senator said he thought this story would be of more use to me than any opinion he had to offer. He declares he sent the friend to Washington especially to bring it, but of course that's only one of his jokes. It seems that there was a skipper of a sailing-vessel, an Italian"—the President called it Eye-talian— "who had been hired to take a certain image of the Holy Virgin to Rome, to be blessed by the Pope and then brought back again to put a stop to some pestilence or other. This image was especially sacred, and priests were on board to guard it, and the skipper had been frightened half to death with the warnings of what would happen if he did not deliver it safely. Well, time went on, and sure enough, what did he do but run the vessel on the rocks. When they got off, they found a hole in her side, at the water line. A storm was raging, and the water began to rush in, and the sailors rushed to the pumps; but the ship continued to fill, in spite of all they could do. All the time, of course, the priests were praying before the image of the Virgin, imploring her to save them. The harder they prayed, however, the worse the storm grew, and the faster the water rushed in, and the lower the ship sank. They made all sorts of vows, and the captain made all sorts of vows, but it did no good—the ship went on settling and settling. And at last, when it seemed that they might go down any minute, the captain suddenly jumped up and began to swear. He yelled for the mate, and he yelled for the sailors—'Yo ho, there!' says he, 'take the Holy Virgin below and stuff her head in the hole!' "

And with that Mr. Lincoln exploded suddenly into a burst of laughter; he was completely doubled up with it—he wrapped his long arms about his knees and drew them up till they touched his face. "The Constitution is my Holy Virgin!" he said, when he could get his breath.

And then, when in the act of saying something more, he came to a dead halt. The laughter vanished from his face, and an expression of solemnity replaced it with a swiftness that was comical. A door at the other end of the room had opened, and two gentlemen were coming in. The President rose, and putting his hands behind his back, stood as before, with his feet braced apart, waiting, submissively, for whatever might be coming.

Of the two persons who had come in, apparently by a private entrance, one was small and slightly built, stooping as he walked; he was quick and alert in manner, and his head projected forward inquiringly, an effect which was accentuated by the fact that it was a very large head, and with a very prominent nose. Allan had seen him in Washington eleven years ago, and knew him at once, though his hair had turned white in the meantime. It was Secretary Seward.

His companion was a quite stately person, bald, and with a fringe of white whiskers under his chin. He was faultlessly dressed, and one had only to look at him to see that he was a man of high breeding—his manner was that of an English nobleman. Allan had seen him somewhere, but he could not place him until he heard the Secretary introduce him. Then he recollected—it was Mr. Adams, the new minister to England, a grandson of President John Adams and son of President John Quincy Adams. He bowed reservedly when introduced, and was taken by surprise when the President put out his hand; he corrected himself so quickly, however, that only a close observer could have detected his surprise, and the President repeated his queer pumping motion once more, and gave two or three more of his queer jerky bows. He expressed his great pleasure at meeting Mr. Adams, and then his private secretary came in with the note for Professor Otis.

The three, who had risen, started to take their departure; but the President stopped them with a wave of his hand. "Don't go, don't go," he said cordially. "Sit down—we are all friends here. Mr. Adams, Professor Otis, of Harvard College."

"I have already the pleasure of knowing Professor Otis," said Mr. Adams.

"And Mr. Jack Otis—one of our defenders. And Mr. Montague."

Mr. Adams bowed again, and the party sat down once more. The President slid down in his chair until his collar rested on the back of it, and crossed his long legs, so that the worn slippers and white yarn socks were again the most conspicuous objects in view. Before long, however, perhaps after catching a glimpse of the Secretary of State, who sat very stiff and solemn, he began anxiously getting erect again, inch by inch, so that no one might notice it—in the meantime not taking his eyes off Mr. Adams, who had begun a little speech.

The new minister was on the point of sailing for England, it seemed, and had come to Washington to receive his instructions. He was very much gratified indeed at the mark of confidence which was implied by his nomination at such a critical hour, and to such a post of danger as the Court of St. James. He trusted that this confidence in him would not prove to have been misplaced.

These were the inevitable things to say, and Mr. Adams was

saying them very gravely, and apparently expecting to say on to the end; but the President interrupted him.

"Oh, that's all right," he said, easily—"make yourself comfortable on that score, Mr. Adams. We have no doubt at all that your services will be most satisfactory."

There was a moment's halt. Then the minister said, gravely, "I have wished to thank you—"

The President stopped him again. "You know," he said, with a sudden burst of confidence, "your appointment isn't my doings, anyway—it's the Governor's." The speaker waved his hand toward Mr. Seward. "It was the Governor's choice, you understand, so it's him you have to thank."

A lifetime of social training, together with the inherited attributes of his two ancestral diplomats, was not enough to enable the gentleman from Boston to conceal entirely his discomfiture. It was only for an instant, however, that he was at a loss; then once more in his cold and impassive manner he began to speak. "Naturally, Mr. President," he said, "in so grave a crisis you will wish to consult with me—"

"Yes, certainly," said Mr. Lincoln, and he gave a slight bow, smiling pleasantly. "You know, though," he added, "the Governor is going to run that part of our business, Mr. Adams. All that there is to tell you he'll attend to, I imagine."

Again there was a silence, this time permanent, so far as Mr. Adams was concerned. The President sat gazing in front of him, rocking his foot up and down. Then all at once he started. "Oh, by the way, Governor," he said, turning to Mr. Seward—"I've decided that Chicago appointment!"

"Yes?" said Mr. Seward.

"Yes, *sir!* I gave it to Harris, after all!"

Again there was a pause. "Funny," continued the speaker, again in his abstract way, gazing into space, "I never had an office give me so much trouble as that one. I think there have been a dozen delegations on it here. There were two men who wanted it, you understand, and the way they set about it was for each to send me charges involving the honesty of the other. And of course I told each about the charges, and demanded that they clear them up, but instead of that—back they came with more charges, each against the other! 'That won't do, gentlemen,' I said—'it isn't a question of the other man; it's a question of *your* man. I want you to disprove *these* charges.' Then they'd go all the way to Chicago, and come back with fresh stories. Of course they wore me out—as I suppose they expected to. I had to appoint the least bad of them."

The President had slid back in his chair again, and was laughing good-humoredly. He was getting to be at his ease again. "You know," he began, all at once, "it made me think of the story of Daniel Webster and the schoolmaster. Did any of you gentlemen ever hear of Daniel Webster and the schoolmaster?"

Nobody had, apparently.

"Well," said Mr. Lincoln, "when Daniel was in school, he was a very careless boy—some called him a dirty boy. His teacher had many times reproved him for not washing his hands. He had coaxed and scolded him, but it didn't do any good—Daniel would come to school with his hands dirty. Out of all patience with him, one day at last he called Daniel to his desk and made him hold up his hands in the presence of the whole school; then he solemnly warned him that if ever he came to school again with his hands in that condition, he would give him a licking he'd never forget.

"Well, Daniel promised better behavior, and for two or three days there was an improvement—his hands looked as if they were washed daily. But the reformation was not permanent, and in a few days his hands were as dirty as ever. The teacher's sharp eyes detected them, and as soon as school had opened for the day, with a stern voice he said, 'Daniel, come here!' The guilty culprit knew what was coming, and his hands began to tingle in anticipation. He stealthily brought the palm of his right hand into contact with his tongue, and, as he walked slowly toward the master's desk, he rubbed his hand upon his pantaloons, in the effort to remove some of the dirt. 'Hold out your hand, sir!' said the master, and Daniel extended it, palm up. 'Do you call that a clean hand?' demanded the teacher. 'Not very, sir!' modestly replied the offender. 'I should think *not very!*' said the master. 'If you can show me a dirtier hand in this schoolroom, I will let you off.' And then, quick as a flash, Daniel thrust out his other hand, which hadn't undergone the cleansing process. 'There it is, sir!' said he."

Never in his life did Allan forget the various heroic attempts which the auditors made to laugh over that story; and when at last the three had taken their departure and come outside of the building, they stood and looked at each other, and Jack Otis gasped, "Jehoshaphat!"

CHAPTER III

Events moved on apace. The States of North Carolina, Tennessee, and Arkansas seceded and joined the Confederacy; and on the 4th of May the Washington government issued a call for eighty-two thousand more men. By this time the voluntary contributions of the North had amounted to some forty millions of dollars, nearly half of what it was estimated would be the cost of putting down the rebellion.

At the South, also, the fervor burned high. Private citizens were raising companies and regiments for the Confederacy, and equipping them at their own expense—there were so many offers the government could not accept one quarter of them, though it was raising an army of a hundred thousand. The Congress had met at Montgomery, and passed a formal declaration of war; also, in answer to Lincoln's proclamation of a blockade of the Southern ports, it authorized President Davis to commission privateers, and it prohibited the payment of all debts due to Northerners, and sequestered property belonging to them.

In the West a desperate struggle was going on for the possession of Kentucky and Missouri. Kentucky was wavering, and her legislature had passed an act declaring "neutrality," and forbidding either of the contending parties to enter her limits—a prohibition which each respected, for fear of driving the State into the arms of the other. In Missouri the masses were for the most part "loyal," but the governor was an active secessionist, and he assembled the State militia, which was in sympathy with him, planning to seize the United States arsenal at St. Louis, and command the city and the State. The commander of the arsenal was too quick for him, however. This officer, a Captain Lyon, a little hornet of a man, got together secretly the loyal men of the city—Germans, for the most part—and after making a tour of the encampment of the militia disguised as a woman, he suddenly descended upon it with six thousand men and took its occupants prisoners. There was some fighting, and a riot in the streets, but the gallant little captain landed most of his prisoners in the arsenal, and was made a brigadier for his exploit.

The Federal troops continued to pour into Washington, and the country was calling for action, murmuring with discontent at the slowness of the authorities. Six weeks and more had passed since the outbreak of hostilities, and still the "sacred soil" of Virginia had remained untouched by a Northern foot. Sixteen thousand of the Confederates were at Manassas Junction, a place about thirty miles from Washington, where the railroad from that city to Richmond was joined by another from the Shenandoah; and in the town of Alexandria in Virginia just across the river from the capital, the Confederate flag was kept floating from a hotel in full view of the White House. Not until it was discovered that the enemy was on the point of seizing Arlington Heights to fortify them and command the city did the authorities move; on the night of the 23rd of May, just after the men of the Fifth Massachusetts had gotten asleep in their uncomfortably crowded quarters, they were turned out and ordered to prepare to march. Amid intense excitement they set out, leaving a good part of their baggage behind them, and in the bright moonlight crossed the Aqueduct Bridge at Georgetown. It was the first act of war, and a breathless crowd watched the march, all in dead silence. It had been hoped to capture the enemy's forces in Alexandria, but these got off by the railroad, and there was only some scattered shooting here and there.

Other troops had crossed by the "Long Bridge," and a regiment of New York "Zouaves" was transferred to Alexandria by boat. This organization, which had been recruited mainly from the firemen of the metropolis, was under the command of a handsome young officer, Colonel Ellsworth, who had been conspicuous in Washington. After he had posted his men he chanced to notice the Confederate flag which still floated from the hotel, and he mounted to the cupola and took it down. As he descended the steps, the proprietor of the place sprang out and emptied the contents of a double-barrelled shot-gun into the young officer's heart.

This act of hatred sent a thrill of horror through the nation. Ellsworth had been a friend of Lincoln, and it is said that when the news came to the President he burst into tears. It seemed too dreadful that a young life had thus been swept out of existence. Columns of poetry were printed in the newspapers, glorifying him as the martyred hero of the nation. And on the other hand the South with equal fervor glorified the hotel proprietor, who had been shot dead by one of Ellsworth's men. He died nobly, it was held, defending his home from invasion and his country's flag from insult.

Fortifications were laid out, and the regiments went into camp, each separately. That of the Fifth was called "Camp Andrew," in honor of the governor of its State. Here began again the long routine of drill and guard-mounting, and of toil in the trenches in the blazing sun, varied only by sudden alarms, and by daily rumors of the enemy's approach. A great many of the regiments were in a state of utter confusion, for most of the officers were politicians who did not know enough about military matters to make out a requisition for stores; many of them also, instead of learning, were lounging about the hotels and barrooms of the capital, and galloping on horseback through the streets, displaying their gorgeous uniforms. There were ugly stories that some were selling government rations, and were in league with sutlers to defraud their men. Under such circumstances it was not surprising that the rank and file were ill-behaved—that the camps were dirty, and that crowds of drunken soldiers swarmed in Washington, fighting in the streets, and begging from the passers-by. Decent men witnessed such things as this, and burned with indignation; but no efforts seemed to count for anything in the saturnalia of incompetence that reigned.

At this time the government had made no regulations concerning uniforms, and each company was costumed according to its taste. Endless was the variety to be seen in the camps—there were some companies made up wholly of foreigners, and most of these had chosen uniforms from their native lands. In the regiment next to Allan's was one in the full regalia of the Bavarian regulars, and every night there was fighting between them and a near-by Irish regiment, "Mike" Corcoran's Sixty-ninth New York, whose colonel was still under court-martial for having refused to parade in honor of the Prince of Wales!

In addition to the confusion of uniform, the equipments of the regiments were hopelessly diverse. Scarcely a battery had two guns of the same calibre, and there were a score of different kinds of tents, and no one seemed to know how to put up any of them. The arms that were issued were of various patterns, many having come from abroad, many being old and worthless; also, there was no cavalry, and consequently no information concerning the enemy in front—there was not even a map to be had of the country, and riding-horses were so scarce in Washington that staff-officers went campaigning in buggies.

Yet the nation had made a mighty effort to raise this army, and the newspapers were wild to have something done with it. Every editor and correspondent had turned strategist, and was planning the campaign—the soldiers planned it in the camps, and the cabinet planned it in Washington. General Scott was in favor of a close blockade and a slow advance of the mighty army that would be ready in the fall; but this did not suit the country, which made fun of his scheme under the title of "Scott's Anaconda," and insisted upon instant action. When the news came that the Confederate government had shifted its capital to Richmond, this, which seemed a direct challenge, set every one blazing with indignation, and made the papers more impatient than ever. The New York *Times* reiterated its opinion that President Lincoln ought to be immediately deposed.

The first battle of the war—a "battle" they called it—came at "Big Bethel," just back of Fortress Monroe, where General Butler had been sent to take command. The result of it was only to increase the clamor—the general sent out three regiments to seize by night a rebel battery, and in the darkness they went astray and fired upon each other, and then were driven back from the battery with the loss of a score or more killed. This seemed like a calamity to the people. So much blood poured out for nothing, they said. So much effort and expense, and only humiliation after humiliation! The gallant Massachusetts lawyer fell under a cloud—for a moment the country even forgot its gratitude to him for the master-stroke of humor of the war.

This was the invention of "contraband." From the beginning the military commanders had had to face the possibility of servile insurrection and the ever present fact of servile elopement. The slaves came pouring into Fortress Monroe by the hundreds, and they all declared that their masters had used them in constructing military works. It was not long before one Confederate officer sent to General Butler a flag of truce demanding the return of one of his servants, under the Fugitive Slave Act: to which the wary lawyer-general made response that he understood Virginia was now a foreign country, and that he did not see how the act could apply. A few days later the North was startled by the tidings that the general had declared that slaves, being "property," and property of military service, were "contraband-of-war!" The phrase settled the question on the instant, for it caught the humor of the country; the Negro who got into the Union lines after that was a "contraband," and he was never sent back.

In the western part of Virginia, meantime, there had been events of importance, and at last a victory for the North. In all the mountainous portions of the Confederacy the hold of Slavery had been slight, and there had developed more or less opposition to secession. In the Northern portions—that is, in Eastern Tennessee and Western Virginia—the Union feeling had proven almost overwhelming; and in the latter, meetings had been held and a convention called at Wheeling, which now declared for the withdrawal of that portion of the State from the Confederacy. To sustain this movement troops were advanced from Ohio, and by a night attack by several regiments upon a place called Philippi, the only Confederate force in West Virginia was routed—a victory which set the North quite beside itself with rejoicing.

That was the way to do it, said the newspapers; and their prodding of the Washington government went on. Most of the volunteers had enlisted for only three months; their time was passing, and they were discontented and indignant—if they were not soon led out against the enemy they would return home, and the army would collapse. The month of May passed, and the month of June, in the sweltering heat of a Virginia encampment, and still there was no advance. "FORWARD TO RICHMOND!" "FORWARD TO RICHMOND!" thundered the New York *Tribune,* in enormous letters upon its editorial page. Day after day it printed this under the title of "THE NATION'S WAR-CRY."

The *Tribune* was a high authority; but there were those who declared the nation's war-cry to be different from this. General Beauregard, the conqueror of Sumter, had been sent to take command at Manassas, and he now issued a proclamation, addressed to the people of Virginia. Beauregard was a fiery little Creole gentleman from New Orleans, and he set to work to "fire the Southern heart," as Yancey had once phrased it. "A reckless and unprincipled tyrant has invaded your soil"—so ran his *pronunciamiento.*—"Abraham Lincoln, regardless of all moral, legal, and constitutional restraints, has thrown his Abolition hosts among you, who are murdering and imprisoning your citizens, confiscating and destroying your property, and committing other acts of violence and outrage too shocking and revolting to humanity to be enumerated. All rules of civilized warfare are abandoned, and they proclaim by their acts, if not on their banners that their war-cry is 'Beauty and Booty.' All that is dear to man— your honor and that of your wives and daughters—are involved in this momentous conflict!"

The Fifth Massachusetts had been drilling ever since the previous January, and so the men regarded themselves as veterans. They took it ill that they should be held back and kept waiting by the raw volunteers who were pouring into camp day after day. So often they had been shaken by the rumors of an advance, and so often been disappointed, that they had given up in despair, and abandoned themselves to swearing at the government. But the delays could not last forever—business was bad and taxes were appalling. Six weeks more had passed, and many of the early volunteers had only a few more days to remain; the rumor of the forward movement then came daily and almost hourly. At last, on the 13th of July, the order was read for the Fifth to pack personal baggage and send it to Alexandria. The camp leaped into life once more.

The three who tented with Allan had not much to send back— they expected to take everything with them, it appeared: a miscellaneous assortment of clothing, toilet articles, slippers, brushes and combs, a harmonica, a spyglass, a jar of preserves, half a box of cigars. Allan concluded after meditation to follow the example of Sergeant Schlemmer, whose outfit consisted of a change of underclothing, a toothbrush, and a tin plate and spoon. The sergeant had by this time become the oracle of half the regiment, being the only man in it who had ever had any experience of war. High officials used to repair to him to have knotty points in the regulations ravelled out; and in the evenings he was generally the centre of a group of open-eyed militiamen, to whom he taught the fine points of campaigning. It was due to Sergeant Schlemmer that theirs was the only company in the regiment whose men were not limping about with blistered feet, owing to the fearful shoes which the quartermaster had given out; the sergeant had taught them to plaster the inside of their socks with soft soap, and be happy. Now he was sitting in his doorway, puffing at his pipe and giving them his advice as to marching—that they should fill their canteens at every stream, they should not straggle, nor waste their breath singing, nor "cut up" in the early part of the day.

"You think we'll have to march so far, then?" some one asked him, anxiously.

"You never know where you are going to march," was the answer. "You may march all night to find the enemy, and all day fighting him, and all the next night running away from him."

"Get food"—that was the sergeant's further advice—"you'll find there's nothing else counts—food and tobacco. You won't march far before you'll see men throwing away their haversacks—cut them open and take the food. Don't take anything else. When you need shoes and uniforms, you can draw them from the quartermaster. But food—"

"You can draw rations, too," suggested some one.

"You can," said Schlemmer, "until the commissary's wagons begin to break down, and the enemy takes to shooting his mules. Then I tell you there'll come a time when if you see a dead man in the way, the first thing you think of is if there's anything on him to eat."

There were two more days of delay; but they were really going to move this time—the thing was in the air. Staff-officers were galloping hither and thither, and all the regiments were astir. The visitors were coming out to the camps in swarms to say good-by, and the men writing reams of letters home. Finally, one afternoon when they lined up for parade, they got their orders—three days' rations, light marching order, and a start at sunrise on the morrow. The regiment broke into a cheer, and they heard it taken up by others in the distance.

It was an army the like of which had never been seen before on this continent—it was full forty thousand strong. One could see it all from the top of the hill—for miles around the country was white with patches of tents, while at night there were thousands of camp-fires, shining like red eyes in the darkness. And at last it was going forth to battle—it was going to drive rebellion out of the land! There were solemn hours in the camps that night, and many of the regiments held prayer-meetings.

In the morning, when reveille was sounded, they tumbled out. It was still dark, but men were laughing and singing, and the morning was cool and damp, and every one's heart thumped in expectation; men swallowed their breakfast in huge gulps. The Fifth—the "steady Fifth," as they called it—was to lead one of the columns of march; and several of the companies had been ordered ahead on skirmish duty. That was breathless work—stealing along through the bushes, where any moment one might come into view of the enemy's outposts. What hunting had any one ever dreamed of that was equal to this hunting of men?

Soon the column was in full swing down the road. It was in vain that the sergeant had warned them to waste no strength in "cutting up" and in singing. They sang until they were hoarse—such delightful songs they had! "The whiskey-bottle lies empty on the shelf" was one of their masterpieces of humor; also they renewed their never-dying resolution concerning "Jeff Davis and the sour-apple tree." There was a company of the regiment from Charleston, and they had a patriotic chorus on the subject of Bunker Hill. Now and then some luckless staff-officer would ride by them, all bright and shiny; and how mercilessly they would guy him, what endless ingenuity in their invention of expletives! At last the wretch would spur his horse and gallop on in desperation—though sometimes, alas, he did not dare to, having perhaps never been on a horse in his life until two or three weeks earlier.

But then the sun rose, and the singing died, and men began to turn red and mop their faces. When the column halted, they no longer played pranks upon each other, but sat down in silence by the roadside. Then it was that things began to be thrown away—the waste would have been shameful, had it not been for a battery of artillery just in the rear. These artillerymen strode jauntily, having no burdens to carry, and they gathered up everything in sight, and laughed and called for more. Pretty soon their caissons looked like the wagons of a traveling peddler—knapsacks and articles of clothing dangling in rows. The man who marched next to Allan swore softly, now and then, hearing from one of the guns of this battery the strains of the harmonica he had carried and had hidden away in a thicket at the last halt.

The army was moving in four columns, upon separate roads, centering at Fairfax Court House; at the hills one could look back and see his own column stretching far into the distance, like a huge snake—gliding with a slow, writhing motion over the hillocks and down into the hollows. The effect of it was indescribably curious—red and blue and yellow and gray and black it was, looking as if the contents of a paint-box had been emptied upon it. Nowhere was there any uniformity, save in one place where a few companies of the regulars had been placed together. These latter marched in good order; but some of the regiments were mere mobs, having been enlisted only a few days, and having come to Washington but a few hours before—and now going out to battle.

Still farther in the rear was the train of white-topped wagons, making one think of the pioneers and the prairies. Among them were also buggies and coaches, filled with civilians who had come out to witness the spectacle—senators and congressmen, diplomats, newspaper men, all eager to be in at the death of "rebellion."

It was a marvellously uncomfortable thing—this army; a thing newly born, palpitating, sensitive, a most dangerous army to stray pigs and cows that ran into it in the thicket. Its skirmishers did not know how to handle their muskets very well, and sometimes in pushing through the underbrush they left the hammers of their guns uncovered and shot each other. There were popping reports in front all through the day, and now and then a volley; whenever this happened, the heads of the columns always halted, and officers galloped madly here and there, shouting orders. There would be an attempt to deploy in line of battle, but almost no one knew the necessary evolutions, and the result would generally be that the regiments got huddled together like sheep in a pen. At such times any man who felt a talent within him did what he could to clear up the confusion.

It was a democratic army; no one paid any particular attention to orders, but every one had his own ideas about the strategy of this campaign, and swore at the commanders and the administration. The person who was responsible for it was one McDowell, a well-meaning and patriotic gentleman, a general in the regular army; but he had never been on a campaign, and at present he was sick, and had almost no staff to help him. To make matters worse, the Secretary of War was present, somewhere, making suggestions out of the infinitude of his ignorance.

All the spies were on the other side, apparently, and no one in this advancing host had any idea of where the enemy was, or how much there was of him. There were only vague reports of enormous hosts, of fortifications at Manassas, and of new regiments coming every hour from Richmond; of General Johnston's army somewhere in the Shenandoah that was hurrying up by railroad. Wide-eyed Negroes had been bringing into the camps accounts of an all-destroying squadron known as the "Black Horse Cavalry"; and every time an equestrian appeared on the horizon, this terrifying name was heard.

But the enemy did not appear, and they bivouacked for the night. Scarcely had they gotten asleep before there were shots and cries, and the drums beat the long roll, and they tumbled out and seized their muskets. Spies, or scouts, or the advance guard of an approaching foe—no one could be certain; but one prisoner was led in, a countryman, excessively frightened, and so the camp settled down once more.

They were up again at dawn, marching cautiously, with skirmishers far ahead, and others cutting trees to clear the road. They were in the enemy's country now—they saw scouting parties in the distance, and there were occasional shots from the hilltops. The houses they passed were all deserted—evidently General Beauregard's proclamation had been taken seriously by the farmers about here. In the afternoon the regiment came to Sangster's Station, on the Orange and Alexandria Railroad—just in time to see a train disappearing with the last of the "rebels," jeering derisively. They slept that night in a field of new-mown hay, without stopping to build any sort of shelter.

The main portions of the army were then a little to the right, at Fairfax Court House. A few miles ahead was a village called Centerville, and beyond this a little valley where ran a stream known as Bull Run. On the other side of Bull Run, as one followed the main turnpike, he came to Manassas Junction, a village of a dozen or two houses, where the camp of the enemy was known to be.

In the morning the expected order to advance did not come. The men were keyed up to a high pitch—they were wild with impatience, and spent their time wandering about, listening, speculating. Where was the rest of the army? And what was the matter with it? How much longer would they be kept waiting here? So the morning passed, and dinner-time came—and then suddenly—men sprang to their feet, their blood bounding. It was a gun.

One, and another, and another! A cannonade! It was two or three miles in front of them, sharp and clear, quick and incessant. They stared at each other; it was fighting—the battle had begun.

On and on it went, and they listened with clenched hands and tense faces. That was a roll! How they were giving it to them! Now and again there would come a lull, and they could hear the spattering fire of musketry, sometimes volleys of it at once. It was a real battle this time—the whole army must be engaged!

And they—what were they doing here? Was there nobody in charge, nobody to see about this? Had they been forgotten entirely? Dense gray clouds of smoke began to rise in the distance, and spread out in a wan haze; and the guns thundered on, faster and faster. Men gathered in little groups, discussing it in whispers.

It was the first time they had ever heard guns in real earnest. It was a wicked kind of sound, harsh and sinister, like the snarling of some angry beast; it set the blood to racing, it got upon men's nerves. Some of them wandered hither and thither, like caged animals; others tried to laugh their nervousness away. Allan noticed that his cousin Jack was white about the lips, and stood in silence, fumbling at his sword. Allan himself was excited to the point of pain—it was as if a thousand needles were pricking him in his fingers and arms. He had come out to see this thing through, he told himself, and he was ready to face it; but to stand there helpless, and just listen! And then suddenly he chanced to notice Sergeant Schlemmer, sitting with his back to a tree, his head comfortably propped and his eyes closed. The sergeant had his pipe in his mouth, as ever; and he would draw it out and half open his eyes, and take in the scene, and then close them again and go on—puff, puff!

A full half hour they heard the firing, when suddenly there were shouts near by, in the next field, where the First Massachusetts was posted. A courier upon a foam-covered horse was seen to dash out of the woods, bringing them orders; they were forming—

they were going to the fight! "Our turn next!" the men thought, and bit their lips, fingering their cartridge-belts, trying their bayonets, and looking furtively now and then at their neighbors, to see if by chance anyone else was as uneasy as they.

So, for another hour or two, and then little by little the firing died away. The musketry ceased, and the cannon-shots almost. What could *that* mean?

They discussed it excitedly. Some one must have been beaten, after that terrible conflict; but they saw no signs of a rout—and if the enemy were retreating, surely, they, the Fifth, would at least get a chance to pursue. They argued this, pro and con, until a straggler came into the camp and brought them the story— that there had been just a "reconnaissance" at one of the fords of the little stream.

And then, while they gazed at each other, feeling so hopelessly like fools, Allan glanced at Sergeant Schlemmer. The sergeant was still puffing at his pipe.

CHAPTER IV

The men slept on their arms. But the morrow came, and the next day, and still they did not move. So they began to growl and grumble again, and set to work making themselves shelters out of poles and boughs. If their commander was going to keep them there indefinitely, he might at least have told them, so that they could keep out of the rain, they said.

The truth was that their commander was working like mad, trying to get his supply wagons up and his army in hand for the coming battle; he had certainly stimulus enough to haste, for the time of some regiment expired every day, and he was liable to lose ten thousand men, the third of his army, within the week. One Pennsylvania regiment had already started back to Washington—"to the sound of the enemy's cannon," as he phrased it in his report. The time of the Fifth was up also, but if there was any man in the Fifth who wanted to go, he had kept the fact a close secret. Pennsylvania men might do that way, but not Massachusetts men.

Saturday evening, the twentieth day of July, the orders came at last. Cooked rations were distributed, and the regiment was ordered to march at half-past one the following morning. Everybody felt that this time it meant business—the death grapple with secession was coming.

The men discussed it, sitting in groups, some of them busily cleaning their rifles. Others, who happened to be of a meditative turn of mind, went apart, feeling solemn. They were students, or business-men, or clerks, these volunteers, and as for fighting, some of them had never been in so much as a fist fight in their lives. A battle was a thing about which they knew through books, a thing that had always seemed as far away and impossible as the Arabian Nights. But now there was going to be one—here! to-morrow! And they to be in it! How strange it was to think about! Bits of incidents they had read would float into their minds—things bloody and terrible—and now suddenly become *real*. One looked at his companions, wondering. Did they *know* what they were going to do—did they realize what it was going to be like? Could it possibly be that they did, and that they did not mind it any more than they seemed to? What uncomfortable people they had suddenly become! And how overwhelmingly you felt your own inferiority—quaking and upset as you were!

Your thoughts fled home; and, dear God, how suddenly homesick you grew! Sick—*sick*—until you could not bear it, and ran off, so that the fellows might not hear you sobbing! And then you brought yourself back by the scruff of the neck to face the music. You thought yourself of some importance, but you were really quite a nonentity—just one private—you would figure just one in the total! There was that last "reconnaissance," for instance—eight or ten killed, so it ran. It did not at all matter which.

You imagined yourself in the battle. You were there, with the bullets whizzing about you—just what would you do? Such a very ticklish feeling came over you; so strangely aware you became all at once—of your *stomach!* Your stomach was such a soft and mushy thing; surely, if man had been intended to go into a place where bullets were flying, he ought to have had some kind of hard coating over his stomach! Now and then in a sudden flash you would realize one of those bullets, and would cave in, as if some one had poked a spear-point at you. Was there any part of you at all that you could imagine being struck by a bullet? Anywhere in the head or body—no, assuredly not there! The arms or the legs might not be so bad, near the edge; but how would it feel to be hit in one of your bones?

Eight or ten killed! You might perhaps take the chance; but then, even eight or ten would not be enough—there would surely be more than that killed in a real battle! Imagine it as being decided in advance—how would it seem if the regiment were to be stood up in line, watching the grisly phantom, Death, coming toward them and touching one on the shoulder here and there. Would the men all stand in perfect quiet and indifference, as they did now? The mere fact that it was not to happen until tomorrow seemed to make it of no consequence at all to them.

Death! *Death!* The devil of a thing it was to think about! Of course, you knew that everybody had to die; but then you had never included yourself. But now you did; and how strange it suddenly made things seem—how ghostly and phantasmal! These men who were moving about in the firelight—tomorrow they might all be gone! They would be here of course, but you would not know about them, and was not that the same thing to you? You were to be added in that total.

And when you were dead, where would you be? There were some men here who believed that they would wake up again, after it was all over; at least they sang hymns to that effect, and tried to make believe that they believed it. An extraordinary sort of idea was that—but still it might be true, anything might be true, in this world. And how curious it was to think of! What a joke it would be if it were true—what a queer sort of fraud it would make life into! All your agonies and uncomfortableness for nothing! Your horror lest a bullet should get you in the stomach—and all the while you could get along just as well without a stomach as with it!

But no, there was not any more speculating about that. When you were dead, you were dead. Yet what a strange dream-creature that made you out! You were so much excited about yourself, you took so much interest in yourself—and all the time you were like the flame of a candle that a puff of breeze might blow out! You were gone in the snapping of a finger—like that! Cold, icy thoughts were those—you grew suddenly frightened, and crept into the circle of the firelight, where there were human voices, living and warm. You put your arms about some one, in a sudden access of friendliness. How kind and tender we ought to be to our fellow-victims of this strange malady, life! And the poor rebels, too—they were in the same fix! Curious that we had nothing better to do in the world than to go shooting at them, and they at us!

After a while you dozed off to sleep. But scarcely had you closed your eyes, it seemed, before somebody touched you, and you heard a muttered word or two, and sat up with a start, and rubbed your eyes. The camp was flooded with moonlight, and men were hurrying here and there, rolling up their blankets, toasting a bit of pork before the fire, or warming some coffee in a tin cup, and stuffing "hard-tack" down their throats. Far off a horse neighed, and everything seemed strange and wild.

The word was given, and the regiment fell into line. In columns of fours it swung out into the road, and the night march began. How men's hearts thumped with excitement, how they wondered what was going forward! Ahead and behind, the road was crowded with men—the whole army was astir, one could hear its tramp and the murmur of its thousands of voices. But not a drum, not a trumpet-call—was it to be a night attack?

Nobody could say. It soon became apparent, however, that if that were the plan, there was going to be a failure. The march was a thing to make any nervous man crazy. They would go half a mile, stumbling on each other's heels, and then they would stand still for half an hour. Then another half a mile—and perhaps a halt of an hour! They fidgeted with impatience; they stood up, and sat down, by turns. They swore, and abused the administration. What sort of an army was this, anyhow, that could not even march? Wasn't there a road ahead there?

They passed through the village of Centerville, and into the Warrenton pike. There the press was greater than ever—the way was hopelessly blocked. The precious hours fled by, and no one did anything. The staff-officers had lost their heads, and kept galloping back and forth on the road, just for spite, it seemed. They ordered the men out of their way, and the men ordered them to hell for their pains.

So it went on, until at last the regiment came to a little road, a mere bridle-path, that turned off to the right, into the forest. They went into this. What could *that* mean—away off to the northwest, directly away from the enemy! They went on and on, for hours, stumbling over the ruts, and coming to a halt again, then being ordered on and stumbling some more. The sky began to redden behind them, and the sun rose, and still they plodded on in this forest road. It was dry, and their marching stirred up the dust, until they could scarcely see for it; it rose in clouds above the tree-tops. It got into their eyes and their mouths and their hair—when their throats became dry and they swallowed they found their teeth full of grit. Very soon they emptied their canteens; and then there was no more water—their throats began to burn and crack, their tongues hung out and they panted like dogs. Some of them, at the halts, lay down and drank the brown-and-yellow water of the forest pools.

An hour or two after sunrise they began to hear artillery, far away on their left. They listened wonderingly—they were marching straight away from it! Presumably they were engaged in some sort of flank movement; but then, the road ought to begin to turn, and instead it went straight on and on! And they ought to make haste—but the column seemed to halt more often than ever. They were walled up in a dense pine forest and they could not see a thing—there was nothing to do but trust to their commanders and plod on, while the sounds of battle raged louder and faster.

Finally they heard shouts behind them, and a staff of officers galloped by. One of them, a fine, imposing-looking man, they recognized as McDowell; he had left his sickbed—perhaps he had gone to hurry things up in front there!

The march grew faster; but also the sun rose and it grew hotter. Men gasped and choked, and some began to fall out. They still heard a battle raging, but they no longer cared about it—what did people bring them out on a mad errand like this for if they wanted them to fight? They could not fight until tomorrow—they were nearly dead. But then on top of it came the command, "Double quick!" and they started at a trot, their equipments jangling and shaking about them—you would have thought it was cavalry coming. One gazed at the heels of the line in front of him, until his head reeled—he had to do that, while running, to keep them from stumbling in the ruts and hillocks of the road. Some staggered to one side and fell down, unable to move.

The rest went on, for hours. The battle had broken out directly to their left. The ground shook with the cannonade, and the musketry fire was incessant. A breeze sprang up, and they began to get the scent of the powder smoke. God, would that road never come to an end! It was now afternoon—they had been marching nearly twelve hours.

The music of the battle took hold of them, however, in spite of their exhaustion, and the pace grew quicker. The road was beginning to turn now, and was evidently going to lead them somewhere. Then suddenly they began to see the end of the woods—there was open ground in front. Before them was a slope and a deep hollow, into which they darted, gasping, "Water!"

It was that little stream, "Bull Run," of which they had heard. They lay down and drank from it like thirsty dogs, they bathed their heads in it—it was hard to make them get up and make room for others. But there was no time to waste—the battle was raging. Staff-officers galloped up, shouting orders.

Beyond the stream there was a slope, and at the top a little brick church; they toiled towards it, and as they came out on the level ground they could see the dull gray cloud of smoke, beneath which the fight raged, some two or three miles away. The road turned sharply here, and went towards it. Other regiments were in sight upon it, just ahead, and they followed at a run, forgetting everything in their excitement.

It was a real battle, there was no mistake; it was a victory, too—the fighting was a mile or two ahead, and yet it had once been where they were! Here and there over the fields they could see the debris of the conflict—dead men and horses, broken-down artillery caissons; and the ground was tramped up where the army had moved. They were driving them back—they were giving it to them! The regiment surged on with a cheer.

But some of the things you saw here were far from glorious. Wounded men were coming down the road, some of them with their heads bound up, some of them ashen-gray and staggering. And then suddenly—underneath a tree—God, what a sight was that! The hospital corps had taken its stand here, and raised its flag; men were lying stretched out in rows—and right in the roadside was one upon his back, with a surgeon bending over him. The man's face was upturned and savagely distorted. He was clutching his sword in one hand, and the cords stood out upon the hand. The surgeon had sliced away the man's trousers, and he was sawing away at his leg. You heard the saw rasp at the bone—ugh! Jack was marching at his cousin's side, and Allan felt him clutch him suddenly by the arm. He shot a swift glance at Jack—the young lieutenant was white, and his hands shook.

The ground over which they were advancing was for the most part waste farmland, full of stumps and broken up with thickets and patches of woods. One could not see the fighting—it was on ahead, upon still higher land; but the din of it rose louder and louder, and here and there they saw stray signs of it—a terrified horse galloping away, some men retreating, an orderly riding a foam-flecked steed. Upon a little knoll stood a group of men, one with a red-and-white signal flag, which he was waving frantically; the enemy seemed to have sight of this flag, for now and then came a shell, bursting near it with a rain of fire and a hovering ring of smoke. The flag waved on, heeding nothing. Sometimes one saw in the open fields little fountains of dirt leap up, as if something had hit there; and several times cannon-balls came rolling over the ground—balls nearly spent and suggestive of tenpins. One came across the road and the men dodged out of the way of it, skipping and laughing; one fellow made bold to catch it, short-stop fashion, and it tumbled him right into the ditch, head over heels, and went on with speed apparently undiminished. The man lay grunting, but nobody stopped to help him. It was his own fault.

There came orders, sharp and stirring. "By head of column, take wheeling distance. First company forward. Guide left. Quick—*march!*" They saw that the regiment in front was deploying; they watched it spreading out, in a long double line, perhaps a quarter of a mile in length. Somewhere ahead a bugle sounded and the line started, sweeping forward, wavering here and there and breaking at obstructions, but closing up again and moving on. It was a pretty sight—the men cheered, and the flags fluttered in front, and behind ran the officers, waving their swords and shouting.

Then came the turn of the Fifth. Down the column ran the order: "To the left into line of battle. By the rear of column, left into line, wheel. Double-quick—*march!*"—and they swung off at a run. How handsomely they executed the manoeuvre—without an instant's delay or confusion—like machinery! Discipline was something, after all, and their bosoms swelled with pride. Then, cheering like mad, they went on. There was a wooded hollow in front of them, in which ran a little "branch," a tributary of Bull Run; they crossed it, leaping over on the stones, or splashing through the water—and then up the far slope at a dash. The battle was just ahead there—and how the thunder music of it throbbed in them, how madly their hearts beat with it! Here were dead men scattered over the ground, and shells came crashing through the trees, splitting the ear with their din—but who cared for things like that? Over another field they sped—ahead of them were bodies of troops moving, reserves waiting, officers galloping. Then suddenly they burst through a thicket, and out upon the Warrenton pike, the same road they had left in the early hours of the morning, over on the other side of Bull Run.

They were halted here, and ordered to lie down. Before them

[270]

was another sudden rise in the land, and upon the plateau at the top —the battle! Still they could see nothing, but they heard the shouts and cries of the combatants, the rattle of the musketry far and near, and the roar of the big guns in the distance. The air here was hazy with the smoke, and choking to the breath; one heard strange whirring noises above his head, as if bees were flying past his ear. Whenever there came a volley, leaves and twigs and bits of branches would fall from the trees and come sifting down upon one's head like snowflakes. Lying so and resting, one had a chance to look about him, and to get the fever out of his blood, and to realize what an unpleasant sort of place he was in. The men hugged the ground closer, and hugged their muskets, and stared with wild eyes, breathing hard and fast. Down the slope came suddenly a young fellow, a mere stripling of a lad, walking like one who was drunk. There was blood on him, and as he went he pulled up his shirt and looked at himself. There was a little red hole in his side, from which the blood trickled; and he felt of it, and poked his finger into it, to see where it went to. Evidently its location did not suit him, for the men heard him cursing like all the fiends as he went by them.

Somewhere now one heard the voice of Sergeant Schlemmer, rising above all the uproar, in a kind of sing-song chant: "Take it easy now, boys, take it easy! Don't get rattled—when you go up to fire, see what you're firing at. Take your time, and aim low. Don't be in a hurry—shooting lots of times don't count for any-thing—you can't scare them with the noise, you have to hit them with the bullets! Steady, now—steady!" And then suddenly down the line they saw the men rising up, and heard the word passed. They sprang to their feet, and biting their lips together, started slowly, in grim silence, up the slope.

Allan rose up also, but he did not go on with them. During the halt he had had time to look about him, and to notice his cousin, whose post was just behind the line. When the order came, Jack had risen halfway upon his knees and there stayed. All the youth and beauty was gone out of Jack's face—he was sick-looking, and old, white as a sheet, and his features drawn. Allan sprang to him.

Jack tried to speak, but his lips trembled so that he could not. "I—I—" he began; but his eyes told the story—they were the eyes of a hunted animal. Allan wrapped his arm about him. "Steady, old man," he said, in a low voice. "Brace up, now!" He darted a quick glance about him. No one had seen them—the regiment had gone on and was halfway up the ascent.

Jack tried to speak again, but his cousin pressed him tightly to him, and muttered, "Come on!" Then as the other still hesitated, he hissed the words, louder and more imperative, *"Come on!"* Then Jack started, and they marched together step by step, up up the hill.

At the top the thicket ended, and here at the edge was the firing line; other troops were giving place to the Fifth, and falling back to re-form—battle-smitten men, some of them wounded and bloody, all of them powder-stained and wild. Allan had time for just one glance; across the level plateau, on the edge of another woods, was the enemy's line, dimly seen through the haze, with men running about, groups gathered where the guns were, and battle-flags waving above. Points of fire shot out from the line, and the bullets hummed through the air, hitting the dust in front, or burying themselves in the trees in the rear. The regiment was in the act of kneeling. "Ready!" shouted a voice. "Aim!"

And then suddenly from somewhere opposite there burst out a cloud of smoke and flame, and Allan heard at his side a crushing, spatting sound, and felt his cousin, whom he still grasped with one arm, half torn out of it. Things smote Allan's face, cutting him, tearing him, blinding him; and over his hands there rushed a flood of something hot and horrible. In a spasm of fright he shook his head free and wiped clear his eyes—staring. Jack—great God, where was Jack! Here was his body, and above it a neck-bone sticking up, and a jaw dangling in front of it; and out of the middle, gushing up as from a fountain—pumping, pumping—a jet of crimson blood!

Allan reeled, and staggered backwards with a scream; and the body lunged forward, a stream of blood gushing forth and slopping over his feet. The sky seemed to grow black before his eyes; the trees danced and swayed, and he clutched his hands over his face. Shudder after shudder passed through his frame—and then, suddenly, with a choking cry, he turned and fled away.

He dashed down the slope again, blind, frenzied, his hands stretched out before him. The battle thundered in his ears, and universal destruction crashed in his soul; he rushed through the woods like a spirit damned, fleeing from the memory of that ghastly sight—that pumping jet of blood. His senses reeled, he was dazed, stunned; when he stumbled and fell he lay upon the ground, sobbing, choking. Oh God, it was too monstrous—it could not be! He seemed to see the red fountain before him still, to feel it gushing over his hands and feet. Blood—he was a mass of it! His face was plastered with blood and brains—there was blood in his eyes, in his nostrils, in his mouth! The scent of it made him suddenly ill, convulsed his stomach so that it seemed to leap up. He began to vomit, sobbing all the while.

He got up again, and went staggering on. Grief mingled with his horror—he wrung his hands and cried aloud—"Jack, Jack!" Oh, how pitiful it was—he saw that face of pain and fear, white and haggard, down there at the foot of the hill. Jack had not wanted to come—had he foreseen what was going to happen to him? So beautiful he was—so tender-hearted and kind! And now —now he was gone! He was dead! And again Allan saw that hellish sight—that bright red neck-bone sticking up, and the pumping jet of blood! Again the shuddering seized him, and he buried his face, and wept aloud.

He was standing still; and suddenly he lifted his head, and flung up his arms, his hands clenched, his whole soul one blaze of rage. He screamed aloud with it, in frenzy; he cursed—he knew not what he cursed: the world where such things were done—the God that had allowed it—the thing itself, that was hideous, demonic, black as hell. He cursed the thing called life— a fearful hatred of it seized him, revolt against it surged up in him. He flung out his hands before his face, to drive back the fury from his presence; he started to run once more, blindly, through the forest.

How far he went he had no idea, nor how long a time passed, nor what was going on about him. The sounds of the battle were still in his ears, the palaces of joy and hope within him were toppling, down into abysmal depths. He lay on the ground in a kind of trance—he sat up again only when a strange sound broke suddenly in upon his consciousness.

That was a kind of snort, close in his ear. He stared and saw, standing not far from him, a big black horse.

The horse looked strange and wild; it might have been one of the creatures of his dreams. There was a pleading, agonized look in its eyes; it understood all, it seemed to say—that it was dumb was only one wrong the more. What was the matter? Allan's eyes were caught by a long, red object which trailed on the ground behind the horse. It turned, and he saw a great, gaping hole in its side. Something had ripped it under the belly, and its entrails were starting out. That long red thing was a piece of them, and when the horse walked he trod upon it and pulled it out further. Allan gave a cry, and the horse a frightened leap, the entrails bulging out still more.

The man turned away and stared around him. The woods here seemed to have been shattered by a tempest; branches strewed the ground, and some of the trunks were riven as if the lightning had struck them. The tempest was still raging, it seemed; shot and shell plunged through the place, crashing through the trees, ricocheting from one to another; shells burst here and there, with explosions that made the ears ring.

Then Allan noticed that there were men in these woods. Some lay dead upon the earth; some darted here and there, seeking shelter. They seemed to be quite mad with fright—they ran blindly, their eyes starting out of their heads. They bounded about like demon creatures; one went close by him, his hands uplifted and his mouth wide with terror. He was clad in the uniform of the New York Fire Zouaves, the regiment of the martyred Ellsworth; he had his musket still in his hand—he did not seem to have sense enough to drop it. He was panting hoarsely as he ran—and then suddenly, espying a great oak tree, he turned towards that, and took shelter behind it, leaning against it, breathing hard. All at once, as in a lightning flash, something smote the tree;

there was a deafening crash, and the man was hurled forward and flung upon the earth.

Allan watched, and saw that the man never moved. Allan did not know what to make of it—what was the matter with the fellow? He went up to the tree, fascinated. A cannon-ball was buried in it, a cannon-ball as big as his two fists, and it was half a finger deep in the wood. But the man! The man had been on the other side of the tree, and the ball had not gone through at all. Allan went over to him—but he was dead as a stone. He was a big, burly man, with a black beard.

Allan went on, dazed. Everything in these woods seemed panic fear—and suddenly fear seized him. Why should he stay in the midst of this inferno—he would get away from it! He was too confused to know which way to go, but he began to run again, aimlessly, crazily.

The woods thinned away, and he staggered up a slope, thick with bushes. The crash and rattle of the conflict seemed to burst on his ears louder than ever here—he turned and ran along the ridge, through more thickets and bushes. Then there was a cornfield, a pitiful, straggling cornfield such as grows in Virginia. It seemed to have been hit by a hailstorm—its stalks were rent and pierced with holes. Something was cutting more holes in them also—there was a constant sound—zip, zip—like the tearing of paper. Also there was a buzzing, as of a swarm of bees—it was the bullets again, Allan knew, and once more he broke into a run. He sped through the cornfield, and then through a little garden patch, and so, in his blind haste, brought up against a fence of palings. Right before his eyes stood a little farm-house.

It was a poor, forlorn-looking place, unpainted, with two or three tumble-down outhouses around it. There were holes in the house here and there; and as Allan looked he saw bits of chips fly off from it. A second or two later the top of its brick chimney crashed into pieces, a fragment of it flying all the way to his feet. More bricks fell upon the roof, and Allan heard a shrill scream from inside.

It was a woman's voice, her cries rising, one after another, louder and louder. Allan listened a moment, and then ran toward the house; he pushed open the door, and looked in.

It was the home of a "poor white." In one corner was a pallet, and on it lay, or rather sat, an old woman. She was in a nightgown, and evidently bed-ridden; she was wrinkled and ugly, and her gray hair was loose about her shoulders. Her hands were flung up into the air, and she was shrieking hysterically. A shot tore through the wall of the house, smashing to bits a jug which stood upon the table at one side; the old woman buried her head in the pillows of the bed, wallowing and tossing about, convulsed and frenzied with terror. Suddenly she started up again and raised her arms; an instant later she seemed to leap straight up into the air, her face transfixed. She gave a little gulp, and swayed, and then tumbled head first upon the floor, where she lay, kicking feebly. Allan, staring, saw a little spurt of blood running out of her side, and trickling along her gown.

Then an inside door of the room was flung open and a young girl dashed in. She saw the old woman, and cried out, rushing to her, flinging herself upon her and clasping her arms about her, weeping frantically. At the same time a man plunged down the stairway from the upper floor of the house—a man with wide-open eyes of fright. He darted one glance at the scene in the room, and then bounded towards the door; he did not seem to notice Allan, but dashed out. As he emerged he drew his hat over his eyes and crouched, bending to one side like a man in a storm of rain. He leaped the fence and disappeared; then Allan turned to look into the room again, where the young girl was still screaming, "Mother! Mother!"

Then suddenly a curious sight. Near the fireplace of the little room were two kittens—tiny kittens, one of them gray, and the other mottled, black and white. And they were playing together; one would lie on its back and the other would bite it, and they would roll over and over. Everything else seemed to fade into nothingness, and Allan found himself watching the kittens. They were so happy and so busy!

CHAPTER V

The bullets continued to spatter the house. Allan noticed this wonderingly, and in a dazed way recollected that he had been trying to get away from them. A man dashed past him into the room; he wore a blue uniform, and had a musket in his hand; his face was grimed and sooty, and there were flecks of blood on it. He ran to the window and crouched there—he thrust out his musket, took aim, and fired.

Two more men entered the room, then half a dozen, trampling and crowding. They were so intent upon their task that they appeared not to see Allan at all; when they spoke to each other it was in quick, gruff monosyllables. They posted themselves here and there, at the windows, in the doorways—one or two bounded upstairs, and still another thrust his musket through a hole in the side of the house. The place began to blaze with musketry, and a blue haze filled the room; Allan stared—he had all at once come to realize that these men wore the uniform of the "Cambridge Tigers."

Half a dozen more flashed past the doorway, running low—flung themselves down on the ground just behind the garden fence, and began to fire from there. Still others were out in the cornfield. A cannon-ball crashed through the chimney, and through the roof of the house, scattering splinters about the room; then a moment later one of the men at a window gave a grunt and tottered backwards. He began to roll about on the floor, pressing his hands upon his abdomen. No one looked at him, save Allan.

Three more soldiers darted through the doorway. One of them was a short, stocky man, with a bush of yellow hair, smeared with blood. He was in his shirt-sleeves, and one sleeve was torn off and bound round his arm, which was also bloody. He carried a musket in one hand, and his face was ferocious. He fired once out of the window, and then turned to shout to the men. "Give it to them, boys!" he roared—"give them hell!" Allan recognized the voice, though he had not recognized the face. It was Sergeant Schlemmer.

The sergeant ran to the doorway; he was calling to some one in the rear. "Come up here! Come up here!" he yelled. His voice rang like a bugle-blast, above all the din; and he waved his musket, pointing. "Post yourselves by that hedge, there!" he cried. "They're trying to get up their guns—shoot at the gunners —pick them off, and be lively!" There was a cheer or two, and then a volley of shots. Allan wondered somewhat; Sergeant Schlemmer seemed suddenly to be in command of the company.

And then, turning into the room again, his eye fell on Allan. "Why aren't you fighting?" he yelled.

"Fighting?" Allan echoed, feebly.

"Fighting!" roared the sergeant. And he rushed towards him, his voice thundering in his ear. "What's the matter with you? What's the matter with you?"

He picked up the musket which had been dropped by the wounded man—who was still wallowing. "Here!" he said; "take this, and go to the window, and shoot!"

Allan took it mechanically, and ran to the window. He put the gun to his shoulder and fired—or tried to. It did not go off. He raised the hammer and fired again; again it did not go off. He repeated the process half a dozen times—he was too dazed to know what was the matter with it. Finally it dawned upon him that he had to load the gun first. He saw the man next to him taking a cartridge out of his belt; he put his hand to the place— yes, he had cartridges also. He pulled one out and stuffed it into the gun. It would not go in. He poked and pushed—what was the matter with it? Then he saw a man biting off the end of one. Ah, yes, sure enough! Allan did likewise.

The cartridge went in then, and he raised the gun and blazed away. Now he knew what to do—he had the run of it, and blindly, in a frenzy, he began tearing off the cartridges with his teeth, stuffing them into the gun and firing them. He did this five or six times, before suddenly he felt himself seized by the collar of his coat and jerked backward with a force that half choked him. "What's the matter with you, you fool?" yelled a voice in his ear.

It was Schlemmer again; and his breath was like a blast of fire. "Matter!" Allan gasped.

"Jackass!" screamed the sergeant. "Where's your head? You're firing up into the sky!"

The other echoed the words again, and the man began to shake him, as a terrier shakes a rat. "I know what's the matter with you!" he thundered. "I saw you run away once, you hound —you want to run away again, don't you? What are you standing there gawking at me for—where are your senses? Coward! Coward! *Taugenichts!*"—and then the furious sergeant exploded into a volley of curses, English curses and German, his breath hot in Allan's face.

And the words—they cut and stabbed into Allan like knives; they went into the deeps of him, where his manhood lay smothered. And it started up, with a bound and a furious cry. "You lie, you lie!" he screamed back. "I'm no coward! I'm as good a man as you!"

"And why don't you show it, then?" asked the sergeant. "Why don't you fight?"

"I will fight!" Allan panted, and he gripped his gun again. "Show me!"

And the sergeant pointed out of the window. "There's the enemy," he said. "Fight!"

Everything was suddenly grown clear as day before Allan's eyes; there at the other side of the clearing, close upon the edge of a thicket, was a thin, irregular line of men in grey uniform, some standing, some kneeling; clouds of smoke floated above them, and points of fire flashed in front of them. Some were running here and there—and across the plain in front dashed horses with cannon trailing behind, also men cheering. They were swinging the guns into position, and limbering up.

The fiends still tore at Allan's heartstrings; but he fought with them now, his soul rising up, towering and furious. It was an effort that was agony, but here in the midst of this nightmare was a duty, a truth, and he clung to it desperately. He had cried out at the horrors of this reeking field—but see, over there were the men who had caused it! The men who had taken up arms against their country, who had come out to kill and destroy. Was it not they with their bullets and their shells that had murdered Jack—that were trying now to murder him? Let them be killed —then there would be an end of it.

He steadied himself, peering through the rifts in the smoke; there—that group about the cannon! He took aim and fired, and then tore off another cartridge, and reloaded, still keeping his eyes upon the spot. So at last he got down to work, grimly, savagely. Hatred boiled up in his soul—ah, to get his hands upon them over there, the ruffians! To shoot them seemed too little to do. Here and there he saw their battle-flags waving—one a South Carolina flag, and flashes of rage blazed in him at the sight.

He was suffocating with the heat of his labor; he dropped his musket and tore off his coat. The sweat was pouring in streams down his face, which was smeared with blood and grime. He wiped his hands upon his trousers—they were so slimy that they interfered with him; then he seized the musket again and went on. The musket was hot, and the barrel burned to the touch; also his eyes burned, they seemed to be leaping out of his head. His ears rang, and now and then he had to grip his hands tightly to steady his brain; he was panting for breath, choking with the fumes of powder. But out there through the billowing smoke he still got glimpses of the enemy's line, that thundered and crackled, and he hung on to the work; either he would go down or they would, he swore it by the God that had made him. He muttered aloud in his fury, he cursed them like a regiment of fiends— sometimes he yelled aloud, though he did not know it.

Then, outside, he heard cheers, and he saw a line of men sweeping across the corn-field. What was the matter? Had the enemy given way? He darted a swift glance about him—into the room dashed Sergeant Schlemmer. "Charge!" he shouted. "Charge!"

The men leaped up, rushed out of the door, climbed out of the windows. "Line up!" the sergeant was yelling, running here and there. "Steady! Steady! Give it to them now, boys—give them the bayonet! Forward!"

And away they went, sweeping down the field like a hail storm. Where they had come from Allan did not know, nor what had started them; but the line ran as far as he could see—and God, how they went! He hardly knew that he was running—he was lifted on wings, he was borne in the arms of a tempest; he shouted till his voice broke, and waved his gun in the air—like a devil in his rage.

Bullets hummed in his ears—but what were bullets? A man beside him gave a grunt and doubled up and went down, rolling over and over. But the line went on—what was a man? Next to Allan was an Irishman, a giant of a creature, red-headed and wild; he and Allan ran neck and neck, panting to be first. They burst through the smoke—there they were, the enemy! Right ahead loomed one of their guns; and suddenly from out its mouth there burst a volcano of fire—with a crash like the splitting of the skies. The Irishman beside Allan seemed to vanish—he flew into pieces, and the blast of the discharge smote into Allan's face, blew him backwards, seemed to shatter his eardrums. There was a roaring in his head, and blood gushed from his nostrils— but he shook himself, he flung himself free from the dizziness; with a roar he plunged into the fight, staggering, half-blinded.

The lines had come together. Rifles cracked, swords and bay-onets gleamed in the sunlight; there were heard the sounds of the contact, swift, sharp, savage: the thud of muskets coming together, of steel clashing upon steel, and cries, groans, and yells. Men were stabbing, slashing, shooting. Furious faces gleamed out at Allan, flashes of fire blazed into his face. Before him was a member of his company, leaping at one who was pulling a pistol; Allan raised his musket and fired, the man went down and out of sight.

Allan paused, loading his musket. A pistol flashed in front of his face, and a man with sword upraised appeared to leap out of space at him. Things seemed to reel, and then suddenly there came a blow, and everything grew black. He flung up his hands and staggered about blindly, plunging on, striving to see, to find his thoughts; then at last he fell down, senseless.

Bits of ideas and feelings were hovering before him; phantom thoughts which he could not grasp. There was a dull pain, but he could not be sure if it was he or some one else that was feeling it. Forms moved before him, strange and mysterious things, bodiless and nameless, but terrible, as in a nightmare. He wondered if he was dead, if these were not the experiences of a disembodied state. So, little by little, he drifted back into consciousness.

He opened his eyes feebly. The first thing he saw was the moon. Then he noticed that everything was still. How strange it seemed—he wondered if he had dreamed it. All that uproar— the thunder of the earth and sky! But then he stirred one hand, and it touched something alive. It groaned. No, he had not dreamed it.

He tried to move again. He raised his head an inch or so. God, what a pain! And he sank back. His brain reeled—the moon seemed to dance and tremble. He put up his hands. There was a thick clot of blood on the side of his head. The blood was cold on the ground where he lay.

He tried again, after a while, and got up on his elbow. Yes, the battle was over. Forms lay about him—all still. A broken cannon was not far away, and beside it a horse, with legs stretched out long and stiff. Some ways off men were moving about; campfires were blazing here and there.

Little by little Allan experimented, and as his senses returned, he managed to get upon his knees. His head burned like fire, and raging thirst devoured him. He suddenly recollected his canteen, and opened it, emptying it at a draught. It was like wine; he felt that he would be able to move. He wanted to move because the stench of blood made him ill. He forgot that the blood was on him.

He crawled a few feet, in a zigzag path, between forms of men; one lay exactly across his way, and he stopped and looked at it. The time was just after sundown, and it would have been twilight but for the moon: between the two there was light enough for one to see plainly—and Allan gave a sudden start. The man lying there was in his shirt-sleeves, and one sleeve was torn off and bound round his arm. He had light yellow hair—it was Sergeant Schlemmer.

Allan stared without a motion. The form was still, but the face looked so quiet! Allan put out a trembling hand, and touched him on the shoulder; he did not move. Allan slid his hand up toward the face, and touched that. His hand leaped back with a start. The face was cold.

The sergeant was dead, then. Allan continued to gaze, fear stealing over him. He was gone away! How hard he had fought, and now he would never fight again! He had given his life—"for freedom"! With a sudden thrill Allan started up and gazed round him. Had he given it for nothing? For the first time now it occurred to him to ask the all-important question—what the issue of the battle had been.

Somebody must have won, or they would still be fighting. And these camp-fires about here—which side did they belong to? If he could know that, he would know everything; but how was he to know? He could hear voices, now and then, in the distance— if he could get to them and find out! But they were so far away! It did not occur to him that he might fall into the hands of the enemy; whichever side had won, it was over, and what did anything else matter?

He got to his feet. The water had refreshed him, and he was able to walk. He went slowly, for every motion was an agony. He walked along the edge of the woods, supporting himself by the trees; it was hard to keep his head—his faculties would start off, and he would have to bring them back.

He went down a little slope, stumbling upon a dead body now and then, and finally he came to a road. He waited here for a time, in the hope that some one or something might go by, giving him the information he wanted. Dead bodies lay here, and broken wagons, and other wreckage, but nothing moving. Allan was about to start on, when suddenly he heard a strange noise in the thicket, and stood still. This noise sounded like the gobbling of a turkey, more than anything, and he wonderd what sort of an animal could be there. It was moving close by in the bushes— twigs cracked, and the branches rustled.

Then the perplexing sound came again, and out of the dark shadows there emerged the form of a man. He had apparently seen Allan; he came toward him, waving his hands before him in a frantic sort of way. The strange gobbling sound came again, and a sudden fear stole over Allan. He was not afraid of anything human just then; but this? And an instant later the moon emerged from a cloud, and he screamed. This man—this thing—it had no jaw! And it came on toward him, trying to talk! For a moment Allan thought it was Jack; but it wasn't, of course, because Jack was dead when Allan left him.

He turned and fled, like one possessed. Once he glanced over his shoulder. It was following, waving its arms, calling!

Allan must have run for half a mile—he ran until he was out of sight of it. Then he sank down and lay watching down the road, to see if it would reappear.

It did not, and after a while he began to listen for something else. He fancied that he heard a stream, and he got up again, and started toward it. The sound of it drew him like a magnet, and when he had come to it he lay down by the ford, and drank and drank, and bathed his face and hands. The blood had begun to ooze out of the cut upon his head, and he bound that up with a strip of his shirt. Then he got up and staggered on.

Across the ford and down the road. A vision of destruction burst upon him. The road was literally piled with baggage; in the ditches on each side there were mountains of it—rifles and blankets, knapsacks and cartridge-belts, harness, clothing, tents, chests of stores, forges—what was there, of all the endless paraphernalia of an army, that had not been distributed along this mysterious pathway? There were cannon tumbled here and there —scores of them—and caissons and artillery wagons, inextricably tangled. Before this Allan had seen signs of a battle of men; but here seemed to have been a battle of things. Did this always happen after a fight? he asked himself. When men got through fighting, did they leave their weapons where they had fought? It was here as if a tempest had smitten an army, and scattered it to the four winds of heaven.

He stumbled along, through it all, picking his way as best he could, striving to figure out what it meant. Gradually as he went on and on, and the signs of it did not cease, the truth forced itself upon him—that it meant a defeat, a terrible defeat for one side or the other. One side or the other had fled in wild confusion! One nation or the other was ruined beyond all hope! But which? Which? He cried aloud in the agony of his uncertainty. Were the Union and its freedom gone forever?

He weighed the chances, as he had left the battle when he fell. Surely his men had been winning—they had been winning all day, before Allan came! Then it must be the enemy which had fled down the road, abandoning everything. And where were they now? Where was the Union army? Had it followed them and passed on? If only it had been light enough, so that he could have examined the debris and made sure!

He staggered on, in torment, until he heard another stream; he crept down to the ford to drink again. Lying there resting, he thought suddenly that he heard voices singing, and sat up and listened. They seemed to be coming down the road, and soon the sounds of horses trotting came with them. Then the riders— there were several of them—rounded a turn, and their voices came to him clear and loud. They were singing with passionate fervor —a song that Allan had never heard before. He listened:—

"The despot's heel is on thy shore,
     Maryland, my Maryland!
His torch is at thy temple door,
     Maryland, my Maryland!
Avenge the patriotic gore
That flecked the streets of Baltimore,
And be the battle-queen of yore,
     Maryland, my Maryland!"

They sang two verses more, and the glory of their singing seemed fairly to lift them out of their saddles. Their tones rang far in the stillness of the evening—they sang like men possessed. As they came into view and rode down into the stream, they were roaring out the last verse of the wild and furious chant:—

"I hear the distant thunder hum,
    Maryland, my Maryland!
The Old Line's bugle, fife, and drum,
    Maryland, my Maryland!
She is not dead, nor deaf, nor dumb—
Huzza! She spurns the Northern scum!
She breathes—she burns! She'll come! She'll come!
    Maryland, my Maryland!"

Then ceasing, the singers burst into loud laughter and cheering. Allan, crouched where he was by the bank, knew the three voices; he knew the three figures, he knew their uniforms, visible in the moonlight. The riders were Randolph and his brother, Ralph, and Ethel's husband, "Billy" Hinds.

They had halted at the ford to let their horses drink. Meantime they drank also—out of a bottle which 'Dolph pulled out and passed to them. 'Dolph was drunk; but whether he was drunk upon wine or battle was more than his cousin could guess. He laughed, he shouted—all the while he was still beating the time of the song with one hand, shaking his head to the "melody unheard." One of his arms was bound up, and there was blood on it, but that did not seem to trouble him as he waved it in the air. He had begun the song again, half to himself, and he finished a verse with a whoop; then, as his brother and his brother-in-law started again, he spurred his horse and leaped upon the bank, and there whirled about, raising his clenched fist. "Come back!" he roared. "Come again, God damn you, and we'll give you more of it!"

Allan thought for an instant that 'Dolph was shouting to him; but then in a sudden flash of horror he realized that it was the *North* he was addressing! "Come just as often as you like!" 'Dolph yelled. "Raise another army—you'll find us here just as long as you want us!" Then the speaker rushed on, to pour out a torrent of profanity upon the heads of his imaginary auditors. He cursed them—the Yankee hounds—by the heavens above, and the earth beneath, and the waters under the earth, and the fire under the waters; he cursed their cowardly fathers and their cowardly grandfathers, their cowardly ancestors from the flood, their cowardly posterity to the day of doom. It was a very symphony of profanity—and from it the shuddering listener on the ground learned at last what had been the issue of the battle, the issue of all his toil and agony, of his cousin's and the sergeant's death. It was the Northern army that had been routed—the Northern army that was gone back to Washington in wild, panic flight!

The three conquerors turned their steeds toward their own lines, and as they rode on they were singing with increasing fury:

"War to the hilt!
Theirs be the guilt,
Who fetter the freeman
To ransom the slave!"